CHRISTI PHILLIPS

"Enchants readers with her world and the detail in which she has immersed it."
—Bookreporter.com on her critically acclaimed national bestseller

The Devlin Diary
A June 2009 Indie Next Notable Book

"Phillips's talent lies in the details. She pulls together a rich tale . . . a story full of historical suspense. In fact, you'll wish there was more of it, you'll wish there was more of her take on the time period she describes so wonderfully."

—Bookreporter.com

"Intricate, intriguing, *The Devlin Diary* is deliciously absorbing. Read it obsessively—it's a story that will wrap you in laughter and tears."

—Perri O'Shaughnessy, *New York Times* bestselling author

"This engrossing tale might have been a page-turner for me except that I found myself lingering on every fascinating period detail Christi Phillips lavished on this first-class historical mystery."

—Anne Easter Smith, author of *The King's Grace*

"Lyrically written, *The Devlin Diary* introduces two of the most witty, gifted, and resourceful heroines you will find between the covers of one book."

—Stephanie Cowell, author of *Marrying Mozart*

The Devlin Diary is also available as an eBook

More praise for Christi Phillips and *The Devlin Diary*

"A thrilling reading experience."

—*Library Journal*

"Spellbinding . . . providing incredible insights into the intrigue, royal secrets, and loves in the court of Charles II."

—*Romantic Times*

"One of the most engrossing novels I've read in a long time."

—Jake Hallman, A Great Good Place for Books (Oakland, CA)

"For the mystery fan who enjoys a double dose of murder mixed with history that overlaps centuries, *The Devlin Diary* by talented author Christi Phillips is one you won't want to miss. . . . This is a tale I'm pleased to highly recommend to any reader of history, mystery, contemporary fiction, and more. . . . A book guaranteed to please."

—ReaderToReader.com

And acclaim for the stunning debut novel from Christi Phillips

The Rossetti Letter
A *Redbook* Magazine Book Club Pick

"Totally engrossing . . . mesmerizing."

—*Redbook*

"Sexy and suspenseful . . . makes you want to hop on the next flight to Venice, book in hand. Reading it is like a visit to that sensual city."

—Janice Cooke Newman, author of *Mary*

"Reading Christi Phillips's lush, beautifully written novel is like enjoying a sumptuous meal in the Venice it describes with such loving detail. You want to savor every moment."

—Ayelet Waldman, author of *Love and Other Impossible Pursuits*

"A complex web of intrigue enhanced by captivating characters."

—*Romantic Times*

"With impeccable research into seventeenth-century Venetian politics, Phillips plots an imaginary literary suspense debut novel contrasted with the delightful modern romance between two rival academics. . . . The parallel [historical] tale gives the reader a compelling look at the mind of an intellectually curious young woman forced into the life of a courtesan. . . . Moving effortlessly from the seventeenth to the twenty-first century and back, Phillips crafts an entertaining story with intrigue, espionage, and romance in both centuries."

—*Booklist*

"Saucy . . . nicely told . . . sure to appeal to many fans of the genre."

—*Kirkus Reviews*

"An enthralling debut . . . conjures vivid period interest."

—*Financial Times* (UK)

ALSO BY CHRISTI PHILLIPS

The Rossetti Letter

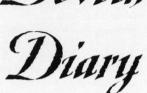

The Devlin Diary

Christi Phillips

GALLERY BOOKS

NEW YORK   LONDON   TORONTO   SYDNEY

G GALLERY BOOKS
A Division of Simon & Schuster, Inc.
1230 Avenue of the Americas, New York, NY 10020

First Gallery Books trade paperback edition April 2010

GALLERY and colophon are registered trademarks of Simon & Schuster, Inc.

For information regarding special discounts for bulk purchases, please contact Simon & Schuster Special Sales at 1-866-506-1949 or business@simonandschuster.com.

The Simon & Schuster Speakers Bureau can bring authors to your live event. For more information or to book an event contact the Simon & Schuster Speakers Bureau at 1-866-248-3049 or visit our website at www.simonspeakers.com.

Manufactured in the United States of America

10 9 8 7 6 5 4 3 2 1

Library of Congress Cataloging-in-Publication Data is available.

ISBN 978-1-4165-2739-8
ISBN 978-1-4165-2740-4 (pbk)
ISBN 978-1-4391-6344-3 (ebook)

In memory of my father,
Don Phillips

No death in England or France was more lamented than that of Princess Henriette-Anne. Since which time dying has been the fashion.

—John Wilmot, Earl of Rochester

PRIMARY HISTORICAL CHARACTERS
(IN ORDER OF APPEARANCE)

Hannah Devlin, a physician

Lord Arlington, Secretary of State and the king's minister

Madame Severin, Louise de Keroualle's mistress of the bedchamber

Louise de Keroualle, a mistress to Charles Stuart, King of England

Jeremy Maitland, a manservant to Lord Arlington

Roger Osborne, a courtier

Mrs. Wills, Hannah's goodwife

Lucy Harsnett, Hannah's maidservant

Hester Pinney, Hannah's maidservant

Theophilus Ravenscroft, a natural philosopher

Thomas Spratt, Ravenscroft's assistant

Sir Granville Haines, a courtier

Ralph Montagu, a courtier and former ambassador to France

Sir Thomas Clifford, Lord Treasurer and the king's minister

Charles Stuart, King of England

James, Duke of York, Charles Stuart's brother and
the successor to the throne

Edward Strathern, a physician and anatomist

Sir Henry Reynolds, a courtier

Jane Constable, a lady-in-waiting to the late Duchess of York

Sir Hugh May, Comptroller of the King's Works

Colbert de Croissy, French ambassador to England

Robert Hooke, a natural philosopher and city surveyor

Dr. Thomas Sydenham, a physician

The Devlin Diary

Prologue

29 June 1670
The Palace of Saint-Cloud, Paris

Urgent to the Rue de Varenne, Paris

The Royal Doctors give her over and so do all that see her. Princess Henriette-Anne took to her bed this morning with a Sickness some say is Poyson. She convulses and screams and clutches her Belly sobbing—it is a Piteous thing to Witness. Most suspect her husband, the Duc d'Orleans, and his lover, the Chevalier de Lorraine, whom King Louis banished to the country only a Fortnight ago. But the King will never condemn his scandalous Brother, even though his sister-in-law is now Tormented by the most excruciating Agonies.

Mors certa, hora incerta, yet all goes on as Before. The courtiers mill about Henriette-Anne's apartments, engaging in idle Discourses, as if this Night were no different from any other. Not one of these tricked-up Peacocks has a care that the Princess's sincere Piety and youthful Beauty will soon be Lost; tho' I must confess that her beauty has quickly Withered, with the repeated clysters and the copious Vomits. The French courtiers—it is a simple task to distinguish them from the English, for their excess of Lace and overbearing Scent reveal them at once—can barely conceal their Astonishment, that a young noblewoman would Suffer so indelicately; and they continually sniff their perfumed handkerchers to mask the Stench that accompanies Death. The Princess's bedchamber, tho' it is grand and overlooks the Palace gardens and the Seine, smells like a charnel-house.

The English contingent—Lord Arlington, Sir Henry Reynolds, Roger Osborne, Sir Thomas Clifford, Sir Granville Haines—are more stoic and less Afflicted. Tho' I detect a Panic amongst them that cannot be attributed to any gentle Sentiment for the Princess. I am almost certain that they are not waiting upon her because she is King Charles's beloved sister and King Louis' beloved sister-in-law, but have remained in France on a secret Purpose.

The efficient overseer of Henriette-Anne's bedchamber, Madame Severin, is as always present. Tonight she is perched at the Princess's bedside, as ominous as a Tower raven, alert to every Sigh and Tremor her mistress makes. Henriette-Anne's fatal Distress has made Madame Severin the very embodiment of Despair and Melancholy, or so it appears; yet not long past I chanced to hear a Quarrel between them, of which I will disclose more when we meet. The Princess's Maids are as mournful as the Matron; they huddle in the corner, red-eyed and fearful, knowing they will be without Employ or Benefactress once their Lady is still and cold.

Only one, the pretty little Breton Louise de Keroualle, seems unconcerned with her Fate. Perhaps the Attention given her by King Charles at Dover was not Lost upon her. De Keroualle is not clever, but she is comely and very Ambitious. She makes much of her Virtue, but I have heard rumors of a past Liaison with the Comte de Sault, a dull Rogue if I ever knew one, and she is poor. Even if she became maid of honor to the Queen she could not make an auspicious Match in France.

I must bring this Missive to a close—more later.

It is now past Three of the clock. Madame Severin has risen and called for the Bishop—the End is near. But no; the Princess motions her back to the Bed, rising on one unsteady Arm to utter a few hoarse Words. Madame Severin looks into the crowded Room, her eyes uncommonly bright in the candlelight.

"Monsieur Osborne," she says, her voice rough with grief.

The courtiers react with perplexed bewilderment, a suppressed ripple of Protest, even outrage. Why Roger Osborne? The Englishman is not a favorite. A friend to King Charles and to Henriette-Anne, to be sure, but someone who arrived late to the Royalist cause. Has the princess forgotten his Parliamentarian past, his work for Cromwell? Perhaps all that matters is that Osborne forgot it quickly enough once Charles was restored to the throne.

Osborne steps out of the crowd, a man of middle Years in unfashionable dark clothes and a cheap Periwig. A large port-wine-colored birthmark spreads its scalloped edges across his right brow. He kneels at Henriette-Anne's bedside, then leans forward to hear her weak rasping Voice. As she murmurs, his eyes grow wide and he shakes his head. Whatever Task she is assigning him, he does not want it, though by refusing he risks a charge of Treason. Henriette-Anne becomes agitated. Madame Severin moves closer, ready to end their dangerous Interlocution. The Princess waves her away, then tugs a weighty gold Band from her finger. She presses it into Osborne's palm. He stares at it as if he has never seen a ring before.

When he looks up, he has the Countenance of a man who has heard something deeply disturbing. The Princess utters a grievous Sigh and falls back onto the bed, her body buckling in pain. Madame Severin summons the Bishop, and the room breaks into a Commotion as the courtiers make way. The Bishop rushes to the bed, but it is all for naught: the Princess's rattle is loud enough for most to hear that she has Dyed. A shocked Gasp resounds throughout the room and the courtiers stop their twittering. The ring falls from Osborne's hand and rolls along the floor, a golden streak of Light. Finally it collides with the wall and falls to one side, wobbling on the rim in ever faster revolutions, its metallic singing filling the sudden silence.

Your dear Friend and my Angel the Princess Henriette-Anne is gone, her Radiance too early extinguished. I will say only this, Letum non omnia finit: *death does not finish everything.*

I remain your most Humble & Obedient, &c.

Chapter One

London, 4 November 1672

SHE LEAVES HER house on Portsmouth Street carrying a wood box with a smooth ivory handle and tarnished brass fittings. It is late afternoon in early November. The street is deserted and cold, and the sunless ground has sprouted scaly patches of hoarfrost; with each step her pattens crack the thin ice to sink into the mud beneath. At the top of Birch Lane she hoists the box to gain a firmer hold—it is heavy, and she is slight—and the constant dull ache behind her eyes becomes a throbbing pain. She has learnt, to her dismay, that the least occurrence can precipitate a headache: a sudden movement, a sound, even a sight as innocent as a bird's wings fluttering at the periphery of her vision. She considers setting the box down, unhitching its scarred metal latches, and searching its neatly arranged collection of bottles and vials until she finds the one that she desires. It is late, however, and she is in a hurry. She continues walking. The small streets she passes through are little traveled; she encounters only a few others who, like herself, appear anxious to reach their destination. Hers is an alley near Covent Garden, and the dilapidated attic room of a house that was once grand. As she crosses Middlebury Street, her breath appears as puffs of white vapor that linger long after she has gone.

When she reaches the Strand she stops, confronted by a street teeming with people, horses, sheep, and snorting, mud-caked pigs rooting in the gutter. The autumn evening is brief and precious, a time for gathering the last necessaries before going home, and the shops and street vendors are briskly busy. The air is blue with coal smoke, rich with the aromas of roasted meat and onions. Underneath is the ever-present odor of the sewer, a narrow, open gutter in the center of the road, where the pigs scavenge. The morning's storm washed away some of the sewage, but the gutters of London are never completely clean. In between the gnawed bones and bits of offal are orphaned puddles of rainwater that shine like mirrors, reflecting nothing but overcast sky.

She pushes back the hood of her cloak; long locks of unruly dark hair break free. In the crush of scurrying people, the limpid brightness of the paned shop windows, the copper lanterns haloed against the darkening firmament, she senses a feeling of contentment tantalizingly within reach. All Hallows' Eve has just passed. This is her favorite season, or once was. In the chilled gray hour before the November night descends she has always felt a kind of magic. When she was younger she imagined that this feeling was love, or the possibility of love. Now she recognizes it for what it truly is: longing and emptiness.

"Mrs. Devlin." A voice rises above the street noise. "Mrs. Devlin? Is that you?"

"Yes," she replies, recognizing the short, ruddy-faced woman in a cotton bonnet and a thick apron, who pushes through the crowd to reach her. She remembers that the woman is a goodwife to a Navy secretary, remembers that she lives with her husband in St. Giles near the sign of the Ax and Anvil, remembers that the woman's mother had suffered an apoplexy and then a fever. It takes her a moment longer to remember the woman's name. "Mrs. Underhill," she finally says, nodding.

"We never properly thanked you, Mrs. Devlin," Mrs. Underhill says as her flushed face gets even rosier, "seeing as we couldn't pay you."

"Do not trouble yourself. You owe me nothing."

"You're very kind," the goodwife says with a small curtsy and bob of her head. "I tell everyone how good your physick is. My mother's last days were more easy because of you."

She remembers Mrs. Underhill's mother. By the time she was summoned, the elderly woman was as frail as a sparrow, unable to speak, and barely able to move. More than a year has passed, but she suddenly recalls holding the woman's emaciated body as if it were only moments ago. "I'm sorry I could not save her."

"She'd lived a long life, Mrs. Devlin. She was in God's hands, not yours." Mrs. Underhill's words carry a gentle admonishment.

"Of course," she says, closing her eyes. The pain in her head has grown stronger.

"Are you all right?" Mrs. Underhill asks.

She looks into the goodwife's eyes. They are clear, green, ageless. She briefly considers telling her about the headaches and the sleeplessness. Mrs. Underhill would understand.

"I'm fine," she says.

"That's a funny one, isn't it?" Mrs. Underhill smiles, relieved to be unburdened of the thought that a physician could take ill. "Me asking after a doctor's health. And you with a whole case full of physick," she adds, looking at the wood box. "I suppose you of anyone would know what medicines to take." She peers across the Strand at one of the street vendors. "Pardon my hurry, but I should be on my way. The master must have his oyster supper every Friday."

They take their leave of each other. As she departs the Strand for Covent Garden, a wintry, soot-filled wind strikes her face. The sky is darker now, and the sense of tranquility she momentarily felt has disappeared, as if it never existed. Inside her head, a bouquet of sharp metal flowers takes root and blossoms. The headache is here to stay, for hours, perhaps days. The medicine case bumps hard against her leg. Many times she has thought of purchasing a smaller, lighter one, but she has not done it. She would never admit it, but she believes that the box itself has healing power. She is aware that this is a superstition with no basis in fact; indeed, she has ample evidence to the contrary. The boy she is on her way to see, a seventeen-year-old apprentice stricken with smallpox, will most likely die before the night is over. For days she has followed Dr. Sydenham's protocol, providing cool, moist medicines where others prescribe hot and dry. The physician's radical new method seems to offer a slightly improved chance of a cure, but she knows that only a miracle will save her patient now, and she has long since stopped believing in miracles. The most she can do is ease the boy's suffering. *Ease suffering.* So she was instructed, but it hardly seems enough. Just once, she would like to place her hand on a fevered cheek and feel it cool, to cradle an infant dying of dysentery and stop its fatal convulsions, to administer medicines that cure rather than placate disease. To heal with her hands, her knowledge, and her empathy. Even a small miracle, she believes, would redeem her.

When she looks up from her ruminations she sees that night has fallen. A coach has stopped at the end of the lane. The bald coachman pulls on the reins, his back still arched, as if he has just brought the horses to a halt. She slows her pace. Something about the coach bothers her, though there's no precise reason for her concern; it's only a common hackney. The door creaks open and a man steps down to the street. He's dressed like a person of quality, but his stance and beefy body are more suited to a tavern brawler. His gaze is so direct it feels both intimate and threatening, as if he knows her and has a personal grievance with her. She is certain she has never seen him before.

"Mrs. Hannah Devlin, daughter of Dr. Briscoe?" he demands. His voice is hard, without finesse, and her first impression is confirmed: he's a brute in expensive clothes. She braces herself, her right hand dipping toward her skirt pocket and the knife concealed there, a weapon she wields with more than ordinary skill. Before her fingers reach the knife she is seized from behind. The ruffian's accomplice wraps his thick arms around her waist and lifts her off the ground so effortlessly that she doesn't have time to think about the strangeness of it all. The first man grabs the medicine case from her and shoves it inside the coach, while the other immediately hoists Hannah through the door after it. She lands on the hard seat facing the back, knocked out of breath. Even if she was able to speak, being confronted with the person who calmly sits across from her would have shocked her into momentary silence.

"Mrs. Devlin," he says. It's both a greeting and a chastisement.

She regards him warily. Lord Arlington, secretary of state, is the king's most trusted minister and the most powerful man in England, after the king. His periwig has more gray in it than she remembers, but his self-important air and the black bandage across his nose, which covers a scar won fighting for Charles I, are the same as ever.

"You carry your father's medicine cabinet," he comments dryly. "How sweet."

Arlington was once a friend of her father's, but that was years ago, before they became enemies. He raps his gold-tipped walking stick on the ceiling and the coach lurches forward.

"Where are you taking me?" Hannah asks.

"To Newgate," he replies, settling back. "You're under arrest."

Chapter Two

THE COACH SWAYS and bounces over the pitted London streets. Hannah steadies herself by gripping the seat, sticky with spilled wine from a past occupant. Like all hackneys for hire, it reeks of ale, human sweat, and stale tobacco. Two small tapers, smoking and smelling of pork fat, light the gloomy interior. The odors combined with the bone-jostling jolts of carriage travel have long cemented her preference for walking.

Across from her, Lord Arlington appears complacent, accustomed or simply immune to any discomfort from the rattling coach. He was the most successful of courtiers, her father once told her, because he was born with the gift of a naturally congenial expression. Those who have dealings with him realize too late that he is not their friend and has no loyalty except to that which brings him power and profit. Even now, as Arlington nears fifty-five and his cheeks have become jowls, his face is boyish and bland, its most distinctive feature being the slender black bandage on the bridge of his nose. Hannah wonders if the king is impressed by this constant reminder of Arlington's service to the Crown. He must be, seeing how high Arlington has risen in twenty-four years, from Lord Digby's messenger to secretary of state. But aside from what looks to be a somewhat pretentious affectation, Arlington is no fop. He is referred to as charming, courtesy of a glib tongue and a knack for languages, but is known to be ruthless, his callous venality glossed over by a sophisticated nonchalance. His Parisian attire is the epitome of style—brocade coat, lots of lace at the cuffs—but unlike the younger court gallants, with their studied casualness and fashionable disarray, Arlington has a Castilian formality, a result of his time in Spain as English ambassador. His hands, sheathed in perfumed gloves, rest lightly on the gold head of the walking stick planted on the floor between his feet. Ragged lines of dried mud ring his high-heeled shoes, and a few related splatters have crept up his beige silk stockings. Hannah stares, momentarily fascinated by the evidence that occasionally Arlington must walk in the street like everyone else. And, apparently, he sometimes rides in a common hackney coach to conceal his activities, although the two dandified thugs just outside the doors, standing on the sideboards and holding fast to the coach like leeches, must attract a bit of attention.

"On what charge am I being arrested?" she asks.

"I should think it would be obvious," Arlington replies. "For practicing physick without a license."

"You can't be serious."

A wry smile briefly raises his sagging cheeks. "Can't I?" With a shrug he sums up Hannah's current predicament: she is his captive, two of his personal ruffians guard her, and the coach is steadily progressing toward Newgate Prison and a squalid cell with no hope of escape. "A woman practicing medicine without a license from the College of Physicians? That is a crime punishable by fines, jail, or both."

"My late husband was a doctor, and as his widow I am entitled by law to adopt his profession."

"I see you have already prepared your defense for the courts. It sounds convincing, but I don't believe that a widow's right to carry on her husband's trade extends to the practice of medicine. Widow or no, all practitioners of physick require a license."

"There are hundreds of unlicensed doctors in London, as you well know. I presume that the secretary of state is not planning on personally escorting each one of them to prison."

"No, I am not. But you are special, Mrs. Devlin. The only child of the great Dr. Briscoe, perhaps the king's finest physician ever."

Is he serious? Hannah wonders.

Arlington reads her expression easily. "You think I jest with you?"

"It is strange to hear you praise my father, as you are the man who had him dismissed from court."

"His own stubbornness and pride brought about his downfall, not I. And he might still be alive today if he'd stuck to his own kind, instead of ministering to the lower classes and the indigent. I was quite distraught when I heard of his death."

"Why am I not convinced?"

"Believe what you will, but your father and I were friends once. I have never forgotten that." He pauses thoughtfully. "Too bad you were not born a man. You could have taken his place at court."

"I have no wish to be at court."

He snorts with derisive laughter. "You actually prefer treating the poor?"

"The poor are as much in need of physick as the rich. I believe it is a worthy calling."

Arlington shakes his head. "Stubborn and proud, like your father." He fixes her with a solemn regard. "Tell me, did he teach you well?"

Why is the minister interested? It is all so strange. After making off with her in the manner of a scoundrel kidnapping an heiress for a forced marriage, then telling her she is under arrest, Arlington appears to want to talk about her education. "Why should that concern you, now that you are taking me to jail?"

"Do not make light with me, young lady. You are hardly in a position to bandy about with your future."

"It appears there is little of my future left for me to bandy about with."

"Your wit may make your friends merry, but be assured it is not welcome here, Mrs. Devlin. A woman should comport herself with greater modesty. Especially a woman such as yourself, who presumes to take on a man's role."

"When did medicine become solely a man's province? I follow my mother's recipe book as often as the *Pharmacopoeia Londinensis*, and I have often found it superior. I shall save my modesty for when I am in jail." She holds Arlington's gaze, daring him to make good on his threat, though she is already beginning to suspect that he will not. There is another reason for this complicated show he's putting on, one that has nothing to do with laws, licensing, or prison, and sooner or later he will tell her. The coach rattles violently. Hannah swallows hard, gulping back the pain. Her headache has settled in and stretched out, working itself into the remote recesses of her brain. Each time the coach joggles and shakes—a regular occurrence, given the condition of the streets— knifing pains radiate from the center of her head. Without thinking she lets her eyes rest on her wood case. The medicine is there, one she has created herself from a variety of herbs, roots, and flower extracts, and, its most vital ingredient, the distilled juice of red poppies.

"Are you feeling ill?" Arlington's ability to sense weakness in others is as sharp as ever.

"Indeed, I am quite well."

His eyes search her face. She can see him adding up the sum of the parts: her sallow skin, sunken cheeks, the dark half-moons under her eyes. "You are in need of a particular remedy, perhaps?" Arlington doesn't wait for an answer. "I have heard—and note well, it is my job to hear everything—that you often purchase poppy syrup from the apothecaries."

"I am not unusual in that." *Papaver somniferum*, the opium poppy, is used in medicines in a variety of ways. Most commonly, poppies are made into a syrup: the blossoms and pods are boiled and the decocted liquid is mixed with sugar water. Less common is the use of opium, the dried sap of the poppy pod, but it is becoming increasingly popular. A few years ago Dr. Sydenham created a preparation of opium dissolved in wine which he christened laudanum, from the Latin verb *laudare*, meaning "to praise," for he considered it the most useful of all medicines. Laudanum has found its way into the London *Pharmacopoeia* and into many of the city's apothecary shops. Either as syrup or as laudanum, the opium poppy is the only thing that allays her agony.

"I have also heard," Arlington continues, "especially from those who have spent time in Constantinople, that the pleasures of the poppy are difficult to forgo, once one has savored them. Could it be you have a secret vice? You can be open with me. It's a debauched age—everyone I know has at least one secret vice, and most don't even bother keeping them secret."

"I believe that opium has more uses than those to which it is presently put." She wants to cite Dr. Sydenham's views on the subject, as he is an esteemed physician, but he is also a notorious anti-Royalist whose political views and modern medical opinions keep him at odds with the College of Physicians. Her father's own association with him was considered, by some, a mark of disloyalty to the king. Her father didn't see it that way, but she knows better than to bring up Sydenham's name with Arlington, so she mentions only her own observations. "I find it especially helpful for my patients with griping of the guts or with consumption."

"So says you, Mrs. Devlin, so says you." Arlington sighs and studies the floor for a moment. "I may regret it, but I'm going to offer you an alternative to Newgate," he says. "I require your services at Whitehall."

"Are you asking me for a favor?"

"Not at all. I am offering you a reprieve, and a temporary one at that, if you do not suffice."

"What is it you want me to do?"

"Not so fast, my girl. First you have a decision to make: Whitehall or Newgate."

As she understands him, she's only one misstep away from jail, even if she does his bidding. What would it mean to be Arlington's puppet for the rest of her life? She can escape him only if he is disgraced and toppled from power, always a possibility for anyone close to the king, but she can't count on that. She restrains a desire to press her fingertips against her throbbing temples. Pain is a great leveler, she finds; it makes her fierce and careless. "I would rather go to Newgate than be forever subject to your whim."

Arlington's affable expression disappears, and he leans forward angrily. "So you'd rather be in jail? Need I remind you that I'm a very busy man, with many important affairs to attend to. I might forget something as inconsequential as your imprisonment for months, even years. I'm told your mother is grown worse since your father died—that she is insensible, that she wanders the streets. Who will provide for her and take care of her if you don't? She'll end up in Bedlam. Only a selfish, headstrong girl such as yourself would make such a choice." He sinks back into his seat, chin up, triumphant. The coach shudders and creaks to a halt. Arlington snaps open the leather window shade: outside is Newgate's humbling façade, a patchwork of impregnable stone and iron.

Her father always said that Arlington was formidable. Now she sees why. "You have no charity in your heart."

"I have charity, Mrs. Devlin. I just never make the mistake of allowing it to interfere with solving the problem at hand."

Chapter Three

WHITEHALL FEELS DESERTED. The coach has deposited them at the far end of the palace, past the King Street gate, away from the main entrance where Arlington is sure to be recognized and his companion remarked upon. The secretary's brutish bodyguards have departed along with the carriage, no doubt on another of Arlington's egregious errands. Hannah and the minister stand in an archway of the high stone wall that edges the street, just outside a circle of flickering brightness cast by a wall-mounted torch. She assumes they are waiting for someone. She assumes. Arlington has revealed nothing.

She sets her medicine case on the cobblestone walk and peers into the moonless night, sensing the emptiness of her surroundings. She sometimes visited Whitehall with her father when she was younger, before Nathaniel, before Sarah. It seems a lifetime ago, but she has not forgotten the general arrangement. Behind the stone wall, a fathomless darkness conceals the bowling green and the privy gardens. On the opposite side of this darkness is a jumble of two- and three-storied palace buildings ranged along the Thames, where only a few scattered windows glow with light. With lodgings for fifteen hundred courtiers, Whitehall Palace is a city unto itself, with coal-yards and wood-yards,

blacksmiths and drapers, kitchens and cofferers, jewelers and hatmak-
ers, guards' barracks and chapels and stables. Typically alight with
thousands of candles that blaze nightly for the king's entertainments
and the courtiers' parties, tonight it has none of its usual bustle and
brightness. Only once before has she seen it so forsaken: in 1665, when
plague terrorized the city and the entire court removed to Oxford.

She leans back against the stone arch. Being out of the coach is a
great relief, but her head still hurts with a vengeance. If she can hold
very still, without speaking, without moving, the pain might retreat
enough to give her a respite of sorts. But that is not possible and will
not be for some hours, she is sure. She finds herself craving the medicine. A few drops would suffice, but she will not reach down, open the
case, and expose her weakness to Arlington.

She glances at the minister's impassive face. Why has he brought
her here—and why in such a way? Could it be that the plague has returned and he is trying to conceal it? But why her? She is no better at
treating the plague than any other doctor. There is no such thing as
a cure, not here, not on the Continent, not even in the Orient, from
whence it came. Her curiosity gets the better of her. "Why is no one
here?" she asks.

"The king is gone to Hampton, and many of the court have followed him," Arlington says. He does not appear to be dissembling.

"For what purpose?"

Her question is met with a tired laugh and a look of incredulity.
"Purpose? No purpose is necessary. He is the king. He may do as he
pleases." As he speaks, a spot of light materializes in the garden. Silently,
they watch it grow steadily larger. Soon it resolves into a man carrying
a lantern. "It's about time," Arlington mutters.

Bearing the lantern shoulder-high, the manservant appears like a
single flame emerging from the darkness, his shining boots and copper-
colored hair ablaze with the fiery light. He draws near, and Hannah
observes his face: clear-skinned and olive-eyed, with a fair brow and
scant beard. He can't be much older than twenty. He has a haughty
nose and a firm, even defiant, mouth—a face she would find aristocratic if he were not in livery. His expression is bereft of emotion, the

blank deference preferred by those who wait upon the high and mighty. Or perhaps it is preferred by the high and mighty themselves: surely Lord Arlington is no easy master.

"You're late," Arlington says by way of greeting.

"Forgive me, my lord," he replies, picking up Hannah's case without being asked.

"Do you know where you are to lead us?"

"Yes, my lord."

The three walk along a path through the privy gardens guided by the lantern's small sphere of light. Without the usual clouds of coal and wood smoke belching from Whitehall's countless chimney stacks, the air is so fresh that she can smell the plantings of thyme and lavender that brush against her skirts. As they get closer to the water, a low, swirling mist carries with it the dank odors of the river: rotting moss and mud and sewage. It creeps between the buildings, into the gardens and into the stone gallery, an enclosed walkway with flagstone floors that connects the long string of royal apartments along the riverbank. Far ahead, at the very end, a curtained doorway leads to the king's suite of semipublic rooms. Larger-than-life portraits of England's past kings, queens, and important ministers line the walls, appearing as huge, humorless ghosts that gaze down sternly upon them as they walk past. An average day would find the stone gallery filled with scheming courtiers, each trying to find a way into the king's good graces for the titles, land, offices, and preferments that are his to bestow. Tonight's tiny parade must seem insignificant to the noble spectators: a minister with a secret, a manservant with a lantern, and a young woman following closely behind, still in the dark.

Arlington's man sets Hannah's case down in front of a large mahogany door. He raises his fist and pounds twice, then bows briefly before he turns and leaves them.

A young maidservant welcomes them inside, meekly scuttling away before they can announce themselves. Lord Arlington doesn't appear to apprehend anything strange in this, but Hannah feels uneasy from the moment they enter. The enormous drawing room is frugally lit, only a few candles here and there, just enough so one can pass through without crashing into the walls or falling over the furniture. But even in the dim light the gilded paneling gleams, the chairs bristle with expensive brocade, the tall mirrors shimmer darkly. Intuitively Hannah knows it's a woman's apartment, but she rules out the queen as a possible tenant. It is common knowledge that the king has provided the pious and sickly Queen Catherine with lodgings at Somerset House a good distance downriver, a convenient arrangement for a monarch whose peccadilloes are public knowledge. The drawing room is certainly fit for a queen, however, and reminiscent of a fairy tale, except that the castle-sized fireplace is cold and the chandeliers are stripped of candles and hoisted up to the lofty ceiling. A suffocating somnolence, suggestive of death or an evil enchantment, permeates the air.

At the far end of the room, a woman suddenly appears, as if—appropriately in this dream-shrouded setting—by magic. It would not shock Hannah to discover that the woman is but a vision. Behind this vision is a solid wall of gilded paneling, or what appears to be solid; could there be a secret door? That she is dressed entirely and rather extravagantly in black seems doubly portentous.

"Has someone died?" Hannah asks.

Arlington shakes his head while keeping his eyes on the specter coming toward them. "Not recently. She mourns her husband."

"How long has he been dead?"

"Some fifteen years now."

An extended, even ostentatious, period of mourning. As the woman slowly comes nearer, Hannah is reminded of a black-rigged frigate steadily crossing calm seas. Her approach is accompanied by a muted trio of sounds: the dull rustle of black brocade; the lisping sibilance of her black slippers on the parquet floor; the heavy jangle of two brass keys that hang from a lanyard tied about her waist, half-concealed in the folds of her velvet mantua. Framing her face is a black silk hood in the French style, shaped with thin wire so that it holds a permanent contour. It billows out from the crown of her head, where it is secured with a large pearl set in gold.

She comes to a stop a few feet away. She is as tall as a man and slender under the layers of skirts and petticoats. Her pale blond hair is pulled back and arranged in curls at the nape of her neck. Her face is breathtaking: fifteen years ago she must have been an extraordinary beauty. Even now, though time has taken its payment, anyone would agree that her naturally dark brows, golden eyes, and ivory complexion——untouched by ceruse or the paint pot, but complemented by a small black patch on the upper rise of her right cheekbone—add up to a face almost pitiless in its perfection. She turns slightly, with a curtsy for Lord Arlington, and Hannah sees the glaring flaw: the lower half of her left ear is missing, and a straight, thin scar runs along her jaw, from the place where her earlobe should have been to just below the left corner of her mouth.

"Madame Severin," Lord Arlington says.

For the third time in as many seconds Hannah feels surprise, for in the minister's voice—this man who reveals so little—she hears both respect and fear. She knows, with a woman's certainty, that Arlington was once in love with the woman he now addresses. "This is the girl I told you about," he says, speaking now with his usual dispassion. "Woman, I mean."

Madame Severin turns to Hannah with a subtle, knowing smile.

"Please come with me," she says.

The bedchamber is at the end of a long hallway. With the exception of a fire in the grate, it is as somberly lit as the withdrawing room. Small pools of candlelight reveal fine tapestries and exotic furnishings: ornamental screens and gold vases and Oriental cabinets. In a huge four-poster bed curtained with rose-colored silk, sinking into a phalanx of downy pillows and covered to the chest with a feather duvet so light and airy that it resembles a bank of clouds, is Louise de Keroualle, the king's mistress.

She is ill. Hannah can sense it more than see it, for she is too far away to make out her face clearly. Madame Severin immediately crosses the room to caress her lady's brow and whisper to her in low, soothing French. In the enormous bed, the king's mistress looks like a fragile doll nestled in a silk-lined box.

"Mademoiselle de Keroualle," Arlington declares softly, confirming what Hannah already knows. "Do you know how important she is to the king?"

"Yes." Like every other Londoner, Hannah is familiar with Charles's colorful and often controversial romantic life. Louise de Keroualle is the king's newest mistress, formerly a maid of honor to his late sister, Princess Henriette-Anne, and now officially a lady-in-waiting to the queen. It's a title for propriety's sake only, as she has no actual duties to fulfill. At twenty-two, the mademoiselle is also the king's youngest mistress and, among the English people, the most resented, being both French and Catholic. She has recently borne Charles a child, her first and his thirteenth. As are three of his other bastards—the king has no legitimate children, not having fathered a child upon his queen—the boy is named Charles. For all her unsuitability in the eyes of a Protestant nation, and amidst rumors that she is a spy for Louis XIV, Louise de Keroualle is acknowledged to have eclipsed all other women in the king's affection. Not that he has renounced all the other women in his life. His longtime love Barbara Villiers, Countess of Castlemaine and mother of five of his children, still resides in a lavish suite near the bowling green and wields considerable political clout, even though she and the king are seldom intimate anymore. Nell Gwyn, the popular orange-seller turned actress, lives in fine state on Pall Mall on the other side of St. James's Park, in a house the king gave to her. Nell's second child by His Majesty is due in December.

It is no secret that Charles Stuart is dominated by the women in his life. Once a woman has control of the king's heart—or, according to court wits Lord Rochester and Lord Buckingham, control of another part of his anatomy—he can refuse her nothing: jewels, titles, land, income from rents, taxes, or the sale of offices. Whatever his mistress desires is hers for the asking, no matter how woeful the state of his perennially cash-strapped treasury. In addition to the gifts of jewelry, clothing, carriages, and houses she has received from the king, Barbara Villiers has amassed an income of over thirty thousand pounds a year, at a time when England is once again at war with the Dutch and the sailors of the Royal Navy go unpaid. The less avaricious Nell Gwyn has acquired three homes: the town house on Pall Mall, Burford House in the Cotswolds, and a royal hunting lodge on the edge of Sherwood Forest. It appears Mademoiselle de Keroualle will profit at least as much as her predecessors; and that's without taking into account the lavish gifts of jewels and money from courtiers, ambassadors, and foreign dignitaries who use these enticements to purchase her influence with the king. Hannah has heard that the new favorite lives more luxuriously than Queen Catherine herself. After seeing only a few of the rooms of de Keroualle's expansive Whitehall suite, she believes it.

"How long has she been ill?" Hannah asks Arlington.

"Three days. And I fear she grows worse."

Initially Hannah thinks that Arlington is professing genuine concern for Mademoiselle de Keroualle, perhaps even a special fondness for her. "The king was displeased that the mademoiselle was unable to accompany him to Hampton," he continues, adding, "I should not like it to happen again." Hannah realizes that what she mistook for partiality is actually the concern of a horse owner for his prize filly. No doubt Arlington has engineered Louise's rise from maid of honor to *maitresse en titre* and has benefited greatly from it. The king's money and the courtiers' bribes pass through his hands first.

Hannah moves closer to look upon the mistress's face. Louise's beauty is the soft, placid sort: wide, dark eyes in a cherubic countenance surrounded by a mass of red-brown curls. If she were well, the rose silk curtains would mirror exactly the shade of her blushing cheeks; instead, a fevered pallor suffuses her skin, her eyes are hollowed, her lips chapped and dry. With difficulty, she lifts her head and looks at Hannah.

"Can you help me?" she asks in her heavily accented English.

"I can try." Hannah looks pointedly at Arlington: she makes no guarantee. As she puts her case down, she wonders how much he knows, or suspects. Hannah announces that she would like to see the patient alone, and that she will need more light.

To her surprise, neither Madame Severin nor Arlington protest. They leave the room with only a single glance between them, sending back the serving maid with two beeswax candles. Hannah directs her to place them on the cluttered bedside table next to a tortoiseshell comb and a pair of ruby and emerald earrings, tossed there as casually as a pair of dice.

She examines the mademoiselle carefully, first checking the hue and temperature of her skin to help determine which of the humors— blood, phlegm, yellow bile, or black bile—are out of balance. The patient is burning up yet complains of chills, indicating a morbidity of the blood. She is languorous, her vital spirits low. She responds to Hannah's litany of questions with one-word answers, and even these seem to require more strength than she possesses.

Hannah takes up one of Louise's wrists to feel her pulse: it's weak and sluggish. Her plump, pale, childlike hand has delicate long fingers and perfectly clean, trimmed nails. A hand that has never known work and never will. Hannah feels it trembling with fever and with fear. The king's mistress is afraid not only of dying, she understands, but more immediately of losing everything: her beauty, her lavish rooms overlooking the Thames, her rubies and emeralds, her monarch's love. And even though Louise de Keroualle is surrounded by wealth of a kind that most people cannot even imagine, a stab of pity pierces Hannah's heart.

She lifts the soft, weightless blanket to make a further examination of the mademoiselle's body, the necessary inspection of her female parts. The mademoiselle gave birth only three months ago, and for this reason Hannah will not bleed her. Even in the overly sanguinary, she has found that bloodletting can increase a new mother's weakness and fatigue, even engender melancholy in some cases. She scrutinizes Louise's thighs for scurvy and her toes for signs of gout. These investigations are routine, however, an afterthought. She has already found exactly what she expected to find, almost from the moment she walked into the room.

"You may rest now," she says, smoothing the duvet back into place. Louise's eyes are closed, her breathing labored but steady; she's already sinking deep into a feverish sleep. Hannah sits down on the embroidered settee next to the bed and opens her medicine case. The removable top shelf contains jars of ointment and bottles of tinctures and syrups. The space underneath cradles instruments: a scalpel and a double-edged knife, called a catlin, for minor surgeries, a lancet for opening veins. She takes out a few simple decoctions of chamomile, fennel, and nettles and sets them on the bedside table. She'll ask the maid to combine them with a pitcher of small beer and instruct her to give Louise one cup every hour, until Hannah returns tomorrow morning with the other medicines the mademoiselle will require.

She extracts the most familiar bottle, a glass vial in the top right corner. This is not for Louise but for herself. The liquid inside is as dark as strong coffee, slightly viscous from the sugar solution and bitter in spite of it. *Papaver somniferum,* mithridate, *diacordium,* tincture of opium, theriac, treacle, laudanum, poppy syrup: so many names for what is essentially the same thing, her salvation. She stirs the contents with a slim glass wand, then leans her head back, mouth open. From the wand she lets six drops fall on the back of her tongue. As she swallows, the acrid taste makes her spine shiver. She has come to anticipate with pleasure this one quick convulsion, for it means that soon she will feel some relief.

Hannah returns the bottle to its place among the others and thinks about what she will say and how she will say it. People seldom profit by being the bearer of bad news. How seriously should she take Arlington's threat of jail? Her father once told her that she should never underestimate what people will do for love or for money, especially at court. She stands and takes a moment to prepare herself before she goes in search of Lord Arlington and Madame Severin, to tell them that the king's favorite mistress has the clap.

Chapter Four

The Tuesday before Michaelmas term

IT WAS A dream come true. Claire Donovan stood, awed and excited, in the center of Trinity College's Great Court, gazing at the sixteenth-century structures enclosing the renowned courtyard. Each spired and crenellated building on the Great Court's periphery was a monument in its own right: the Tudor brick-and-mortar Great Gate, the vine-covered Master's Lodge, the imposing, peaked-roof hall, the elegant chapel. Until yesterday, she had seen the college only in photographs.

Claire had always hoped to teach in a venerable academic institution, but until her fateful trip to Venice four months ago her ambition had never vaulted beyond Harvard's ivy-covered walls, much less all the way across the Atlantic to England. She sighed audibly with pleasure at her surroundings. It didn't get much more venerable than this. Founded by Henry VIII in 1546, Trinity's antecedents stretched all the way back to 1317. Her new place of employment was not only one of the oldest schools in Cambridge but also the largest and traditionally the most aristocratic, being the college of choice of the British royal family. Its graduates included six prime ministers, numerous prize-winning physicists and mathematicians, world-famous poets, celebrated philosophers. Its members had tallied up over thirty Nobel

Prizes, more than most countries. Here at Trinity, Claire marveled, Francis Bacon had cut his teeth on philosophy and law, and Dryden had sharpened his wit. Here, Tennyson had composed his first book of lyrical poetry, and A. A. Milne had penned the light verse he'd been famous for before *Winnie-the-Pooh*. Here, Isaac Newton had secretly written the *Principia Mathematica*, and Lord Byron had famously kept a pet bear. It was also here, she reflected, that Virginia Woolf had been ignominiously barred from the library (at the time, women were not admitted unless accompanied by a fellow), and here that Soviet spies Kim Philby and Guy Burgess had begun their infamous careers. Well, no one could accuse the place of being uneventful.

The last rays of sunlight slanted across stone paths and green lawns, transforming the chapel's ivory-colored façade into a palette of buttery yellows and burnished golds. The house of worship's spiky stone spires pointed up to the heavens like a row of lit torches against the twilight sky, and the courtyard's gently splashing fountain cast a long, dome-shaped shadow across the grass. Groups of tuxedo-clad men walked along the paths, talking and laughing in a carefree manner. Occasionally they were joined by a woman, who, like Claire, wore a long gown and looked a little unsteady on her high heels. They were all headed to the same place: a huge, medieval arched doorway adjacent to the hall.

The college's one hundred and sixty fellows—or many of them, at any rate—were gathering in Trinity's grand dining hall for the annual fellowship admission dinner. Each year, three or four new fellows were sworn in, and a banquet was given to introduce them to all the other fellows. Although Claire wasn't precisely a fellow—as a temporary lecturer, her status was different—she had generously been included with the other newcomers. She discreetly hiked up the top of her strapless, copper-colored satin formal another half inch and headed with the rest through the doorway and to the hall.

The hall's lofty hammer-beam ceiling, elaborate Elizabethan wood-work, and bay-windowed alcoves were impressive even when the hall was unadorned. Tonight, the three long, narrow dining tables travers-ing its generous length were blanketed in white linen and sparkled with fine china and the school's best silver. On a short riser at the north end of the hall, the High Table waited for its illustrious guests. Above it, a sixteenth-century copy of Holbein's life-sized painting of Henry VIII gazed magisterially down upon the room. Scores of candles filled the air with a glimmering luminescence; the milling, chatting, formally dressed fellows filled it with the pleasant anticipatory hum of a special occasion. People had already begun to sit down. There were no place cards, so everyone sat where they pleased, except at High Table, which was reserved for the master, the vice-master, the bursar, the junior bursar, the librarian, the dean, and a few of the senior fellows. Claire eagerly looked around for a familiar face to sit next to, without success. But then, there were only two faces that Claire would recognize: Hoddy, or Hoddington Humphries-Todd, a history fellow she had met in Venice, and Andrew Kent.

She was here because of Andrew Kent. Four months earlier, Claire had traveled to Venice to attend an academic conference after she'd discovered that a Cambridge historian was going to give a paper on the same topic as her unfinished dissertation, the 1618 Spanish conspiracy against Venice. The speaker had turned out to be Trinity fellow Dr. Andrew Kent, an accomplished historian whose first book, *Charles II and the Rye House Plot,* had been translated into a dozen languages and made into a BBC miniseries. During their five days in Venice, Claire and Andrew had cracked a four-hundred-year-old mystery involving Alessandra Rossetti, a courtesan caught up in the conspiracy.

First, however, they'd had to overcome their mutual antipathy. Claire had initially thought Andrew pompous, highly critical, and overly competitive. Happily, she'd spent enough time with him to learn that beneath his cool English reserve he was also thoughtful, kind, occasionally funny, often brilliant, and fully deserving of the awards and accolades that had been showered upon him. He'd believed in Claire and the results of her research so completely that he'd stepped aside to let her give the final lecture on the Spanish conspiracy, an act both generous and encouraging. Not to mention the fact that he'd coughed up three thousand euros of his own money to bail her out of a jam when she'd mistakenly taken one of Alessandra Rossetti's diaries out of the Biblioteca Marciana, the Venice library.

He'd offered her the temporary position at Trinity, and they'd begun a friendship of sorts.

Exactly what sort she couldn't yet say. Throughout the summer, as she'd been completing her dissertation and preparing to move to England for the next nine months, they had corresponded almost entirely by email. The tone of Andrew's electronic missives had been friendly but not personal, and she had responded in kind. Anything else would have been unthinkable, really. As far as she knew, Andrew was still involved with Gabriella Griseri, the glamorous Italian television presenter. And now he was Claire's colleague, and a relationship of that sort would be unwise, wouldn't it? She certainly didn't want to do anything that might jeopardize her new job. It was a teaching position any newly minted historian would kill for. Claire could think of a half dozen former classmates who were probably gnashing their teeth with envy—and no one more loudly than her ex-husband Michael, an assistant professor of ancient history at Columbia University. Claire allowed herself a small, satisfied smile. She'd made certain that he'd known about her new job before she'd left home.

"Dr. Donovan." Claire heard the words, but the name didn't register; she was too busy looking for Andrew.

"Dr. Donovan."

Claire scanned the other side of the room.

"*Dr. Donovan!*"

She turned around. "It's you," she said.

"Didn't you hear me?" Andrew Kent asked.

"Of course I heard you."

"I said your name three times."

She reddened slightly. "I'm not used to it."

"Your own name?" He looked alarmed, as if he was having immediate regrets about hiring her.

How did Andrew Kent so easily manage to make her feel idiotic, inept, and irritated simultaneously? Claire took a breath and tried to remain calm; now was not the time to let an instant retort get the better of her. "I'm not accustomed to the *Dr.* Donovan," she explained. "For one thing, the ink on my degree is barely dry. For another, only physicians are addressed as 'doctor' in the U.S." She didn't add that at American universities it was considered pretentious for someone with a PhD to use the title of Doctor, but she figured that Andrew Kent already knew that. At Trinity, everyone with a PhD was known as Doctor: it was *de rigueur*. After that, only the most accomplished rose to the level of Reader; Professor was reserved for those at the very top of the academic heap.

Andrew nodded. "Yes, and in England we address surgeons as 'Mister.'"

"Why is that, anyway?"

"I'm not entirely sure. Perhaps we don't want them to forget that they were once barbers."

Claire laughed a little, Andrew smiled, and for one long, golden moment they were the only two people in the room. Perhaps it was the tuxedo, but he was even more handsome than she remembered. His dark, unkempt hair had been cropped and tamed, and his skin had a sun-kissed glow that was quite attractive. No more Scotch tape wrapped around the broken earpiece of his eyeglasses, either. In fact, no glasses at all. His large, inviting brown eyes regarded her warmly. Claire was reminded of a certain evening in Venice, a certain cobbled street, a certain few words that Andrew had said to her. What were they? "You're the most argumentative, obstinate, infuriating, exciting, and fascinating woman I've ever met"? Yes, that's exactly what he'd said; she hadn't been able to forget it. She knew he hadn't intended to say it, but there was no escaping the fact that he had. Her heart beat faster at the memory. Or was it racing because she was finally here, seeing him again?

"You're looking well," Andrew said. He cleared his throat. "That's a very nice gown."

"Thank you." Claire had paid way too much for the dress, but she liked the way its shimmering, copper-colored satin brought out the gold highlights in her brown hair and hazel eyes. She wondered if he'd noticed; it was impossible to tell. "Very nice" was probably the most effusive compliment she would hear from him. Andrew was English, after all, but she was prepared to make some allowances for that. She only hoped that they didn't become mired in the awkward small talk that always seemed to precede their real conversations.

"And how was your journey?" he asked.

Oh, dear. What could she say about a six-hour flight and a taxicab ride from Heathrow to London? Nothing terribly exciting, that was certain. She assured him it had been fine, though uneventful. "And your book?" Claire asked. "How's it coming along?"

This was more than a polite question; in fact it was something she deeply cared about. The subject of Andrew's book-in-progress was the 1618 Spanish conspiracy against Venice. He had already asked Claire's permission to quote from her dissertation.

"Very well, in fact," he replied, noticeably relaxing. "Ever since I returned from Venice, everything seems to be falling into place. Like it's writing itself, although I'm hesitant to say that out loud for fear of invoking some kind of jinx. Thank you for sending your dissertation on, by the way. I've found it enormously helpful."

Claire felt herself blushing, just a little.

Andrew cleared his throat again and looked as though he was about to ask Claire a question. She leaned closer in anticipation. Before he could speak, they were interrupted by an attractive woman who put her hand on Andrew's arm. "Andy, I've saved us a seat right next to Richard and Paula," she announced. Her manner implied that Andrew's coming away with her at once was a matter of urgent necessity.

Not that Andrew appeared to notice this. He calmly thanked the woman and turned back to Claire. "May I introduce Dr. Carolyn Sutcliffe, modern and medieval languages. Carolyn, this is Dr. Claire Donovan, the—"

"New temporary lecturer from Harvard," she finished for him in a nasal yet plummy voice that Claire suspected became even plummier when she was speaking to Americans. "Of *course* I know who she is." Carolyn Sutcliffe offered her hand for a limp handshake. She was about Andrew's age, Claire guessed, in her late thirties or thereabouts, petite, with dark auburn hair that curled under at the nape of her neck. She wore a long, scoop-neck black dress and a short strand of pearls. "Andy and Gaby have told me *so* much about you."

Gaby? Who on earth was Gaby? Claire's confusion must have been evident in her expression, for Carolyn quickly explained.

"Gabriella Griseri," she said. "We go *way* back. She's one of my *dearest* friends."

Such dear friends, Carolyn seemed to be saying, that she was willing to stand guard on Gabriella's boyfriend whenever the Italian bombshell was absent, and keep him safe from the clutches of undeserving American women. Carolyn's hand still hovered over Andrew's arm like a raptor's claw, ready to snatch him away at the earliest opportunity.

Claire decided she'd been much too kind in her first assessment; or perhaps it was Carolyn Sutcliffe's pushy demeanor that made her seem less attractive. But she was obviously a woman and basically presentable, if one overlooked the slightly manic gleam in her eyes. Which apparently Andrew did, for he didn't seem to resent Carolyn's company at all.

"I suppose we should all sit down," Andrew said. He looked at Claire. "Would you like to—"

"There's an empty seat right next to ours," Carolyn interrupted, offering Claire her first sincere smile. "Why don't you join us?"

"Thank you." Perhaps, Claire conceded, Dr. Sutcliffe wasn't so bad after all. They set off in the direction of the long table in the middle of the hall.

"You'll sit next to one of our most senior fellows," Carolyn added. "You'll have *such* fun."

When they arrived at the table, Claire discovered that the available chair wasn't "right next" to Carolyn and Andrew but across the table from them. While within view of each other, it would be nearly impossible for Claire and Andrew to carry on a conversation. She took her place next to an elderly gentleman whose name, she soon learned, was Professor Humboldt Residue, natural sciences.

"Delighted to dine with such a lovely young lass," Professor Residue said at the top of his lungs. His speckled, age-spotted head lacked hair, but there were healthy tufts of it growing in his ears. He smiled broadly at Claire. How could she rebuff such an enthusiastic welcome? Especially since Hoddy, the only other person at Trinity whom she knew besides Andrew Kent, didn't seem to be present.

The empty place at her left was soon filled by another fellow closer to Residue's advanced age than her own, a Professor Oswald Hammer, law. Unlike his friend, he had retained all of the hair on his head and a good deal more of it on his face, in the form of two mutton-chop sideburns that seemed to Claire colonial in nature, as if Professor Hammer had once served the British Raj. The two men greeted each other genially. As they appeared to have much to say to each other, Claire offered to move to allow them to sit in adjoining seats.

"Absolutely not," Professor Hammer protested.

"Wouldn't hear of it," Professor Residue insisted.

As the food arrived and wine began to flow (a battalion of waiters delivered and disposed of plates and refilled glasses with fluid ease), and the ambient noise in the hall grew steadily louder, Professors Hammer and Residue began to talk over her, leaning forward over the table and practically knocking their heads together in their desire to communicate. They spoke English, but Claire was thoroughly bewildered by the subject of their discourse. Their lively conversation's intelligibility was not improved by Professor Residue's obvious hearing impairment.

"The First and Third made a good showing in the Bumps last year, did you hear?" Professor Hammer shouted.

"Of course I heard," Professor Residue shouted in reply. "Do you think I'm deaf?"

"I meant, did you hear the news?"

"Did they win or lose?" Residue repeated. "Are you mad? They won, of course. It's the First and Third, by God," he said, banging his fist on the table.

Claire gazed longingly at Andrew Kent. He appeared to be having a perfectly enjoyable time with Carolyn Sutcliffe. They were probably talking about perfectly normal things in perfectly normal voices in a perfectly normal language. Once or twice she'd seen Andrew glance in her direction, but only briefly and never in any meaningful way. He hadn't tried to catch her eye or ask how she was doing or make an attempt to rescue her from her present company.

As Claire looked around, she realized that most of the fellows were not old duffers like Hammer and Residue but colleagues who fell into a broad age category between thirty and sixty-five. The fellows, or members of the college, were not just teachers but also the custodians of Trinity's past, present, and future, who collectively managed the school's day-to-day educational operations and its general business, including its various trusts and endowments and its legendary prodigious wealth. She had heard that underneath the college's stone buildings lay vaults filled with the many gifts—silver tea sets, gold bars, priceless antiquities, and the like—bequeathed to the college over the past four and a half centuries. Secret rooms as rich in treasures as Aladdin's cave. She wondered if it was true.

Claire also noticed that there were very few female fellows among this sea of black dinner jackets and bow ties. From where she sat, without craning her neck too noticeably Claire could count only eighteen women, including herself. Granted, there were probably a few more at the table behind her, and a few others who weren't attending the dinner; still, that meant there were probably no more than thirty female fellows out of a total one hundred and sixty. Even at Harvard, which had not matriculated women until 1972, female faculty were much more numerous than this. She hadn't known until now that Trinity was still such a predominantly male preserve.

Claire's sudden realization made her feel self-conscious. She worried that her strapless gown was showing a bit too much décolletage, and she unobtrusively tried to pull up the top of her dress—an impossible task, it turned out, while sitting down. Not that the gentlemen flanking her appeared to notice her discomfort; they were much too caught up in their discussion.

" . . . he was bowled a googly and caught at silly mid-off," Professor Hammer shouted.

"No matter what the rest of the world says, cricket's an *exciting* game," Professor Residue passionately agreed, his left hand wildly gesticulating in spite of the full wineglass in it. Claire leaned back as the professor's drink splashed onto the white tablecloth.

She suffered through the soup, the appetizer, the palate-cleansing sorbet, the main course, and the salad, a third party to a passionate dialogue about cricket, in which she comprehended very few words except for *jolly good, fancy that,* and *bugger off,* the last of which they said with startling frequency.

Dessert was served along with dessert wines and coffee, and the master, Sir Gerald Liverton, Lord Liverton of Loos, K.B.E., F.R.S., F.B.A., O.M., M.I.5, stood up to address the assembly and introduce the new fellows. Claire had already been informed by the junior bursar that as a temporary lecturer, she would be acknowledged last. She took a sip of sauterne and, with only the slightest twinge of anxiety (she'd already downed three glasses of wine), waited her turn.

"Whatever happened to old Ossery?" Professor Residue leaned across Claire and inquired of Professor Hammer in a loud whisper.

"The old bugger's standing for MP."

"And last," the master said, "please welcome Dr. Claire Donovan, who comes to us from Harvard University, where she has just earned her doctorate in history."

"Not old Ossery! The man doesn't know his arse from his elbow!"

"We have the great privilege of Dr. Donovan's company for the next three terms, during which she will supervise and lecture in history in her chosen area of study, early modern Europe . . ."

"That's never prevented anyone from becoming an MP before," Hammer chuckled. Residue joined in, his hand waving wildly about. This time, the port splashed directly on Claire's dress: directly on her beautiful, expensive, never-before-worn copper-colored satin gown, dead center between her breasts.

She looked down at the spreading stain. Should she use her napkin to dab at it? Her hand went to her lap, then froze. It hardly seemed appropriate to dab at one's own breasts on such an occasion, and in such august company. It was bad enough to be completely paralyzed as to what to do, but then Claire discovered something worse: when she looked up from gazing down at her cold, wet, wine-colored chest, she found that everyone seated nearby was also gawking at it. Andrew Kent's eyebrows rose with mild shock; Carolyn Sutcliffe's pursed mouth barely suppressed a smirk.

As the master's voice faded away, Claire heard the applause and knew she must stand up to be acknowledged. As she rose from her chair she could feel one hundred and fifty pairs of eyes turn to stare at her; she could feel the wine spreading like a bloodstain across the strapless bodice of her gown, its deep rubicund hue matching the color that must surely be rising in her cheeks. This was the moment she'd been imagining for months now: a dream come true, she thought ruefully.

Somehow she'd never imagined it quite like this.

Chapter Five

First week of Michaelmas term

"STOP LAUGHING, MEREDITH," Claire said. The sound that issued from her cell phone was bright, twinkling, and occasionally punctuated by an uncharacteristic snort. Uncharacteristic for Meredith Barnes, anyway. The assistant dean of Forsythe Academy, a preparatory school in Claire's home town of Harriot, Massachusetts, was tall, slender, glamorous, and almost completely unflappable. A deep, sexy laugh, yes; Claire had heard that plenty of times. Or even a light, lively giggle, bubbly as sparkling wine. But never a snort.

"It isn't funny," Claire added, even though she knew quite well that her protests were having little impact. "It nearly ruined my dress. It would have been ruined except that the first dry cleaner I took it to said they had lots of experience getting wine stains out of expensive fabric. Apparently it happens all the time here."

Snort.

"You're not making me feel any better." It wasn't the first time Claire had provided an occasion for her best friend's amusement. How come it never happened the other way around? Meredith never seemed to attract the sort of odd and embarrassing situations that Claire did.

"I'm sorry." Meredith's laughter settled down into a few intermittent chuckles and gasps. "And no one said anything?"

"Not a word. For the rest of the evening, people simply ignored this huge red splotch on my dress."

"Maybe they thought it was a fashion statement."

"God knows what they thought. I certainly don't. They're not at all like Americans, who are so willing to tell secrets to perfect strangers that they seem to enjoy broadcasting the most intimate details of their lives on national television."

"That's a point in England's favor."

"True."

"But that woman—"

"You mean Carolyn Sutcliffe?"

"I think she deserves another name, one that rhymes with witch," Meredith said. "She put you next to that old guy on purpose. She knew what was going to happen to you even before you sat down."

"She couldn't have known that he was going to spill wine on me."

"She knew *something* bad would happen."

After the dinner had ended, all of the fellows had gone to the Master's Lodge for a long-standing tradition of after-dinner brandies and introductions: each older fellow was expected to introduce him or herself to each new fellow. It had been exhilarating in a way—the first time she had ever met one hundred and fifty or so people in one night—but unfortunately it had meant that she and Andrew hadn't been able to talk, at least no more than the same polite banter she'd exchanged with the other fellows. She had felt frustrated by this, but Andrew hadn't seemed to mind. "I wish I could read people better," Claire said. "I can't tell what they're thinking. Except for Dr. Sutcliffe, who appears to hate me simply because her friend does."

"Do you really care what they're thinking?"

"Of course I care." Well, there was at least *one* person whose thoughts she would have dearly loved to know, but he was as enigmatic as all the others, perhaps even more so. Why hadn't Andrew Kent made an effort to sit next to her at the dinner? After all, he was practically the only person at Trinity she knew. Didn't he feel some responsibility to take her under his wing? "I'm just not so sure I'm going to fit in," Claire admitted.

"Why not?"

"For one thing, I'm not a man. I looked up the roll of fellows, and among the total one hundred and sixty, only twenty-seven are women. That's approximately sixteen percent—only one woman for every five point nine men."

"Really? What does nine-tenths of a man look like?"

"Don't mess with me. Among the students, the split is fairly even, about fifty-fifty. But among the fellows, women are a distinct minority. Minorities are a distinct minority too."

"So it's still an old boy's club, is it?"

"Appears that way."

"You can't let that intimidate you. In fact, it should spur you on to greater achievement. Your success isn't just about you, it's about all the women who come after you."

"That's occurred to me already. It's not exactly helping to alleviate my stress."

"I know you, Claire," Meredith said seriously. "And I know that you of all people have what it takes to make a success of this opportunity."

"I wish I felt as confident as you." Claire looked around at her set of rooms, or set, as it was called: a small suite that consisted of a main room with a dining table for four and a cozy armchair and floor lamp; an adjacent office with a desk, bookshelves, and a computer; and a bedroom and bath. The windows of the main room and the office looked over New Court, so called because it was a mere two hundred years old. Her set was larger, more light-filled and generally much more pleasant than she had expected her college living quarters to be. She couldn't complain. Everything was terrific, really. Except that Trinity College was so different from American colleges, from the architectural design of the school itself (a succession of courtyards where both students and fellows lived and taught) to the curriculum and style of teaching. If she had landed a job at an American university, she would have understood the environment and the people at once; God knows she'd been in school long enough.

"It isn't just being a woman and a minority that worries me," Claire explained. "It's being an American. It's being *me*. I have a habit of saying exactly what I think at the moment that I think it."

"Oh, that." Three thousand miles across the Atlantic, Claire imagined her best friend's head bobbing in agreement. "Yes, you might want to keep that in check," Meredith offered.

"You think?"

"Don't be cheeky."

Claire quickly learned that supervisions—one-on-one, hour-long teaching sessions held in a fellow's set of rooms—were the primary mode of instructing students at Cambridge colleges and were considered the cornerstone of Cambridge's academic environment. In theory, undergraduates were taught by all members of the faculty, even the most senior. In practice, the junior members of a department bore the brunt of the supervisions, some of them carrying a load of twenty students a week or more. Perhaps because she was so new to Cambridge, Claire was assigned a mere twelve, for which she was grateful. They arrived at her set Monday through Thursday afternoons, three students per day, beginning at one o'clock. Claire was required to assign an essay each week, and each week the students were required to turn it in twenty-four hours before their meeting. Claire read and marked them in advance of the supervision, at which time she would go over each student's paper, offering insights and tips on how to improve it. In addition to the supervisions, once a week she helped a small group of first- and third-year students prepare for their Historical Practice and Argument paper, during which they would discuss questions such as, What is the difference between history and myth? The students weren't expected to attend any other classes per se, although there were numerous lectures and seminars on constant offer. The first-year undergrads would not have to take a test until the end of their second year.

It was a system that expected a lot from young students: superior writing skills, the ability to work independently, and, Claire soon realized, a certain maturity that was not always present in eighteen-year-olds. She quickly ascertained that her students could be neatly separated into two camps: those who were inordinately well prepared and those who apparently planned to make no effort at all, except perhaps for the effort involved in making up excuses for missing supervisions or not completing their work on time.

In addition to the supervisions, Claire was required to lecture once a week in one of the small, nondescript lecture rooms in the history faculty building. Most important of all, she was expected to research and write papers in her field of study, papers that would be published in the appropriate journals, then published in the appropriate anthologies. In time, she would have to write a book of her own. The publish-or-perish sword hung above every academic's head, but in truth she looked forward to the day when she'd be working on a long, complex project. For the time being, however, Claire concentrated on doing her job and learning her way around the college, the town of Cambridge, and her new life.

Within a few days she discovered that her new position was accompanied by numerous, often intriguing, perquisites. Two she'd known about before leaving the United States: like the fellows, she was lodged and fed at the college's expense. But dining in hall at High Table with the fellows, more than a few of whom, like Professors Hammer and Residue, had already achieved an august and tweedy dotage, was an experience slightly more daunting than she'd anticipated. It didn't help that portraits of Francis Bacon, Isaac Newton, John Dryden, and Lord Tennyson gazed upon her reproachfully, as if they'd known she was an upstart American and suspected that she was way out of her league.

A couple of Claire's privileges struck her as whimsical, indicative of the idiosyncratic character of a four-hundred-and-fifty-year-old institution. She had the right to order wine for her own private reserve. It would be kept in Trinity's extensive wine cellars, rumored to be vast beyond measure. And, unlike students or tourists, she was allowed to walk with impunity on the patchy but highly regarded grass that grew in the college's courtyards. Other benefits, however, were rich with promise. The fellows' key, or F key as it was commonly known, was presented to Claire soon after her arrival by the junior bursar, who informed her that the F key unlocked doors and gates to places that were off-limits to students, such as the Fellows' Garden and the Fellows' Bowling Green, and an unknown number of other sites, both interior and exterior, that were hidden amongst the hallowed stone buildings, arched doorways, leaded glass windows, and creeping ivy of Trinity's medieval environs. Places, he seemed to hint, rendered almost magical by their secret, restricted nature.

But her most enjoyable perk so far was the simple pleasure of going into the Combination Room—that veritable bastion of school (male) tradition, with its wing-back chairs, dim green-glass lamps, and neatly pressed copies of the *Times*—to help herself to a cup of tea from the coffee, tea, and sherry service always at the ready. The tea was served in a china cup and saucer, and stirred with a silver spoon; here one would never find modern atrocities such as Styrofoam cups or plastic stirrers. Tea, Claire learned, was one of the more hospitable aspects of an often chilly country and could always be counted on to provide warmth and comfort.

At present Claire was in need of both, for she had just given her first lecture.

"Underwhelming," would be a nice word for it; a "flop" was probably more accurate. There'd been a grand total of one student in the room, and even he had arrived late, mumbling something about Boat Club tryouts as an excuse: hardly a propitious beginning to Claire's Cambridge career. As soon as she had finished, Claire had fled the lecture room and made her way downstairs to the faculty meeting room on the second floor, where she was dismayed to discover that the hot water dispenser was out of order.

Behind her, a throat cleared. "You have to strike it," a woman said.

Claire turned around. The woman nearest her sat on a sleek leather couch, reading a copy of the latest *English Historical Review*. More academic journals were stacked on the coffee table: *Past & Present, Continuity and Change, Early Science and Medicine*. No doubt each one of them contained an article or two by members of the history faculty. On the wall above the woman's head hung a bold, colorful example of Expressionist art, possibly the only painting in the entire university less than two hundred years old. Indeed, the meeting room resembled a spread from an IKEA catalog, incongruous when compared to the rest of Cambridge but in keeping with the architecture of the Sidgwick Site building. In a university town where most college structures were made of stone and dated as far back as the fourteenth century, it seemed a fluke—or perhaps it was purposefully ironic—that the Cambridge history faculty was housed in a modern glass and steel building designed in the 1960s. At the far end of the lounge, floor-to-ceiling windows offered a dizzying view of a small car park and, beyond that, a rather glorious vista of the gently curving River Cam.

The history fellow seemed so engrossed in the journal that at first Claire wasn't certain she had spoken. Then the woman raised her right hand and made a fist to demonstrate. "You have to hit it," she said, briefly glancing over the top of her half-frame reading glasses. Duly instructed, Claire knocked on the dispenser, which spewed forth a measured stream of hot water, precisely enough for one cup of tea. In it she steeped a bag of Earl Grey, then looked for a place to sit down.

"How did it go?" The woman barely glanced up from her book.

"How did what go?" Claire asked.

"Your lecture." This time she favored Claire with eye contact.

Claire reckoned she should probably get used to the fact that as a new fish in a fairly small pond, others would recognize her before she recognized them. She certainly didn't recognize the woman who was speaking to her. She was in her late forties or early fifties, Claire guessed, but blessed with one of those high-browed aristocratic faces, slightly horsey but very appealing, that seemed impervious to time.

"It was terrible," Claire confessed. "Only one student showed up."

"That's one more than Isaac," she responded with a tilt of her head and a raise of her eyebrows. A few gray strands lightly streaked her chestnut brown hair, which was worn in a fashionable, shoulder-length blunt cut. She was fit, as though she walked a great deal, rode a bike daily, or was a yoga fanatic, any of which was possible in Cambridge.

Against the tawny, lightly freckled skin exposed above the V-neck of her beige cashmere sweater, a tiny, rose-colored pearl dangled on a thin gold chain. A pair of stylish wool slacks bared trim ankles and new, unscuffed black leather flats. She possessed a no-nonsense elegance, in her simple but expensive clothes, and she radiated intelligence and a brisk self-sufficiency.

"Isaac?" Claire repeated.

"Newton, of course," she replied as if everyone was, or should be, on a first-name basis with the father of modern physics. "He was a Trinity fellow for thirty-three years, and there's no record that anyone ever attended his lectures. Apparently he just spoke to the walls." She paused thoughtfully. "Although I doubt that Science and Religion in Early Modern Italy is ever going to have the same impact as the theory of gravity or the invention of calculus."

"No, I suppose it wouldn't," Claire said.

The woman removed her reading glasses, folded the earpieces carefully before setting them on top of the journal, and fixed her bright hazel eyes on Claire. "Have any of the students put your bicycle in a tree yet?"

"No."

"Oh." The woman sounded disappointed. "Well, there's still time," she added reassuringly. Her eyes narrowed slightly. "You don't remember me, do you?"

"I'm so sorry. There were so many people—"

"No need to apologize. No one ever remembers what happens during those dinners. The fellows can drink enough wine in one night to launch a battleship." She held out her hand. "Elizabeth Bennet, social history, Britain, nineteenth century."

"Elizabeth Bennet?" Claire repeated. Elizabeth Bennet as in *Pride and Prejudice*? she wanted to ask but didn't, suddenly intuiting that this was an obvious and stupid question. Unfortunately it had already been implied in her tone. She could see that at once by the look of annoyance on Elizabeth Bennet's face.

The fellow sighed and fiddled a bit with her glasses. "Yes. Elizabeth

Bennet as in *Pride and Prejudice*. If you say she's your favorite character from literature, I'll scream." She shook her head. "The Jane Austen revival of the past fifteen years has made my life a misery."

Claire had no idea how to respond. In less than five minutes, she felt as though she had managed to put not one but both feet in her mouth.

"So tell me," Elizabeth said, "which was she: proud or prejudiced?"

"Prejudiced. Darcy was proud."

"Well done."

A man breezed into the lounge and walked over to join them. "Lizzie, I was wondering if you'd received my note. So who's this we have here?" he said with an inquisitive glance at Claire.

"She's the new lecturer," Elizabeth replied. A sour expression crossed her face as she put her glasses back on and opened the *English Historical Review* once more. "She's filling in for Emily Scott while she's on maternity leave. If you had been at the dinner you would know this."

He turned to Claire. "My deepest apologies. If I'd known that someone as pretty as you was going to be there, I never would have missed it. Derek Goodman," he said, offering his hand.

He didn't add his title or field of study, as he probably knew there was no need. He was Derek Goodman, Claire marveled, the renowned author of *Reform and Revolution: The Roots of British Democracy* and *Heads Will Roll: Capital Punishment during the Reign of the Tudor and Stuart Kings*. Derek Goodman, one of the leading lights of the Cambridge history faculty, a reputed genius and a former wunderkind who'd received his PhD at twenty-five. Ever since, he'd been writing books and articles on British history at an extraordinary rate, and he was published in all the best journals and invited to all the best conferences.

Claire introduced herself, unable to conceal her admiration. As she shook Dr. Goodman's hand, he looked her up and down in a way that was discreet enough but was also unambiguously sexual, something that most men would know better than to attempt. She suspected that Derek Goodman was accustomed to getting away with it, for not only was he brilliant, he was handsome. Movie-star handsome. Short, curly black hair that contrasted dramatically with his startling, mesmerizing blue eyes. Confident, charming, of above-average height and way-above-average sexiness. His book jacket photos, while stunning, didn't do him justice. The images Claire recalled must have been taken some years earlier. He now looked to be three or four years short of forty, and a face that had once been a bit too pretty had taken on a craggy masculinity that was accentuated by his two-day-old beard and the striped wool scarf wound around his neck, one end thrown rakishly back over the shoulder of his navy blue blazer. Under that he wore a white Oxford cloth button-down shirt and a pair of well-worn but well-fitting jeans.

"You're American," he said with delight. "A gorgeous American in our midst. Whatever shall we do with you?" His blue eyes twinkled mischievously. Damn if she didn't feel a bit weak in the knees.

"Keep your dogs in the kennel, Derek," Elizabeth said without glancing up. "She hasn't been here long enough to know that you're the most unscrupulous man in Cambridge."

"I love you too, Dr. Bennet," he said sarcastically, though he seemed completely unfazed by her criticism. He went on speaking to Claire as if Elizabeth hadn't said a word. "It must have been you I saw moving in last week. G staircase in New Court?" At Claire's nod, he looked at her with an even warmer enthusiasm. "My set is right across from yours."

"You might want to keep your door locked," Elizabeth remarked, moistening a fingertip and flipping a page.

"Don't mind her," Derek said. "We had a fling years ago and she's never gotten over me."

"Don't you wish."

"Has anyone taken you on a pub crawl yet?" he asked Claire.

"No."

"Then allow me. After dinner in hall tonight. We'll start out at the Rat and Weasel and make the circuit all the way 'round to the Mad Cow." In spite of the unpleasant associations that rats, weasels, and mad cows brought to mind, Derek Goodman made the prospect of going on a tour of Cambridge pubs seem immensely enjoyable.

"You've come in too late in the game on this one, Dr. Goodman," Elizabeth said. "I believe she's already spoken for."

"Is this true?" he asked Claire.

"I'm not quite sure what she—," Claire began.

"Didn't Andrew Kent hire you?" Elizabeth asked, peering up at her.

"Yes."

"He's bent over backward to make sure that you've got everything you could possibly wish for."

Claire felt her face flush. Andrew Kent bent over backward for her? But he'd hardly even talked to her; they'd had only one conversation since she'd arrived. What in the world did Dr. Bennet mean? And why was she so snide about it, as if there was something inherently wrong with being hired by him?

Perhaps, Claire realized with a sudden, sinking feeling in her stomach, Andrew Kent was known for hiring women in whom he had a personal interest. It occurred to her that she could be the most recent in a long line of research assistants and junior fellows, an appalling thought. One thing was certain: she was already the subject of speculation and gossip. Perhaps it was unavoidable when you were the new fish in the pond. Pond? Ha. More like goldfish bowl.

"But I hardly know Dr. Kent." Claire shook her head. "It's not like that at all."

"So sorry," Elizabeth said in a way that didn't sound even remotely apologetic. "I guess I'd got completely the wrong idea."

"So you're available tonight after all?" Derek asked.

"No, not tonight. I have an, um, appointment," she stammered.

"An appointment?" he said skeptically.

"Yes, an appointment." Claire set her cup and saucer on the counter. "Goodness, look at the time! I've got a supervision back at my set in fifteen minutes."

She backed out of the lounge, smiling and offering a few words about how pleased she was to meet them, and made a rapid retreat down the stairs. An appointment. What a lame excuse. Of course she didn't have an appointment that evening.

She had a date with Andrew Kent.

Chapter Six

4 November 1672

HANNAH WALKS THROUGH Louise de Keroualle's suite until she spies Lord Arlington and Madame Severin taking wine in a small sitting room. How is she going to explain the mademoiselle's illness? She knows of no delicate way to phrase it; perhaps she should remind them that the news could well be worse. At least she is a physician who understands the difference between the clap, as it is known in England, and its more virulent cousin, syphilis, commonly called the pox. Hannah has seen patients with both complaints and knows that a misdiagnosis can easily be made, even by experienced doctors. This misunderstanding sadly increases the sufferer's anguish, as the treatments for the pox and the clap are quite different, and one does nothing to dispel the miseries and sad consequences of the other disease. Woe especially to he who has gonorrhea, or running of the reins (for it is believed that the unwholesome urethral discharge comes from the kidneys), and is recommended by some quack doctor to a course of treatment for the pox, which consists almost exclusively of preparations containing mercury: mercury lotions, mercury pills, mercury enemas, mercury steam baths. The metallic chemical has shown some efficacy in arresting the development of the pox, but its effects are loathsome: excessive salivation, nausea, fluxing, blackening of the gums, loosened teeth, hair loss, melancholia, frenzy, even mental derangement. And of course it does nothing to cure the clap, which, left untreated, can cause barrenness in women and, in men, strangury, an inflammation of the prostate—occasioning a discomfort even greater than that which was experienced at the beginning. The lengthy, expensive cures for the pox are often taken at private spas or baths on the outskirts of London, because in spite of the fact that the diseases of Venus are rampant in all classes of society, they are socially stigmatizing.

Every physician in London is all too aware that venereal disease is epidemic, but no one knows how many Londoners die annually from the pox or from complications of the clap. The relatives of the dead often bribe the searchers, elderly women hired by the parish to record the cause of death, to overlook any sign of venereal disease upon the late beloved. In this way, the Bills of Mortality—published each week by the parish-clerks of London, and given in a monthly report to His Majesty the King—have included, along with the usual number of deaths from Fever and Consumption, fatalities of a strange and mysterious nature, such as Timpany, Rising of the Lights, and Vapors in the Head.

Her father's mentor, Dr. Thomas Sydenham, was one of the first physicians to make clear the distinctions between the two diseases. Charles Briscoe built upon Dr. Sydenham's illuminating observations of the disease process and, like him, often set aside humoral theory in favor of his empirical findings. Both men believed that illness was caused not by an imbalance of humors but by an outside agent working on the body. The patient's imbalance was simply another symptom of disease. This departure from traditional Galenic theory was controversial, but it had some impressive results. In the course of his years with the permissive English court, both in France and in England, Dr. Briscoe developed, by popular demand as it were, a special serum and a method of treatment for the clap that enjoyed a reputation for being as sure as it was secret. And Hannah is the only one who knows it.

If she wasn't so overcome by the manner in which Arlington chose to make off with her, she might have realized sooner why she was suddenly so necessary to him, why he chose her instead of one of the court

doctors. Arlington knew, or at least suspected, what afflicted Louise before he abducted Hannah.

When she enters the sitting room and informs him and Madame
Severin of her diagnosis, he does not look surprised.

"It is not the pox, then?" Madame Severin asks.

"No, but there is still cause for concern," Hannah replies. "She has
an extreme exacerbation of the clap such as I have rarely seen. If she
survives, she may no longer be able to conceive."

"*If* she survives?" Madame Severin turns reproachfully on Arlington,
speaking angrily in French. "You told me that she had a secret cure, that
it was infallible."

"Madame Severin, you should be aware that Mrs. Devlin is fluent
in the French tongue." The minister's voice is steady, though Hannah
notes a strain of irritation underneath: he does not brook being spoken
to in such a way. "Her mother is French and her father raised his family
in France during the king's exile, as any good Royalist, such as her father
once was, would have done. I beg you to be more discreet."

Hannah senses Madame Severin's cold fury at Arlington's reprimand, but the mistress of the bedchamber is too experienced a courtier
to show her displeasure. And what does the minister mean by that dig
at her father: a good Royalist as he *once* was? She knows that her father
became disillusioned with the king after the Restoration, but so did
many others. What happened between him and Arlington?

"Do you have knowledge of your father's secret cure or not?" the
minister inquires, keeping to the point. He is, as he said, a busy man.

"I do, although I am hesitant to call it a cure. I don't believe that
he ever ministered to a woman as seriously ill as Mademoiselle de
Keroualle, so I cannot guarantee its efficacy in all cases. I can only assure you that I will do my best to help her."

"Your best had better be perfect," Arlington warns. "Excepting the
king, Mademoiselle de Keroualle has no better friends than Madame
Severin and I, and we intend that she shall receive the finest care, for
her own sake as well as the king's."

And for your own sake as well, Hannah adds silently.

"Obviously," Arlington continues, "we cannot conceal that the mademoiselle is ill, but we require discretion concerning the nature of her illness. We will put it about that she has a contagious ague and does not want to expose the court doctors and thence the entire court to her infirmity. Do not let it be known that you are your father's daughter. We will say you are a childhood friend with knowledge of physick, here out of mercy.

"We'll expect you tomorrow morning," he says as he escorts Hannah to the door of the mademoiselle's suite. She is met there by his manservant, who leads her back along Whitehall's shadowy paths through the privy gardens and to the street, where a carriage awaits: Lord Arlington's own carriage this time, an ostentatious vehicle of gleaming black lacquer generously trimmed with gold. As the horses break into a canter, Hannah realizes that the poppy syrup has begun its merciful work. The coach bounces over a deep pothole, swerves and lists, and she hardly feels anything. The pain she does feel seems distant, almost as if it is happening to someone else.

She turns her gaze from the window to look across the carriage at Arlington's man, her unwanted chaperone. What is his name? *Jeremy,* he said, *Jeremy Maitland at your service.* As she intuited earlier, he isn't a ruffian, he's too thin and fine featured, but in spite of his appearance he sports a deep cut across the back of his left hand. She hazily wonders how it happened. More important, it's poorly dressed; the tattered bandage is soaked with blood.

"Have you seen a doctor for that?" Hannah asks.

"This?" He raises his hand as if he hasn't noticed it before. "It's only a scratch."

"People can die from scratches." The coach rocks and the hood of her cloak settles around her shoulders.

"Not me." As if he feared he might have been rude, he adds, "I've never had much use for doctors. Most of them do more harm than good."

"Regrettably, that is too often true. *Ars longa, vita brevis,*" she says, then remembers that Maitland is a servant; he will not have any Latin. She translates Hippocrates' adage: "'The art of healing is long, and life is short.' There is much I don't know, but I can help with that if you like."

"You're a doctor?" he inquires as if he does not quite believe it, but is impressed in spite of his stated dislike for the profession. It makes her want to boast a little, even to confide in him, but she remembers Arlington's strict demand for secrecy and thinks better of touting her expertise.

"I have some knowledge of physick," she answers cautiously, "and have medicines right here in my case." The coach shakes and the glass vials jiggle against the wood box as if on cue.

"All right then." He holds out his hand. She takes it and gingerly unwinds the bloodied bandage. The cut looks new, a few hours old at most. His hand is surprisingly strong and uncalloused. She opens a jar of ointment of yarrow, good for healing wounds and inflammations.

"This may burn a little," she warns as she dabs it over his injury. To her surprise he makes no outcry and does not jerk his hand away. She looks at his face, expecting to see the hurt registered there, but he is composed. "You weathered that well," she says, using a linen cloth from her cabinet to bind his hand.

"As I said, it's only a scratch. I've suffered much worse. But you've done a fine job, I see," he says, turning his cleaned, bandaged hand in front of his face. "And now, Doctor, what is my payment to be? What do I owe you for saving my life?"

His questions are innocuous, but there's an underlying impertinence in Maitland's manner. Hannah looks away, suddenly self-conscious, aware of the plainness of her wool dress, her simple linen petticoats, her disheveled hair, how tired she must look. There was a time when she would have countered his youthful impudence with a smile and a riposte, but now it only makes her ill at ease.

"I do not charge for such trifles. As you said, it is nothing."

Her cool, reserved manner is not lost upon him. "Have I offended you? Perhaps you think me too familiar."

"There is no harm done, Mr. Maitland. But you are quite young to be so bold."

"I will soon be twenty-one," he protests.

"And I am just turned twenty-five, and a widow."

They travel on in awkward silence for a few minutes before the coach comes to a stop outside her house. "May I see you inside?" he asks.

"It isn't necessary." She hears the coach driver jump down to the street. As soon as he opens the carriage door, she pushes her way out. Maitland exits after her. "It is late, Mr. Maitland," she says. "You should go home and sleep."

"I don't sleep." His eyes search her face. "Neither do you."

His behavior is so impertinent that it could get him dismissed from Lord Arlington's service, though he does not seem like the sort who is forward with all women. The young Mr. Maitland appears instead to be naively passionate, sincere, and vulnerable, so she withholds her censure. But it is late; she is tired, although not sleepy; she is feeling the effects of the poppy syrup; and she fears that her impressions are not sound. How did he guess that she does not sleep? It's unnerving. It creates an unwanted complicity with him, as if they share a secret. But to encourage this intimacy would be unkind, for she has no intention of allowing it to go any further.

"Good night, Mr. Maitland." She unlocks the front door and lets herself in, waiting there until she hears the sound of the coach fade away. How small and plain her dining room and parlor look now, after Whitehall, after Mademoiselle de Keroualle's grand apartments. Yet she can't help breathing a sigh of relief that she is gone from there and is home, if only briefly. These quiet hours of the night are her favorite time: no carriages rattling past, no cries from the water-sellers and the fishmongers and the assorted peddlers of food, drink, and coal who patrol the streets during the day. She has spent many nights alone in her bedroom, reading her medical books and recording her daily observations, listening to the shudders and sighs of the house as it settles. She likes the sensation that the house itself is slumbering, enfolding its inhabitants within its walls. She can tell, just by listening, that they are all in their beds: Mrs. Wills, Lucy and Hester, her mother. She would love to tiptoe up the creaking stairs to her attic room and try to sleep. Instead, she glances out the front window into the empty street, listens for the "All's well" cry of the night watchman, and picks up her medicine case once more.

Chapter Seven

JENNY DORSET HAD good luck before in an alley off Fleet Lane, earning five shillings from a gent stumbling home after an evening in the White Hart Tavern. Not really a gentleman, more like a middling sort, she corrects herself. And then, because she is honest with herself even when it rankles, she admits that he wasn't even a middling sort, just some poor bloke who'd won a few coins at cards and was too drunk to count when he put the money in her hands. But in the dark, standing up in the alley, what difference did it make, gent or bloke? No difference to her purse, at any rate. Money is money, the winter's coming on, she's got a new mouth to feed. As she looks for a dark niche near the tavern, she thinks of little Jack, her Jackie-boy, that tiny, red-faced, wizened little monster she grudgingly loves. Soon she finds the place she remembers, an alcove just beyond the light from the lanterns outside the White Hart. Not so out of the way that no one will walk by, but private enough that a man might be persuaded to satisfy a need before he goes home to bed. She looks up and down the alley for any sign of another petticoat or a folded fan, the wanton's stock-in-trade. She's the interloper here, a part-timer, and if any of the regular Fleet Lane whores find her on their turf, they'll beat her and run her off.

Confident that she's alone, she settles back into her chosen spot and fends off the cold with a few cherished fantasies. Jenny Dorset is still young enough to believe that it's only a matter of time before a gentleman comes along and takes her away from her life of never enough—never enough food, never enough warmth, never enough amusement—and away from her despised and servile drudgery as a seamstress's assistant. It's not such an outlandish idea: she's always been pretty, everyone says so, even since the baby was born, and she is not yet eighteen. She knows that gentlemen are sometimes seen slumming 'round here, swords clattering at their hips as they make their merry way from tavern to tavern. And why shouldn't she dream? The king himself has taken an actress as one of his mistresses and put her up in a grand house in Pall Mall with servants and coaches and every manner of luxury. Everyone knows that the only difference between an actress and a common strumpet is that actresses have the advantage of strutting their wares upon a stage.

Jenny is thinking about how this fine gentleman will be so overcome by her beauty that he will forgive her for her youthful indiscretion, the result of which was little Jackie, when three men exit the tavern. It must be packed to the rafters inside: when the door opens, Jenny hears a riot of booming voices, clattering dishes, raucous laughter. The door shuts heavily behind them. The sounds of the tavern fade, and tobacco smoke laced with the sour smell of beer wafts through the alley. As the men stand together under a dim lantern light, Jenny takes their stock. Disappointingly, they're not grandees: no lace, no swords, no bigwigs. Roundheads, she decides, Parliamentarians who wish to take power away from the king. Not that Jenny cares much: men are men. Even the most pious Protestant can't resist a bit of twang now and then.

"You're playing a dangerous game, Osborne," one of them says to another. The man he addresses has a wicked birthmark upon his brow, larger than a crown and so dark it's nearly the color of blood.

"I have an unrestricted charter to travel between England and France signed by Arlington himself," says he. "Not to mention my patroness in France." The two other men—one portly and one thin, both older than the one called Osborne—share a cautious glance.

"But they're Catholics," the thin one says with distaste.

"All the better to cover our activities. I tell you, gentlemen"—
Osborne lowers his voice—"ever since the princess made me a party to
this Devil's pact I have had more freedom than ever before. Why should
we not use it to further our own ends?"

They talk some more, their voices so low Jenny can't make out
the words, then the men split up without so much as a by-your-leave.
Osborne walks toward her. He's better dressed than most men here-
abouts, but somber-like, and not, by the looks of him, much of a tippler.
He is old, at least thirty. Not exactly what she had hoped for in the way
of custom, but just as she makes up her mind to tap his cheek with her
fan and give him a sly wink, another whore steps out of the shadows.

She stands between Jenny and her mark, and she is tall enough
that the hood of her cloak obscures the lower half of his face. Even so,
Jenny can see him—light falls on the pair from the tavern's upstairs
windows—and in Osborne's eyes she sees a surprise that equals her
own. He's so befuddled by the harlot's sudden appearance that Jenny
nearly laughs out loud, stifling herself when she remembers what will
happen to her if the old bawd discovers her. "I've got something for
you, Mr. Osborne," the whore says in a sultry, dulcet-toned voice.

Osborne tries to shake her off, but she turns with him so that they
remain face-to-face, his back angling toward the alley wall. His voice
rises enough for Jenny to hear his anger: "I'm not going to—," he cries,
but then the whore makes a sudden lunging movement and he breaks
off in the middle of the sentence. Jenny very nearly laughs again—she's
never seen a man so rattled by a whore—as he staggers back a few steps
and bumps into the wall. Osborne's hands clutch at his stomach just
below his left breast. A black liquid gushes through his fingers. Jenny
sees the terror in his eyes as he looks at his hands and then into the
harlot's face, and catches a glimpse of the shining blade flashing from
the folds of her cloak. Osborne continues to stare at his attacker, his
mouth open in mute horror. He manages to stutter, "I know you . . ."
just before she stabs him again, low in the belly this time, then rips the
knife up through his abdomen to his chest. His eyes roll back, blood
spills from his lips.

Jenny claps her hand over her mouth, afraid she'll scream and give herself away. Osborne's body slumps to the ground. The whore squats down and quickly removes the gloves from his hands. On the smallest finger of his right hand is a gold band. She attempts to pull it off, but the ring won't budge. Jenny's eyes grow round as she watches the whore bend back the entire finger—it makes a sharp cracking sound, like a stout branch snapped off a tree—then cut it off with the knife, as expertly as a butcher chopping off a chicken leg. Then she grabs onto the finger next to it and slices it off, too.

Quivering with fear, Jenny shrinks into the shadows, making herself as small and invisible as she possibly can. She must have gasped, though, because the whore suddenly stops and looks around. She stands, slipping the severed fingers into her cloak pocket. Then she turns toward Jenny, the bloody knife still gripped in her hand.

Jenny can't tell whether the woman is young or old; she wears a vizard, a black fabric mask, that conceals the lower portion of her face. Above it, her eyes are enraged, terrifying. Jenny is too petrified to speak, even though she wants to. She wants to say that she has no money, no jewels. That she is not yet eighteen. That she has a little baby named Jack, her Jackie-boy.

But all she can do is stand there and shiver.

Chapter Eight

First week of Michaelmas term

THE MOMENT CLAIRE saw Hoddington Humphries-Todd standing in Nevile's Court near the short flight of stairs leading up to the hall, she knew that, in essence, Andrew Kent had stood her up. "Darling!" Hoddy said, bending his lanky frame to give her a friendly buss on the cheek. "How lovely to see you. Something's come up and Andy's busy this evening. But he did say he'd try to make it up to you soon. In the meantime he's asked me to be your escort. That's if you don't mind," he concluded with an irresistibly lopsided grin.

"Of course I don't mind." Claire was delighted to see the history fellow, and she sincerely hoped that he hadn't noticed her fleeting look of disappointment.

Possessed of a natural panache, Hoddy was looking exceptionally well, still radiant with a late-summer tan and dressed somewhat unseasonably in a dapper linen suit, as if he refused to believe that summer had ended. One glance at the sky would have convinced him otherwise. In the past few hours, the cold but clear autumn weather had been transformed by a bank of storm clouds that glowered with menace, casting a preternatural, rather medieval gloom over Trinity's Tudor gates and stone spires.

"I take it you've already had the incomparable experience of dining at High Table," Hoddy said.

"Yes."

"Given that you will have many other opportunities to do so over the next three terms, what say you we blow this joint and go out for a hamburger and a beer?" He folded his arms over his chest and shivered. "Someplace with a cozy fire," he added. "Alitalia lost my luggage, and this is the only decent suit I've got."

"Now that's a real burger," Hoddy said as the waiter set down two plates with towering stacks of toasted bread, thick, juicy beef patties, and sides of crisp lettuce, fresh tomato, and perfectly browned fries—no, in England they were called chips, Claire remembered. They sat across from each other in red leather club chairs a few feet away from a crackling fire in a wide brick hearth. Overhead, the beam and plaster ceiling glowed with the warm firelight, which winked cheerfully on the mullioned windows overlooking Green Street.

"It's not so easy to get an honest-to-God hamburger in Cambridge anymore," Hoddy informed her, carefully adding the garnish to his two-fisted dinner while eyeing it with carnivorous zeal. "Many of the cafés and even some of the pubs have gone vegan and serve some sort of wheatgrass-soybean-hemp concoction. I wouldn't recommend it unless you enjoy the taste of cardboard combined with garden trimmings." He fell silent as he took his first bite, his eyes fluttering closed with pleasure. "Even Italy, home to what I am convinced is the finest cuisine in the world, cannot seem to master the art of the burger."

They ate in companionable silence until finally Claire pushed her plate away. Hoddy was looking satiated too.

"You were in Italy all summer?" she asked.

"Except for three weeks in Mykonos and Crete."

"And here I was feeling sorry for you in that flimsy suit."

"This flimsy suit cost a pretty euro, I'll have you know. Anyway, my holiday in Greece was much too brief. I spent most of the summer in Rome. I could complain that it was too hot and there were too many cars and too many tourists and it would be true, except that it was bloody fabulous in spite of all that. I haven't quite returned yet, if you know what I mean."

A certain melancholy in his voice and expression made Claire wonder if it was Rome he was sad to leave behind, or someone in Rome.

"You weren't at the dinner," Claire remarked.

"I know, I was very naughty, and I've already received a dressing-down from the vice-master. But I couldn't help it. I stayed in Italy a bit longer than I'd planned. I had a quite remarkable experience, in fact," Hoddy continued in a cheerier tone. "Some friends of friends turned out to be filmmakers shooting a film at Cinecitta, and I was given a small but important role in it."

"You acted in a film?" Claire asked, impressed.

Hoddy preened a bit. "A watershed moment for Italian cinema, I daresay."

"What role did you play?"

"I believe I was billed as 'Bullet-Riddled Corpse, Number Three.'" He popped the last of his chips into his mouth. "The director said that I had an uncanny ability to appear dead. I don't know if it was a compliment to my acting prowess or to my Englishness. In any case, it was a great deal of fun." His smile faded. "However, I didn't ask you here to tell you about what I did on my summer vacation."

"No?"

"No. All the new fellows are paired up with an older fellow, who is supposed to make sure they're getting along all right. Originally Andrew was going to do it, since he's the one who brought you in, but he has so many responsibilities, what with being committee chairman, group leader, et cetera, et cetera, et cetera, he has found this first week of term to be exceptionally busy and has asked me to take over. So, how are you getting on?"

"Fine."

"Everything in your set of rooms okay?"

"Wonderful, in fact."

"Yes, it's a nice set. I believe Charles, Prince of Wales lived in it when he was here in the nineteen sixties."

"Really?" Claire gulped.

"Yes. And before that, Lord Tennyson. Quite some time before Charles, obviously."

"Obviously."

"You've been allocated your computer and printer?"

"Yes."

"You know where the laundry room is?"

"Yes."

"You've read your 'Brief Guide for New Fellows'?"

"Cover to cover. However, I think that 'Brief' should be deleted from the title."

"Point taken." Hoddy scowled and scratched his head. "It appears you don't need me at all."

"That's not true." What she really needed to know had nothing to do with the things covered in the "Brief Guide." Exactly why had Andrew Kent hired her? Was Elizabeth Bennett's comment an indication of what everyone else thought? Why did Andrew seem to be avoiding her? Was he still involved with Gabriella Griseri? Perhaps all this was well beyond Hoddy's advisory role. She stared pensively into the fire and was aware of him studying her.

"So you met Derek Goodman today," he said.

"How did you know that?" She felt her face flush with the memory of their encounter: his charm, her susceptibility to it, her abrupt and graceless exit.

"I heard it from Toby Campbell, who was told by Radha Patel, who heard it from Liz Bennett."

"Are you trying to tell me that everything I do will be noted and commented on?"

"Cambridge is a very small place. Everything *everyone* does is noted and commented on. I have discovered, often the hard way, that one of the most important elements of academic success is learning to get along with the disparate personalities one is forced to work with, sometimes for decades. And, in the case of the history faculty at least, not only disparate but highly neurotic, egotistic, and obsessive."

Claire blanched. "Are they really that bad?"

"Those are their *good* points."

"Great." She'd landed in deep waters, way over her head. "I don't think everyone gets along as well with others as you do. Dr. Goodman and Dr. Bennett seem to hate each other."

"Doesn't mean much in their case. They fight and make up on a near-weekly basis."

"You mean they're involved?"

"No, just friends. When they are friends." He drained the last of his beer from the glass. "I've been around long enough to know where most of the bones are buried. You can ask me anything"—he leveled a sly look at her—"about anyone."

"I see. You're not here to tell me how to get to the laundry room, are you?"

"No."

Claire didn't want to come right out with her most pressing question, so she tried to think of a subtle way to phrase it. "When we were in Italy in June, Dr. Kent was involved with someone named Gabriella . . ." She waved her hand in a vague manner that suggested she couldn't remember the last name. " . . . something or other."

"You mean Gabriella Monalisa Arianna Griseri, the stunningly beautiful and accomplished Italian countess and television presenter?"

"She would be the one, yes."

"What is it you want to know?"

"I was just wondering . . . only casually, you understand . . . if by chance they were still seeing each other?"

"I don't know. Sorry to disappoint. Usually my romance radar is on full alert, but this summer I was happily involved in my own and didn't have much time to devote to anyone else's. But I have heard that Gabriella has been to London a few times in the past months to talk with people at the BBC. They're considering her for the same sort of program she had in Italy, a kind of cultural chat show. And apparently Andy was introducing her 'round, as he knows lots of people in television ever since his book was made into a miniseries."

If Andrew Kent was helping Gabriella make a move to London, Claire mused, their relationship must be serious. No wonder he'd been avoiding her.

"But I get the feeling that there's something else on your mind."

"It's something Dr. Bennett said." Claire shook her head. "At first she was being sort of nice, and then—"

"She stung you with a zinger?" Hoddy nodded sympathetically. "Yes, I've been on the receiving end of that barbed tongue a few times myself. She's got a bit of a chip on her shoulder, but I can't say that I blame her entirely. She's one of the first women to attend Trinity in nineteen seventy-seven, when the school finally became 'mixed,' as we say. Something they don't like to advertise, as it brings to mind the college's antediluvian practices. She was one of the first female fellows as well, which couldn't have been easy. More intelligent than most of the men here, but she hasn't progressed up the career ladder as fast. Liz tests people. She likes to see how tough they are. Don't let her rattle you and you'll win her respect."

"She said that Andrew had 'bent over backward' for me. Essentially she implied that he had hired me for reasons that have nothing to do with my credentials."

"So that's what's bothering you." Hoddy leaned forward to speak confidentially. "Here's the thing. There's been a bit of talk. Andy went out on a limb to make sure you'd have all the privileges of a fellow even though you're not precisely a fellow. He pulled a few strings—"

"What strings?"

"Like your set of rooms, for instance. They're especially nice. Temporary lecturers don't usually merit a set at the college."

"I see." Claire bit her lip. So some of the fellows had good reason to resent her even before they met her. Great. "Hoddy, do you think he hired me for the wrong reasons?"

"I can't pretend to know what's on Andy's mind, but I can say this: of all the people I know, he's the one I can always count on to go by the book. He's a Boy Scout. Always has been. He's a right stand-up guy, our Andy, upholder of school, country, and tradition. Sex, drugs, and rock and roll seem to have passed him by like an express train.

It's as if he spent his entire youth standing on an empty platform at Victoria Station with the *Times* folded under his arm, humming Rachmaninoff."

That wasn't Claire's impression of Andrew Kent at all. Yes, he could be a bit stuffy and pompous sometimes, and he always assumed that he was right—something that was bound to annoy Claire, since she was usually right, of course. But she suspected that Andrew was not always so proper as Hoddy believed. In Andrew Kent she sensed a kindred spirit: someone who had followed the rules all his life but who secretly yearned to rebel and break free of convention. She had imagined that she could help him do this; that they could help each other. They had certainly disregarded some rules to uncover the truth of the Rossetti letter.

"You make him sound boring," Claire complained.

"Sometimes I think he is." Hoddy shrugged. "But that's just me. I spent *my* entire youth dancing half-naked in discos, like every other normal homosexual. What is more to the point is that I believe Andy hired you because in Venice he saw, as did I, a young historian with a great deal of promise. Regardless of what his personal feelings may be, he would never do anything against the rules."

"What are the rules?"

"Regarding personal relationships?" At Claire's nod, he continued. "Students, for obvious moral, legal, and aesthetic reasons, are completely off-limits. You don't have any interest in eighteen-year-old boys, do you?"

"None whatsoever."

"Girls?"

"Ditto."

"Relationships between fellows are not strictly forbidden, but they are strongly discouraged."

"Fellows never get involved with each other?"

"I wouldn't say never—but rarely, and seldom with good consequences."

"But some fellows live at the college for years."

"Yes, and when they marry, or partner as the case may be, they move out. Only the master's wife and family are allowed to live with him at the college. A good number of fellows, usually those with families, live in town. But while one is a resident fellow, sexual relationships are seriously frowned upon. Especially if the other fellow is also another fellow." He mustered a wry grin.

"I'm sorry."

"Don't be. It's not nearly as bad as it was. Cambridge is very open-minded these days. There seem to be militant lesbians everywhere one turns. And the rugby teams no longer practice the age-old tradition of dunking queers in the fountain. Good thing for them, too, because the lesbians would beat the crap out of them."

"Still, it hardly seems fair."

"Perhaps it isn't. But as you know, the colleges were originally set up much like monasteries and the fellows took vows of celibacy. I don't think the practice was stopped until sometime in the nineteenth century. The idea that fellows would have sexually intimate relationships was anathema to the whole concept of learning. Times have changed, but the place is still somewhat hermetic. As you've already discovered, it's difficult to keep secrets here. Understand, I've never pretended to be anyone other than who I am, but I have long found it politic to keep my professional and personal lives scrupulously separate."

"Hence Italy."

"Hence Italy."

"But you must get lonely sometimes."

"Sometimes I do," he said with a sigh and a faraway look in his eyes. "Happily, Rome is lovely at Christmas."

Chapter Nine

Second week of Michaelmas term

A FEW DAYS later, with no further word from Andrew Kent, Claire decided it would be best to follow Hoddy's example and keep her personal and professional lives separate. But although Andrew might be easy to avoid, there was no avoiding the college's unspoken but clear expectations: that she should prove herself a diligent, working historian. A *brilliant* historian would be even better, but for the time being she was willing to settle for conscientious and hardworking. She needed to research and write at least one paper, preferably two, during the next three terms; otherwise, she wouldn't be asked to stay on at Trinity permanently. And if she wasn't asked to stay on, what would she do? Go home and apply for jobs at small, out-of-the-way colleges in the States? That would be a considerable letdown after this.

In spite of Andrew Kent's less-than-open-armed reception and in spite of her new colleagues' occasional spite, Claire had already fallen in love with Cambridge. It offered a perfect blend of historic academia and quaint, centuries-old charm. The cobblestone streets of the pedestrian-only town center were lined with cafés, pubs, bookstores, and boutiques. For awe-inspiring grandeur, she had only to step inside the King's College Chapel. A satisfying atmosphere of medieval mystery lurked in the shadowed lanes and narrow alleys near Clare College and Gonville and Caius. The bucolic Backs—the gently sloping back lawns of the colleges that edged the tree-lined River Cam—provided an ideal setting for a few peaceful, stolen moments or an impromptu picnic while watching punters make their way upstream. In October, the trees of Cambridge leafed yellow and red, and the afternoon sunlight acquired a golden nostalgic glow; the very air seemed filled with the exhilarating yet comforting feeling that Claire always associated with the return of autumn and the beginning of school.

If she wanted to stay, Claire thought as she trudged from New Court to Nevile's Court, she'd have to crack some books.

She began her search with a short trip to the Lower Library, Trinity's student library located on the ground and basement floors of the north wing of Nevile's Court. It had an unexpected, airy modernity, its arched windows and large fluorescent ceiling panels shining abundant light over maple bookcases, Danish wood tables, and beige Berber carpet. Computer terminals were scattered around the study carrels, with a bank of four terminals along one wall in the back. Its general collection included textbooks, required reading, reference books, and periodicals. Claire went to the reference section to peruse a few of the history journals—the *Annual Bulletin of Historical Literature, Continuity and Change,* and the *English Historical Review*—for an overview of what other historians had recently written about. Once she came up with a subject, she'd have to check carefully to make sure no one had already covered it.

But first she had to decide on something. She preferred to write about people, not trends or statistics. For her dissertation, Claire had researched the life of Alessandra Rossetti, a young Venetian courtesan who, in the early seventeenth century, had written a letter to the Venetian Council warning them of a possible attack by Spanish forces. Discovering who Alessandra was, what she'd done, and finding the answer to her heretofore unknown fate had been an exciting coup for a young historian. In the aftermath of the Spanish conspiracy, as it had become known, the artistically talented Alessandra had left Venice for

Padua, where she'd earned a living by producing botanical drawings for the university.

Claire knew there was little chance she'd come across another story as dramatic as the Spanish conspiracy. Even so, she had to begin somewhere. If Alessandra had earned an income as an artist, perhaps other women had done so, too. Perhaps she could write about women who'd worked as professional artists in the seventeenth and eighteenth centuries. Claire checked a few sources on the college's online database, then left the Lower Library to walk up a flight of stairs.

At the top of the stairs, a wide doorway led to the Wren Library, Trinity's architectural showpiece and one of Christopher Wren's earliest commissions. When it was completed in 1695, it was the most magnificent library in all of Britain. Three hundred years later, the adjective still applied, Claire marveled. Massive dark oak bookcases arranged in thirteen bays lined the long walls of the large, rectangular space. Above the bookcases, a procession of tall, arched windows rose up to the thirty-seven-foot coffered ceiling. In the wide center aisle, black and white marble tiles set in a diamond pattern led the eye to the southern end, where a white marble statue of alumnus Lord Byron posed poetically below a stained-glass window. With its classically influenced design, lofty elegance, and air of timelessness, the Wren Library was a sort of Palladian temple dedicated to books.

Of which it had a unique and unusual selection, dating from as early as the eighth century, in a variety of languages including Old English, Middle English, Latin, and Greek. The books and manuscripts that the Wren Library had amassed over the past three hundred years included a tenth-century copy of the Epistles of St. Paul, numerous illuminated medieval manuscripts, an eighteenth-century collection of Shakespeariana, a few of Milton's poems in his own hand, and early printed books on subjects ranging from alchemy to zoology. Almost all had been acquired through the bequests and donations of private collectors, many of whom had been either masters, alumni, or benefactors of the library, who rested more peacefully knowing that their private collections would be kept intact in one of the world's most beautiful book depositories. The books were still shelved according to collection.

The most valuable works were kept in gated, locked bays, two at each end of the library.

Claire stopped at the unoccupied inquiry desk just inside the entrance. While she waited for the librarian's return, she looked over the neat display of items set carefully upon the desk's weathered surface: a leather blotter; a small, square pad of white notepaper; a wood container with pencils; a hand-cranked pencil sharpener; a fifty-year-old telephone with a dial. No computer monitor or keyboard, not even a liquid gel pen. Even the sign that proclaimed the librarian's name—MR MALCOLM PILFORD—revealed its aged origins with a typeface from a bygone era.

It was like looking at a diorama from an earlier age, but Claire knew that the librarian's ascetic desktop was not only the result of time and circumstance, but also library policies and procedures. Libraries such as the Wren—libraries intended for scholars, that is, not lending libraries—had strict rules about what was allowed inside. Even the ultramodern, multimillion-pound British Library did not tolerate ink pens or any extraneous personal possessions in its reading rooms, most especially totes or backpacks that could be used to squirrel away precious library property. Pencils, laptops, and paper notebooks were the only items permitted inside, and guards posted at the doors checked readers on their way in and on their way out. The Wren had none of the British Library's accoutrements, such as guards or cloakrooms, but it was assumed that the people who used the Wren Library were Trinity College fellows, who were trustworthy and could leave any inessential items behind in their sets.

Claire had arrived with a brand-new, spiral-bound notebook, two pencils, her keys, and her one concession to modern life: her cell phone. Turned off, of course. Not that she had to worry about disturbing anyone. Only one other scholar worked in the library this morning, a young woman who sat at a table behind Byron's statue. Even though academics from other universities and colleges could, with permission, use the Wren Library, Claire was under the impression that this permission wasn't requested very often. Indeed, the library seemed to be underused. There were fewer than twenty active history fellows and only a handful of history graduate students at Trinity, so she didn't have much competition for the collections kept within it. Claire's temporary lecturer status bestowed upon her the privilege of browsing the stacks: an almost unbelievable, heady freedom that she wouldn't enjoy at any other comparable library.

At the far end of the room, behind Byron's statue and below the stained-glass window, a man appeared from behind a heavy velvet curtain that draped a tall, wide doorway. He stopped to say a few words to the woman sitting at the table, whose long brown hair was pulled back into a thick, frizzy ponytail. He briefly placed an avuncular hand on her shoulder, then looked up to see Claire waiting. He walked toward her in a way that conveyed the perfect balance of authority and servility: he didn't rush obsequiously or rudely lag. His measured footsteps encompassed precisely one marble tile per stride; one white, one black, one white. He was clearly the master of this realm, but one who was more than happy to assist all who entered.

"May I help you?"

Claire introduced herself, and the librarian beamed at her with genuine welcome. "It's a pleasure to meet you," he said, and Claire was almost taken off-guard by the warmth of his greeting. Mr. Pilford appeared to be at least seventy, but even so, given the age of some of the other fellows, he was younger than she'd expected and much more sprightly. He had a fine head of short silvery hair; though a small man, he carried himself proudly, with a kind of military vigor. He looked jaunty in a tweed jacket, hunter green sweater-vest, and striking blue-and-green-striped bow tie. His round, black eyeglasses were a sort she'd seen only in photographs of James Joyce.

"What can I do for you this afternoon, Dr. Donovan?"

"I'm interested in a folio in the Barclay collection," said Claire, consulting her notes. "In particular a letter from a woman named Mary Beale, a court painter of the late seventeenth century." She showed him the folio's class number, scribbled in pencil within the faint blue lines of the white notebook paper.

"May I ask what you're researching? I may be able to find other, similar items for you."

"I'm looking for primary sources about or by female artists."

"Which era?"

"Early modern."

The librarian squinted and looked up to the ceiling, as if he was searching the crowded archives of his mind. "The Barclay isn't a bad place to start. There are many items in it that haven't been cataloged yet, so there's no telling what you may find." Was it Claire's imagination, or did Mr. Pilford's eyes glimmer with a mysterious excitement? "You may also want to look at the Sir Henry Puckering collection," he went on, then shrugged, palms up. "We haven't fully cataloged it, either, although the Puckering arrived three hundred years ago, just after the library was completed. Both collections are in R bay, down at the end."

Claire walked along the wide center aisle past the magnificent dark oak bookcases and their leather-bound arcana, past the Grinling Gibbons–carved coats of arms, past the marble busts of Newton, et al., gazing down from on high, past the display tables where especially prized items—Shakespeare's first folio and A. A. Milne's original manuscript of *Winnie-the-Pooh* among them—were exhibited under glass. The ponytailed woman working at the table behind Byron's statue closed her laptop as Claire approached.

"I'm sorry," she said. "I'll be out of your way."

She hardly looked at Claire as she spoke. She wore a long, full skirt that brushed against her ankles and, over that, a man's gray cardigan sweater that drooped like a dirty sock on her slight body. The pockets bulged with crumpled tissues. She kept her eyes on the table as she closed her three open books and carefully arranged them into a small, neat pyramid.

"You're not in my way," Claire replied.

"I'm not supposed to take up space needed by a fellow."

"It's not a problem," Claire said. The young woman appeared too old to be an undergrad; she must have been a graduate student. "There's plenty of room for both of us."

But the young woman tucked the laptop under one arm and managed to get her books under the other. "Sorry," she apologized one last time before turning her back to Claire and scurrying away to the librarian's desk.

Claire shook her head and returned to the task at hand. The baroque, wrought-iron gate to R bay was locked. Claire turned to look for Mr. Pilford, then remembered her keys. As the junior bursar had promised, the F key fit easily into the lock. The gate creaked as Claire pulled it slowly open and stepped into the dusky light of the book bay. Thirteen-foot-tall bookcases crowded with volumes of every size surrounded her on three sides. The larger books were placed on the roomier lower shelves and the smaller books on the upper, which were so high that she would have to stand on a bench to reach them. The literary works were sheathed in a variety of calfskin, pigskin, and morocco bindings; many of the spines had raised markings, or were embossed and gilded. Faint gold curlicues, ornate borders, and family crests glimmered in the shadowy light. She breathed in the books' familiar, invigorating aroma: dust, tanned leather, moldering paper, ripening vellum—a scent Claire had long come to associate with knowledge and secrets.

Although she was a logical, practical person, she believed that in books there existed a kind of magic. Between the aging covers on these shelves, contained in tiny, abstract black marks on sheets of paper, were voices from the past. Voices that reached into the future, into Claire's own life and heart and mind, to tell her what they knew, what they'd learned, what they'd seen, what they'd felt. Wasn't that magic?

She decided to begin with the folio she'd come in for, though she soon discovered that it wasn't so easy to find. Most of the books in R bay had been printed and bound long before anyone had thought of conveniently stamping the title on the spine. In fact, she'd read that when the library had first been built, the books had been shelved the other way around. The page ends had faced out, while a "board," or covered cupboard at the end of each bookcase, contained a list of the nearby volumes. Unfortunately, the lists had been abandoned in the early eighteenth century. Now, as then, finding a particular work entailed taking it off the shelf and opening its covers.

The books in the Earl of Barclay's collection were marked by a crest of castle and lynx, easily distinguished from Sir Henry Puckering's escutcheon of clarion and crow. Claire spent nearly an hour searching before she found the correct folio. One had to proceed slowly with old books to keep from damaging them. Some libraries required the protocol of white cotton gloves (which they provided), but most simply expected clean hands and gentle, professional treatment. Inside the bay, a square oak table designed by Christopher Wren featured a built-in, four-sided revolving book stand in its center. Quite ingenious, Claire thought as she propped the folio upon it.

The folio wasn't a published book but a collection of letters, mounted on sheets of thick, yellowing paper, much like a scrapbook. Unfortunately there was no mention of whether the letters had been collected contemporaneously or if they'd been assembled much later. Most of the letters seemed to come from the last two decades of the seventeenth century and were composed in a variety of hands. Claire supposed they must be related in some way, but there was no explanation of how. A collection of family letters, no doubt. About two-thirds of the way through, she found the epistle from the court painter.

18 February 1678

My dear Lady Barclay

This is to confirm that you and your husband will be sitting for portraits at my studio on Pall Mall commencing March 1 and everyday thereafter (excepting the Lord's Day, of course), until such portraits are finished. The fee for each is £10 which Mr. Beale tells me is agreeable to you.

I remain, &ct.,
Mrs. Mary Beale

It was evidence of a working, income-earning female artist, but hardly enough to base a paper on. Claire looked through the remainder of the folio without finding another letter from the painter or any other mention of her. She stood up, returned it to the stacks, and looked around, feeling overwhelmed. She hardly knew where to begin. It was tempting to start on one side and methodically work her way around through every single bookshelf, but even taking a cursory glance at each volume would take days. She could simply choose books at random, she thought, or make a game of it by choosing one book from every shelf. She had to face it: without a comprehensive catalog, there were no shortcuts. She decided to examine the first book on the left side of each shelf, a methodology that would make it easier to begin again exactly where she finished.

The first was an illustrated tome from the Puckering collection: *The royall game of chesse-play: sometimes the recreation of the late King, with many of the nobility,* published in London and written by Gioachino Greco in 1656. The second came from the Barclay: *Recherches anatomiques et physiologiques sur la structure intime des animaux et des vegetaux, et sur leur motilite,* Paris, René Henri Dutrochet, 1684. The third, Barclay again: *Experimental philosophy in three books: containing new experiments, microscopical, mercurial, magnetical. With some deductions, and probable hypotheses, raised from them,* London, Theophilus Ravenscroft, FRS, 1670. And again, Barclay, this time a seventeenth-century work on surgery: *Chirugia spagyrica / Petri loannis Fabri doctoris medici Monspeliensis. In qua de morbis cutaneis omnibus spagyrice & methodice agitur, & curatio eorum cita, tuta, & iucunda tractatur,* Toulouse, Pierre-Jean Fabre, 1626. The next book, from the Puckering collection, had a long, explicatory title typical of the era: *The mysteries of opium reveal'd / by Dr. John Jones, . . . who I. Gives an account of the name, make, choice, effects, &c. of opium. II. Proves all former opinions of its operation to be meer chimera's. III. Demonstrates what its true cause is . . . IV. Shews its noxious principle, and how to separate it; thereby rendering it a safe and noble panacea; whereof, V. He shews the palliative and curative use,* London, John Jones, 1701. The following book was another medicinal work: *Organon salutis. An instrument to cleanse the stomach, as also divers new experiments of the virtue of tobacco and coffee: how much they conduce to preserve human health,* London, Walter Rumsey, 1657.

To reach the highest shelf, Claire stood on one of the bay's four small benches and stretched her hand up as far as it could go. Even so, her fingers could just barely touch the desired volume. She felt a bit like

Alice in Wonderland, struggling to grasp a key off a tabletop that was steadily rising higher and higher. She slowly and very carefully eased the book out of its tight, confined space. But as she gently coaxed it into her hand, she dislodged the volume next to it, which landed on the floor below with a muffled, dust-rising thud. Claire froze and held her breath, waiting for the sound of Mr. Pilford's footsteps.

When it was clear that the librarian hadn't heard the unfortunate result of her overreaching ambition, Claire stepped down from the bench and picked the book off the floor. It was a volume about three-quarters of an inch thick and approximately five by seven inches in size, bound in plain, honey-colored leather, unmarked except by the scars and blemishes of age. A book so unprepossessing that she imagined at first it was a schoolboy's workbook. Claire opened the cover to find the first page with nothing upon it but a date, handwritten in English and faded with time: *November 1672.*

She sat down at the oak table to look through this mysterious volume more carefully, propping it up on the book stand. Every page after the first was a puzzle, handwritten in a language she'd never encountered before. It wasn't Latin, it wasn't Greek, it wasn't Hebrew, and it certainly wasn't English. It looked more like a set of alchemical symbols or algebraic characters, but it clearly wasn't mathematical. There were no sets or subsets of equations, just a series of strange, singular characters written in neat straight lines that marched smartly across each page.

It must be some sort of code. In Venice, she'd discovered encrypted letters written by Alessandra Rossetti, and she, along with Andrew Kent, had deciphered them. Ever since, Claire had had an interest in codes and ciphers. In the seventeenth and eighteenth centuries, documents were frequently encrypted. Everyone—ambassadors, kings, merchants, mistresses—used codes in their communiqués, and often in their private papers and ledgers as well. It was the only way to keep one's secrets secret. But even that didn't always work, as code breakers were as common as code makers.

But this didn't look like a ledger. It was something private and personal, a journal or a diary, perhaps. The pages were not numbered, but the journal appeared to be about sixty to seventy pages long. She carefully turned the yellowing sheets; about halfway through she discovered a second page bearing the date December 1672. It was written in the same delicate, elegant script. A woman's diary? Instinctively, Claire felt it was a woman's. Had anyone else ever deciphered it? Or had it sat here for hundreds of years, a voice immured inside this library for centuries, waiting for someone to discover it? Waiting for her, in fact?

Hmmmm . . . what if she wrote a paper on encryption in the seventeenth century? A big subject, to be sure, but perhaps this discovery would provide a special insight or a new slant. That was if she could break the code and uncover its meaning, of course.

Claire settled in for the long process of copying it by hand. She couldn't take it out of the library, and she didn't want to have it photocopied. Not because she was afraid it would be damaged—Mr. Pilford and his associates were accustomed to working with old, fragile materials—but because she didn't want to subject it to such cold public scrutiny. She already had proprietary feelings about it. It took a while to get the hang of the letterforms, if that's what they were, but after a couple of hours it began to feel like second nature, and she was working at such a steady pace that she anticipated copying half the diary by closing time. Certain characters were repeated often enough for Claire to be sure that it was some sort of code. But what it meant was completely beyond her.

"Dr. Donovan."

Claire nearly jumped off the bench. The librarian stood in the open gateway. "Mr. Pilford." She restrained a desire to shield the book and her notebook from his sight.

"Didn't you hear the closing chime, Dr. Donovan?"

"No," Claire admitted. "Is it six o'clock already?"

"Indeed it is. The library is closed. Not to mention that it's time for my tea."

"Of course, Mr. Pilford."

"Please put the books back exactly where you found them."

"Yes, Mr. Pilford." The librarian looked harmless enough, but there was enough starch in his manner for Claire to get the message that disobedience would not be tolerated. With some reluctance, she closed the diary and placed it back on its high shelf. Then she left the library, taking the path around the back of the Wren and walking in to New Court through the west gateway.

Derek Goodman was on his way out. "Dr. Donovan," he said with obvious pleasure at seeing her again.

"Dr. Goodman." Claire had been in the library for hours without a break, and she felt unguarded, as if he'd just caught her waking up from a nap. She hoped she hadn't been twisting her hair into knots, as she sometimes did while she was concentrating.

"How are you getting along?"

"Fine," she said.

"Really?" His eyes narrowed as he studied her face. "I'm not sure I believe you. You look like you haven't seen a ray of sunshine or had a bit of fun since you got here. I'm afraid you've discovered that Cambridge is not always the friendliest place in the world."

"No, it's been great," she said with as much sincerity as she could muster.

"Are you busy tonight?"

Claire had hoped that Andrew Kent had called her sometime during the day, but this was hardly the time to check her cell phone, no matter how badly she wanted to. What were the chances he'd actually called? Based on recent experience, they were pretty slim, she decided. "No, actually, I'm not."

"You're a beautiful woman, it's Friday night, and you're all alone. You mean to tell me that you're having a good time?"

"Well, I've been working all day in the Wren Library—"

Derek laughed. "That's what you call fun? You know what they say about all work and no play."

Claire nodded. "Makes for a very dull—," she began.

"Swot, git, and a boffin," Derek finished for her.

"A what?"

"I'll be happy to explain each of these colorful expressions to you if you'll join me for a beer in the pub."

"Now?"

"Do you have something better to do?" Derek smiled and Claire felt that odd weakness in her knees again.

No, she certainly didn't.

Chapter Ten

5 *November 1672*

THE FIRST SOUNDS of the morning are indistinct, transformed by sleep into dream metaphors: angry bees buzzing, waves crashing, trees felled by bolts of lightning. Eventually the sounds reach deep into her slumbering consciousness and Hannah raises her head from her desk. She fell asleep just before dawn with her face resting on her open journal, apparently in the act of writing. Directly downstairs the argument continues, and even though she can't hear the exact words, she can distinguish her mother's elevated, insistent voice and Mrs. Wills's deeper, patient response. Hannah already suspects how it will end, and she remains still for the short time necessary for her hunch to be proven correct: her mother lets loose with a flurry of words, her bedroom door slams, and the key turns in the lock. Mrs. Wills stands outside on the landing, pointlessly jiggling the doorknob while muttering under her breath the most scathing oaths her conscience will allow.

These sounds of discord and unhappiness have woken Hannah, but they have not surprised her; she hears them too often. She picks up a dressing gown from her untouched bed and wraps it around her night shift. Even in her attic bedroom, receptacle of all the heat that rises from the basement kitchen and the half dozen fireplaces downstairs, November mornings are cold. She briefly looks in the small mirror next to the armoire. Her hair is wild and she has a smudge of black ink on her cheek. She moistens a fingertip and rubs at it, to little avail. Without further effort she leaves the room, stopping on her way to the kitchen and knocking on her mother's door, one floor below.

"Go away," her mother shouts.

Hannah's shoulders sag and she momentarily stands mute, unsure of what to do. "Mother, it's me, Hannah."

"I'm not receiving any visitors this morning."

I'm not a visitor, I'm your daughter, she wants to shout in reply but doesn't, partly from embarrassment—they might hear her downstairs-—and partly from sheer futility. Her mother seldom recognizes her anymore. Charlotte D'urfey Briscoe came from a well-to-do family in Montpellier. She grew up headstrong and spoiled, so that her desire for knowledge—and for the young English physician studying at Montpellier's renowned university—was indulged, even approved, in the manner of parents too old or too tired to protest. After they married, she moved with Hannah's father to Paris, where his practice included members of the exiled English court. Once Charlotte was a physician as skilled as Dr. Briscoe, even though, like Hannah, she had no legal sanction to practice. Hannah remembers their years in France as happy ones, but it's a child's perspective: she knows now it couldn't have been easy. Charlotte gave birth to three children after Hannah, none of whom survived past the cradle, and the subsequent move to London was difficult for her. In contrast to Paris, it was polluted, crowded, and unsafe. Then came the Plague and the Fire. After 1666, both Hannah and her father noticed that Charlotte was often confused and forgetful. Her sickness of mind progressively grew worse, and after Hannah's father was killed, Charlotte deteriorated further. She had sudden changes of humor and could be unreasonable, even violent. At other times she was as sweet as a kitten, happy to putter in her room upstairs, drawing pictures or arranging flowers. Sometimes she escaped their vigilance and left the house to roam the streets. Kind neighbors would find her at the markets or at an apothecary's, befuddled and lost, and bring her home. Londoners' hatred of the

French and of Catholics meant that it was never entirely safe for a
Frenchwoman, especially one not in full possession of her senses, to
wander around alone.

The only person whose company Charlotte truly enjoys is Lucy
Harsnett's, their youngest maid. As Hannah groggily makes her way
downstairs, past the second floor with Mrs. Wills's and Hester's rooms,
then past the ground floor parlor, she wonders why Lucy is not upstairs
with her mother. When she reaches the kitchen she discovers the reason: there is some sort of row going on. She can feel the stormy aftermath in the air, can see it in their faces. Mrs. Wills looks pinched, as if
she's still mentally muttering curses; Lucy and Hester Pinney, the other
maidservant, sit on the bench at the kitchen table and pick sourly at
their breakfast of cheese, bread, and herrings.

Hannah spies a tray with an untouched plate of food on it. "Has my
mother refused her breakfast again?"

"Even Lucy couldn't tempt her," Mrs. Wills replies with a curt nod.
"Lucy told Mrs. Briscoe we didn't have any hen's eggs this morning and
your mother became much distressed. Then I went upstairs to try to
smooth things over, but she got even angrier and then"—Mrs. Wills
looks darkly at the two girls—"she locked me out, because someone
left the key to her door inside her room."

On closer inspection, Hannah notices that Lucy's blue eyes are
swollen from crying and the pale residue of tears streaks her peaches-
and-cream complexion. She's a pretty, sweet-tempered girl, whom
Hannah's mother dotes on. Charlotte would be content to brush Lucy's
long golden hair for hours, if Lucy would allow it, and frequently seems
calmed just by gazing upon Lucy's perfect English-rose beauty. Lucy is
often troubled when Charlotte is too unreasonable to be soothed by
her presence, but apparently something more than that is causing her
unhappiness today.

"I'm not the one who left it there," Lucy sniffs.

"I didn't leave it there, either," Hester adds vehemently.

"You *must* have been the one who left it there," Lucy says. "I know
better than to let her have the key."

"But I'm not the one who's always in her room, you are."

"You did it on purpose," Lucy says, indignant. "You're trying to get me into trouble, just because you're jealous."

"Jealous of you? Why would I be jealous of someone who's too stupid to remember what she's done?"

"Girls, that's enough," Hannah orders. Why could she not be the mistress of a congenial household, as her mother was when she was able?

The maidservants fall into an uneasy silence. Hester's a year older than Lucy, but at sixteen she's still scrawny and gangly, with dark ginger hair and freckled skin. She'll never be a beauty like Lucy, to whom it is her misfortune to be continually compared. As the girls have gotten older—they've both been in Hannah's service for six years—Hester has grown increasingly resentful. Hannah isn't sure that Hester is aware of it as such, but she sometimes overhears her saying unkind things to Lucy, and of the two Hester is more often in need of reprimand for leaving the washing out, or neglecting to turn the beds, or staying out too long on errands. Often Hannah thinks that having the two girls in her house is like living with a benevolent spirit and an angry one. But they won't be with her forever. The parents of both girls are deceased, and, as their employer and guardian, she'll have to begin thinking about dowries for them soon. She glances at Hester, who lowers her smoldering eyes to her plate. That's if anyone will have her.

"I'm beyond caring which of you did it," Mrs. Wills says. "Finish your breakfast, pick open the lock on Mrs. Briscoe's door, distract her, and get the key back, or else neither of you will be allowed out to the market this morning."

"Yes, ma'am," the girls answer dutifully.

Although she's finished scolding the girls, Mrs. Wills is still angry; Hannah can tell just by the way she stirs the simmering pot on the stove. Hannah is also fairly certain she knows why the goodwife is seething, and she attempts to curtail Mrs. Wills's upcoming lecture with a diversion. "We should get another key made. I'll keep it in a secret place, so if she locks herself in again we'll be able to open the door. Why don't you summon the locksmith today?"

"I thought we didn't have the money."

"We do now."

Mrs. Wills taps the wooden spoon on the rim of the stew pot and sets it aside. She turns to Hannah, who instantly realizes that her best effort has failed. "And where were you all night, without so much as a note to keep me from worry?"

Mrs. Wills is an excellent, though somewhat stern, goodwife who's been with Hannah's family since they moved to London, but Hannah wishes that she would remember that Hannah isn't twelve anymore, and that she is de facto mistress of the house. "I went to see young Matthew, Mr. Polk's apprentice."

"You were there all night?"

"I stayed with him until he died."

Mrs. Wills frowns. Lucy and Hester exchange a troubled look. "He died of the smallpox," Hannah explains. "We've all had it. There's no danger to any one of us."

"And what of the danger to a woman who insists on walking about at all hours of the night?"

"I keep to the lighted streets and I carry a knife."

"So does everyone else. Just last week a curate was found dead at the Inns of Court. He'd been robbed of every stitch on his person and had his throat cut from ear to ear."

"Mrs. Wills, please, the girls—"

The goodwife looks somewhat chastened but holds her ground. "Keeping the truth from them won't make them safe, it will just make them foolish. Doesn't a day go by in this city without somebody getting robbed or killed. Your father should have known better, and so should you."

"I was merely trying to comfort the poor boy."

"You have more to think about than just your patients," Mrs. Wills adds needlessly.

"Yes, I know." Hannah stands over the gurgling pot, inhaling its savory aroma. "Is that beef in there?"

"We got a good price for it," Mrs. Wills says defensively. Their budget doesn't always include money for meat.

"It smells divine." Hannah has learned from long experience that the best way to get on the good side of Mrs. Wills is to compliment her cooking.

"It's for dinner," she says. She brusquely waves Hannah away from the stove, but she has a raised brow and a pursed lip, which in her case passes for a smile. "Noon sharp. Mind you're here for it."

The apprentice behind the counter at the Blackhorse Alley apothecary shop holds up his hand. "Please, Mrs. Devlin, you go too fast for me. What were the last three you mentioned?"

"Twelve scruples guaiacum powder, two ounces tincture of roses, and sarsaparilla extract, six ounces."

With a quill, he scratches a few cryptic marks onto a scrap of paper. "Is that all?"

She's already requested more than fifteen different simples—medicines of only one ingredient. She prefers to make her own compounds, creating unique combinations for each patient and their particular symptoms. Mademoiselle de Keroualle's treatment will consist of a gentle herbal purgative, some hartshorn mixed in rosewater to ease the pains of fever, and an electuary—a medicine made with honey—with the diaphoretics guaiacum and sarsaparilla to bring on a cleansing and fever-reducing sweat. This will be followed, as soon as the patient is able, by soothing herb-infused baths and a steady administration of her father's remedy, a complex blend of more than twenty herb, flower, and root distillations. She nods to the apprentice, who turns toward the back of the shop with his scrap of paper. "Wait," she says, mentally calculating the coins in her purse. "Would you add syrup of poppies, two ounces, please?"

"Yes, ma'am."

The apprentice disappears through a curtain into the back room. The public portion of the tiny shop is only ten feet wide and half as deep. It's not much more than a doorway opening into a small room filled by a U-shaped wood counter and, behind that, floor-to-ceiling shelves. She's the only person in the shop, but it feels strangely occupied. Lining the walls are glass and ceramic canisters filled with the raw materials of the apothecary's art: hartshorn and dried toads; gnarled ginger root, peony root, and mossy tufts of fern; birds' nests, doves' tails, swallows' eyes, and crows' beaks; snails and mouse tails and a jar of pale gold liquid innocently labeled Puppy-Dog Water.

The apprentice pops his head out from the curtain. "Mr. Murray wants to know if you'd like London treacle instead. He says it's quite good, he made it only yesterday."

London treacle is a compound that includes opium, along with sixty other ingredients. Originally, many centuries ago, it was created as an antidote for poison. That it is entirely ineffective for this purpose has in no way reduced its popularity; the London *Pharmacopoeia* recommends it for maladies ranging from ague to Saint Vitus' dance. "No, thank you. Just the poppy syrup, please."

"Yes, ma'am."

Hannah looks outside and catches her faint reflection in the window. It startles her. At first she doesn't recognize it as herself: shadowed eyes stare out of a ghostly countenance without a spot of color anywhere, not even in the pale line of her mouth. She wonders how others see her, if she is beginning to appear as haunted as she feels. The headache is still with her. It's a near-constant presence, an enemy that temporarily retreats only to regroup and attack with greater force. Some mornings it will disappear for two hours or even three, lulling her with the false promise of a day without pain. But gradually it creeps back again. At times her awareness of it will come upon her suddenly, in one sharp, blinding jolt, and she will realize that the headache has been with her for hours, that everything she does and has done, every effort, every movement, every word she has spoken, is and has been informed by pain.

She tries to remember when her affliction began. Not, she is certain, while her husband, Nathaniel, was still alive. Even during the long vigil of his fatal illness—smallpox that struck him down before he was yet four and twenty—she cannot recall being troubled so. And Sarah? The months she had with her daughter were among the sweetest of her life. Bittersweet, as Nathaniel did not live to see his child born. Tears she remembers, many tears, especially after Sarah succumbed to a fever, but headaches? No. This distemper did not

begin until after her father died. Yes, she thinks, it must have started
sometime in the past year.

Like many doctors, Hannah is a recalcitrant patient. She allowed
weeks to go by, expecting the intermittent pain to go away again on
its own, before making a concerted effort to cure her own ailment. As
the headaches became more frequent, she sampled many remedies,
staying up late at night to peruse by candlelight every recipe book she
could find—the *Pharmacopoeia,* Culpeper's *Herbal,* Gideon Harvey's
The Family Physician, her own parents' notes and observations—until
her eyes ached as much as her head. At least, she tried those cures that
seemed the least informed by superstition: concoctions of cephalic
drugs such as amber, clove, cinnamon, rosemary; cold plasters and
hot plasters; the distilled water of vervain; chamomile flowers moist-
ened with warm milk. She had stopped short of shaving her head and
anointing it with a paste made of myrtle, oil of roses, and ground bee-
tles, or extracting the mind's morbid humors by attaching a leech to
her nostrils and letting blood, as was sometimes recommended. After
months of experiment, she has found that opium is the only medicine
that alleviates her pain, temporary though its effects may be.

She's still waiting for the apprentice to return when Lucy and
Hester walk into the alley with a young man she has never seen before.
They stop at the clearing where Blackhorse Alley meets Carter's Lane.
They are on their way to market, empty baskets on their arms, laughing, dawdling, killing time. She doesn't mind. She remembers, if only
remotely, what it is like to be young, though she can imagine the sharp
words Mrs. Wills would have for them. She should remind her not to
be so severe with the girls.

The young man is tall, fair, sturdily built. She supposes he is handsome by the way Lucy is smiling up at him and laughing, but they are
on the other side of the alley and she cannot make out his features.
Hester hangs back from the other two, silent and watchful, but that
is always her way. And it's clear that he's smitten with Lucy, but then
everyone is.

After a few minutes he tips his hat to the girls and walks on. Arm in
arm, Lucy and Hester cross the alley and pass by the apothecary shop.

Instinctively Hannah steps back from the door. An odd response, she supposes, but as they walk past she is thankful they don't see her.

"Why don't you ever say anything to him?" Lucy chides Hester. "He probably thinks you're simple."

"It doesn't matter," Hester says. "It isn't me he fancies."

"Mrs. Devlin." The apprentice holds a tray with an array of small glass bottles and packets of powder. "Two shillings, ten pence," he says as he places it on the counter.

"Is that all?" The tariff is less than she expected.

"Begging your pardon, ma'am, but Mr. Murray says we're all out of poppy syrup for today. He only has the treacle."

Her disappointment feels almost like panic. She is due at Whitehall, and now she will have to go to another apothecary. She tries to think of one along the way, perhaps one in Westminster, for surely she will not get through the day without a few drops.

"Are you all right, ma'am?"

She assures him that she is fine. How odd. People have been asking her that question a great deal lately.

Chapter Eleven

"YOU, SIR, ARE a cheat and a dog!" Theophilus Ravenscroft attempts to straighten his small, stooped frame to its most imposing height as he confronts Christopher Mead inside the optician's shop on Long Acre Street. "Six pounds fifteen for a faulty microscope! It is too much to be borne."

"And you, sir," Christopher Mead replies with equal antipathy, "are a wastrel and a blight upon all instrument makers, who torment themselves to come up with better and more powerful devices for your use, only to see them mishandled and abused."

"This instrument"—at Ravenscroft's urging, his young assistant Thomas Spratt offers up the broken pieces of the microscope in question—"is so obviously deficient that it can't stand up to a long night of work and one—only one, mind you!—accidental collision with the floor."

"If you drop a glass, sir, it will break. Any child knows that."

"If it were only a two-penny drinking cup I had purchased from you, I would not be here now, Mr. Mead. But as you see . . ." He takes the eyepiece from Thomas's hand and puts it under Mead's nose. "This 'scope is broke at the jointure to the arm, which should be sturdy enough to handle a bit of knocking about. Not to mention that the lens"—he removes a sharp fistful of tiny glass shards from his pocket and sprinkles them on the counter—"is in pieces."

In spite of Ravenscroft's incontrovertible argument, Mead responds in his usual mulish manner. "How am I to know what really happened?" he asks, stubbornly crossing his arms across his chest and jutting his chin. "Perhaps you threw it on the floor." He glances at the broken glass. "Then stomped on it. Your volatile temperament, Mr. Ravenscroft, is well known."

"My temperament is well justified. I pay a high price for the best, and I expect nothing less. A philosopher cannot achieve greatness if he is forced to work with inferior tools. How can you call yourself a craftsman when you produce instruments as are not fit to be used? Do you not feel an obligation to provide your finest work for others' experiment and inquiry? Odd's Fish, man, do you not *care*?"

His fit of spleen makes little impact on Mead. The optician runs his fingers though his disheveled hair and sighs impatiently. And rather rudely too, Ravenscroft thinks. He and Thomas arrived at the shop at ten of the clock to find Mead upstairs asleep in his bed, looking as though he'd just been turned every which way but loose. Disgraceful. It is shockingly apparent that men are no longer concerned with mastering their art or with achieving perfection. All the young bucks are lazy and more eager to play the fop and the gallant than to attend to the business of furthering knowledge. Has it always been so? Ravenscroft searches his memory—a mysterious region full of light and shadow, but a place where, more and more often, what is illuminated seems insignificant—but he cannot recall that such carelessness was the fashion in his youth. The world has become full of incompetents and mediocrities and ignorant coxcombry fools.

"Mr. Mead," he says firmly, drawing himself up (which places the crown of his head no higher than Mead's chin), "you would be wise to spend less time fondling your mistresses and keep a mind to your craft, and thence to your customers, for the other fellows of the Royal Society will follow my lead in this matter and take their business elsewhere if I am not satisfied." He is not certain this is true. The members of the

Royal Society are more inclined to lead than to follow; their fraternity
contains a healthy measure of anarchy at its core. But it cannot be dis-
puted that the majority of Mead's customers are Royal Society fellows.
Who else but a natural philosopher intent on examining the wonders
of the world and the heavens requires a relatively newfangled invention
such as a microscope or telescope?

Mead sighs again, less impertinently this time. "What is it you want,
Mr. Ravenscroft?"

"I insist that you build a new microscope for me. This one will
not do."

"You insist, do you?"

"Yes, sir."

Mead scowls, but Ravenscroft knows that his threat is too genuine
for the optician to ignore. "As you wish, then," Mead sullenly replies.
"But do not imagine that I will do it right away."

"Do you really think he'll make you another?" Thomas asks as they
walk past the shops of wheelwrights, carpenters, metalworkers, gla-
ziers, and clockmakers that populate this West London neighborhood.
Ravenscroft buttons up his coat against the bitter wind. It's nearly two
miles back to his house on Bishopsgate Street.

"Of course." He glances quizzically at his assistant. "Did you think
he would not do as I asked simply because we engaged in a bout of
verbal fisticuffs? Not to worry. Mead and I have the same argument at
least once every few months. Natural philosophy is a fractious business.
If you are afraid to make yourself heard, you will not go far."

The two men, one young and one old, make a droll pair. The philosopher has never been handsome; even as a child, he lacked the sort
of appearance that would endear him to others. His absence of vanity and a good deal of parsimoniousness are evident in his apparel,
from his poorly clad feet (shoes, very worn rust-colored pigskin, twelve
shillings, over fifteen years old) to his body (topcoat, coffee-stained
wool, one pound, secondhand store on Gracechurch Street) to his head
(periwig, matted gray hair, two pounds ten, castoff from another of his
Cheapside barber's customers). Ravenscroft's slight and slightly crooked

figure moves swiftly ahead at a jerky but determined pace, his shoulders hunched deep into his coat, fists shoved into pockets, his head hatless in spite of the cold. Beside him, the fair-haired, fair-featured, and strapping Thomas Spratt lopes along, his long stride nearly two of his employer's, his ungainly feet as outsized as a puppy's.

Thomas is the son of an acquaintance from Garraway's, Ravenscroft's favorite coffeehouse in Exchange Alley near the Old Exchange. He became Ravenscroft's assistant only two months earlier, when the position was suddenly vacated in the usual manner: Ravenscroft threw his former assistant out on his ear. Although the philosopher is not prone to excessive praise, he would admit that so far Thomas has exhibited the qualities he sought: "a sober and virtuous young man, diligent in following direction." He has artistic skill as well and has already proved himself a capable draftsman and copyist. His daily duties include preparing trials and experiments, copying Ravenscroft's drawings, and doing errands. In exchange, Ravenscroft houses him, feeds him, and allows his maid Nell to launder his clothes, a trade that is greatly in Thomas's favor, he believes; for surely he is learning much that he can profit from later on.

"You must be willing to stand up for your convictions, Thomas, and forge ahead with a free and open mind," Ravenscroft tells his assistant, finding himself in a rather expansive mood following his altercation with Christopher Mead and so offering another of the impromptu lessons he feels are such a necessary part of his work as a man of science. "I have found that truth more often resides in what is newly discovered than in the theories of the past. Only last week in Mead's shop I was introduced to an old coot, one Mr. Hobbes, who would not be persuaded that a microscope afforded a closer view than his own spectacle glasses; and who pretended to see better by holding his spectacles in his palsied hand, which shook as fast one way as his head did the other. That is what happens when people cleave tight to ancient beliefs: they do not even credit what they see with their own eyes. The old fool would not allow himself to be convinced that optical instruments further our sight, and so he will never have the sublime pleasure of witnessing the fiery details of a comet as it streaks across the sky, or seeing the crisp, pockmarked face of the moon, or the fascinating, impossibly intricate anatomy of a bee, a beetle, or a baboon. The natural philosopher has three faculties: sense, memory, and reason, and all of these may be improved upon—our senses most profoundly by the instruments we create to expand them."

They turn into Harper's Lane, passing a heavily laden horse cart slowly creaking along to market, and dodge the mud thrown up by the horse's hooves as they skirt the piles of stinking refuse that litter the road. Low in the sky above them a smudge of pink the color of a pig's bladder momentarily peeks through the clouds. The reddened sun, courtesy of the miasmic coal smoke that continually blankets London, flares briefly, then is swallowed up again by the heavily overcast sky. The blustery autumn wind reddens the tips of Ravenscroft's ears, and in the damp air he feels the presence of impending rain: a day for omens and portents.

As they near the Fleet Bridge, Ravenscroft becomes aware of the pains in his swollen feet, his knobby knees. The cold, damp weather aggravates his gout. Happily he is on speaking terms with some of London's finest physicians and apothecaries, all of whom give him frequent advice for his gout, his vertigo, his neuralgia, his excessive wind, his costiveness, his megrims, and his melancholy, as well as recommending the latest and most modern treatments. In addition to the usual prescription of vomits, purges, and bloodletting, Ravenscroft has tried innumerable patented "waters," distillations, and cordials; tinctures of wormwood, solutions of iron oxide, and fomentations of frog spawn; white wine infused with dried peacock's dung and powdered stag's pizzel; as well as the inhalation of the fumes of a burnt horse's hoof. He has experimented with all these many treatments and more, separately and in combination, but for some reason his health never seems to improve. Not that it is likely to as long as he lives on Bishopsgate Street, he reflects bitterly. A coaching inn has lately been built on what was an empty plot next to his house, and every day he is forced to breathe in the suffocating stink of the stables and jakes.

The only odor worse than the one he suffers daily is the one that assaults his olfactory sense now, at the foot of the bridge that crosses the

Fleet Ditch. Once a river cascading from the green hills and meadows of Hampton Heath, the Fleet has for centuries been London's largest open sewer, a turgid morass that flows thickly to the Thames, carrying with it waste of the meanest kind: human and animal excrement, offal from the slaughterhouses, poison from the tanneries, food slops, garbage, drowned rats, dead dogs. He looks north, where pigsties and cheap, hastily built timber dwellings line the muddy banks. After the Fire, wood houses were outlawed in the City, but they have managed to proliferate outside the walls in the poorer areas. These Ditch-side abodes, inns, and taverns shelter the lowest sort—cutpurses, whores, thieves, and worse—and those too poor to live elsewhere, for no one readily chooses to reside near the Fleet and its noxious exhalations.

A few splintering planks shore up the sides of the riverbed adjacent to the bridge.

"What is that?" Thomas asks Ravenscroft.

"The remains of a rebuilding project begun after the Fire," he replies. "Christopher Wren, surveyor-general of the King's Works, and Robert Hooke, city surveyor, were commissioned by the king to turn the Fleet into a navigable canal." The work progressed in fits and starts, he explains, then finally stopped altogether, as Wren and Hooke were not able to come up with a satisfactory method of cleaning and dredging the ditch. Busily engaged all over London in rebuilding much of the city, the pair has allowed the project to lie fallow, much to the distress of the king.

They climb the stairs to the top of the bridge and stop for the momentary ease of Ravenscroft's aching knees. He looks south toward the Thames, a wide pewter-colored streak that shines dully in the distance, making silhouettes of the new houses and heaps of rubbish that characterize the post-Fire city. He rubs impatiently at his watery eyes, rheumy from lucubration, then slips on his spectacles (lenses ground by Christopher Mead, he thinks with a pang of annoyance), and glances down at the opaque river. The detritus that the Fleet carries daily bobs along on the mud-brown current: a goat's disembodied head, a gray mass that looks like pig's intestines, a furry black thing that might be the hide of a curly-haired dog or an old periwig. Only God and the Devil know what is underneath the surface of the water; the cellar sweepers and the night-soil men too often dump their noisome cargo into the Fleet. It is nothing less than a river of shit. No wonder Mr. Wren and Mr. Hooke have given up.

Like Ravenscroft, Wren and Hooke are fellows of the Royal Society. He is acquainted with both men and is in no doubt as to their extraordinary abilities, though he has wildly differing opinions of their characters. Wren is a gentleman and a genius; Hooke is capable, indeed, but a boaster and a braggart. He is perhaps the world's most annoying man: Ravenscroft has only to hint at a new discovery to ensure that Hooke will claim to have found it first.

He has learnt that the only way to avoid such trouble is to keep his own counsel and not speak to the man. Not an easy task, as Mr. Hooke is the society's curator of experiments and so attends nearly every weekly meeting of the natural philosophers, mathematicians, astronomers, physicians, chemists, and noble patrons who comprise the membership of the Royal Society. Even though Hooke is busy enough for three men, he apparently finds time to discover the secrets of everything under the sun, at least according to himself. But if that is true, Ravenscroft would sometimes like to ask, why is Hooke continually at the coffeehouses, gabbling on for hours with others of Ravenscroft's own acquaintance? He hesitates to call them friends, because there are so many in addition to Hooke with whom he no longer speaks. The perfidy and treachery of natural philosophers is beyond that of the worst assassins and spies. He cannot count the number of times he has been close to gaining the recognition he deserves, only to see it snatched away by another.

Ravenscroft crosses to the other side of the bridge and rests his palms on the cool, rough stone of the waist-high balustrade. As he gazes north, he envisions the Fleet Ditch unsoiled, its waters clear. No one living has seen it so. What if he could find a solution where Wren and Hooke could not?

This thought produces a sense of excitement Ravenscroft has not felt in years. The king would no doubt consider this a scheme of the highest importance, as it would make possible Mr. Wren and Mr. Hooke's canal project. That he would do anything to Mr. Hooke's benefit is slightly galling; but what a blessed change it would be for London to have unsoiled water and fresh air where now there are only noxious, pestilential miasmas. Not to mention that clearing the Fleet of its filth would secure his fame at last. Why, he might even be awarded a knighthood!

But he cannot dawdle here all day, dreaming. He has plenty enough work to keep him occupied already. As he turns away from the river, something in the water catches his eye. When he looks back, whatever it was is already lost, pulled under by the river's vortices. Strange, but he thought he'd seen a woman's dress—no, not a dress but a woman. A young woman, her inert body supple as a rag doll in the river's rolling current. He stares hard through his spectacles. It was just a dress, he decides. Or perhaps it was a figment of his imagination.

No, there it is again. He gasps and points. "Thomas, look."

Below, a woman's body washes up against the bridge piling nearest the riverbank. The current traps her there, wrapping her lifeless form around the narrow support like a horseshoe, hands stretched above her head as if trying to touch her toes. Thomas bolts down the stairs, intent on rescue. As he wades into the shallows under the bridge, others too spy the body in the river and rush to his aid. Two men help him drag her out of the water and onto the muddy riverbank. By the time Ravenscroft makes his way over, a small crowd has gathered; they stand in a circle around the body. Thomas rolls her onto her back. Her vacant eyes stare blankly up to the sky. She is soiled by the filth of the river, but the knife wounds in her chest and the terrible gash across the base of her throat are unmistakable. From the crowd, an outcry arises that sounds to Ravenscroft's ears like the noise made by a flock of seabirds, and everyone begins talking at once. Through the babble of voices he hears a woman's sorrowful twitter and sigh. "Why, it's Jenny Dorset," he hears her say, her voice breaking. "It's little Jenny Dorset."

Chapter Twelve

Second week of Michaelmas term

"A *swot*," Derek Goodman said good-naturedly, "is a nerd who's always studying. A *git* is an annoying idiot, and a *boffin* is a geek—usually the sort who works with test tubes or calculators, but if you spend too much time in the library you could be taken for a boffin." He took a sip from his pint of Guinness. "Any other English slang words you care to know?"

"That'll do for now," Claire said, smiling. They sat in the Eagle Pub at a window table overlooking St. Bene't's church, built before the Normans invaded England. A few weathered gravestones rose up from the lush, grassy churchyard at odd angles, like crooked teeth.

"Too bad. I was hoping to impress you with my vocab. When I was fourteen, we moved back to England after being away for some years, and I could hardly understand what people were saying. So I compiled a comprehensive list of slang words, from *oxters*—which are armpits, by the way—to *wellied*, which can mean 'drunk' or 'wearing enormous gumboots.' I was definitely a swot—and a boffin, too, I imagine."

Claire laughed. She hadn't imagined that someone as accomplished and intelligent as Derek Goodman could also be so down-to-earth and funny. She liked his self-deprecating humor, and he seemed more vulnerable than she would have thought from their first meeting. But maybe her first impressions had had more to do with her own prejudice about extraordinarily handsome men—that they were facile, selfish, shallow—than they had with reality. Wasn't that the kind of prejudice pretty women always faced? It wasn't fair or open-minded, two traits on which she prided herself. It was clear that Derek Goodman's extroverted charm came naturally to him, and his looks were only one part of the whole attractive package.

"You didn't grow up in England?"

"Not entirely. My father was a diplomat. We lived in eight different countries before my brother and I turned ten. Mostly European countries, East and West. Well, except for the year when my father had a falling out with the prime minister, and we were sent to Papua New Guinea." His startling blue eyes met Claire's. "I know what it's like to be an outsider in a foreign place," he said. "It's not easy being the new kid here, is it?"

"Not always, no," Claire said. She was too proud to say it, but to herself Claire admitted that she'd been lonely. If it hadn't been for Hoddy's company, she would have had no one to talk to. No peers, anyway. "Besides Dr. Humphries-Todd, you're practically the only person who's been friendly to me."

Derek burst out laughing. Claire watched him, slightly wounded.

"Sorry, I'm not laughing at you," he explained. "It's just that everyone makes the same mistake. I certainly did. When I first came up to Cambridge I thought, 'What a lovely little college town. So quaint, so charming.' Which it is, on the surface, but don't let it fool you. Underneath, Cambridge is a university town full of scheming academics. It's a hotbed of rivalries, jealousies, grudges, resentments, paranoia, backstabbing, lust, greed, and envy, with the occasional bit of arse-kissing thrown in. But what am I saying? I'm going to scare you away before you've had a chance to unpack your suitcases." He laughed again, then assumed a mock-serious expression. "Welcome to Cambridge, Dr. Donovan," he said gravely. "You're going to love it here."

They shared a pleasant pub dinner while learning a bit about each other's pasts. Derek Goodman's was by far the more fascinating of the two. With his diplomat father, he'd lived in twelve different countries by the time he was fourteen. He spoke eight languages, he said, then amended that number to seven and a half, as his "Serbo-Croatian wasn't really up to scratch." He brushed off his two books lightly, saying they'd come about simply because once he found a subject that interested him, he found it difficult to shut up about it. He made writing sound as if it were as effortless as breathing. Her dissertation had required considerably more exertion than that, Claire said.

"I heard you pulled off quite a coup in Venice," he remarked. "Gave Andrew Kent's lecture for him."

"It wasn't like that. He asked me to speak in his stead."

"You must have done something right or he wouldn't have asked, and you wouldn't be here." Derek shook his head, smiling. "I wish I had been there—in Venice, I mean. I would have loved to have seen Andy upstaged." He caught the waiter's eye and gestured for another round of beers. "And now? Are you working on a paper?"

Claire related the events of her day: how she had pursued an idea about women artists and then discovered what looked like a private diary instead.

"Written in code?" Derek asked, intrigued. "Do you have any idea who wrote it, or what it's about?"

"Not at all, I'm afraid."

"Did you have it copied?"

"No, but I copied some of it by hand. I thought that if I could decipher it, I could use it as the basis for a paper on encryption."

"Not a bad idea," Derek mused. "No, wait—I think I saw an article about something similar in *Past and Present* not long ago. I believe it was about coded communications in the seventeenth century. That's right, it was written by that wanker Charles Buford over at St. John's. By the way, just so you know, Trinity and St. John's have a rivalry that goes back about five hundred years. You shouldn't have anything to do with them."

"Why?"

"Because everyone at St. John's is a wanker, that's why," Derek said as if it had been self-evident. "I'm sorry to be the one to break the bad news, but I think your idea for a paper has been done already. You may want to reconsider." He frowned at the look of disappointment on Claire's face. "Sorry, didn't mean to take the wind out of your sails. But better to find out sooner rather than later."

"Yes."

"If there's any way I can help . . ."

"Would you mind taking a look at it?" If Derek was familiar with this sort of code, she might save herself some time.

"Not at all."

Claire opened her notebook and handed it to him. "I tried to follow the letterforms as faithfully as I could. I suppose I should have had it copied, but—"

"You didn't want to share your discovery?"

"I suppose that sounds pretty naive."

"It's perfectly understandable."

Claire contentedly watched him pore over her notes. This was exactly the sort of moment she'd come to Cambridge for: to work with other historians who loved history as much as she did. She'd imagined Andrew Kent sitting in the chair opposite hers, but Derek Goodman was an excellent substitute. "Have you ever seen writing like that before?" she asked.

"No, it's new to me." He gave the notebook back to Claire. "I will warn you not to get your hopes up too much, however. Things like this have a way of turning out to be more prosaic than they first appear. This could simply be notes from a church sermon or even someone's laundry list. The collections in the Wren have been around a long time. Most things of import were documented long ago. That's why you don't see too many other fellows in there."

The evening air was cool and misty as Claire and Derek Goodman walked back to Trinity. "There was a graduate student in the Wren Library today," Claire mentioned as they passed through the college's main gate. "She left right after I arrived. I worried that I'd done something to upset her."

"Lots of frizzy brown hair and very baggy clothes?"

"Yes."

"Rosamond Mercy. Don't take her behavior personally. She's like that all the time. She's working on her PhD and . . . well, *neurasthenic* is the nicest word for it, I suppose. She's bright, but she hasn't got much of a personality. Rosamond Mousy, I call her."

They walked into New Court and crossed to G staircase. Claire stopped just inside the arched doorway. "I had a very nice evening," she said.

"May I walk you to your door?"

"Not tonight, Dr. Goodman."

"Dr. Goodman? Let's dispense with that formality, at least."

"Derek," Claire said, "as you pointed out earlier, I'm new here. Which is a very good reason to be even more circumspect than I might normally be." She'd also had two and a half beers, about one and a half over her limit. It wasn't only that she wasn't ready to trust him; she didn't completely trust herself, under the circumstances.

"I must admit I'm terribly disappointed," Derek replied. "You have a lovely set." The gleam in his eyes underscored the double entendre.

He was being naughty, as the English might say, but he was much too cute for her to complain about it. Claire smiled instead. "Did you really expect to get invited upstairs with a line like that?"

He shrugged. "I didn't think it would hurt to try." He moved closer. "Claire, I just want you to know that I know what it's like to be new here. If you ever need help with anything, anything at all, I hope you won't hesitate to ask me." Derek wasn't smiling anymore. His blue eyes focused on hers. "I don't make this offer to just anyone. But when we met I felt we had this instant connection."

He was going to kiss her. Claire knew it at least three long, breathless seconds before he glanced down at her mouth and moved in for the kill, and she didn't stop him. Why didn't she stop him? Perhaps because she'd had one and a half beers too many. Or perhaps because Derek Goodman was handsome, brilliant, and completely irresistible. He was also, Claire discovered soon after his lips touched hers and his tongue began gently exploring, a front-runner for the title of World's

Best Kisser. For a while she was aware of nothing but the sensation of his mouth on hers. In the remote region of her mind still capable of logical thought, she wondered how long it had been since she'd kissed a man. *Too long* was the most accurate answer she could come up with. Then one of his hands slid south from her waist and the other began moving north toward her—

"Derek."

At the sound of the man's voice, low and accusatory, they jumped away from each other. Andrew Kent stood just outside the archway.

"What the hell are you doing, Derek?"

"We were just chatting." He raised both hands in the air in an attitude of supreme innocence, a suspect without a weapon.

"You weren't just chatting." Although Andrew seemed in complete self-control, Claire could see that he was furious. It was evident in his perfectly straight shoulders that looked broad enough to burst through his Burberry coat, evident in his voice, and, most especially, evident in the way he avoided looking at Claire. Above the stark white collar of his shirt, two spots of color blazed brightly across his cheeks. Derek was only one flippant remark away from being grabbed by the throat and dragged out onto the lawn. "Dr. Donovan is a new fellow, and you've no right putting the moves on her. You know the rules."

"She's not really a fellow." Derek had overcome his initial surprise and now just seemed irritated.

"The rules still apply."

"Well, of course we must always follow the rules, even when they make no sense. Old stick-in-the-mud Andy." Derek looked at Andrew with one eyebrow suspiciously raised. "And why were you coming 'round this time of night?"

"I was simply stopping by to make sure that Dr. Donovan had everything she needed, and so forth."

"And so forth?" he insinuated.

"Grow up, Derek." Claire had the distinct feeling that it wasn't the first time the two men had had an argument like this. "By the way," Andrew went on, now sounding more exasperated than angry, "Fiona

Flannigan has registered another complaint about you with the vice-master. You've got to stop calling her that ridiculous name."

"Flush is upset? Oh, come on. You don't take her seriously, do you?" Derek looked at Claire, his eyes shining with mischief. "Get this," he said, barely able to restrain his laughter, "Fiona Flannigan is a history fellow at Clare College who's writing an entire book on—how can I say this politely?—sewage."

"It's a book about the first public sanitation systems in London," Andrew explained.

"Exactly," Derek said. "It's a book about shit." He turned to Claire. "Everyone calls her Flush Flannigan."

"You've got to stop it," Andrew insisted. "The students look to you for an example. Even the freshers are starting to call her Dr. Flush. She doesn't find it funny."

"What do you expect me to do about that?" Derek shrugged, palms up. "Some people have no sense of humor."

"Derek, if you don't clean up your act, you'll soon discover that even your brilliance will not save you. There's only so much bad behavior the college will tolerate."

Derek sighed. "Andy, you are such a joy-killer."

"I'll walk you back to your set," Andrew said to Derek. It wasn't an offer; it was a command.

"Good night, Dr. Donovan." Derek took her hand and kissed it lightly. "Thank you for a lovely evening."

Andrew's expression was grim as Derek ducked past him. Andrew glanced once, briefly and inscrutably, at Claire.

And then he turned and walked away.

Chapter Thirteen

Third week of Michaelmas term

"ALICE LARKIN'S DAUGHTER was in a *riding* accident and *broke* her leg," Carolyn Sutcliffe explained to Claire as they sat in Carolyn's well-furnished set. She spoke in a manner that suggested this was highly *confidential* information and that Claire should be hanging on to her every *word*. "Poor Alice has had to take a leave of absence. Her supervisions will have to be *split up* among the other fellows, and I'll be taking over her role as the history department's director of studies until she returns."

Carolyn Sutcliffe's unstated but clear message: she was now Claire's boss. Not something much to Claire's liking. She had made a point of avoiding Carolyn ever since the fellowship admission dinner, and she wasn't warming to her now any more than she had the night they'd met. It wasn't easy to cozy up to someone who quite obviously disliked her; but even if Carolyn was more agreeable, Claire would have a difficult time regarding her as a friend. She behaved as though she was at the center of some monumentally urgent matter or had been entrusted with a secret mission. She continually wore a self-satisfied smirk, as though she had just done something worth bragging about or said something incredibly witty. Frankly, Claire couldn't imagine Carolyn doing either of those things.

"Of course, her leave of absence may be *extended*, depending on the *severity* of her daughter's injuries," Carolyn added.

"Of course," Claire echoed. In spite of a two-mile run this morning, she felt groggy. For the past three days, a thick, drizzly mist had swallowed up Cambridge, turning streets, buildings, trees, and river into dream-like, mind-numbing shades of gray. It was the sort of drizzle that didn't seem heavy enough for an umbrella, but on the running paths the air had been so dense that she hadn't been able to see more than ten feet ahead. The weeping willows along the riverbank had dripped with condensation. "Can you tell me again what the director of studies does?"

"The DOSes are in charge of supervisions," Carolyn replied. "We assign students to the fellows. Or temporary lecturers, as the case may be." She spoke as though the job was a terribly tiresome burden, even though it was obvious that she was delighted at the prospect of wielding power, and perhaps especially delighted at wielding power over Claire. A phone rang in the set's other room, and Carolyn sprang from her chair to answer it.

"Gaby!" From where Claire sat, she could easily hear Carolyn's brassy, loud greeting. It was followed by a flurry of Italian, also loud, speaking the usual formalities: *How nice to hear from you. I was thinking of you only yesterday.* Even in a foreign language, Claire noticed, Carolyn still managed to sound posh and self-important.

Gaby must have been none other than Gabriella Griseri, of course. The Italian countess was Carolyn's friend and, as of four months ago at least, Andrew Kent's girlfriend. She was also the woman who had falsely accused Claire of stealing a four-hundred-year-old diary out of Venice's Biblioteca Marciana. Claire had good reason to dislike Gabriella, and the countess had made it abundantly clear that the feeling was mutual. Claire settled back quietly, prepared to amuse herself by listening for anything of importance.

Carolyn stepped into the open door, phone in hand. "You speak Italian, don't you?"

"Yes."

"Anything else?" she breezily inquired.

"Spanish," Claire answered truthfully.

Carolyn disappeared again and began speaking French. Claire wasn't entirely ignorant of the language, but as she strained to listen, Carolyn's strident voice dropped a few decibels as well. She couldn't make out much. Twice she heard Carolyn say, "Andy," and once she heard her mention "BBC." In between were a few indistinct but enthusiastic murmurs.

Carolyn soon returned, even more smug than before. "Gaby just told me the most *marvelous* news. You remember Gabriella Griseri, don't you?"

"Yes." Claire didn't bother pointing out that Carolyn knew very well that she knew Gabriella.

"She just landed the most *fabulous* job," Carolyn gushed. "Her own half-hour chat show on the BBC. Andy will be *so* proud." She smiled at Claire as if challenging her to refute it. Her intent was so obvious— *don't you dare interfere with the happy couple!*—that Claire didn't even deign to acknowledge it. When she didn't respond, Carolyn got back to business. "Where were we? Oh, yes, Alice Larkin's supervisions. She was in charge of sixteen students. I'm going to assign three to Radha Patel, three to Toby Campbell, and the remainder to you."

"Ten students?"

"You've only *twelve* at present. Others have taken on more than that at times."

But not currently, Claire read between the lines. Carolyn Sutcliffe was assigning more students to Claire than to anyone else in the department. Another ten students would bring her total up to twenty-two. She'd be teaching so much that she'd hardly have time to research and write. Even with her current load, she hadn't done much. She'd looked for the article that Derek Goodman had mentioned, but she hadn't found it. And she'd gone back to the Wren twice to work with the diary. She'd copied everything but the last ten pages. She berated herself for not being more diligent when she'd had time. How was she ever going to find time now, with twenty-two hours of supervision and twenty-two papers to read every week?

"Is there a problem?" Carolyn asked in a way that made it clear she couldn't care less if there was.

"I won't have much time to do research."

"I don't see the need. You're a temporary lecturer, not a research fellow."

"I'm still a historian. I'm working on a paper about encryption in the seventeenth century. How am I going to be able to write it while supervising twenty-two students?"

"I'm sure I don't know, but I hardly think it matters."

The gloves were off, Claire realized. Obviously Carolyn Sutcliffe valued her friendship with Gabriella so much that she was willing to undermine Claire's ability to do her job by trying to make it difficult for her to write a paper, maybe even by making it difficult for her to perform well as a supervisor.

"In any case," Carolyn went on, "I believe that another of the fellows is writing a paper on the same subject, so it's just as well for you to leave off."

"Someone else is writing about seventeenth-century codes and ciphers?"

"Yes."

"Who?"

"Derek Goodman."

Claire strode across the Backs toward Sidgwick, where Carolyn had told her Derek was lecturing. Her pace was brisk, her mind troubled. Was it possible that Derek Goodman had asked her to go out with him just for the opportunity to poach her work? It seemed absurd, but he was the one who'd told her that academics were ruthless.

In the past week since the kiss, she'd been avoiding both Andrew Kent and Derek, and she wasn't looking forward to confronting him. She suspected they had been avoiding her too. On the Trinity College website she had found a paper entitled "Sexual Relationships between Junior and Senior Fellows" that spelled out all the possible consequences of such a liaison, and none of them were good. Perhaps all Andrew had had to do was mention "disciplinary action" to Derek and he'd stopped pursuing her. She spotted him emerging from the fog while walking across the Backs of Queens' College.

"How could you?" Claire demanded as soon as she was within speaking range.

"How could I what?" Derek grinned innocently.

"You know very well what." All the way from Nevile's Court, Claire had been unsure of what she would say, but now that she was face-to-face with Derek Goodman her anger untied the knot in her tongue. "You stole my idea."

He guffawed. "Don't be ridiculous."

"Carolyn Sutcliffe just told me that you're writing a paper on seventeenth-century codes."

"And what's this to do with you?"

"I told you that I was writing about it. You stole my idea for a paper."

"Come on, now. Do you really think I need your help to generate ideas?"

"I showed you my notes from the diary I found. Are you saying that you thought of it before I did?"

"Of course I did."

"If that's true, why didn't you tell me the night we went out to the pub?"

"I know better than to share my ideas with other historians."

"But why would you want to write a paper on a subject that was just written about by some"—Claire paused as she tried to recall the word—"'*wanker*' at St. John's?"

"Oh, that." He shrugged. "I may have misremembered."

"Misremembered?" Claire said incredulously. She was temporarily stunned speechless by the depth and breadth of his deception. "You made it all up, didn't you? It was all a big lie, from the moment you asked me out to telling me that a paper like mine had already been written."

"I think your imagination is working overtime, Dr. Donovan. Surely I've got better things to do than wine and dine junior fellows and press them for ideas. Anyway, ideas are easy; it's the execution that's hard. I don't see that my paper and yours have anything at all to do with each other."

"You mean you're still going to write it?"

"Write it and publish it, I imagine. I've got a greater knowledge of sources, and I daresay I can churn out a paper much faster than you can. I know editors at all the journals. All I have to do is make a phone call and they'll make space for anything I choose to write. And once my paper is published, no one will be interested in publishing yours."

Claire felt as if she'd been knocked breathless. She'd heard of ruthless ambition before, but she'd never encountered anything like this. He'd made a preemptive strike to destroy the competition even before she'd had a chance to compete. And not only had Derek Goodman completely deceived her but he also showed no remorse for his behavior. "You can't do this," Claire said. "I'll lodge a complaint with the vice-master."

"Go right ahead. It's your word against mine. Who do you think he'll believe? A fellow who's been with the college for fourteen years, or a temporary lecturer who's been here less than a month?"

Derek smiled again, but Claire didn't find it at all charming anymore.

The door to Andrew Kent's set was at the top of E staircase in the Great Court. Claire raised her hand to knock, then hesitated. She had decided against going to the vice-master to make a formal complaint against Derek Goodman. If Andrew Kent could have a private word with Derek and tell him to lay off the writing of (and the stealing of, Claire thought darkly) her paper, then all of this could be handled very quietly, no fuss, no muss, no repercussions. Not that she was worried about what was going to happen to Derek, but she knew it wouldn't look good for a new lecturer to make accusations about one of the fellows, no matter how true it might have been. The cards were stacked against her.

But how was Andrew Kent going to react? She lowered her hand. If he hadn't seen her kissing Derek Goodman (the kissing debacle was how she thought of it now), she could have counted on his trust in her. They might not have known each other well, but certainly he knew her well enough to know she was not a liar. But now? What must he think of her?

Claire worried that she'd lost Andrew's good opinion entirely. Maybe he was even sorry he'd hired her. After all, he hadn't bothered getting in touch with her since the debacle, and he'd given her no opportunity to explain. Not that she was sure she could explain. What would she say? "I was just standing there innocently, and he kissed me"? Not exactly the truth. "I was feeling lonely and I let him kiss me"? Closer, but still not the whole enchilada. "I thought Derek Goodman was extraordinarily attractive until I discovered what an underhanded snake he is"? That more closely approximated the truth, but how could she prove that there had been a devious motive behind Derek Goodman's kiss?

Maybe she shouldn't say anything to anyone. She could turn around, go back to her set, and pretend none of this had ever happened. She could supervise twenty-two students a week and try to find another subject for a paper—if she ever found time to go to the library again. Except it was so patently unfair. Even if it hadn't happened to her, Claire would have been outraged by Derek Goodman's behavior. It was simply wrong for an older, seasoned academic to charm, manipulate, and steal from one of his younger colleagues. And as he'd said, he'd been a fellow for fourteen years. Claire had a sneaking feeling that she wasn't the first person he'd used in this way.

But did she really want to open this can of worms? What would Derek Goodman do once he found out that she'd told someone about his misdeed? Clearly, Claire decided, she should think on it a bit longer.

The door opened and Andrew Kent stood in the doorway, dressed in a brownish tweed jacket, similarly colored slacks, a tan button-down shirt, and a green tie. Not a bad ensemble for a man who sometimes dressed as though he were color-blind. He sported a new pair of glasses that reminded her of 1920s intellectuals, rather dashing in their vintage style, and his hair was mussed, as if he'd been running his hands through it. He was, in fact, the epitome of the absentminded professor, the sort who is sexy without being aware of it. At the moment she wished she didn't find Andrew Kent so incredibly appealing. It simply made this particular encounter more awkward.

"Were you going to knock, or were you planning to stand there all afternoon?" he asked in a way that was not entirely welcoming.

It reminded her that Andrew Kent was not so much absentminded as acid-tongued. "I hadn't decided yet," Claire answered in an equally frosty tone.

"Why don't you come in while you're making up your mind?" Andrew said as he stepped back from the doorway.

His set consisted of only two rooms, a sitting room and an office. Andrew lived "out," or off-campus, with his young son. Through the windows she could see across the Great Court to the chapel on the other side. She could also see the path leading up to the doorway of E staircase. Andrew had seen her coming in. *Great,* she thought, feeling foolish. He'd known she'd been standing outside his door the whole time.

Inside, the sitting room contained a pair of large leather chairs with tufted backs, and a few well-stocked bookcases along one wall. A collection of framed photographs covered the top of a mahogany side table. Most appeared to be of his son, Stewart, and they charted his growth from infant to the present, about ten years old, Claire estimated. He was a redhead, or ginger-haired, as they said here. Must take after his late mother.

"Is something wrong?" Andrew asked, closing the door behind them.

"What makes you think that?"

"One, you've never come to visit me before, and two, the unhappy expression on your face."

Not for the first time, Claire wished that she weren't so transparent. "I'm having a problem with one of the fellows." She decided to sound out Andrew first before giving specifics.

"What kind of problem?"

"This other fellow is writing a paper on the same topic I'm writing on—only I'm pretty sure that he wasn't writing it until after I told him about my own paper and showed him my notes."

"Pretty sure?"

"Entirely sure."

"Can you prove it?"

"No, but it's true. I just spoke with him about it. He doesn't even try to conceal the truth—he just said that he'll write it faster and publish it first so that my paper doesn't stand a chance."

"Is it Derek Goodman, by any chance?"

"How did you know?"

"Let's just say you're not the first to have these sorts of issues with him."

"Then perhaps I should go to the vice-master."

Andrew shook his head. "Not a good idea."

"Why not?"

"Because you're new here and he isn't. Because he's a Trinity graduate and you're not. Because you're American and he's English. Because you're a woman and he's a man. There, I've just said all of the politically incorrect stuff—I suppose I shouldn't have, but unfortunately it's all true. If he refutes your claim, you might not get a fair hearing."

"He said it would be my word against his." Claire paused, feeling overwhelmed. Of all the things she had imagined going wrong in her new job, she had never imagined this. "So what can I do?"

"What is it you want?"

"I just want to be able to write the paper."

"And publish it?"

"Hopefully, yes."

Andrew picked up his cell phone and punched a few keys. "I'll put this on speakerphone."

Claire heard the phone ringing at the opposite end, then Derek Goodman's voice. He didn't bother saying hello. "I told you, I won't sit on another damned committee, Andy."

Andrew ignored his insolent manner. "Do you have a minute, Derek? I need to talk to you."

"A minute, but no more," he said with a sharp laugh. "I'm timing you." Interesting how obvious Derek's rudeness was when it was not offset by the charms of his person.

"Dr. Donovan tells me that you're writing a paper very much like hers, on the subject of—?" he looked to Claire.

"Seventeenth-century codes and ciphers," she answered.

"Seventeenth-century codes and ciphers," Andrew told Derek.

"Is that so?" Derek replied snidely. "I beg to differ. She happens to be writing a paper that is very much like mine."

"She said she showed you her notes."

"Rubbish. It's complete fiction."

"Why would she lie about this, Derek?"

"Could be any of a number of reasons. Number one of which is that she asked me to come up to her set and I said no. Hell hath no fury and all that."

Claire gasped at his bald-faced lie.

"Somehow I don't think that's the case, Derek," Andrew said.

"For Christ's sake, how am I supposed to know why? All I can tell you is that she's lying. We went out for a beer and had a snog, which you may recall, Andrew, as you so rudely interrupted us. We never even discussed work." He paused. "And I see that our time is up. Don't call me again unless it's about something important."

Andrew closed his phone and returned it to his pocket. "Charming as usual. Well?"

At first Claire was too stunned to say anything. Finally she blurted, "He's the one who's lying. It wasn't like that at all—I never asked him to come up to my set."

"I understand that Derek is, er, difficult," Andrew said, "and that this is a difficult situation, but I'm afraid there's not much I can do without some kind of proof."

"That's it? He's 'difficult,' it's a 'difficult situation,' but there's nothing you can do? Derek Goodman is a shameless liar and a thief to boot. You might have at least warned me about him. That's if you'd ever bothered to speak to me."

"Oh." Andrew seemed at a loss for words. "I'm sorry about that." He looked down at the floor. Was that guilt or embarrassment in his expression? "I've been really busy."

"Too busy to make me feel welcome?" Claire asked. "Just why did you hire me, anyway?"

"Because you're a fine scholar and I thought you would be an asset to the college."

"That's the only reason?"

"Of course that's the only reason."

Of course. Why had she ever thought there had been something more? Her imagination had run away with her. Andrew Kent was a senior fellow and she was, for all intents and purposes, a junior fellow. There were rules about that. Rules that Hoddy had already told her Andrew would never transgress.

"If you can come up with proof that you were writing on this subject first and showed him your notes," Andrew said, "I promise I'll have him brought up before the disciplinary committee. In the meantime, the best advice I can give you is to steer clear of him."

"Avoid him? That's all you're going to say?" Claire huffed as she turned toward the door. "I'm sorry I bothered coming here."

Chapter Fourteen

5 November 1672

THOUGH THE KING remains at Hampton, the courtiers have returned to Mademoiselle de Keroualle's. Her drawing room has come to life again, with the chandeliers, the candelabra, and the palatial fireplace ablaze. A maidservant, this one a quick-limbed girl of no more than thirteen, leads Hannah past the bewigged men at the card tables, engrossed in high-stakes games of Basset, and a few who lounge on the furniture, talking and taking snuff. By the time they reach the end of the hallway, the withdrawing room's light music of harp and viola has faded away, along with its steady drone of animated voices. When the maid ushers her into the mademoiselle's bedchamber, she is reminded of the drowsy, enchanted silence of the previous night. The only sounds that disturb the stillness are the hiss of the wood fire and the swish of the maidservant's skirts as she hurries from the room.

The curtains are drawn open, revealing two large windows with an expansive view of the wide, gray river and the lowering sky. Slow and stately, barges and boats glide up- and downstream. The room itself is extravagantly designed, rather more so than Hannah realized last night. Everything in it—the curtains, the chairs, the custom-made Aubusson carpets, the paneled walls decorated with gold filigree—is tinted in shades of rose. No doubt in sunny weather this is a flattering color for Mademoiselle de Keroualle, but in the cold light of an overcast autumn morning it takes on a bluish-gray hue, which Hannah cannot help comparing to the bloodless pallor of a corpse's lips.

She goes directly to Louise's bedside. The mademoiselle accepts her presence without a word, her heavy-lidded eyes glancing up once in recognition, then closing again. She seems little changed from the night before. Her lips are so dry that they are cracked and bleeding. On the nightstand is an empty glass but no pitcher of beer or any other potable liquid. Has no one been tending to her? The maid returns with more wood for the fire and Hannah asks her to fetch some small beer. She returns with it as Hannah is turning out her pockets, unloading the various potions and powders she has brought for Louise's care. She pours a glass of beer and holds it to the mademoiselle's lips, rousing her from her febrile sleep, urging her to drink. Louise looks at the glass, then at Hannah, and turns her face away.

"Madame," she whispers, along with a few words that Hannah can't make out. "Madame . . . ," Louise says again, followed by a barely audible murmur in French. What was it? It sounded like *madame . . . try to . . . poison.*

"What did you say?" Hannah leans closer. "Mademoiselle—"

"What are you doing?" Madame Severin has entered the room and is striding toward her. "Give me the glass," she demands.

"Pardon?" The forcefulness of Madame Severin's manner takes Hannah off-guard.

"Give me the glass." Madame Severin holds out her hand.

Hannah reluctantly hands the glass to her. She isn't certain about what the mademoiselle just said; indeed, it could be fever-induced madness, but it has made her wary of Madame Severin nonetheless.

"Why will the mademoiselle not drink?" Hannah asks.

"She drinks from no one's hand but my own."

"Why have you not been giving her beer as I instructed last night?"

"She did not wish to drink as often as you said she would."

"You must make her drink, even if she does not wish to. She must take in enough liquid to quench the fever that rages within her. And what of the decoctions I left here? Did you put them in the beer?"

"No. I am having them tested."

"Tested for what?"

"For poison."

"I am a doctor. I am here to heal her, not to poison her."

"I will take no chances with the mademoiselle's life."

"If you mean to save her, I must begin her treatment at once. Your delay has caused her more harm than you realize."

Madame Severin continues to gaze at Hannah as if trying to take the measure of her. "I'm not sure that you understand what it is like to be a Catholic in your country, Mrs. Devlin," she says. "Although the king has graciously created the Declaration of Indulgence, which allows us freedom of worship, there are many who are resentful that we follow our faith, especially that we do so here in Whitehall."

"My mother is a Catholic and my father was an adherent of the Anglican Church. I myself am a physician first. I do not concern myself with my patients' beliefs, only with their bodies."

"You do not believe that it is through God's grace that we are healed?"

"Not entirely, no. No more than I believe that we die because we have provoked God's wrath. I have seen too many innocents die to believe that."

Madame Severin still seems unsure.

"I suggest that you trust me," Hannah says, "and allow me to do what I was brought here to do."

"Then tell me about these." Madame Severin points to the array of medicines on the nightstand.

Hannah holds up each medicine as she gives instructions for its use. "This tincture and this powder must be mixed in with the beer— three drops and two grains to every pint. The mademoiselle will need more blankets and fresh linens every few hours. She should begin perspiring a great deal. It is beneficial for her to do so, but try to keep her dry and warm. These are herbs for an immersion bath as soon as she is able. She must be given one spoonful of this syrup every four hours until she is well, starting now."

Madame Severin takes the bottle containing the electuary, removes the cork, and sniffs. She tips the bottle over and cautiously tastes the sticky drop that appears on her fingertip. She savors it a moment and, apparently finding nothing that arouses her suspicion, returns the bottle to Hannah. "Very well, Mrs. Devlin. But you should be aware: if any harm comes to the mademoiselle, harm will come to you."

Hannah brings a chair closer to the bed and takes up her post. The mademoiselle's illness is a type that is slow to release its hold and requires careful vigilance. If she had thought that the king's mistress, with her staff of servants, with her "dear friends" Lord Arlington and Madame Severin, would not be assiduously attended, she would have stayed longer last night. Madame Severin's behavior is very odd. Hannah can't decide if she has been overly protective or negligent. Her fear of poison seems exaggerated. But is it really? Mademoiselle de Keroualle is the king's current favorite: that alone could create enough envy and malice for a hundred poisoners.

The minutes and the hours go by slowly, unheralded. Even though the king is known to be fond of them, there are no clocks in the mademoiselle's room. The passing of the day is marked by Madame Severin's punctual return every half hour, to give Louise drink and medicine at Hannah's instruction. Although Hannah would never describe her as amiable, Madame Severin seems to have grudgingly accepted her authority.

Hannah has little to do but watch the slow-moving river barges and the placid features of Mademoiselle de Keroualle. Surely this is the most unusual sickroom she has ever been in. High-ceilinged, well-kept, and well-aired, the mademoiselle's Whitehall bedchamber lacks odor, or, more specifically, bad odors—the pungent, sweet smell of sickness and death, which is one of soiled linens and close-stools and mortifying flesh, so thick and ripe you can choke on it. The places where Death creeps in are nothing like this: perfumed sheets, sachets of lavender and rosemary, the faint, pleasant hint of wood smoke. Even Louise's skin smells good, like clover honey and nutmeg. No wonder the king enjoys spending time here.

By the afternoon the mademoiselle has not improved, so Hannah calls for a basin and lets a few ounces of blood from a vein in her ankle. Not enough to affect her much, but enough so that if anyone asks, she will be able to say that she did so, just as any doctor licensed by the College of Physicians would do. Soon after, the diaphoretics begin to take effect, and Hannah calls for the maid to change the silk sheets.

"She is still ill," Hannah tells Madame Severin as she prepares to leave. "It could be days or weeks before the mademoiselle is completely well. If she takes a turn for the worse, you should send a coach for me. Otherwise, I will return tomorrow."

"Has Lord Arlington given you leave to go?" Madame Severin asks.

"I believe he trusts I will do whatever is necessary," Hannah replies. If not, he certainly knows where to find her.

"You have been with the mademoiselle?" a man calls out to Hannah as she walks through the withdrawing room.

She stops and looks back over her shoulder to see the source of the inquiry: a large man stuffed into a small armchair. His bland pudding of a face is dominated by a bulbous red nose; his right hand has a death grip on a wineglass. When he sees that he has her attention, he enthusiastically slurps the remaining contents of the glass and struggles to his feet. Although he is too advanced in years to be mistaken for one, he is dressed as grandly as any gallant, with a towering periwig of shining black curls and a richly embroidered waistcoat that strains against his ample stomach. His ceruse-whitened skin is accented by two black patches, one on his chin and one just above his left eyebrow. As he walks over to Hannah, he ogles her with unabashed curiosity, such as he might display toward a contortionist's exhibit at Bartholomew Fair. "You have been in to see her?"

Hannah looks around helplessly. She hoped to leave without being noticed, and more particularly without being questioned.

"I thought no one was allowed to visit her," he continues loudly, capturing the attention of another courtier nearby. "She is very ill, you know."

Hannah scrambles for a reply. "I have recently been afflicted with the terrible ague from which the mademoiselle now suffers and am therefore in no personal danger."

The courtier frowns, perplexed. "How can you be sure?"

"Sir Granville," the other courtier says as he joins them, saving her from the necessity of a reply, "who is this you're interrogating?" He is an attractive man of thirty or so. Hair lighter than her own, with darker, cocoa-colored eyes. His clothes are unmistakably French, but his open, intelligent expression marks him as a man of good judgment.

"Why, she is a young lady!" Sir Granville replies.

"I am pleased to see that your university education has not undermined your ability to discern that which is obvious." He wears an ironic smile and has the merest suggestion of amusement in his eyes—enough for anyone with perspicacity to notice but not so much that his target will take offense. She likes him in spite of her general wariness toward courtiers. Her father had no good opinion of most of the courtiers he met, but she's willing to give this one the benefit of the doubt for coming to her rescue. Hannah sizes him up more carefully. He wears a wig, of course—no man of quality would appear at court without one—but it's not so big as to be absurd. No makeup or patches. And his attire, while fashionable, well-tailored, and, no doubt, expensive, is subdued and sophisticated.

"I beg your pardon?" Sir Granville says.

"Have you not introduced yourself, Sir Granville? Oh, the manners of the young people at court these days." He arches his brow for Hannah's benefit. "Allow me. Young lady, this is Sir Granville Haines, and you are—?"

"Mrs. Devlin."

"Mrs. Devlin," he repeats with a short bow. "I am Ralph Montagu, His Majesty's most loyal servant—"

"And veritable scoundrel," Sir Granville adds.

"—and, until recently, our country's ambassador to France. Please excuse Sir Granville's impolite behavior. As he is one of the king's physicians, I fear he is overcome with his concern for Mademoiselle de Keroualle's health."

"I am indeed," Sir Granville says. "I have heard she is in grave need of a doctor."

"But not you, certainly, Sir Granville. I'm sure you would not like Mademoiselle de Keroualle's need for a grave to be increased?"

"Well, I . . . I don't . . . indeed, sir!" he stammers. "You make no sense. As for the mademoiselle, I have it on good authority that only three days ago she was completely given over to madness and hysteria. There can be only one possible cause, of course: fits of the mother."

The former ambassador looks delighted with the diagnosis. "Do go on," Montagu says encouragingly.

"Fits of the mother," Sir Granville intones, eager to enlighten them, "whereby a woman's womb rises through her body"—he demonstrates with a slow rise of his hands—"and lodges in her head, thereby occasioning episodes of hysteria and fainting, such as were witnessed in the mademoiselle only recently."

"Sir Granville." Hannah knows she should remain silent, but she cannot. "Have you ever found this amazing condition in a patient you have yourself examined?"

"Examine a patient!" Sir Granville snorts. "A real physician has no need to examine a patient!"

"But even a short perusal of medical literature reveals that there is no evidence that a womb has ever detached itself from the surrounding organs and traveled through a woman's body to her head. Surely, if this had ever occurred, a body with a womb in a place where it did not naturally belong would have been discovered and recorded at some point in history, yet this has never happened. Moreover, Dr. Sydenham himself has noted the same type of hysteria in both men and women, by which he deduces there must be some other cause. Or do you suppose there are wombs within men's heads too?"

Underneath the white maquillage, Sir Granville's face turns an alarming shade of pink. "Well, I never! Wombs in men's heads! Dr. Sydenham, of all people!"

Hannah regrets her outburst as soon as it is finished; she is hardly accomplishing her goal of going unnoticed. Even the worldly Montagu looks a little surprised at her opinionated speech, but he politely intercedes and smoothes the elder physician's ruffled feathers.

"Sir Granville, will you not tell us about your new medicine? I believe I heard you mention it only recently."

"Yes, of course," Sir Granville says, recovering his composure. "It cures wind, gout, agues, and all pestilential fevers, the great pox, the smallpox, the plague, rheumatisms, the bloody flux, fits of the mother, frenzy, fanaticism, disturbed dreams, and any other discomfiture of the mind. Sir Granville's Clyster and Julep, I call it."

"So it is both an enema and a beverage?" Montagu inquires.

"Quite right," Sir Granville says.

"How convenient." Montagu's expression is one of barely suppressed mirth. Hannah avoids meeting his eye, for fear of behaving shamelessly; she can barely keep her countenance as it is. Luckily, Montagu has the situation well in hand. "Mrs. Devlin, did I hear you say that you must be leaving?" he breezily inquires.

"What?" Sir Granville says.

Montagu bows his head slightly and winks at Hannah. "Please allow me to escort you," he continues.

Hannah can't think of a time when she's witnessed—or worse, been a party to—such frank impertinence, but she can't deny she's very grateful for it. "Thank you, Mr. Montagu."

Montagu takes his leave of Sir Granville, Hannah honors him with a small curtsy, and they quickly make for the door. Once outside, they burst into laughter.

"You were most impolite," she chides him.

"Not me! It's my business to be polite. As you shall see. Please allow me to escort you to your carriage." They begin walking along the stone gallery in the direction of the palace courtyard and Whitehall's main entrance.

"I have no carriage."

"Then please allow me to see you home."

"It isn't necessary."

"At the very least, you must allow me to walk you to the gate."

"If you must."

"A reluctant acquiescence." Montagu puts his hand to his heart, but he is grinning. "I am wounded. Women so seldom understand the great harm they do, just by their lack of regard for men's finer feelings."

Hannah laughs. "I think you are not so easily wounded."

"But you do believe I have finer feelings, don't you? That's a good start. Tell me," he says with a half smile, "what did you think of Sir Granville?"

"I cannot believe that that man is a physician," Hannah answers vehemently. "And the king's physician as well! Please tell me it isn't true, or our entire country is in grave danger."

"I'm afraid it is true," Montagu replies with a resigned laugh. He looks at her quizzically. "Do you always speak your mind in such a forthright manner?"

"I suppose I do, yes."

"That isn't a healthy habit for a courtier."

"I'm not a courtier."

"But here you are at court. So you must be, at least for now. You are absolutely right about Sir Granville, of course. He's one of the stupidest men I have ever met, but he is very wealthy and has long been a staunch supporter of the Crown. Therefore his position is secure. But do not fear. Even the king realizes what a buffoon he is. The last time he was ill and called for a doctor, he specifically asked for anyone except Sir Granville."

"'Even the king . . . , '" Hannah repeats. "You say that as if the king is less discerning than other men."

"Have you ever been in His Majesty's presence?"

"The King? Why, no. My fa—" She stops herself in time. "I saw him walking with his ministers in St. James's Park once years ago, but that is all."

"Perhaps you will discover for yourself the depth of His Majesty's understanding." He pauses and, less jovially this time, asks, "What do you think of the black widow?"

"Madame Severin?"

"Yes."

"I was told that she mourns her husband. Surely that is not something to ridicule."

"In most cases, no. But Madame Severin did not love her husband; she hated him." He laughs heartily at the look of surprise on Hannah's face. "You must never forget, Mrs. Devlin, that this is the court of Charles Stuart and nothing here is ever what it seems to be."

"If she hated her husband, why is she still in widow's weeds?"

"'Tis all vanity. In her youth, Madame Severin was one of the most beautiful women to grace this earth. The reason she still wears black is that she wants no one to forget that she was once the most stunning woman in France, and that men fought and died for her."

"You can't be serious."

"What I say is true. Madame Severin's story is a fascinating one. Her family, though aristocratic, wasn't wealthy, and her dowry was small, but she was so beautiful that no one cared. There were many suitors for her hand. Her parents, being mercenary like all the French, married her off to the richest. She was sixteen, and he was more than twenty years her senior.

"The marriage was never happy. Severin was a man of passionate temper, quick to anger and given to frequent rages. A man like that does not so much love as possess. Madame Severin made him suffer in return, in the way she was most able: she made him jealous at every opportunity, and there were many opportunities. Monsieur Severin was forced to become a capable swordsman. When word got round how good he'd become, it put a damper on Madame Severin's love life. But then she caught the eye of the finest duelist in France—and Monsieur Severin was dead within a month."

"He was killed in a duel?"

Montagu nods. "Madame Severin was not yet nineteen. She rejoiced in his death, but she was not to be a merry widow for long. Severin's riches turned out to be a sham, and the creditors gathered like packs of dogs at her door. They took everything she owned. Her new lover, the man who had killed her husband, was even more jealous than Severin. One night, after he'd seen her with another man at a party, he decided that the only way to stop her flirtations was to make her less beautiful. So he sliced off her ear and cut her cheek with a rapier."

"That's barbaric."

"Yes, I suppose it is. But do not feel sorry for her. Princess Henriette-Anne, who was soon to be wed to the Duc d'Orleans, took pity on her and asked her to be one of her ladies. It didn't take long for Madame Severin to rise to mistress of the bedchamber. Some years later, she arranged to have the duelist killed; he was set upon by some supposed highwaymen. Some people even believe she killed him herself. It will never be proved, but I think it behooves her to remain in England. And here she thrives. Madame Severin is ideally suited to being a courtier. Her ability to charm and deceive was well honed during her marriage."

"You pass a harsh judgment upon her."

"No harsher than what is warranted."

They approach the main gate. "You seem to know much about many people, Mr. Montagu."

Montagu gives her a sidelong glance. "You have no idea."

The courtyard swarms with crowds as people of all types, from the highest noble to the most humble apprentice, pass in and out of the gate at Whitehall Street, the main thoroughfare leading into the palace. The only requirement for entry to Whitehall is a decent suit of clothes, and even that minimal condition is waived in some cases. A few of the king's guards and the red-coated horse guards, whose barracks and stables lie just across the road, stand duty, but they seldom harass anyone. Carriages, sedan chairs, and hackney coaches for hire line up in front of the Banqueting House.

"Again, may I escort you home?" Montagu asks.

"No, really—"

"But I insist." His light, mocking tone is gone. He directs Hannah's attention to one of the hackney coaches on the street. Maitland stands by the door, waiting for them.

Hannah realizes at once that Lord Arlington has arranged this—not just the coach but also Montagu's presence at Mademoiselle de Keroualle's and even, perhaps, the former ambassador's solicitousness. She tries to hide her disappointment, though she fears she is unable to completely do so. "I see."

"Do not be alarmed, Mrs. Devlin." Montagu takes her arm and escorts her through the milling crowds. "Your secrets are safe with me."

Chapter Fifteen

Observations of my second visit to Mademoiselle de Keroualle, at Whitehall:

She continues quite ill with unremitting fever, pain in her loins, heat in her urine, and extreme lethargy. I am more firmly of the opinion that she has the running of the reins. There is only one possible source of this sickness. Lord Arlington has not said so directly, but as he delicately put it: "The mademoiselle's affections have been engaged by no one but His Majesty." Last night I asked him and Madame Severin if she had felt poorly before the pain and fever commenced. The Mistress of the Bedchamber replied that as long as a fortnight ago Mlle. de Keroualle had complained of discomfort, but did not imagine that she could be vexed with a disease of Venus by way of the King. I said that it has been my experience and the experience of my parents before me that sickness does not make distinctions of class, wealth, or goodness of character, to which Mme. Severin took some offense, thinking that by this statement I considered Mlle. de Keroualle no better than a lady of the town. Lord Arlington had to assure her that I did not mean such a thing. It seems we are always to be at cross-purposes to one another. Mme. Severin is clearly *anxious to establish her mistress's loyalty to the King; and at the same time she does not want to anger the King by making known the result of his profligate behavior. I can understand her reluctance but I cannot agree with it, for it has allowed Mlle. de Keroualle's illness to continue and take hold with great force. I did not ask how the King himself fares; it is understood that he must suffer from the same complaint, although in a lesser degree; and from Arlington's expressions I gathered that this is not the first occasion.*

At Mlle. de Keroualle's I met Ralph Montagu, who has been lately recalled from France, where he served as ambassador. He is charming, which is cause for circumspection; but is that not a trait which all diplomatists must nurture? He, like Lord Arlington, is employed in keeping my enterprise at Whitehall clandestine; I appreciate this necessity, though it gives me reason for worry, and from Lord Arlington I fear no good will come to me, as no good came to my father. Mr. Montagu is possessed of an excellent understanding and very well favored, and has a wit which I fear with less restraint would be wicked indeed. He put down in a most satisfactory manner the presumptions of one of the King's doctors. I suppose his treatment of Sir Granville could be considered cruel by some, but I believe this man to be the worst sort of physician, whose small amount of book learning only serves to inflict a great amount of suffering upon anyone unfortunate enough to be his patient. If my father were still alive, I'm sure he would have felt as I did.

Her father. Hannah puts down her quill and presses her temples between her thumb and fingers. It's been more than a year since her father died, a year ago September. Not died, precisely, but was killed, the victim of his own charity: Dr. Briscoe was visiting a patient in one of the poorer parishes when he was robbed and left for dead. One by one, the people she most loved passed away: her husband, Nathaniel, her daughter, Sarah, her father. Hannah's mother left in spirit long ago, though she remains in body, and Hannah has nothing on which to place the blame: a sickness of the mind, or of the soul?

If only there were someone whose mind and counsel she could

consult, could rely upon. Mrs. Wills is too busy with the work of the household to be a confidante, and she has never shown great interest in medical matters. The girls are too young; they look to Hannah as a mother of sorts. Since her father died, she's had no one to talk to. No wonder she scribbles in this diary every night: to create a listener, a sounding board, a place where all her thoughts can be expressed without encountering judgment or censure.

Hannah yawns and stretches. The events of the day have been wearying. To find syrup of poppies, she had to go to two more apothecary shops, and even so she was able to purchase only a small amount, a few days' worth at most. To make up for the possible shortfall, she'd also bought some laudanum, Dr. Sydenham's creation of opium and wine. Generally laudanum is stronger than poppy syrup, and must be used more judiciously, but she feels better knowing it is close at hand. She has taken only a few drops of syrup today, just enough to reduce her pain while keeping her mind clear. She wouldn't have gotten through the trip to Whitehall without it. But now it is night, and, keeping to its usual pattern, the headache has grown worse. She looks across the room to her workbench, a plank table as big as a door placed under the eaves. The brown bottle that contains the poppy syrup is just one of the many bottles and jars and dishes set amongst the jumble of her medicine-making apparatus, the mortars and pestles, the pill-making board, the alembics.

In the beginning, the poppy syrup helped her sleep, but its soporific effect has ebbed away over time. More often now she feels restless and unsettled after taking it; the pain is lulled and quieted, but she is not. The only answer, she knows from observing patients, is to administer a larger dose. Perhaps switching to the laudanum would help. There are dosing instructions for tincture of opium in the notes her father kept while working with Dr. Sydenham, she recalls. She is about to get up and look for his bound journal when she hears a knock on the door.

"Come in," Hannah calls.

The door opens slowly. Hester reluctantly takes a few steps inside. Her freckled face has a pleasant, coppery glow in the candlelight. Hannah notices the creases ringing the bottom of her flannel overskirt;

Mrs. Wills has let out the hem twice, and it's already too short again. Hester is growing so fast that she's all arms and legs, like a newborn foal. She holds a blue ceramic cup of something steaming that smells of nutmeg. "Mrs. Wills made you a posset," she says, offering the cup awkwardly. "To help you sleep."

Hannah has tried to keep her late nights and nocturnal perambulations a secret from the rest of the household. Obviously she hasn't been entirely successful.

"Thank you, Hester." Hannah takes the cup from her. The posset is made of hot milk, honey, red wine, and spices. It would no doubt be good for her, but she does not, at this moment, feel like drinking it. She puts it on the writing table next to her diary. "You may sit with me for a few minutes, if you like," she says, knowing that her offer will almost certainly be turned down. Hannah hasn't given up hope, however, that one day Hester will be less apprehensive.

Hester can barely conceal her panic. She has never enjoyed being in Hannah's room; in fact, she is afraid of it: the bundles of herbs drying in the rafters; the jars of mysterious liquids and powders; the ceramic canisters of dead, dried insects and animal parts; the bubbling alembics; the strange aromas; the stacks of aging, leather-bound books. Hannah tries to see it through Hester's eyes: less of a bedchamber than a combination of apothecary's shop, alchemist's warren, and a place with, perhaps, a darker purpose. Hester's family moved to London from the countryside, and Hester has retained many of the small-town prejudices that she was born with, even though Hannah has insisted on educating both of the girls. Hester believes in bizarre and morbid occurrences, such as bewitched girls who vomit pins and hanks of horsehair, or men who fall under an evil spell and are compelled to dance a jig until they die. Even though Hannah has tried to point out the improbability of such events, Hester's belief in the occult is hard to dislodge.

"Please excuse me, ma'am. Lucy and I are busy with our Latin grammar." She has given the one excuse that always works with Hannah: she is studying. Mrs. Wills doesn't think much of Hannah's educational curriculum for the girls. Especially the Latin, she says, is a waste of time and tutors' fees, but Latin is still the language of scholars and Hannah wants Lucy and Hester to have the ability to read widely, regardless of their path in life. Although admittedly neither of them have taken to it with the enthusiasm that she did.

"And how are your studies progressing?"

"Very well, ma'am." It is a dutiful answer and a predictable one. It's also a lie: the last time Hannah quizzed the girls they were woefully inept. But that isn't what bothers her most. No matter how she tries, she can't get past Hester's reserve. It's as if all the girl's darker emotions, her resentment and anger and fear, have turned inward to fester and grow. She worries that someday Hester will do something terrible, something worse than lying or shirking her duties or tormenting Lucy, something so bad it will be irreversible. But her head throbs and she can do nothing about it now.

"All right, you may go." Hester is out of the room as soon as the words are out of Hannah's mouth.

She looks at the posset, still steaming in the cup. No, it won't do. It won't do at all. She crosses the room to her workbench and picks up the bottle of poppy syrup. Eight drops this time. Maybe ten. Maybe more.

Chapter Sixteen

Fourth week of Michaelmas term

STEERING CLEAR OF Derek Goodman was more easily said than done, Claire soon discovered. They lived and worked in the same small universe: New Court, hall, the history faculty building. Only a week after her maddening conversation with Andrew Kent, Claire was standing in the dinner buffet line trying to choose between the meat and the vegetarian entrées (roast pork loin or cannelloni Provencal?), when Derek Goodman entered the hall and took a place right behind her.

"Hello, gorgeous," he said.

"Are you speaking to me?" Claire asked, incredulous.

"Of course I'm speaking to you. Do you see anyone else around here who's gorgeous? Except me, of course," he added with a wink. He glanced over at the elderly waiter who stood near the buffet table, presumably to help the fellows spoon food upon their plates. "Not that you aren't a fine-looking man, Mr. Digby."

"Thank you, sir."

Derek turned back to Claire. "What do you say to dinner tomorrow night? And none of this Dutch treat business you Americans go for, it's all on me."

"I hardly think—"

"But why wait until tomorrow to do what we can do today? Why don't we pile up a couple of plates with enough sustenance to keep us alive 'til tomorrow morning, and go back to my set?"

"Are you insane, or do you just have a very bad memory?"

"Now why would you want to hurt me by saying something like that? I thought we were getting on so well."

Claire put her plate down on the buffet table. She could hardly believe what she was hearing. How dare he act like nothing had happened? Derek Goodman was a piece of work, all right—an egomaniac and a complete narcissist. "Have you forgotten that you stole my idea for a paper and then lied about it to Dr. Kent?"

"*I* lied?" Derek's voice shot up a few decibels; every head nearby swiveled to stare at them. "I'm not the one who's the liar here. Just because you found me attractive and wanted to *shag*"—at this, more heads turned—"and I said no, you're going to tell lies about me to the other fellows?"

"What?" Claire gasped. "You *are* insane. Or completely unconscionable."

"Did you really think you could get away with it?"

"Get away with what?" Not only the fellows at High Table but also the students were listening with rapt interest.

"Slandering me. Just because you're American and you're young and pretty you think you can say whatever you want and get away with it. Well, you're not going to get away with stealing my paper—"

Claire could recall being this angry only once before: when her (now ex) husband Michael had announced that he was in love with another woman on the day of Claire's mother's funeral. She'd had the same response then as she did now. Before she was completely aware of what she was doing, she clenched her right fist and aimed. She knew it connected when she heard Derek Goodman's yelp of pain.

"Bloody hell!" Derek's hands flew to his face, where a bright red mark spread across his cheek. "She hit me! Did you see that, Mr. Digby?" The waiter looked too shocked to form words. Derek pointed an accusing finger at Claire. "She bloody hit me!"

Stunned by what she had done, Claire stood frozen in place. A few seconds passed before she realized how quiet the hall had become, and that everyone in it was staring at her. She felt a hand on her shoulder and glanced up to find Hoddy at her side. "You best get out of here," he said, steering her toward the door.

Once they were outside, Hoddy looked at her with dismay and concern. "Now why did you go and do that?" he said. "Derek was just egging you on."

"I know, but what he *said*—"

"I heard what he said. Unfortunately, so did everyone else. What's been going on with you two, anyway?"

The following morning broke foggy and gray, with a somberness that suited her mood. Claire looked out her window onto New Court, empty except for a few sparrows that flitted from the tree in the center to the lawn and back again. Much like her thoughts, which kept returning again and again to the events of last night.

After leaving hall, Hoddy had spirited her away to his favorite café in town for dinner. Claire had sworn to him she'd never lost her temper like that before—well, only once, anyway. She should have known better than to allow Derek Goodman to goad her like that. Twice now she'd fallen for his manipulative behavior, but this time had been worse than the first: there'd been lots of witnesses, most of whom were probably convinced that she was unstable, angry, and violent.

But she couldn't deny that she had acted in a highly unprofessional manner. She supposed there were worse things than having a public argument and punching a man in the face, but at present she couldn't think of any. It didn't really matter that Derek Goodman had sorely deserved being punched. Claire asked Hoddy if it might be possible, in stereotypical English fashion, for everyone to simply pretend that it never happened?

Unhappily, Hoddy's response was a firm no. She'd have to make a formal apology to the master and the vice-master if she wanted to be back in everyone's good graces. She drew the line at apologizing to Derek Goodman. But she would have to let the others know she'd made a mistake, that she regretted letting her anger get the better of her, and

that it would never happen again. She wanted to ask Hoddy exactly
how she should word it, but it was much too early in the day to ring
him and ask.

Indeed, some mind-clearing exercise was in order. She donned
her warmest workout clothes, tied on her Nikes, and headed for the
Backs. The gravel and dirt paths along the river were perfect for jogging
and cycling. The hours before breakfast tended to be the quietest, and
she was already becoming acquainted with a number of other early-
morning enthusiasts like herself. From her stay in Venice, she knew that
Andrew liked to run in the morning, and she harbored a faint hope
that she might see him. Certainly meeting him casually would be easier
than going to his office again.

She cut across the lawn behind New Court and took Trinity Bridge
over the river. She planned to run to St. John's, then turn south to go
all the way down to Queens' College and make the loop back to Trinity.
But on the path ahead, at the intersection of the Cam and a tiny stream
that fed into the river, a small crowd had gathered. A few uniformed
constables kept the joggers and cyclists away from a police car and a
black van that had driven off Queen's Road and onto the grass. The
back doors of the van were thrown open. On the ground, medical per-
sonnel were busy strapping a man onto a gurney. Claire peered past the
heads of the others watching but managed to get only a partial view.
Someone must have suffered a heart attack, or perhaps a jogger had
been hit by a bike. Whatever had happened, it must have been serious;
she could tell just from the hushed silence of the onlookers and the
solemnity of the scene. She craned her head and saw, as the paramedics
lifted the gurney and walked it to the van, that the body was encased
in a blue nylon body bag. Serious, indeed. A sort of sigh went through
the crowd as the paramedics pushed the gurney inside and closed the
doors.

As the van drove away, Claire spotted Andrew Kent on the far side
of the stream. He was wearing his running gear, and he was talking with
a pretty blond woman in a black raincoat, black jeans, and boots. She
was almost as tall as he, and as they spoke their heads leaned together
in a friendly, familiar way. Seeing him immediately brought back her

regrets about yesterday, and, oddly enough, stirred some vaguely proprietary feelings. Who was the blonde, and why was she talking to Andrew in such an intimate manner?

"All right, everybody," one of the constables announced, "it's time to move on. There's nothing more to see." With a few soft murmurs of protest, the crowd began breaking up. A woman in pajamas, a dressing gown, and knee-high Wellingtons pushed past Claire. Her face was pale and her eyes were red. At first Claire didn't recognize her.

"Dr. Bennet," Claire called as she quickly caught up with her. "What's happened?"

Elizabeth stopped and looked at Claire blankly, as if she didn't know her. Then a flicker of recognition glimmered in her dulled eyes.

"Derek Goodman is dead," she said.

Chapter Seventeen

12 November 1672
Whitehall

To the Rue de Varenne, Paris

After first begging your Forgiveness for my long silence, I hope you will appreciate that these past weeks have been filled with Obligations and Duties attached to my new office of Master of the Great Wardrobe, a position which cost me prettily but has yet to Reimburse me for my Pains.

For more than a month now I have been back at Whitehall, and a miserable Prospect it is. The long, sodden English winter has already begun and the Palace is none the better for it. As you have never had the dubious Pleasure of a visit to our Monarch's favorite Residence, I shall provide you with a Picture: it is a jumble of disparate buildings, courtyards, and galleries without Cohesion or Style, having been built at various times by various Kings, and generally allowed to fall into Ruin during the Interregnum. From where I now sit in my Lord Arlington's chambers, I have what is considered one of the finest Views, encompassing the Palace's main courtyard and the relatively new Banqueting House, but nothing here compares to the serene and well-planned Palaces of King Louis; even that rustic hunting Lodge at Versailles he is currently

*rebuilding is more luxurious than the most part of Whitehall.
However, this in no way lessens the Machinations, Bribery, and
tooth-and-nail Struggles of courtiers to procure rooms here. There
is never enough for the Scores who want to be near the King and
the opportunity for Advancement, as the only way to achieve
Wealth is to be here at the center of power. My own lodgings are
near the river on the Scotland yard, and their Condition is such
that I am already wistful for my former digs in Paris in your excellent and very gracious home. My Whitehall rooms are flooded
at least once a Year, and stink of the Thames and the cook-smells
from the nearby privy Kitchens.*

*The King's finances being what they are—even after the Stop of
the Exchequer earlier this year, when the Crown refused to pay the
interest on its outstanding loans and so Bankrupted some goldsmiths
and turned the City upside down—he has but few funds set aside
for Improvements, except to his own suite, of course, and those of his
family and his Mistresses. The best lodgings by far are those occupied
by Mademoiselle de Kéroualle, installed near the King in what used
to be the Queen's quarters. The young Mademoiselle seems determined to reproduce the Louvre in her extensive suite; in less than two
years, she has had it redecorated three times. Speaking of whom, I
have much to tell—but for the moment my Lord beckons, and I must
be at his Service.*

*It was nothing, really; he asked me to fetch a Clerk so he could
dictate a letter, a Task which he is now engaged upon. I have largely
closed my ears to him so that I may write to you undisturbed, but
a few words pierce my self-imposed Deafness: "beggaring bastards,"
and "indigested vomit of the sea," he says, which indicates to me
that he is writing to someone about the Dutch. He does not hate the
Dutch, but it behooves the King to be at War with them at present;
and whatever the King wants, Arlington supplies, regardless of his
convictions (although I am not entirely certain that my Lord has
any). Indeed, Arlington has a Dutch wife whom he loves immod-
erately for reasons no one can Fathom. She has no Beauty and her
marriage Portion was so meager that it was spent almost at once.*

They are always a step away from Ruin and live well beyond their
Means, for they love fine things and love to Entertain, but my Lord
Arlington was not born to Wealth and so finds it necessary to cling
to Office for his income. I believe it is this, rather than reasons of
Religion or Politics, that makes him believe France the best pattern
in the world; the more absolute Charles's power, the more my Lord
is free to Benefit as he can, without interference from Parliament.
He is lately much aggrieved by the King's appointment of his for-
mer protégé Thomas Clifford to the office of Lord Treasurer, a post
which he coveted for himself. He feels Betrayed and now considers
Clifford a most ungrateful Wretch. But he has only himself to blame,
for though the King values him highly, His Majesty is also well aware
of my Lord's spendthrift ways, and for this reason made Clifford
Treasurer instead of him.

Arlington has a great estate at Euston where the King's year-
long courtship of Mlle. de Keroualle was finally Consummated, with
much Direction given to the pretty little Breton by my Lord and Lady
Arlington. They staged a mock Wedding between the Mademoiselle
and the King, to make her the more easy about giving to the King
the only Riches she possessed without in return becoming Queen.
Of course now that she has given the King a child (one of thirteen
at last count, although there may be more who are unknown or
unrecognized; the King's fecundity is such that when he was once
addressed as "the father of the people," Lord Buckingham quipped,
"Yes, a good many of them"), the news of her Triumph has spread
throughout England and the Continent, and no woman could be
more self-pleased than she.

Until of late, when matters have taken a decided Turn against
her. It is mainly for the following (although what I have written
above also requires your utmost Discretion) that I ask you to burn
this Epistle once you have read it. The King has passed on to the
young Mademoiselle an Affliction which he likely got from some
backstairs doxy. Arlington and Madame Severin go to great lengths
to keep this matter Private, though you know as well as I this sort
of Secret cannot be Concealed for long. And when it is known, there

will be jockeying for Power such as has rarely been seen, as every
Minister tries to capture the King's attention by dangling in front
of him yet another Miss. "And howe'er so weak and slender be the
string/Bait it with a Whore, and it will hold a King."

They have gone so far as to bring in a doctor whom no one would
recognize or even suspect of practicing Physick. She is the daughter—
yes, daughter—of Charles Briscoe, whom you may recall performed
the Post-mortem on Princess Henriette-Anne; and who confirmed
that there was no Poison in her, but that her death came about by
Natural Means. Though this was no Comfort to the King, who, when
told of his sister's demise, collapsed with Grief. Dr. Briscoe was re-
nowned for (among other remedies and skills) his curative treat-
ment for the Clap. Many courtiers availed themselves of his Service,
even my Lord Arlington, I believe, in his incontinent years before his
marriage.

I must end this for now, but promise to write again soon. I will
forgo the excessive Compliments and Praise of a less familiar corre-
spondent in the knowledge that our intimacy is above the common
niceties of strangers. Please know that I remain

Your most Humble & Obedient, &c.

Arlington dismisses his clerk with a wave of his hand as Ralph Montagu dusts his letter with powder and waits for the ink to dry. The window provides a desolate view. Miserable English rain pours down on the palace courtyard, on the Banqueting House, on the offices of the king's ministers and secretaries, stewards and masters, comptrollers and clerks; miserable English rain pours down on the workshops of barbers and carpenters and laundresses and cooks. God's balls, Whitehall is a dismal place. Once he earns enough in bribes from his newly purchased office, he will build a house for himself in the French style such as no one in London has ever seen.

Montagu stifles a yawn. On days like today his grand future feels much too far away. He folds his letter in two and suddenly remembers that he is supposed to be meeting someone. He has little inclination to go out in the rain. No matter, she will wait. They always do. This fact used to surprise him, but no longer.

Instead of stirring himself from his chair or going out into the inclement weather, he thinks of Mrs. Devlin. He noticed the resemblance between Hannah and her father. It wasn't their appearance so much as the fact that they both seemed to possess lofty principles—in itself, a rare quality these days—tempered by kindness, although neither was inclined to suffer fools. He smiles to himself as he recalls the way she spoke to Sir Granville. The man might never have the courage to address a woman again—most surely a victory for womankind.

Montagu is drawn to Hannah, although she is not really his type. He regards her as a little too thin, not coquettish enough; and he generally prefers fair-haired, not dark-haired, women. Nevertheless, Mrs. Devlin has captivated him. He cannot help but like the quick understanding in her warm brown eyes. He likes even more the promise of her lush mouth; indeed, her lips are almost too full, as if in defiance of her fine-featured but angular face. A tiny fox's face, wise and sharp, looking out from under all that raven hair. And she has something few women have: learning combined with passion. He wonders what it would be like to kiss her. Would she be equally passionate then?

A woman like Mrs. Devlin would set him down whenever she thought he deserved it, however, which makes him uneasy. Montagu knows that he deserves setting down all too often. Still, he is attracted to her. There is something in her eyes, something more than just her quick wit. He has to think for a moment before he hits on the answer: her eyes had seen too much suffering. He has never considered before how something like that could leave a person marked, but he is sure of it now. He remembers Dr. Briscoe from Paris; yes, the same eyes. Passionate, strong, perceptive. The kind of eyes it's easy to get lost in. Montagu reminds himself that Hannah is not his type, and then it occurs to him that he may be getting tired of his type.

His meandering thoughts are interrupted when a solitary figure enters the courtyard. The man angrily strides across the rain-soaked square without hesitation, as if he were impervious to the storm, the head of steam on him noticeable even at this distance.

"Trouble this way comes," Montagu says.

"Clifford?" Arlington asks. At Montagu's nod, he gestures at the back of the room. "Go on," he says, "get behind the curtains."

"What have you done with him?" Clifford shrieks.

"Done with whom?" Arlington says.

"Osborne, of course."

Sir Thomas Clifford has a rather pretty face, Montagu decides, even when it is red with rage. It's not the first time he's seen the Lord Treasurer in a temper; he habitually resorts to shows of anger in order to achieve his ends. Although no one else on the king's privy council believes that Clifford deserves the king's favor, he has it, and as long as he does his tirades must be endured. Although a tirade delivered soaking wet, while wearing a wig that looks like a drowned muskrat, makes his performance somewhat comical.

Arlington appears genuinely bewildered. "I've done something with Osborne?"

"Don't act the fool with me, I know you too well. Osborne was supposed to be here three days ago with the money from France, and I've not had one word from him. What was his price, Arlington? How much did you pay him to relieve him of the king's gold?"

"Good Lord, man, calm down." Arlington appears genuinely concerned. "I've no idea what you're talking about."

"I've got Castlemaine and Severin and that brat Monmouth all banging on my door wondering where their money is. Why don't I send them over here so that you can explain?"

"Are you telling me that you don't know where Osborne is—or the money? He keeps a room on Drury Lane. Have you checked there?"

"He hasn't been seen there since he left for France three weeks ago."

"I'll have it looked into, then."

Sir Thomas eyes him suspiciously. "If you're lying, I swear to God I'll take you down to the Devil with me. And you know very well I can." He looks to the back of the room, where Montagu is concealed. "And that goes for you too, Montagu," he calls. "I know you're there. I used to stand behind those curtains myself. Take care that you see what being Arlington's favorite will get you—a stab in the back." Clifford storms out, slamming the door behind him.

Montagu comes out from hiding. "You honestly don't know where Osborne is?"

"For God's sake, man, I am to be guilty of every black deed some idiot dreams up? I don't have a clue where he is." Arlington sighs. "Trouble this way comes, indeed."

Chapter Eighteen

18 November 1672

HANNAH LOOKS ON with the other courtiers and their footmen as the king sits down next to Louise de Keroualle's bedside and presents her with a golden box. When his mistress opens it, her eyes light up and she favors him with a joyful yet tender smile.

"Your Majesty, they are the most beautiful jewels I've ever seen."

She displays its contents to the courtiers, Louise's and Charles's closest intimates: Lord Arlington, Lady Arlington, Madame Severin, and the king's brother James, Duke of York. Nestled within the box's velvet innards are two extraordinary necklaces, one of diamonds and one of pearls. The courtiers make the appropriate murmurs of appreciation and delight, much like a well-mannered audience attending a private play.

"A love token for my little Fubsy," the King says, calling Louise by the pet name he has given her—Fubsy meaning plump, for her well-rounded figure—and chucking her under the chin.

"We're humbled by this impressive act of random generosity," Madame Severin says, offering the words that should have rightly been spoken by her lady, who is already busily engaged putting the strand of diamonds on her neck. The others smile and nod, even though they all know that the king is attempting to make amends to Louise for the sad effects of the last gift he inadvertently gave her. An objective outsider might think that it was the least he could do, but among those most concerned there is immense relief. The king's actions are seldom taken for granted, as no one, even Arlington, is ever entirely sure of the course he will take.

Hannah has observed His Majesty for more than a week now, and she is beginning to understand what her father meant when he once remarked that the king was full of idle potential and contradiction. In appearance, Charles Stuart is supremely regal: well over two yards high, he towers over both women and men, and is very fit and vigorous in body, even now, at forty-two. He is sometimes referred to as "Charles the Black" because of the dark intensity of his eyes and hair, inherited traits from his French ancestors and his de Medici grandmother. His visage is saturnine and stern in repose, with a curling, sensual mouth and deep lines from nose to chin. But the king's manner is never imposing or rude; indeed, his severe expression is greatly softened when he speaks. He is unfailingly polite and chivalrous, treating both the low- and high-born with equal consideration and respect. His court is marked by a relaxed openness that would be unthinkable in France. Anyone, even a servant, is allowed to approach His Majesty, and everyone in London knows that if they want to speak to the king they have only to go to St. James's Park of a morning, where they will find him taking the air. His life at Whitehall is at best semiprivate.

The king prides himself on being easily accessible to his people, yet his ministers can seldom pin him down. He takes an unusual interest in natural philosophy, and can spend hours experimenting in his laboratory or observing the movements of the stars, yet he insists on continuing to touch for the King's Evil—the laying on of the royal hands to cure scrofula, a disease of the lymph nodes in the neck, a tradition that began with King Edward the Confessor in the eleventh century—thereby encouraging his subjects to believe in superstitions. He discourses on many topics but appears to have no profound understanding of any one in particular. A few times now Hannah has seen a glimmer in his eyes that she took for a sharp intelligence, only to be disappointed by his subsequent remark. Twice when this happened she caught Ralph Montagu's eye and remembered his words: "*You may see for yourself the depth of the king's understanding.*" Hannah wishes that she had not. She has little enough to believe in.

Of course he is the king and he may do as he pleases, but Hannah is sometimes shocked at his capriciousness. He is followed everywhere by a pack of small, liver-spotted spaniels that continually yap and run in circles at his feet; he so indulges them, they are allowed to relieve themselves indoors. A harried sergeant of the hawk trails the dogs with sponge, mop, and bucket. And the king is too often in the company of the young rakes of the court, some of whom are no better behaved than the dogs, for he will forgive almost any indecency if it is accompanied by beauty or wit. He attempts at all times to keep himself amused by empty and vulgar conversations and mirth. He abhors seriousness, and has a habit of taking out his pocket watch and checking the time whenever he is bored or vexed by someone's company. The more experienced courtiers will scatter the moment they see him reach for it, not wanting to be in any way associated with the king's displeasure. He does not seem to mind, or even to be aware, that people think him frivolous and foolish. Hannah had not thought it possible, but she has actually felt something approaching pity for Lord Arlington, who constantly waits on the king, attempting to get him to do this or that, and whose strain is always apparent, as the king seldom puts his mind to business.

But ever since His Majesty returned from Hampton a week ago and came at once to see Louise, sitting by her bedside for more than an hour, Lord Arlington's spirits, along with those of the mademoiselle's household, have brightened considerably. And as the king has returned to his daily routine of visiting the mademoiselle for an hour or two after his morning exercise—a hotly competitive game of tennis, a bracing swim in the river (while his servants wait, shivering, on the bank), or a walk in St. James's Park, so brisk that the courtiers pant to keep up—Louise has brightened, too.

Hannah doesn't much like the transformation. Her own sensitivities have been worn slightly raw by the mademoiselle's treatment. She has been in attendance on Mademoiselle de Keroualle every day for nearly a fortnight now, remaining by her bedside for hours, spooning syrup (under the watchful eye of Madame Severin) into her mouth, providing her with physick and guiding her slow return to health. She has washed the mademoiselle's feverish body and arranged for soaking tubs to be brought to her room, has applied plasters to her loins and helped her to the close-stool. Even though she has little in common with the mademoiselle besides being French-born, Hannah felt sympathy for her and believed that she might even feel a sort of kinship—a belief that vanished as soon as Louise opened her mouth and began speaking. The mademoiselle's conversation lacks warmth, wit, discernment, or interest, as Louise is capable of discoursing on one subject only, and that is herself.

"Why isn't the Countess of Castlemaine or that impudent whore Nell Gwyn suffering instead of me?" she complains in her thickly accented English. "Why not Queen Catherine herself?" She utters this blasphemy without shame. "She already has one foot in the grave." Louise believes that when Queen Catherine dies, the king will marry her and make her queen: a belief no doubt encouraged by Arlington but shared by no one.

The mademoiselle spends the morning choosing the perfect dressing gown and arranging herself in a studied dishabille, so that she can appear to be caught charmingly off-guard, still in bed with her lustrous hair being brushed by two maidservants, when the king and the courtiers arrive. Otherwise she talks only of the gifts the king has given her, and the ones she hopes he will give her. She also speaks of her desire to return to France and sit on a tabouret in the presence of the French queen, the highest honor to which a French noblewoman can aspire. It seems that Mademoiselle de Keroualle is intent on having her revenge on everyone in Paris who once snubbed her. Apparently their numbers are legion. Although Louise is twenty-two and the mother of three-month-old Charles Fitzroy, old enough to act like a woman, she behaves like a child. She resents Hannah's presence and refuses to take her medicines (unless the king is watching), makes a fuss over her baths and plasters, dissolves in tears and tantrums at least once an hour, and tries the patience of everyone except Madame Severin.

Hannah knows that at least some of Louise's vexatious behavior is due to her fear and unhappiness at being so unfairly afflicted (for which she has some sympathy), but it is difficult to face day after day. Hannah eagerly looks forward to the time when she will not be tending to the king's mistress, but recently she has come to suspect that Louise, in spite of her dislike of medicinal baths, will draw out this drama for as long as possible. Her indisposition has captured the king's interest. Hannah knows that the mademoiselle will do anything, even pretend to remain ill when she is not, in order to keep it.

"Mrs. Devlin, it is already half past ten," Madame Severin reminds her. "Is it not time for my lady's morning medicine?"

"Yes, of course." Hannah requests to be excused from the king's presence and goes to the sitting room adjacent to the bedchamber. On a trestle table she has set out her syrups and powders. Though Louise makes a pretty show of taking her medicine in front of the king, she refuses to have the vials and jars on the table next to her bed, "like a sickly old lady."

Hannah uncorks an empty vial. As her father taught her, she fills it half-full with a dark, thick medicine from one bottle, sprinkles in a few grains of a foul-smelling powder, then mixes them together with a lighter, honey-colored syrup. Not mixing the solution until the last moment, just before its administration, contributes to its more potent constitution and is one of the secrets of his remedy. Although everything Hannah does for Louise bespeaks her profession, at court she is never referred to as a doctor or a physician. Every courtier Hannah meets regards her and refers to her as the mademoiselle's childhood friend who just by coincidence happens to have some knowledge of healing.

What matters most at court, she has learnt, is what is unsaid, what everyone knows but is never acknowledged. The courtiers refer to Louise's "ague" without irony even though Hannah is certain that each of them (with the possible exception of Sir Granville Haines) is fully aware of the malady from which she suffers. But not in word, gesture, or expression would any one of them ever reveal what they know to be true. They are actors of a most sophisticated type, more convincing than any she has ever seen on a stage, perhaps because the consequences of making a mistake are so great. To acknowledge openly an unspoken truth is to risk banishment from court; to be unaware of the tacit realities, the secrets and lies that are the court's most valuable currency, is to be labeled a fool and never truly allowed to enter.

"How is my favorite doctor?"

"Mr. Montagu!"

Ralph Montagu offers her a proper bow and not-so-proper grin, clearly as pleased to see her as she is to see him. Indeed, Hannah cannot imagine being at court without him, as she would be very lonely without his company. Montagu's friendship and good humor have made her time here much more enjoyable than she thought it would be.

"Have you heard the latest?" he asks confidentially, standing shoulder to shoulder with her at the table. "Thomas Killigrew, director of the Theatre Royal and the king's appointed fool, told His Majesty that his matters were coming into a very ill state, but yet there was a way to help all. And then he did say, 'There is a good honest able man that I could name, that if Your Majesty would employ and command to see all things well executed, all things would soon be mended; and this is one Charles Stuart—who now spends his time in employing his lips and prick about the court, and hath no other employment. But if you would give him this employment, he were the fittest man in the world to perform it.'"

Hannah gasps. "He said that directly to the king?"

Montagu nods. "The king's leniency is such that he laughed instead of sending Killigrew to the Tower. Unfortunately the king profits none by Killigrew's criticism but turns his attention only to his pleasures."

"Mr. Montagu," Hannah warns, "His Majesty is in the other room."

"Not to worry, my dear." Montagu peers through the doorway. "He's well out of hearing range. But I have to say that everyone understands Killigrew's frustration, myself included. I spent the earlier part of this morning with the king at the park, where he and the Duke of York made sport of watching the geese mate in the pond, taking bets on which two would pair up. It is sadly true—the king is a fool and the duke a governable fool."

"Mr. Montagu! It is dangerous for you to speak so."

"Don't worry, I know how to look out for myself in this den of iniquity. And in fact I am already bored by the subject. Tell me, Mrs. Devlin, if I were a gander and you were a goose, would you take a turn around the pond with me?"

Hannah smiles in spite of herself. "I believe you take great pleasure in trying to shock me, Mr. Montagu, and so I refuse to be astonished by your very wicked remarks. I will also say that I suspect that underneath your scandalous exterior there's a better man waiting to get out."

"What tells you this?"

"My woman's intuition, I suppose."

"That can scarcely be argued with."

"I daresay not."

"You haven't answered my question, however."

"Which question?"

"About the goose and the gander."

Hannah smiles slyly and turns away from him. "That is because it's time to give medicine to a certain young lady."

Montagu follows Hannah into the bedchamber, where the Duke of York is holding forth about the play he saw the day before. James is a fair-haired, less swarthy version of his older brother, by conventional standards more handsome than Charles, but in Hannah's view, his good looks are negated by his haughty manner. The younger Stuart is proud, vain, and from all accounts less clever than the king. This has not dimmed his attractiveness to women, however; being successor to the throne is a powerful aphrodisiac. He has cut a swath through the court nearly as wide and deep as the king's.

Popular opinion is against James, Duke of York being next in line for the crown, for he is an avowed Catholic, but Charles will have no one but his brother as his successor. As long as the king has no legitimate offspring, no one can gainsay him. As time goes on, an heir is looking less and less likely, and James more and more possible. It occurs to Hannah that the king avoids a great deal of trouble and court intrigue by not having a legitimate heir and by having a successor that few people want to see on the throne. Perhaps he is not quite as foolish as he appears.

Hannah crosses the room, bottle at the ready, to give the medicine to Louise. The mademoiselle opens her mouth to the spoon willingly, like a baby bird being fed.

The king clears his throat. "Mrs. Devlin, will my little Fubsy be well enough to dance a coranto before long?"

"I believe she is much improved, Your Majesty."

"How many days?"

"It may be more appropriate to measure her recovery in weeks instead of days, Majesty."

"Weeks? I do not want to wait weeks."

Hannah has little doubt that he is talking about something other than dancing. The mademoiselle would be better off if the king no longer favored her with his attentions, but saying so will endear her to neither of them. Or to Lord Arlington, she realizes, as she sees him looking at her fearfully. "I am sure Your Majesty is well aware of the severity of the fever the mademoiselle has suffered. If she continues to improve as rapidly as she has, I should think that she may be dancing again in two weeks."

"Two weeks," he repeats. From his mouth it sounds like a death sentence. "I think not. I think . . ." His eyes rove from Hannah to Louise and back again as the courtiers hold their breath. "I think she will be well enough in ten days."

She cannot believe it, but the king is trying to bargain with her, as if the mademoiselle's health were only a matter of opinion and personal interest. "Two weeks, Your Majesty," she says firmly.

"Perhaps your physick is not as effective as it should be, Mrs. Devlin. Might it not be made stronger, so that it can work more quickly?" The king gives her one more chance to say what he wants to hear. Arlington appears as though he's about to have an apoplectic fit.

She disappoints them both. "Even the best physick must be given time to work, Your Majesty. I believe it will require two more weeks." She looks him in the eye, and for a split second she feels certain that he fully understands exactly what she means: the mademoiselle is to be left alone for this length of time. She hopes he has been able to discern her secondary message, that he will remain continent before climbing back into the mademoiselle's bed and so not expose her to illness again. But

Charles Stuart's eyes are blank and inscrutable, and she can't be at all sure that he comprehends her meaning.

The king turns away from her. His interest is seldom held for long. It appears that he is going to speak again, but instead he is distracted when the bedchamber door opens and one of the king's guards is let into the room. He swiftly walks up to Arlington and the king and bows.

"Your Majesty, my lords, forgive me for my interruption. There has been an accident on Whitehall Street, and we have not been able to find a doctor."

"Have you called on Dr. Pearce or Dr. Fraser?" Arlington asks.

"Both, my lord, but they are not in their rooms, and no one seems to know where to find them. My captain thought you might know their whereabouts. There is no time to waste—a man has been badly injured."

"What about Dr. Goddard?" Arlington asks.

The young guard looks embarrassed. He whispers into Arlington's ear.

"I see," Arlington says, nodding. "He's in his cups," the minister informs the king. "What about the apothecary?" he asks the guard.

"His shop is closed."

"Wait." The king raises his hand, and everyone falls silent. He looks at Hannah. Arlington seems to know at once what the king is considering.

"I don't think that is a good idea, Your Majesty."

"Why should we search any further? We have a fine physician right here, one who is very decided in her opinions and seems to be quite sure of herself. What say you, Mrs. Devlin? If you can treat this man, I will grant you the two weeks you request for your physick to work. If not, I will insist that the mademoiselle be cured in ten days."

"Majesty, we have tried to be discreet about Mrs. Devlin's presence at court," Arlington says.

"You mean it's a secret?"

"Yes."

"Then everyone is sure to know." He turns to the guard. "Where is this man?"

"We took him to the tack room in the stables, sir. It was the closest shelter we could find."

Chapter Nineteen

THE KING BRISKLY leads the way through the courtyard to the palace gate, the phalanx of courtiers behind him scrambling to keep up with his long stride, dogs barking at their heels. Accustomed to the king's pace, Arlington slows down for a moment to speak to Hannah. "If you disappoint the king in any way, I will be made most unhappy," he warns. As he returns to his place at the king's side, Montagu falls into step next to her.

"Did my Lord Arlington mean that I should fail?" she asks.

"No, he means that the king is testing you," Montagu says, pitching his voice low so that she alone can hear. "I have seen His Majesty do this before. Do not hesitate to do whatever you must do. If you vacillate or are uncertain, he will see it as weakness, and it will give him good reason to banish you from court."

"I will not be altogether unhappy about that."

"But Arlington will be. Beware of him. He may seem reasonable, even harmless at times, but I assure you he never is. He will make good on his threat."

They cross Whitehall Street and enter the king's stable-yard. From inside the stables they hear a commotion of shouting and protest, then one man's voice rises above the others. "Lay off me, you damn black-guards!"

Hannah and Montagu follow the king and the others through an open door, finding a tack room with bridles and reins hanging on the walls and, in a corner, a stack of saddles in need of repair. On a table in the center of the room, under the shabby glow of a rusted iron chandelier, four of the king's guards attempt to restrain a fifth man, who lies on his back on the table. "For God's sake, hold him down!" the captain shouts to the three others. The man on the table—not a guard but a rougher sort, dressed only in a torn wool tabard—is strong enough to require the combined effort of all four.

"I'll crawl out of here on my hands, you bloody bastards, but I won't have some drunken sawbones hacking away at my leg!" he shouts.

"You'll stay here until we find a proper doctor to take a look at you," the captain replies. He is a man of twenty-five or so, of apparent good sense. His voice is heated as he speaks to the injured man, but he appears to have a difficult situation somewhat under his control. "We've already sent for—"

Lord Arlington stamps his walking stick on the stone floor and clears his throat. "His Majesty the king," he announces.

At his words the guards look up and spring instantly to attention. The injured man stops thrashing. "The king?" he says with amazement, as though he is dreaming.

Charles walks over to the captain and motions for Hannah to follow. The captain bows low. "Your Majesty, we are honored by your presence—"

The king waves him silent. "What has happened here?"

"This coachman fell from his post at the back of a carriage, and was hit by another that was coming along directly behind. It wasn't the other's fault, they couldn't have stopped in time. Not to mention that it's not yet noon and this man here is as drunk as a lord." He peers past the king. "Begging your pardon, Lord Arlington."

Arlington purses his mouth but doesn't respond. The guards move aside as the king steps up to the table and leans over the coachman. "What is your name, man?"

"Nat Henley, Your Majesty." His spasmodic shaking is an involuntary response to intolerable pain. "I assure you, Majesty," Henley says, sweating and trembling, "this here hurt is nothing much. I'm a hardy fellow, I'll be healed by tomorrow with no more than a whore's blessing, 'scusing your pardon. No need for a doctor, surely—"

"Mr. Henley, I've brought a physician to examine you."

He gulps, and his shaking grows worse. "You are most kind, Majesty."

Hannah steps forward, and Nat Henley's flushed, sweating face comes into view. His skin is reddened and rough; his nose appears as if it's been in more than one scuffle in the past. His thinning hair barely covers his large head, but in spite of his advanced age Henley looks as strong as a stevedore. His shoes and pants have already been removed, revealing muscular thighs and the bloody mess that was once the lower half of his left leg. Henley's glance skips over Hannah, then roams the room.

"Where is the doctor?"

"She's standing right next to me," the king says. "Can you not see her?"

"But that's a woman!"

"Indeed she is, Mr. Henley."

"But—but that's not possible!" Nat Henley's eyes dart around the tack room as if looking for an escape, or perhaps for someone to reassure him that what he'd heard was a jest or a lie. "It's a sin against nature, it is!" he protests. "I'll not be worked on by a woman, by God!" He pushes himself up from the table, but the guards are on him fast, one to each limb, and they wrestle with him as they did before the king's entrance. Henley's face suddenly turns pale, and he stops struggling against his captors. He breathes rapidly a few times, then his eyes roll up to heaven and he falls back onto the table in a dead faint.

"Thank God, he's finally out," one of the guards says as they release him and relax, remaining in place in case Henley should wake again.

The king turns to Hannah. "I had not imagined that a woman physician could be so effective." He raises his brow slightly. "Well done."

The guards find benches for the king and his entourage to sit upon. While they are being seated—the tack room being transformed into an operating theater of sorts—Hannah walks around the table to better inspect Nat Henley's leg.

It is brutally injured, that much is obvious even before she removes the blood-soaked rag that's been wrapped around the wounded limb. With it she wipes away some blood from the calf so she can more clearly assess the damage. Both bones of the lower leg are broken beyond repair. Their splintered ends are visible, having burst through the torn skin about four inches below the knee. The anterior and lateral calf muscles are cut and bleeding, but the posterior muscles and tendons are still intact and connect the knee to the ankle. The foot is twisted around so far that it is nearly facing backward. It is astonishing that Mr. Henley was able to withstand the pain as long as he did before passing out.

She is in no doubt about what must be done: the leg will have to be amputated. It is not possible for Henley to survive this injury. The bones cannot be set, and so there is no way for it to heal on its own. His chance of surviving the operation is perhaps fifty percent, perhaps not even that, but without it he will certainly die.

"Well, Mrs. Devlin?" the king says. "What do you make of it?"

She turns to face him and her audience, three rows of pale faces in the shadows: the king and Arlington, Montagu and the other courtiers, their footmen in the back. The king appears unusually interested: he is known to have an interest in medicine, particularly in the surgical arts. This is not uncommon among kings, who are always looking for new ways to solve the problems of injury and disease among their fighting forces, but Charles is more involved than most monarchs, visiting hospitals, the Barber-Surgeon's Hall, and the College of Physicians to witness surgeries and dissections, and allowing the Banqueting House to be used as a site for anatomical trials upon cows and sheep, trials in which he sometimes takes part. Perhaps the king looks upon Mr. Henley's misfortune as another opportunity for experiment. Arlington looks seriously annoyed. Most of the courtiers seem to be anticipating some sort of entertainment. What kind of place makes a spectacle out of a man's suffering? It reminds her again that she does not really belong here.

Just as she is about to speak, she is aware of a disturbance in her vision, a bright, wavy line that crosses her sight like a flash of lightning. Her head has ached all morning, and now, with the tension of the moment and apprehension of the task ahead, it has grown worse. In her pocket she has a vial of poppy syrup which has become her constant companion, but she will not be able to use it now, not here. She steals a glance at Mr. Henley, and an idea occurs to her. Usually strong drink is all that's given to a patient under these circumstances, but according to the captain, Mr. Henley is already drunk, and it might be worth a try. With effort, she steadies herself and speaks.

"Mr. Henley's leg needs to be amputated." A murmur goes through the small crowd, but the king says nothing. "This is the best time to operate, while the patient is still suffering from the shock of the injury. It will cause him the least amount of additional pain." She pauses, focusing her thoughts. "Obviously, I do not have any surgical instruments with me. Are there any here at court?"

"You intend to perform the surgery?" Arlington asks, alarmed.

"Mr. Henley will not survive long without it."

"Have you ever amputated a leg before?"

"No, my lord. But many times I assisted my father, and as you know, he was a skilled surgeon."

"Excellent," the king says decisively. "Let's see what she can do, Arlington. I daresay you've never seen a woman cut off a man's leg before."

"I've never seen a monkey cut out a kidney stone before, but that does not mean I should like to," Arlington answers sourly, but he calls his footman over and instructs him to go at once to the king's laboratory and bring back a set of surgical tools.

Henley stirs and moans, as if to remind them that he is still among the living. Hannah imagines that her patient is only slightly less frightened than she is. She has often done the small surgeries—let blood, lance boils, sew up wounds—that most physicians know how to perform. She has amputated frostbitten toes and gangrenous fingers, and she once removed the ear of a man who was troubled with a tumor.

And once, with her father, she helped cut off a man's badly broken arm. She knows what needs to be done, but she has never before amputated a leg, and certainly not the leg of a man this size. Cutting through muscle and bone, especially bone, is difficult; it requires strength. She is not certain that she can do it.

"Captain, I'll also need a box of straw to put below the table to catch the blood, some linen to make pledgets and bandages, and a few threaded needles for the ligatures—"

"Your Majesty!" A familiar and unwelcome voice calls from the doorway. Sir Granville Haines enters, followed by another man. Sir Granville instantly spots the king and hurries across the room to make his humble obeisance. "A thousand apologies for not being available the moment you summoned me."

"I summoned you?"

"I was told you were in need of a court physician, and I—" He catches sight of Hannah. "What is she doing here?"

"I asked her to attend to the coachman," the king answers.

Sir Granville squints at Henley, not believing what he sees. "But that man needs his leg cut off!"

"Yes, and Mrs. Devlin is going to do it."

"Majesty, I must protest! With all due respect, sir, all the physicians of your court—nay, London—will be up in arms over such an outrage. Surely you will not endorse this affront to our dignity."

"From what I hear, Sir Granville, you affront your own dignity every day."

The courtiers laugh. Sir Granville is not amused. "The College of Physicians will be in an uproar, make no mistake," he warns.

Lord Arlington cocks his head to speak into the king's ear. Charles listens for a while, then sighs. "Enough, enough," he says to Arlington, and then, as if to himself, "as usual, someone has managed to take the fun out of my fun. What do you suggest we do, Sir Granville? There seem to be no other doctors available, and Mrs. Devlin insists that she has the requisite skill. Not to mention that it is the king's desire to see a woman perform such a feat. Would you deny me my amusements, Sir Granville?"

"Oh no, Majesty, never," Sir Granville grovels. "I am only thinking of the future of medicine and how to protect our esteemed calling from those who are unworthy." He looks pointedly at Hannah. "Edward, if you please," he says after a moment. Sir Granville's companion comes forward and bows before the king. "Your Majesty, may I present my nephew, the Honorable Dr. Edward Strathern. He is an excellent surgeon recently returned from his medical studies in Leyden. I propose that he perform this operation."

Edward Strathern bears little resemblance to his uncle, being more soberly attired and modestly bewigged. No ceruse or patches, either, but he has a self-satisfied air that Hannah dislikes at once. She catches a vain glint of gold braid on his cuffs and lace on his cravat. She knows Strathern's type instantly: a university-trained physician with his head full of a thousand useless theories and no experience in the real world. He's no older than twenty-eight, she guesses, thirty at most. Now he's come to court to claw his way up, under the auspices of his well-connected uncle. She grants that he'll need all the help he can get: even if he's twice as clever as Sir Granville, he'll still be an idiot.

The king clears his throat. She supposes he will ask Strathern to list his qualifications. Surely he will require more than Sir Granville's endorsement. "Dr. Strathern," the king says, "how did you find the ale in Leyden?"

"Not nearly as good as English ale, Majesty."

What a ridiculous charade. The man has probably never even held a knife. Surely the king won't allow him to operate, but she reminds herself that he is called Dr. Strathern and, no matter how accomplished she becomes, she will always be Mrs. Devlin. The footman arrives, out of breath and carrying an elegant carved wood box.

"Your Majesty," Hannah interrupts, but she receives a warning look from Arlington.

"Of course, of course, we must not delay," the king says. "I have decided that the two physicians will work together."

Hannah can hardly conceal her shock and dismay. What if Strathern makes a mess of it? She is even more appalled when she sees the doctor looking at her in precisely the same manner. She turns away, takes the instrument case from the footman, and opens it. Inside is a double-bladed catlin knife, a scalpel, a lancet, and a fine-toothed saw. The instruments are a bit small for this particular task, but they appear new and well made. She takes out the catlin knife and places the box on the floor near her feet, where she will have easy access to it.

"Captain, would you have your men position Mr. Henley so that the injured part of his leg is off the table?" she asks. "Dr. Strathern, if you would take hold of his ankle, please?"

Though Strathern is standing beside her, he does nothing. Hannah feels the king's, and everyone else's, eyes upon them. The physician turns his back to their audience and speaks softly. "His Majesty said that we were to work together."

"Yes, and you can help by holding the patient's ankle," she whispers in return.

"I think I should perform the surgery."

"You are ambitious, aren't you? I happen to be more qualified for this task than you."

"And how do you know that?"

"Dr. Strathern, you do not look like a surgeon."

"Pardon me for saying so, but neither do you. And yet here we are."

"I have performed many surgeries in the past, including the amputation of an arm." She is exaggerating slightly, but with good reason.

"You have?"

"Yes."

"Oh." Strathern seems surprised. "The truth is I am not precisely a physician or a surgeon."

"Then what are you?"

"An anatomist."

"You dissect dead bodies?"

"Yes."

"Mother of Christ," Hannah lowers her voice even further. "You'll kill him."

"And how do you deduce that? A man's body is designed the same whether he is living or dead."

"There is a great deal of difference between operating on a dead body that feels nothing and a living man who will most likely be screaming and thrashing about in pain."

Is she imagining it, or does he blanch just a little? It gives her a strange sort of pleasure. "You must make the incisions very quickly," she continues, "so as to cause as little suffering as possible. Can you do that?"

He hesitates. "In truth, I'm not accustomed to working in haste."

"Then I will resect the skin and muscle, and perhaps you could saw the bone." She doesn't look at him while she waits for an answer. She doesn't want him to know that by agreeing he'll be doing her a favor.

"All right then." Strathern looks down at his coat. "We'll need aprons." One of the guards goes off into a corner of the tack room and returns with two blacksmith's aprons. Hannah gives the captain her vial of poppy syrup.

"When Mr. Henley wakes," she says, "which he probably will, instruct your men to hold him as still as they possibly can. I know this will be difficult, but you will be doing him a service if you remain strong."

"Yes, ma'am."

"When Mr. Henley opens his mouth, pour this in. Half will be fine to start, but he is a big man and may require more. It should make him calmer and easier."

Hannah double-checks the position of Henley's body. His injured leg juts off the table. Dr. Strathern holds his ankle, while his other limbs and his shoulders are firmly secured by the guards. "Is everyone ready?" she asks, and she receives nods all around. "Your Majesty, we will begin." She takes a final measure of Henley's calf and lightly places her knife for the first incision.

"You're too low on the leg," Strathern whispers. "The bone is shattered closer to the knee."

"We're not going to resect the bone here," Hannah says, annoyed. "Just the integument. We'll need as much healthy tissue as we can salvage to form a stump." She turns her attention to the task before her. "Don't interrupt me again."

She quickly makes an incision halfway around the leg, about a quarter-inch deep; and then another in the opposite direction, so that the two incisions nearly meet—or would if the leg were not broken. Henley groans loudly and instinctively tries to pull his leg away, surprising Strathern most of all, who looks on uneasily as the leg moves in his hands.

"Captain, the medicine, please," Hannah says.

The captain lifts Henley's head and tips the vial into his mouth. "How much?"

"All of it."

Henley gags on the syrup and spits some of it out. He moans and tries to move, then finds that he can't. His eyes flick open as his consciousness returns.

"My leg!" he screams. "My sodding leg. You bloody bastards. My God, it hurts!" The guards struggle to keep him still as Henley's sobs rack his body.

"Hold his leg down harder, there just above the knee," she commands the guard closest to her. He complies, and she raises the knife again. She feels a ring of perspiration break out on her forehead and the annoying tickle of a single bead of sweat as it rolls down her face. Only a profound resolve keeps her hands from shaking. She gently separates and slices through the muscles one at a time, working through the peroneus, the soleus, the tibialis. This is the most agonizing part of the surgery, and under her knife Henley trembles violently. She has never caused anyone so much pain before; it is nothing less than horrible, yet she knows it must be done. As she cuts the tendons, Henley is still sobbing and moaning, but she can feel his anguish subside a little. With any luck he will be unconscious again before they saw off the jagged ends of the broken bones. She severs the last bits of muscle, tendon, and skin. Arterial blood spurts forth, splattering her and Strathern. Their audience gasps. The sound seems to come from very far away.

She turns to the other physician, who now holds Henley's foot and ankle in his hand. Their eyes meet, and she sees that his are a deep blue-gray, intense, and intelligent, a fact which registers in her mind with a simultaneous sense of surprise. Strathern's face and forehead are streaked with blood; at some point he must have wiped one of his hands across his brow. For a moment they do nothing more than look at each other, at their blood-splattered selves. In God's name, what have they done? Have they just killed a man or let him live? It is impossible to know. Then Strathern lowers his gaze to the severed limb in his hands. It's already turning blue.

"Put it in the box," Hannah says. Without question and without emotion, Strathern places Henley's foot into the box of bloodied straw. He opens the instrument case and removes the saw, then straightens and regards the amputated leg in front of him with a practiced composure.

The rest of the operation goes smoothly. Nat Henley lapses into blessed unconsciousness. Hannah ties off the bleeding blood vessels. Using thin strips of fabric, she retracts the severed muscles up toward the knee, and Strathern saws off the jagged ends of the bones. They form a stump by overlapping the muscles and skin and sewing them into place. Hannah rips up the rest of the sheet to use as a dressing. Nat Henley is lifted from the table and carried to a cot set up in a corner of the tack room.

The king stands and stretches. Arlington waits anxiously for his verdict. If the king banishes her from court, Hannah thinks, so be it. She would be happy to see no more of it. Arlington can do whatever he will with her.

"Excellently done," the king says to the two physicians. Arlington's relief is immediately evident. "Dr. Strathern, I hear you are in charge of the new anatomy theatre at the College of Physicians."

"Yes, Majesty."

"I wish you well. Please keep me apprised of your work there. I am always interested in the latest discoveries. Mrs. Devlin, you have earned your two weeks. But the court will have a dance then, I will insist upon it." He takes out his pocket watch. "It's time for dinner. Who's joining me?"

The king departs, followed by the group of pale-faced courtiers, none of whom looks in the mood to eat.

"This should keep you in good stead with Arlington," Montagu manages to whisper to her on his way out. "You might be disappointed that you'll be kept at court a while longer, but I'm not."

The room empties, and Hannah searches the operating table for her bottle of syrup. Even a few drops would help ease her pain. She finds it on the floor, without the stopper. It is disappointingly empty. She puts the vial in her pocket and goes over to check on Mr. Henley. Dr. Strathern is covering him up with a wool blanket that smells strongly of horse.

"What will you do with the foot?" he asks. It has been wrapped in a section of sheet and placed in a clean box of straw beneath the cot.

"It isn't mine to do anything with. If Mr. Henley lives, he can bury it himself, and if he does not, his family can bury it with his body. You didn't think you would have it for one of your anatomical studies, did you?"

"Despite what you may have heard, anatomists are not grave robbers. Not all of them, anyway. The captain told me that Mr. Henley has a brother living somewhere near Cheapside. They are going to try to find him, and when they do, I will ask him if he thinks Mr. Henley would like to contribute to our understanding of the human body."

"By giving you his foot to dissect? I hardly think he will agree."

"It doesn't do any harm to ask."

"I think he's already been through enough."

"I do realize that, but this is a medical issue, not a personal one."

"Many physicians believe that the study of anatomy will never help discover the causes of illness."

"I cannot say that I agree with them. I believe that all knowledge is valuable, even if we are not certain to what use this knowledge shall be put."

"Dissection for dissection's sake? It seems to me that you are over-eager to cut up this man's foot."

"It seems to me that you were overeager to cut off his leg."

"He would die if we had not done so."

"And now? How much chance does he have of surviving?"

"At least he has a chance, which he did not before." She is suddenly very angry, but her head hurts too much to think straight, to form the words of contempt she feels. With some surprise, she sees that Dr. Strathern is angry too.

"Mrs. Devlin, I was expected for dinner at noon, an engagement for which I am already late," he says stiffly, "and I cannot possibly arrive looking like this." He looks down at his blood-splattered hands and clothes. "If you'll excuse me," he says, turning on his heel and walking out the door.

Chapter Twenty

Fourth week of Michaelmas term

THE MASTER TAPPED the microphone and called for quiet before addressing the few hundred students and fellows assembled in the hall. "For those of you who have not heard, I am very sorry to tell you that one of our most esteemed and beloved fellows, Dr. Derek Goodman, died this morning."

The noise in the hall instantly rose to a clamor, necessitating another plea for silence. Claire sat next to Hoddy, whom she had called as soon as she had returned to her set. His displeasure at being awoken so early had been quickly overcome by shock at the news. Andrew stood with a group of fellows in the empty alcove where the buffet was served. They all wore a similar expression of sad incomprehension.

After the hubbub died down, the master continued. "Apparently Dr. Goodman was out walking late last night when he fell and hit his head. We are all saddened by his death. At the present time, I have nothing more to tell you, but I would like to introduce Detective Sergeant Hastings, who will be handling the inquiry." He stepped back from the microphone, and the blond woman Claire had seen Andrew talking to earlier stepped up.

"As Lord Liverton said, I'm DS Portia Hastings with the Criminal

Investigations Division. On behalf of the Cambridgeshire Constabulary, I'd like to offer our sincere condolences on the loss of your colleague and teacher." The detective appeared to be close to Claire's age, give or take a year or two. Her black jeans were topped by a fitted, men's style shirt, also black. She wore her straight blond hair parted to one side, so that it dipped in a light golden curve across her brow. The blond hair looked natural, as did she; she used very little makeup, perhaps none at all. With her fresh, vibrant good looks, she didn't need any. As Portia stood behind the mic in front of such a large assembly, Claire sensed her lack of fear and innate confidence. "We have no reason to believe that Dr. Goodman's death was anything other than accidental," she said. "However, I would like to speak to anyone who saw him or spoke to him yesterday."

A rippling murmur went through the hall. Claire turned anxiously to Hoddy. "I'm sure you've nothing to worry about," he whispered. Then he looked up and saw how many people were craning their necks to stare at Claire.

Hoddy squeezed her arm and told her to sit tight. He got up and went over to Andrew, with whom he carried on a short, whispered conversation. Soon he was back at Claire's side.

"You're going to have to speak to the detective," he said. "She already knows a bit about what happened. Andy says they'll expect you in the vice-master's office at four o'clock today."

"Andrew's going to be there too?"

"It's for the best. You're a foreigner, she's a detective. The master has asked Andy to be the police liaison. The detective's an old friend of his."

No wonder they had looked so friendly earlier. "This really is a small town, isn't it?"

Hoddy shrugged. "I tried to tell you."

In all Claire's years as a student, she couldn't think of an occasion when she'd been sent to the principal, but as she entered the vice-master's office, she felt as if she had been summoned for a reprimand. She gave her name to a secretary, who lifted a telephone receiver and announced her to whoever was assembled in the office beyond the closed door. Even before it opened, Claire's palms felt damp.

She was relieved to see that the only people present were Andrew Kent and the detective. Andrew greeted her politely but with a formal reserve. The detective rose as Claire walked in. Andrew introduced her as Detective Sergeant Hastings, which the detective quickly amended to Portia. They each sat down in one of the cushy, slip-covered chairs in the vice-master's spacious office.

As Portia leaned forward, her long hair fell over her shoulders and she unselfconsciously brushed it back. She was even prettier close up, Claire noticed, a green-eyed blonde with dewy skin and peach-colored lips.

"Can you tell me about your argument with Dr. Goodman?" Portia's manner was pleasant but serious.

"Just yesterday or the whole story?"

"The whole story."

Claire began with finding the diary in the Wren Library, running into Derek Goodman and going to the pub with him, showing him her notes and then confronting him after she'd found out that he was writing a paper on the very subject she had been researching. She didn't stop until the embarrassing end, when she hit him in the face.

"Do you often get into heated arguments?" Portia asked.

"No, of course not." Claire glanced at Andrew, and remembered that it wasn't completely accurate to state that she never got into arguments. "Well, not like that."

Portia scratched a few lines in her notebook. "Did you see Dr. Goodman again last night?"

Claire shook her head. "No." Andrew seemed intensely interested in her answer. "No," she repeated.

The detective opened a leather-bound portfolio on the coffee table in front of her. On the top was a standard-size sheet of paper. Portia handed it to Claire, who looked at it with wonder: it was a Xerox copy of one of the encrypted pages from the diary. At the bottom of the page, someone had scrawled, *I told you so—now PAY UP.* The last two words were not only capitalized but underlined as well.

"This is a copy of a paper we found in Dr. Goodman's coat pocket," Portia said. "Is that your handwriting at the bottom?"

"No."

"Do you know whose it is?"

"No," Claire answered, "but this is a page of the diary I told you about." She turned to Andrew. "This proves Dr. Goodman was lying."

Portia looked askance at Andrew. "It's a copy," he said with an apologetic shrug. "I'm afraid it isn't proof."

"You think I'm lying?" Clare asked.

"I didn't say that I don't believe you. I just said this piece of paper can't be considered proof that the diary exists. Just because these marks look like they were made with ink and a quill doesn't automatically make them old. The original could have been written five hundred years ago or five minutes ago. Until we have our hands on the original, there's no way to know for sure. I believe that's Dr. Goodman's handwriting, by the way."

Portia took the paper back from Claire. "Do you know what this is, or what it says?"

Claire shook her head. "No."

"It's tachygraphy," Andrew said. "It's an old form of speed writing, or shorthand, that was popular in the seventeenth century. Pepys used it."

"Peeps?" Portia asked, her brow furrowing.

"Samuel Pepys," Andrew explained. "He was secretary to the Admiralty, and he kept a personal diary from 1660 to 1669. It was written in shorthand much like that. It wasn't translated and published until the early nineteenth century, however. It caused quite a stir among the Victorians, as he wrote very frankly about his private life. In his later years, Pepys amassed a sizable library, which is now kept at Magdalene College."

Portia smiled thinly. "Thank you for the history lesson, Dr. Kent." She rattled the page in her hand. "Do you know what this says?"

"Not offhand, no."

"If I make another copy for you, can you find out what it is and what it says?"

"I can try."

The detective turned her attention back to Claire. "Do you carry your mobile phone with you?"

Claire nodded.

"May I check it?"

Claire felt the blood rush to her face. Yesterday was embarrassing enough, and now she was being treated like someone with something to hide. She took her phone from her purse and gave it to the detective, who quickly scrolled through the menu and looked at Claire's list of recent calls. Finding no calls to or from Derek Goodman, she snapped the phone shut and handed it back. "What's going on?" Claire asked.

"Nothing, really," Portia said. "I'm simply being diligent in my job. I don't know if it's true in America, but in England accidental deaths are investigated as a matter of policy. I'm trying to put together a time line of Dr. Goodman's actions last night. It may help us understand why he was walking around on the Backs at two in the morning." Her glance shifted to her notebook for a second and then back to Claire.

"Do you take any drugs?"

"Excuse me?"

"Do you take any medications?" she repeated. "Prescription drugs, perhaps?"

"No."

"Street drugs?"

"Is this really necessary, Portia?" Andrew asked.

"It is, in fact. I received Dr. Goodman's toxicology screen earlier this afternoon."

Andrew looked worried. "He was drunk, wasn't he?"

"With a blood alcohol level of point ten, yes, I'd say so," she replied tartly. "But that's not the half of it." She shuffled through the papers in her portfolio until she came to the desired report. "He also tested positive for marijuana, Xanax, Vicodin, a couple of antidepressants, and cocaine."

"Good Lord." Andrew paled.

"He was a walking pharmacopoeia."

"I had no idea," Andrew said. "I mean, I knew he drank, but . . . did you find any of those drugs in his set?"

"Only a couple that he had prescriptions for. Which makes me think he might have been at a party last night. Where or with whom I don't know yet. If you hear anything—"

"Of course I'll let you know."

"The department's under a lot of pressure to make this go away quietly."

Andrew sighed and rubbed his forehead. "I'm not surprised. I'm sure the master is already imagining the headlines: 'Trinity History Fellow, Author, and Drug Addict Dies.' Not exactly good for admissions."

"I know how you feel about your school, Andrew, but we're not going to be able to sweep this under the rug." Portia handed Claire a business card. "If you think of anything else, please ring me, or you can stop by the station."

They stood and shook hands, and Andrew walked Claire outside. The blustery wind swept Andrew's tie up and over his shoulder, and he tugged it down into place again. They faced each other awkwardly, both at a loss for words.

"Well," he finally said, "I've got to get on. I've got another meeting." He glanced down at the ground, then at his watch. Clearly he didn't want to discuss anything. So this was what resulted from the English fashion of pretending things never happened.

Not so satisfying after all, Claire discovered.

That evening, she was comfortably ensconced in the chintz-covered wingback in her set when she heard a knock on the door. She opened it to find Andrew standing outside.

"May I come in?" he asked.

"Of course."

He walked inside and looked around her set, his eyes lingering on the photo of Claire and her mother propped on top of the low bookshelf, the student papers stacked on the dining room table, the open book resting on the arm of the chair. Andrew moved closer to scan the title: *Watching the English: The Hidden Rules of English Behavior.*

"Studying the native culture?" he inquired.

"Yes," Claire answered honestly, although she felt slightly embarrassed to have been found reading the book, as if he'd caught her peeking into his personal life—going through his medicine cabinet, for instance, or looking him up online. Or perhaps it was simply embarrassing to need a book to tell her why people who spoke the same language as she did were so unfathomable to her.

"Have you learned anything about us?"

"Quite a lot."

"Such as?"

"English people talk about the weather to disguise their social unease. Tea is considered a near-miraculous beverage that can soothe almost any ill. It's possible to tell someone's social class by the way they eat peas."

"Really?"

"Really."

She'd learned that it was considered rude to ask direct questions, even questions Americans would take as a mark of friendliness and sociability, such as, What do you do for a living? or, Where do you live? She'd learned that introducing yourself to a stranger was considered offensive. (No wonder English people talked about the weather so much, she'd thought when she'd read that: almost every other topic was off-limits.) She'd also discovered that many English people would rather commit suicide than boast about themselves or their achievements, and that people who did boast about their achievements (or simply mentioned them, even) were thought to be either vulgar or American, and usually both. Claire had read that English men, especially those in the upper classes, were notoriously inept at conducting romantic relationships. *That* chapter she had read with great interest.

"Why are you here?" Claire asked.

"I'm afraid I have some rather bad news," Andrew replied. "About Derek. DS Hastings called about an hour ago with the results of his postmortem. The cause of death appears to be drowning. Considering the variety of drugs that he ingested along with copious amounts of alcohol, I suppose it shouldn't be surprising that Derek Goodman drowned in less than a foot of water. However, the coroner found a few small bruises on his face and neck."

"What does that mean?"

"It means," Andrew said, "that someone held him down."

"With all those drugs in his system, I wouldn't be surprised to learn that Derek Goodman was dancing around on the Backs stark naked and singing tunes from *Brigadoon.*" Hoddy raised his cup to his lips for a tentative sip; the freshly made tea was still steaming hot.

Claire stirred milk into her mug of Earl Grey. "It certainly explains some of his erratic behavior. Portia Hastings said that if he hadn't drowned he might have died from an overdose."

"Yet they're convinced it's murder."

Claire nodded and sighed. "Apparently so."

They sat comfortably, if not contentedly, in Claire's set, looking out at New Court and the melancholy drizzle that had been coming down all morning. The tree in the center looked cowed under the constant rain, and all the small, twittering birds had disappeared. Where did they all go?

"Andrew told me that the master actually wanted to suspend me, just to make a show of taking some action," Claire informed Hoddy. "He convinced him not to do it by claiming that as an American, I would sue the college for wrongful dismissal. It's not very nice to know that I still have my job simply because Americans are believed to be overly litigious. Not to mention that people seem to be terribly suspicious of me now. Every time I go to hall, I feel like everyone's whispering and staring at me."

"There's a reason why you feel that way," Hoddy said.

"Why?"

"Because they *are* whispering and staring at you. People always believe the worst—it's more entertaining." He sipped his tea with greater confidence. "I think it's time we took some preemptive action."

"Such as?"

"We could go to the Wren and take another look at that diary."

"What good would that do?"

"You said that Derek had copied a page from it, yes?"

Claire nodded.

"And he'd written something at the bottom?"

"'I told you so—now pay up,'" Claire quoted.

"Sounds as if something in the diary was used to settle a bet. I say we get the diary, have it copied, and transcribe the whole thing. We may be able to determine with whom Derek made the bet."

"You think the person he made a wager with is the person who killed him?"

"I don't know, but it would at least focus attention on someone else for a while."

Chapter Twenty-one

18 November 1672

"So you met the king," Arabella says breathlessly after Edward sits belatedly down to their midday dinner. Her lips and cheek, deliciously warm, perfumed, and soft, are tantalizingly close to his own, but in her parents' dining room he can take no advantage of his fiancée's proximity.

"The king will not soon forget his first encounter with Dr. Edward Strathern!" Sir Granville exclaims just before stuffing a venison pasty into his mouth. Edward's uncle has long been a friend of Arabella's family. Arabella's parents, Sir William Cavendish and his wife, Frances, are positively aglow with the news of their future son-in-law's triumph. He feels almost brutish for being unable to share their enthusiasm, but the events of the morning have produced no feeling of victory in him. Instead he is acutely aware of failure and the lack of medical knowledge, his own and the world's at large.

"What was he like?" Lady Cavendish asks Edward.

"Who?"

"The king, silly," Arabella answers. She's wearing that expression that makes him feel as if he's just said something foolish, as if everyone else knows the thing of which he is so ignorant. Although he's the one with an education (granted, Cambridge was a waste of time, with its ancient fellows and its hidebound fidelity to Aristotelian philosophy, but his years in Paris and Leyden were well spent), Arabella possesses an intrinsic understanding of things he cannot always fathom: fashion, the theater, poetry, why it is necessary for one's carriage to travel anti-clockwise while circling Hyde Park. Her seemingly effortless charm in a variety of company is a trait he admires. That she is not high-born makes it more charming still, for it alludes to something ticking in that brain of hers, something more than how much braid is proper to use on one's clothes, or which lace maker is á la mode. Sir William is not a courtier per se, but the son of a tailor whose wealth and title are of recent vintage. His fortune comes from his massive lumberyards at Wapping and Rotherhithe, which supply the Navy. This is a boom time for shipbuilders, as the Dutch are able to sink English ships as fast as the Navy can build them. The Cavendishes' house on Piccadilly, built less than a decade ago, is constructed of twenty-two different kinds of lumber, many of them exotic. Six different woods, from places as far-flung as Brazil and Ceylon, can be seen in the dining room alone. New visitors are required to take a tour of the thirty-eight-room mansion, led by Sir William, who can explain in detail the difference between hard woods and soft woods, and the intricacies of grain.

"I cannot tell you," Edward replies. "I didn't take much notice of him." He almost adds that he was too busy sawing off a man's leg, then realizes that it isn't an appropriate subject for the dinner table. He is surprised, though, when everyone else laughs.

"Didn't take much notice!" Sir William repeats. "Edward, that's rich."

"The one thing a courtier must take notice of is the king," Sir Granville adds.

"I do appreciate your patronage, Sir Granville, but I have no need to be a courtier. I've already acquired the position I most wanted, director of the new anatomy theatre."

"But Edward," Arabella says, "think of the society you'll be in—that we'll be in—if you become one of the king's doctors. Surely it's better than being surrounded by dead bodies all day long."

"Don't be so certain, my dear," Sir William says, and Lady Cavendish silences him with a look.

"But my choice is based on my desire for knowledge, not better society," Edward says. "Surely you understand that, Arabella."

Judging by her expression, Edward isn't certain that she understands at all. A meager but irrefutable morsel of doubt about his future creeps into his soul. Edward's elder brother Hugh, who became the Earl of Barclay when their father died five years ago, made some objections to Arabella and her parvenu parents when Edward first told him of the engagement, but he relented when he learned of the size of Arabella's marriage portion. Their own inheritance was nearly destroyed in the Civil War. Although much of it was restored along with the monarchy, their wealth does not begin to compare to Sir William's. But these matches of aristocracy and money are so commonplace now that no one takes exception anymore. And as Edward pointed out to Hugh, their title is not so old or so grand, but one of many that Queen Elizabeth bestowed on the middling class in the late last century. In truth, Edward pays little attention to differences of rank and has always been glad that as the second surviving son he does not have to bother with issues of title or inheritance, which has given him the freedom to pursue his studies.

Edward gazes at Arabella's lovely but anxious face. She seems about to embark on one of her curt speeches, but she is given no opportunity.

"Did I hear Sir Granville say that the other physician was a woman?" Lady Cavendish interjects brightly.

"Odious woman," Sir Granville says. "Mrs. Devlin is immodest to a dangerous degree. She styles herself a physician, and a surgeon, and an apothecary, and heeds advice from no one. Why the king allows this upstart behavior from a woman I know not, but he should nip it in the bud, or before long she'll be styling herself queen. Or king. Or the pope."

The others laugh and Edward joins in, though not quite so merrily. He had had approximately the same thoughts of Mrs. Devlin, not that she was odious so much as immodest, but he dislikes hearing it said, especially by Sir Granville. Just hearing her name spoken makes him feel uneasy. Why the mention of her name should provoke any feeling in him whatsoever is a question he prefers not to answer.

"I must say," Edward speaks up, "she proved herself a competent surgeon."

"But her presumption is not to be believed. The woman is a discredit to her father," Sir Granville says. "Do you remember Charles Briscoe? I introduced you to him in Paris."

"I remember," Edward says. "He was a remarkable man and a fine doctor."

"Yes, it's a tragedy," Sir William says.

"What's a tragedy?" Edward asks.

"Didn't you know?" Sir Granville says. "He was killed last year. It must have been around the time you left for Leyden."

"Not just killed," Sir William adds, "Dr. Briscoe was murdered. His body was found near the Fleet Ditch, cut open from stem to stern. Apparently he'd been visiting a patient late at night, and was overcome by a thief who struck him down on the spot. But the murderer was never discovered."

"One of the king's physicians had a patient who lived near the Fleet?"

"He'd left the court by then, hadn't he, Sir Granville?"

"Left the court?" Edward asks. "Why?"

"No one knows," Sir Granville says with a shrug. "My dears," he addresses the ladies, "let me tell you about the necklaces that the king presented this morning to Mademoiselle de Keroualle. One of diamonds and one of pearls. Together worth more than twelve thousand gold guineas."

As Arabella and Lady Cavendish swoon over the latest news from court, Edward tries not to think about Mrs. Devlin. But of course trying not to think about something makes it that much more compelling. He cannot forget the moment when Mr. Henley's leg was cut in two. He simply stood there, holding the foot like a fool, but he couldn't take his eyes away from hers. It was as if—his own mind mocks him for thinking this—he saw into her soul. And what he saw was brilliant, breathtaking, and deeply disturbing.

But he must not think of her. He looks up from his plate of roast peacock and stewed oysters and tries to appear interested as Sir Granville regales the others with stories of court ladies past. "Lady Myddleton, now there was a great beauty, even surpassing the recent Mrs. Stewart," Sir Granville says. "She was very fine, in both her face and body. And I recall that even in her old age, she did not look ugly." He dabs at his mouth with his napkin. "When seen at a distance, of course."

Chapter Twenty-two

THE SIXTH DUKE of Norfolk plans to tear Arundel House down soon, it being so old and dilapidated as it is. Even so, Theophilus Ravenscroft thinks it a superior setting for Royal Society meetings. Much better than their previous accommodations at Gresham College where Mr. Hooke resides, which provides the curator occasion to assume undue importance and give himself airs. Situated near the Maypole between the Strand and the Thames, Arundel House is unimaginatively built but boasts an impressive garden, populated by ancient Greek and Roman statues, that descends in terraces to the river. Two of the property's previous owners were beheaded for treason, endowing the place with an intriguing ambiance of terror and tragedy. The present duke seems more interested than his forebears in staying on the good side of the Crown, not being desirous of surrendering his title, his head, or his excellent collection of ancient art.

Ravenscroft enjoys wandering Arundel's dim, musty galleries and closets to savor these exquisite pieces of the past, for even though the Royal Society meetings are generally held in the downstairs parlor (for experiments requiring additional space, flammable substances, or live animals, they will remove to one of the galleries or to the dining hall), the duke cares not if they roam the house. For this, and for his generous gift of the Arundel House library, Ravenscroft and the other fellows are willing to overlook the duke's popery and the fact that Norfolk does not really care for natural philosophy unless it provides him with an extravagant display of fire, explosions, or blood. In this he is not unlike many of their noble members. This popular inclination tends to steer their weekly investigations away from inquiries of the more subtle sort, but without the annual dues and occasional largesse of the wealthier fellows, the Society would cease to exist.

"Make way, Ravenscroft," says Dr. Lindsey, shouldering past him through the narrow doorway to claim a seat.

"I take up but little room. Surely you can find a better way 'round," Ravenscroft retorts, keeping to himself the words *You giant ass*, which he so longs to say. Here they are all gentlemen, so-called. He looks over the group of twenty-odd chairs arranged in front of a wood pulpit. Although the Royal Society has more than two hundred members, meetings are usually attended by a dedicated core of twenty to thirty men, most of whom are philosophers. The exceptions are courtiers Sir William Brouncker, their president, and Sir Robert Moray, who aid them at court by making certain that their proceedings are well represented to the king (also a fellow and their most distinguished patron, whose promises of attendance and funding have often been made but never fulfilled).

Behind the pulpit hangs a large, disintegrating tapestry, so tattered and worn that its landscape of castle and glade can barely be made out, and so riddled with mold and dust that it constitutes a bodily hazard. During his lecture on the exotic plants of Ceylon last week Ravenscroft was overcome by a fit of sneezing so violent that he banged his face on the pulpit and everyone laughed. He bestows on the tapestry a particularly withering look. Although some of the chairs are as yet unclaimed, he is stymied about where to sit and remains at the back of the room, weighing his limited options.

He refuses to occupy the empty seat next to Mr. Creed, who made sport of his Otocousticon, saying it was only a great glass bottle broke at the bottom, with the neck held to the ear—although Creed was as excited as any of the fellows to hear the amplified sound of splashing oars in the Thames through the Arundel gallery windows. He cannot abide being next to Dr. Pell, who took issue with his discourse on fish gills, or Sir John Finch, who will not credit him for being the first to question the existence of phlogiston, a hypothetical substance wrongly believed to be an essential element of fire. The seats are filling up fast, but it's difficult to make a decision: Mr. Atkins is a snake, Mr. Jones is a dog, and Mr. Pepys is a horse's ass who knows nothing about natural philosophy and can't keep his hands off the tavern wenches. Mr. Audibrasse steps around Ravenscroft on his way to a chair and says, "Excellent entertainment you provided last week, Ravenscroft. I can still see the lump on your forehead."

Buffoon. At last Ravenscroft spies a man who is above reproach and sits down next to him. "Dr. Strathern, welcome back."

The young physician turns to him with a look of genuine warm regard. "Mr. Ravenscroft. How good to see you."

"How was Leyden?"

"Most interesting. The university was well supplied with cadavers."

"That's excellent, indeed. You studied with Dr. Verbrugge?"

"Not only studied but was his primary assistant."

Ravenscroft favors him with a rare smile. "Doesn't surprise me at all."

Strathern has known Mr. Ravenscroft since his return to London after graduating from Cambridge. Even then, Edward knew that his interest tended to anatomy and not the practice of physick. In years past, they often went to Tower Dock to buy fish and other creatures from the incoming ships, taking them to Ravenscroft's laboratory to study. Edward would perform the dissections, and together they would sketch the body, its various systems and parts, and inspect the tissues under a microscope. Once Ravenscroft impulsively purchased a dead dolphin-fish that was too heavy to carry to his house on Bishopsgate, so they took it to a coffeehouse instead, where they cut it up and studied it. Another time they bought a live raccoon. Owing to its charming character, they could not kill it, so Ravenscroft kept it as a pet until one day it bit him on the finger and ran away. Although

the older fellow is a man of strange, unsocial temper, who is quick
to take offense where none is meant, Strathern has always enjoyed a
friendship with him based on common interests and mutual respect.
Ravenscroft possesses a wide range of knowledge and excellent drawing and mechanical skills, and no one is more focused than he in the
pursuit of knowledge. That he has not received the accolades and
acknowledgement he deserves has something to do with his unique
ability to turn perfect strangers into enemies, and a sort of bad luck
that has always plagued him.

Whether Mr. Ravenscroft's bad luck is the source of his pessimism
or the result of it, Edward knows not. He notices that Mr. Hooke is not
in attendance tonight, and as a consequence Mr. Ravenscroft appears to
be in a pleasant mood. At least he is until he looks at Mr. Jones, sitting
in front of him, who every few seconds vigorously scratches his head.
Ravenscroft makes a point of moving his chair back a foot and suggests
that Edward do likewise.

Mr. Henry Oldenburg, their secretary, assumes his place behind
the podium. His ponderous manner and German-accented English
belie his quick understanding and excellent command of European
languages. Because of Mr. Oldenburg's unceasing industry, the Society
receives news of discoveries, observations, and inventions from natural
philosophers all over the world, and dispatches their own.

"Good evening, gentlemen," Mr. Oldenburg begins. "Welcome all to
the weekly assembly of the Royal Society of London for the Improving
of Natural Knowledge. Tonight I will read an account of an experiment
made by our esteemed fellow, the Honorable Mr. Robert Boyle. Next I
will offer a summation of a new book by Fellow Dr. Thomas Willis. My
third topic is an epistle from a Monsieur Denys in Paris.

"After I have concluded these matters, Dr. Pell will kindly tell us
about the progress of his trial of transfusion; then Mr. Slingsby will give
us a discourse, both mathematical and philosophical, on the experiment of raising great weights by the breath."

Mr. Smethwick clears his throat and catches the secretary's eye.

"Oh, yes," says Mr. Oldenburg, "Mr. Smethwick will enlighten us
with a lecture on the history and generation of Colchester oysters."

Mr. Oldenburg begins as he promised, with Mr. Boyle's account of the varying weight of the atmosphere upon bodies in the water, and a summary of Dr. Willis's book, concerning the pathology of the brain and the diseases that affect it. Last, he takes up the letter from Monsieur Denys in Paris.

"'Dear Sirs,'" the secretary reads, "'we are now busy, at the order of King Louis, making experiments, whence the world is like to receive great benefit. Here hath been found out an admirable essence, which being applied to any artery whatsoever, stops the blood instantly without any need of binding up the wound. We have first experimented it upon dogs, then made trials upon men; and it succeeded with them as well as it did upon dogs.'"

Ravenscroft nudges Edward. "Do you think there's any truth in it?" he asks.

"I don't know. I can only say that I could have used a blood-stopping essence earlier today."

Mr. Jones scratches his head again.

"I fear the man has fleas," Ravenscroft whispers.

"Monsieur Denys ends his letter by offering to send some of his essence for a trial. I'll pass his request to our curator, Mr. Hooke, along with the others he has not had time for recently," says Oldenburg, frowning and setting the letter aside. "Dr. Pell, please tell us how you're getting on with your transfusion experiment."

Pell stands to address the group. "I have found a man who, for twenty shillings, has agreed to have some of the blood of a sheep let into his body. It is to be done on Saturday next."

"Dr. Pell, what do you propose to discover from this trial?" Mr. Atkins inquires.

"The man has a frantic nature, and I believe that the sheep's blood will have a calming effect on him, by cooling his blood."

"I don't believe that sheep's blood will have any effect at all, being a creature inferior to man, and not possessing a soul," says Mr. Smethwick.

"But the sheep's gentle nature and passivity may be passed on to him, nevertheless," Mr. Creed offers.

"I have heard a story about Dr. Caius that rebuilt Caius College," adds Sir Robert Moray, "that when he was very old he lived only upon the milk of a wet nurse; and while he fed upon the milk of an angry, fretful woman, he was so himself, and then being advised to take the milk of a good-natured, patient woman, he did become so."

"But that is nutriment, not blood," Mr. Jones says.

"However, we all know that blood can take on humors, and become hot or cold," says Dr. Lindsey.

"Perhaps only the blood of men can be affected by humors," says Mr. Slingsby.

"For God's sake, Jones, stop scratching," Ravenscroft says.

"What will happen to the sheep, Dr. Pell?" Mr. Atkins asks. "What if, instead of the sheep's soothing humors being transmitted to the man, the man transmits his frantic nature to the beast?"

"I'm not putting the man's blood into the sheep," Dr. Pell answers, exasperated.

"What if you kill the man?" Mr. Atkins presses.

"I'm not going to kill the man! I'm only going to put in twelve ounces of the sheep's blood, about as much as can be administered in a minute by watch. He is a healthy man. Though a little cracked in the head, he should be able to give us an account of what alteration, if any, he does find in himself."

"He will not be able to tell us much if he finds himself bleating like a sheep," Mr. Audibrasse points out.

"Gentlemen, please—," Mr. Oldenburg says.

"Honestly, Jones, you should have left your damned wig outside," Ravenscroft says.

"Bloody hell!" Mr. Jones pulls his periwig off. "I told the wigmaker it had nits, I told him to comb it out, but it's still crawling with vermin."

Everyone in the room falls silent. They all stare at Jones's stubble-covered head and at the mass of curled hair in his hands. Everyone except Ravenscroft.

"A comb," Ravenscroft says to himself, just loud enough for

Edward to overhear. "Of course, a comb!" He rises and makes ready to go. "Good night, Dr. Strathern. It was good to see you again."

"You're leaving?" It's customary for the fellows to adjourn to the Turk's Head coffeehouse on Chancery Lane after their meetings.

"Yes, I must leave right away," Ravenscroft says as though suddenly distressed. And before anyone can utter another word, he is gone.

Chapter Twenty-three

18 November 1672
Whitehall

To the Rue de Varenne

The English court is as Depraved and addicted to its Pleasures as the French, and no one in it more so than the King. Tonight's entertainment at the Duke of York's Palace of St. James has brought together the curdled cream of court Society: the King and the Duke, of course, and their faithful dogs Lord Arlington, Sir Thomas Clifford, and Sir Henry Reynolds, among others. And so I find myself amongst a bunch of sodden Wits, pox-ridden Rakes, loutish Lords and so-called Ladies who have come to see a performance by the King's company of players. They are temporarily without a stage of their own, as their theatre on Drury Lane burnt to the ground last December. Each of the courtiers has already swilled a bottle or two of French wine and stuffed themselves with roasted Larks and sweet-meats and candied fruit. They loll about on cushions on the floor or drape themselves over couches. Considering the familiarity of some, they seem to mistake the couches for their own beds.

The private stage at the Duke of York's residence is not large, but it makes up for its diminished size with extra Finery: velvet curtains, gilded woodwork, gold candelabra footlights. The backdrops *are the artful Work of the best court painters. But the theatre's big-gest advantage is that it is open only to the intimates of the Duke and the King. No mixing with the noisy hoi-polloi, the crowded stinking bodies, the masked and vizarded Strumpets in the pit.*

Mr. Killigrew bounds onto the stage in full riding gear, urgently calling for his horse. Mrs. Howard, an actress whose best Features are amply displayed above the low edge of her Bodice, inquires of him, "Sir, where do you go in such a hurry?"

"To Hell," he answers boldly, "to fetch up Oliver Cromwell to look after the affairs of England, for his successor is too busy swiving."

Everyone, including the King, is made merry by this. Louis would never allow his crown to be debased by mirth and raillery, but Charles Stuart's soul is as bankrupt as his Exchequer. After that devil Cromwell is hounded back to Hell, where he belongs, Mr. Wycherley recites scurrilous Verses concerning the men and ladies of the court, which are very Droll and make everyone clutch their bellies, agog with Laughter. Then Mrs. Howard returns in a rollicking scene in which she plays a young French miss (can you guess who this is?) who swears she will have no more Commerce with that known Enemy to virginity and chastity, the Monarch of Great Britain.

The Duke of York laughs loudest at this, even though he is an enemy to Virtue as villainous as his brother. Now that his wife the Duchess Anne has died (some say from the Pox that he gave her, some say from her own Immensity, for she was as wide as a pregnant heifer), he makes free with all of her Ladies while the King and his ministers squabble over his choice of a new wife: the successor to the throne will have no one but a Catholic and they say the country will not abide it. All I can say is that the Princess who makes her new home in this place will be aggrieved indeed.

Lord Rochester leaps onto the stage and announces he will read his Prologue to another author's play, titled The Empress of Morocco. *He says that the play is best forgot, except for the Part he writ. Rochester is a pet of the King's, for he is pretty and witty, but he dares too often to speak the Truth, and make Satires of the King's whores, and seeking revenge they Scheme and Plot to undo him. They need not bother; Rochester is his own worst enemy. He himself boasts he has not been Sober two hours together in the past five years, and he offends the King as often as he pleases him. Tonight he is as much in his cups as ever, his fine clothes wrinkled, his wig askew, a bloodred glass of Tent spilling from his hand. He is a clown, yet people listen when he begins to recite.*

"Who can abstain from Satire in this age? What nature wants I find supplied by rage. Some do for pimping, some for Treachery use; But none's made great for being good or wise. Deserve a Dungeon, if you would be great, Rogues always are our ministers of state. Mean prostrate bitches, for a Bridewell fit, with England's wretched Queen must equal sit."

No one laughs at the end of his speech, and all eyes look to the King. Will His Majesty ban Rochester from court again and send him off to rusticate at his estate in Adderbury? Then Sir Henry Reynolds pipes up: "Rochester, why do you abuse this age so? It's as pretty an honest, drinking, whoring age as a man would wish to live in."

The King guffaws, and everyone laughs. Rochester has his Reprieve, but the Playacting is over for the evening. Most are sprawled about in various stages of Drunkenness. Those who are not already asleep swill more wine and gobble Sweets, or sneak away in illicit Pairs to the shadowy corners of the Palace or to the brisk outdoors and the dark, hidden places of St. James's Park.

Sir Henry Reynolds leaves the theatre and scurries after one of the Queen's ladies, following her down the gallery that leads to the palace Garden and the park. She is an unusual choice for him, for he is infamous for his Addiction to common wenches, and for spreading a Doctrine that it is cheaper and safer to lie with common wenches than with Ladies of Quality.

But that is hardly the worst thing he has done.

The young lady leads him on easily, she laughing softly and keeping a few paces ahead, he huffing and puffing through the Garden and then into the park. Once he is in the wilderness he loses sight of her, but perhaps Escape is what she had in mind from the start.

"My Lady Caroline," he croons. "My little dove, do not be so

coy, I have not the patience for it." He takes a few steps forward into the darkness, then pulls up short. "What are you doing here?" he demands. "I have no use for your company."

"If there were any justice in this world, Sir Henry," says I, "your parts would be displayed on pikes above the London Bridge."

When I first thrust the knife into his chest, his wide-eyed Expression is almost comic, as if he were about to snap his fingers and command one of his servants to fetch him a glass or a pipe. But on the second strike, the one that flays open his Innards, he utters a deep and wavering moan; and so I must cut his throat as well, so that Lady Caroline and the other courtiers in the park will not be alerted.

For after I lay him out on the ground there is much Work to do.

Chapter Twenty-four

Fourth week of Michaelmas term

CLAIRE UNLOCKED THE gate to R bay, and Hoddy followed her inside.

"It's the second book on the top shelf," she told Hoddy as he pulled one of the benches over to the bookshelf. He climbed up on it and, being six inches taller than Claire, easily took down the volume and handed it to her.

"This isn't it," Claire said as she opened the cover of the book Hoddy had given her and read the title: *Enchiridion medicum = An enchiridion of the art of physick.*

"What do you mean, isn't it?"

"This isn't the diary." Claire got up on the bench next to him and perused the top shelf. "It doesn't seem to be here."

She and Hoddy methodically skimmed each of the other bookshelves in R bay, climbing up and down benches when necessary, running their fingertips over the books' spines. Twenty minutes later, they still hadn't found the diary. "Time to call in the cavalry," Hoddy said at last.

Mr. Pilford was seated at his desk. "Dr. Donovan and I are looking for what we believe is a diary written during the late seventeenth century," Hoddy told him. "Does it sound familiar to you?"

"I'll need more information than that, certainly. Do you know which collection it's in?"

"The Barclay collection," Claire told him. "We know the year it was written, 1672, and that it was written in code—well, tachygraphy, or speed writing, similar to the sort Samuel Pepys used. We also know that Dr. Goodman was probably the last person to look at it."

"Dr. Goodman?" The librarian repeated the name in a tone dripping with acrimony, self-righteousness, and an underlying horror, as if he'd just discovered something nasty smeared on the bottom of his shoe. His warm demeanor instantly turned cold. "Dr. Goodman was in the habit of taking books from the library without notifying me," Mr. Pilford testily informed them. "And now he has died without returning them. It's simply not on. In my long career as a librarian, Dr. Goodman was the worst reprobate I have ever encountered. Always rooting around in the stacks, holding on to books for months at a time, putting them back in the wrong places. He treated the Wren like his own private library. I tried many times to have him banned from here, but he always managed to pull rank." Mr. Pilford had worked himself into a fit of anger. The pupils of his eyes narrowed to two silvery points. "Serves him right, what happened."

"Surely you aren't suggesting that Dr. Goodman deserved to die because he didn't follow correct library procedure," Hoddy said.

Mr. Pilford's lips puckered and his bushy silver eyebrows rose high on his forehead. "It's a library. Its contents belong to everyone. It's a sacred trust."

"I see," Hoddy replied, chastened. Apparently Mr. Pilford thought death was a light sentence, in view of the crime.

"What I'd really like to know," the librarian went on, "is when I'm going to get everything back."

"Very soon," Hoddy assured him. "I'll make sure of it myself."

"What do we do now?" Claire asked as they made a hasty retreat.

"Just follow me," Hoddy said, "and look innocent."

Hoddy took out his key ring when they got to Derek Goodman's door in B staircase. "The F key opens *all* the doors?" Claire asked.

"This isn't an F key," Hoddy replied. "It's a copy of one of the bedder's keys."

"What are you doing with a bedder's key?"

"Let's just say I came across it in my travels." Hoddy unlocked the door and they quietly slipped inside.

"Good Lord," Hoddy and Claire said in unison.

They took in their surroundings with a mixture of awe and dread. If the diary was here in Derek's set, it wasn't going to be easy to find. The main room was filled with reading matter: old books, new books, academic journals, magazines, bound dissertations, and piles of paper that looked suspiciously like lengthy, unbound manuscripts. The texts filled the bookshelves that lined the walls, overflowing into stacks on the tables and countless thigh-high heaps on the floor.

Hoddy walked over to the curtains, carefully keeping out of sight of the windows, and slowly drew the drapes closed.

"Why do I get the feeling you've done this before?" Claire asked.

"Draw the curtains?"

"Sneak into someone else's set."

"Ask me no questions and I will tell you no lies." Hoddy stopped to look around at the incredible profusion of books and other reading materials in the room. "One thing's for certain," he said. "No one could accuse Derek of being a slacker."

Claire took a few steps farther into the room along a path that had been carefully carved out from the stacks of books. On the wall opposite the windows, poster-size enlargements of Derek's two book covers were displayed, along with a giant black-and-white head shot of himself. The photographer had managed to capture the devilish gleam in his eyes and his not-quite-benign smile. "No one could accuse him of excess humility, either," she added.

Hoddy suggested they begin in the study, using the logic that Derek's most recently used materials would be near his desk. No doubt it was the reasonable thing to do, but Claire wondered if he felt, as she did, a certain sense of relief once they were out of sight of Derek's photographic gaze. Unhappily, the adjacent study was even more densely packed than the front room. "It looks like he's got half the library in here," Hoddy remarked. A path less than a meter wide led to a desk that faced a window overlooking New Court. The desktop was empty except for two items, an antique brass lamp and a glass paperweight shaped like an egg. Strangely empty. No computer, Claire pointed out.

"He didn't use a school computer," Hoddy said. "He preferred his own laptop."

"Shouldn't it be here?"

"I suppose, unless he had it with him . . ." *when he died,* Hoddy implied without saying.

"You think he was carrying his computer around at two o'clock in the morning?"

"Could have been. Maybe that's why—"

"You believe someone killed him for his computer?"

"It's possible," Hoddy replied, although he didn't sound completely convinced of it himself. "Or perhaps the police have impounded it. That's probably the more reasonable conclusion." He shook his head and made a sound that mingled disbelief with incomprehension. "When Andy first told me that he'd been murdered, I thought, 'Why would anyone want to kill Derek Goodman?' Then almost as quickly I thought of a half dozen reasons."

"Such as?"

"He annoyed most everyone he met. He always assumed he was the smartest person in the room. He felt compelled to seduce every woman who got within arm's length of him. It didn't matter if they were someone else's girlfriend, wife, sister. Even mother, I believe, in an instance or two. He was always crowing about his accomplishments and belittling everyone else's. He could be a complete ass, behave in the most appalling ways, and he never cared about the consequences. At least he never cared about the consequences for anyone else. In short, Derek Goodman considered himself the center of the universe around which all the other paltry stars and planets revolved. Does that explain it?"

"Very well. But why didn't you tell me this about him before, when we had dinner?"

"You didn't ask. I didn't think you'd be so susceptible to his charms."

"Charms, indeed. Knowing what I know about him now, I only wonder that he wasn't murdered years ago."

"I suppose. It's hard for me to believe that he was killed by someone he knew, because I *know* most of the people he knew. These aren't the kind of people who kill other people just because they're annoying. I mean, if that were true, human beings would quickly kill each other off until there was no one left." Hoddy took a breath and looked around. "Tell you what. I'll check the closets if you'll search the bedroom. Then we'll work through this mess together."

Derek Goodman's bedroom was bigger than the bedroom in Claire's own set, large enough to contain a double bed with a few feet of space along each side. In contrast to the other rooms, it was uncluttered to the point of being austere. No books or boxes of manuscripts and journals on the floor. The bed was carefully made up, the silver-gray silk duvet and matching pillowcases smooth and unwrinkled. Two black lacquer bedside tables each held a lamp with a sleek silver base and gray lamp shade. Ivory silk curtains with a thin gray stripe draped the window looking out to the Backs. A twenty-inch flat-screen TV was mounted on the wall facing the foot of the bed.

Hoddy slouched in the doorway. "Very Zen Buddhist, in a Calvin Klein sort of way," he announced. Which was the true reflection of Derek Goodman's personality—the slightly mad, obsessive book collector, or the suave, urbane seducer? Certainly, Claire thought, this room was less of a surprise than the others.

"Nothing in the closets," he went on. "So this is where he went to get away from all the books. Have you looked under the bed yet? Or in the dresser?"

Claire shook her head. "I feel a bit weird about going into his underwear drawer."

Hoddy made a quick check of the dresser while Claire peeked under the bed. "Nothing under here," she reported. "Not even any dust bunnies."

"The bedder has been here," Hoddy said. "The rubbish bins are empty."

Claire gave the bath the once-over. Nothing unusual there. Like the bedroom, it clove to the "less is more" doctrine. Spotlessly clean, with only one of each necessary item in the bathtub/shower stall: soap, shampoo, shaving gel, disposable razor. Only a few miscellaneous things remained in the medicine cabinet: more disposable razors in blue, orange, and pink; a bottle of contact lens solution; athlete's foot spray. No prescription medicine bottles; the police must have taken them. Claire closed the mirrored cabinet door and saw Hoddy standing behind her.

She turned around. "This is kind of creepy."

"Yes, it is."

"I hate the idea that when I die, strangers will be looking through all my things—"

"And drawing conclusions and making judgments."

"Yes." She shuddered at the thought.

"It's a good argument for having children, though, isn't it? At least it won't be a stranger, it will be your own child."

Claire mulled it over. "I can't decide if that's cynical or practical."

"Perhaps it's both."

"Did Derek Goodman have any family?"

"A brother, who lives in Los Angeles. He's supposed to be here for the memorial service," Hoddy said as he walked back toward the study. Then he stopped, his gaze fixed on the bedroom door.

It was open, but they could both see that something was attached to the back, a large sheet of paper or a poster of some kind. Another one on the wall. Hoddy swung the door on its hinges as Claire moved closer.

Thumbtacked to the door and to the wall behind it were two maps of London—not current maps but copies of old maps. One was from December 1666, showing the devastation of the City after the Fire. The other had been drafted even earlier, in 1658, and included not only London but also Westminster and a bit of St. James's Park. On each of the maps were small red stick-on dots. When Claire looked closely, she saw that the dots were numbered.

"They're in the same location on both maps," Hoddy pointed out just as she noticed it herself.

The dots numbered one and two were placed east of the Fleet River, number three in St. James's Park, four near Pall Mall, five—with a question mark next to it—in Southwark, and six, again near the Fleet.

"What's that?" Hoddy asked. They both held their breath and listened anxiously as a key turned in the lock of the front door, and someone stepped inside.

Chapter Twenty-five

19 November 1672

DR. STRATHERN IS already there when Hannah arrives in the morning to check on Mr. Henley. Strathern sits on a three-legged stool next to the cot, gazing upon Henley's face. At first, before her eyes recover from the sharp, stinging aroma of the stables and the murky light of the tack room, she thinks they are engaged in conversation. As she gets closer, she sees that that is not possible.

Strathern looks up when he hears her footsteps and, seeing her, rises to his feet. They don't bother with greetings but in silence keep their eyes turned to their patient. The horse blanket has been carefully drawn back, exposing Henley's upper body and his bandaged leg. His eyelids have been mercifully shut.

"When did it happen?" Hannah asks. She guesses within the past two hours. Mr. Henley is pallid but has not the blue, marblelike appearance he will take on once the blood in his body collects in his lower extremities.

"About an hour ago. The captain said that Henley had been resting peacefully when he suffered a violent convulsion and died."

"He never woke up?"

"Apparently not."

"I should have stayed," Hannah says. "I might have stayed if not . . ." She trails off. If not for her headache and her need for poppy syrup. After she got home she discovered that she hadn't any left, so she took laudanum instead, which lulled her into a deep, hallucinatory sleep. When she woke up, she felt fatigued, as if she had traveled great distances in the night. But the pain is bearable now, almost gone, as if it had been wrestled, tamed, and trapped in a small corner of her brain.

"Even if you had stayed, you could not have saved him," Strathern points out. "What do you imagine you would have done?"

"Changed his plaster and given him a syrup, and told him that these measures would ease his pain and speed his healing."

"And if your medicines did nothing?"

"I would tell him that they were working, regardless of their actual efficacy."

He looks at her quizzically. "Do you believe that simply saying it makes it so?"

"In the absence of true medicine, a few harmless lies and our sympathy may be the most we can offer."

"You surprise me. I would not have thought that you had so little faith in your profession."

"How long have you been studying medicine, Dr. Strathern?"

"For the best part of the past eight years."

"I have been studying all of my life. At the same time that I was learning to read and write, I was making plasters and pills with my mother. Indeed, I cannot recall a time when I was not doing so. It's not that I have so little faith but that I have discovered, through my parents' practice and my own, that there are few treatments for illness that consistently produce the results we strive for. What is taught in the English universities appears in many cases to do more harm than good. My father had the good fortune to study with Dr. Sydenham, who believes that physick cannot be taught from books, but only by observation and practice. His is the example I follow."

"I have heard a story about Dr. Sydenham, in which a young man asked which books he recommended to his medical students and the doctor replied, 'Don Quixote.'"

Hannah smiles. "That is a true story."

"It may surprise you to learn that I share his views. I belong to a society of like-minded men—other physicians, natural philosophers, chemists, astronomers—who believe that all philosophic theories should be developed after careful observation, not before."

"The Royal Society?"

"Yes."

"I have heard of it, and its motto—*Nullius in verba*."

"'Nothing in words.' It means, in essence, that we don't base our beliefs on untested theories. We have rejected the old way of natural philosophy, in which philosophers simply debated and believed that the truth existed in whichever theory was the most elegant. We believe that only close observation of the physical world will lead us to the truth. First we inquire into the properties of things, then slowly proceed to hypotheses for explanations of them."

"It sounds extraordinary."

"The meetings are quite remarkable," he continues, eyes shining with enthusiasm. "We discourse on anatomy, astronomy, botany, the properties of light, air, magnetism—anything and everything that man can investigate. Sometimes we conduct experiments, or the fellows will give accounts of their own trials."

"I must admit I'm rather envious. I should enjoy being part of such a learned society." It occurs to her that this is the first time she has had a conversation about the things she cares about most, medicine and philosophy, since Nathaniel and her father died. The three of them spent their days practicing physick and continually shared their observations, speculations, and discoveries, each of them contributing to an ongoing dialog that ended with her father's death. She is acutely aware of how much she misses them, their minds, their thoughts. And how much she misses her mother, too, whose presence—whose very self—has gradually slipped away. Suddenly Hannah realizes how terribly alone she has felt. She finds herself wondering how Dr. Strathern regards her. Most men think her immodest for having interests beyond her home and family. Even the desire for greater knowledge is considered immodest, and immodesty is considered a woman's greatest fault. Dr. Strathern may be forward-thinking and a proponent of the new philosophy, but that does not mean that his attitude regarding women is different from any other man's.

"I suppose you think it odd for a woman to be interested in these matters."

"It seems quite natural coming from you. But I think you are unlike anyone I have met before. Of all the women I know, you would be the one most welcome in the Society."

"Thank you." She is surprised by the sting of tears in her eyes. It feels as if it's been a long time since someone has seen her for who she truly is. She hides her emotion by covering Mr. Henley's body with the blanket.

Strathern's glance slides down to the dead man's foot, still in the box of straw underneath the cot. His chest rises and falls with a small, resigned sigh. "Mr. Henley's brother is coming to take him to be buried," he says. "Unfortunately I can't stay any longer. The king has asked me to handle the terrible tragic business of last night."

"What tragic business?"

"You have not heard? Sir Henry Reynolds was brutally attacked and killed in St. James's Park."

"Sir Henry?"

"Did you know him?"

"I know of him. My father mentioned him a few times. I know it's wrong to speak ill of the dead, but I don't recall that he ever said anything good."

"I'm to do the postmortem. His body has already been taken to the college, so I must go."

Oddly, though, after stating his intention to depart, Dr. Strathern does not do so. He stands awkwardly, glancing at his hands, at the floor, at any place other than directly at her. "I was very sorry to hear about your father. He was a fine doctor." He finally looks into her eyes. "And so are you. Do not think badly of yourself. You did well by Mr. Henley, Mrs. Devlin—as well or better than anyone I know. I would have cut too high on the leg," he admits. "An anatomist has no need to think about how people will heal."

Mr. Henley's brother arrives to retrieve the body. Hannah gives him money to help with the burial at their parish church in Aldgate. He accepts it with thanks and a polite nod, but the charity does not assuage her feelings of remorse. After he carries the dead man away in a wheeled handcart, she stands at the door of the tack room for a long time, looking out at the stable yard.

The yard is filled with the red-coated King's Guards, both foot and horse, and their well-groomed mounts. She should have realized when she arrived this morning that something was amiss, just by the increased show of force at Whitehall, a palace normally undefended and lax in its security. A search is being launched for Sir Henry's murderer. The urgency is apparent in the voices of the guard captains as they round up their men, in the shiver and nervous stamp of the horses. If her father had remained a courtier and had been murdered in St. James's Park, instead of being a doctor to the poor who was struck down near the Fleet, would the same have been done for him? She cannot help feeling resentful, for surely no great effort was made to find the man who killed him.

Hannah pulls her hood up as she walks through the yard, skirting the men, the horses, the squawking chickens that run loose. She thinks of Dr. Strathern, who left gracelessly without saying good-bye, and wonders if she will see him again. There will be no cause for it now that their mutual patient has died. She regrets that this is so; her initial impressions of him were ill founded. Dr. Strathern is nothing like his uncle, that much is certain, and his philosophic beliefs intrigue her. But what kind of man makes a career of dissecting bodies?

She weaves through the crush of sedan chairs and carriages on Whitehall Street to pass through the main gate into the palace courtyard, with hardly a glance from the sentry. Even though the King's Guards are out in force, admission to the palace is as easy as ever. Courtiers and carpenters, London merchants and foreign dignitaries, the king's councilors and his cooks, numerous lords, ladies, footmen, and maids hurry to and fro on their individual affairs. As she approaches the covered walkway leading to Mademoiselle de Keroualle's apartments, a young lady of the court in a silk gown and velvet cloak falls into step with her.

"Mrs. Devlin," she says softly, "please walk with me." She glances about warily and, convinced there is no one watching them, gestures for Hannah to follow her out of the courtyard into a quieter corridor. Although all of the young court ladies are handsome, this one is prettier than most, with black hair, angular but pleasing features, and intense dark eyes. Eyes in which Hannah perceives cunning, guile, and furtiveness. Or perhaps she's been at court too long already to so quickly accredit such base emotions to someone she doesn't know.

Hannah stops as soon as they find an isolated spot. "Who are you?"

"My name is Jane Constable. I'm one of the maids to the late Duchess of York. I'm told that you are a doctor."

"Yes." There seems little point in trying to keep it concealed any longer.

"I need your help."

"What kind of help?"

"I am an unmarried maid. Perhaps you can deduce for yourself."

Hannah lowers her voice. "You are with child?"

Jane glances around nervously. "Careful, there are ears everywhere."

In court vernacular, the early termination of a pregnancy is known as "slipping a calf," a nonchalant phrase for something Hannah is aware is neither simple nor easy. Although many midwives, physicians, and apothecaries are willing enough to prescribe an herbal means of inducing abortion, it is illegal, and the penalty if caught—for the mother and for the doctor—is steep. It occurs to Hannah that Jane could have been sent by someone, perhaps one of the court doctors, to embroil her in a scheme that could get her banished from court, prohibited from practicing physick, sent to prison, or worse. Already the court physicians are set against her, if Sir Granville is any indication. If her treatment of Louise is successful, the king and Arlington will favor her, which will only expose her to more scrutiny and jealousy. It occurs to her just how dangerous success might be. "I'm sorry, I can't help you," Hannah says, turning away.

Jane clutches her arm. "Wait! Do not be so hasty. Do you understand what will happen to me? As soon as my belly begins to swell I'll be banished from court, sent to the country, and branded unmarriageable for life. Only the king's whores can have bastards without paying a price." She laughs bitterly. "And then they're made dukes, of course."

"The father of the child has not offered to marry you?"

"Of course not. Have you not seen for yourself the manner of men at court? They look upon maids of honor only as amusements, placed here for their entertainment. This man—the father—was charming and kind, and I thought at first he was unlike the others, but he is not. The courtiers require us to be easy prey, but they will not marry us, not unless a great deal of money is involved in the match." She looks at Hannah, her black eyes pleading. "Surely you have helped women before."

"Just because I am a woman does not mean that I am especially skilled in such matters. But I have heard that Dr. Fraser—"

"If I go to a court doctor, everyone will know. It's because you're not a courtier that I came to you. Don't you know of a potion that helps a woman slip her calf?"

"There are certain herbs that are known to help bring on the terms, but they are not meant to be used on pregnant women. They are powerful and can be quite dangerous. If taken in too large a dose, they can cause your death."

"I'm willing to take that risk."

"But I am not. I could be hanged just for helping you."

"Then what am I to do?" Jane's mouth quivers and her feral eyes swim with tears. Either the girl is sincere, or she's an excellent actress. Perhaps she's wrong to distrust her. Hannah thinks through a list of potential abortifacients. They are all dangerous; poisonous, actually, if not handled correctly. "Please, do not make yourself unhappy," Hannah says, "lest others discover the cause of your sorrow. Give me a day or two. I may be able to come up with a safer solu—"

Jane catches sight of something behind Hannah and suddenly bolts, her skirts sliding around the corner and quickly out of sight. Hannah turns to find Mr. Maitland walking toward her. He stops a few feet away and bows. "Mrs. Devlin, Lord Arlington has bid me to say that your presence is desired at Mademoiselle de Keroualle's."

"I was on my way just now."

"It would be my pleasure to escort you." He smiles contritely at Hannah's hesitation. "Please do not be alarmed. I promise to behave with perfect propriety. I have long hoped for the opportunity to apologize for my actions of that night. Especially as you are such a fine doctor." He holds up his cut hand. "See how well it has healed."

"So I see. As you have comported yourself in a gentlemanly manner ever since, I see no reason not to forgive you." She adds a smile to soften her words.

"I hope it will not surprise you to learn that I am a gentleman's son," Maitland says.

"Now that I consider it, no, I'm not surprised. But how did you come to be in Lord Arlington's service?"

"My father, like many Royalists, was ruined in the Civil War. He never overcame the blow, and he died when I was very young. I was fortunate to have patrons such as Mr. Montagu and Lord Arlington. They paid for my education, and so now I serve as their man-of-all-bidding. But it is only the beginning. They promise to sponsor my rise at court so that I may one day return my family to the high rank it once enjoyed."

"You have long been associated with Mr. Montagu?"

"All my life. He was a friend of my father's."

"And what is your opinion of him?"

He glances slyly at her. "I believe he has a high regard for you."

"You did not answer my question," Hannah replies, laughing at her vain attempt to pry information from him. "I see you can be discreet when it suits you."

"When it suits Mr. Montagu, more like," Maitland replies. "Yes, ma'am, I am aware that it does not serve to bite the hand that feeds. Especially when there are so many others that need biting," he adds with a wicked grin.

"You remain bold in your thoughts, Mr. Maitland, if not in your actions. If you continue in such a way, you will become as much of a rake as the others here."

"Do you speak with approbation or with admiration, Mrs. Devlin?"

"A little of both, I suppose, for men enjoy freedoms that women may never share, but only men are capable of causing such great harm as they do." She stops before they turn into the stone gallery and looks for Jane Constable, but the girl is nowhere to be seen.

Chapter Twenty-six

"I've come to talk with the comptroller," Ravenscroft says. "Is Sir Hugh in his chambers?"

"Yes, but he is sitting with others presently," the clerk replies.

Ravenscroft offers his letter of introduction. "I come directly from Sir Robert Moray."

The clerk quickly reads the letter's few scrawled lines and, with a perturbed sigh, rises from his chair. Though young, he has an acerbic look about him, as if his only pleasure comes from exercising what small power he has. "Wait here," he says, nodding at a pewlike bench along one wall.

Ravenscroft sits as the clerk crosses the antechamber to Sir Hugh May's door. As comptroller, Sir Hugh holds the purse strings to the King's Works, the branch of His Majesty's government that oversees building projects in and around Whitehall and the City. As he waits, the injurious effects of only a few hours' sleep begin to settle in his bones. Last night he rushed home from the Royal Society meeting, his mind frantic, as if his inspiration was something fragile that would break if he did not bring it immediately to life. He ignored young Thomas's greeting and Nell's offer of supper, and shut himself up in his study, making sketch after sketch until he completed a practicable set of plans. After a nap in the early morning, he awoke feeling happy and benevolent, as if he had drunk the nectar and dreamt the dreams of gods—for inspiration surely must have a divine source. He decided that he would go at once to Sir Robert, his influential Royal Society colleague. He washed with heated lavender water and donned his best coat, his finest periwig, and a lace cravat he had been saving for just such an occasion. Then, with an easel and his drawings under his arm, he set out from the Old Swan stairs on a wherry to Whitehall.

Where he was shunted about from clerk to clerk, each one more officious than the last, before sitting briefly with Sir Robert and being sent to Sir Hugh. The part of the palace near the Scotland Yard that houses the King's Works has changed little since King Henry's time, except that the rooms have been partitioned to accommodate the additional secretaries and copyists made necessary by the Fire. It is a warren of tiny nests, each one filled with a scribbling clerk. As he leans his head back against the wall he can hear them scratching and scrabbling like mice. The rooms are dismal and cold, with wood-paneled walls and leaded-glass windows placed very high up. In clement weather the windows do little to dispel the gloom, and on cloudy days such as this one they admit almost no light at all. Even though each has a shilling's worth of tapers on his desk, to a man the clerks sit with crooked backs, squinting at barely legible documents only inches away.

The close air and the tallow smoke make him drowsy. When the clerk finally grants him an audience with the comptroller, he feels slightly dazed, like a grateful supplicant ushered into the light. Sir Hugh has beaten back the darkness of his chambers by placing candles all about: it's as bright as a chapel.

"Mr. Ravenscroft, pleased to make your acquaintance," he says with a vigorous handshake and a smile. The comptroller is hale and hearty, about fifty, with a sanguine complexion and a jovial, informal air, but like all successful courtiers he wears expensive rags and a scent stronger and more complex than simple lavender water. Ravenscroft suspects that Sir Hugh's warm welcome has little to do with his unassuming self and much to do with the comptroller's wish to supplant Christopher

Wren as surveyor-general. It did not go over well with the older architect when the king appointed the young Mr. Wren above him.

"This is my under-clerk, Mr. Urquhart, and my cousin Sir Richard
Davies," says Sir Hugh. Mr. Urquhart is a man of about thirty with
a round face and a reticent manner. Sir Richard is an old, vainglori-
ous fellow covered in lace and brocade, with shoes so tall he teeters on
them. His periwig is shaded a youthful dark brunette, even though his
face and neck are more wrinkled than a basset hound's. "Sir Richard
has come to us for help with plans for his new house on Pall Mall."

"Adjacent to the residences of Sir Philbert Whigby and the Duke of
Albemarle," Sir Richard says, chin rising with conceit.

"It is my pleasure to make both your acquaintances, I'm sure"—
actually, Ravenscroft is not sure of this particular pleasure at all—"but
I had rather thought that this would be a private sitting, Sir Hugh." He
indicates the roll of papers under his arm. He has not presented his
designs to the Society yet; anyone could embezzle his plan and call it
his own.

"Of course, Mr. Ravenscroft." Sir Hugh explains for the others. "Sir
Robert tells me that Mr. Ravenscroft has a unique new scheme for the
Fleet. As a philosopher and a member of the Royal Society, he is ever
watchful that his ideas do not fall into a competitor's hands."

"I have heard of this Society," says Sir Richard, his powdered jowls
and turkey's neck wobbling. "You're one of those fellows who weighs
air, and enjoys dropping things from very great heights." He chuckles
and looks to the two others as if he has just said something clever.

"That is the opinion of those who are ignorant," Ravenscroft curtly
informs him. "Experimental philosophy involves the careful study of
nature, for the purpose of comprehending its true laws and processes.
Only in this fashion is it possible to discover the truth. Those who trivi-
alize our work are generally found to have no understanding of it."

Sir Richard's jaw drops. Sir Hugh quickly steps in to heal the breach.
"Mr. Ravenscroft, I can assure you that we have the utmost respect for
your pursuit of philosophy, and that no one here will appropriate for
themselves that which is not theirs. Sir Richard meant nothing by his
banter," he says with a pointed look at his cousin. "Now, if you would

be so kind as to begin your discourse." Sir Hugh and Sir Richard recline in the chamber's two upholstered chairs, and Mr. Urquhart perches on a stool next to a secretary's desk in the corner.

Ravenscroft sets up his easel and attaches his diagrams, unrolling the first of the series and pinning it flat. "Gentlemen, you see before you my rendering of the Fleet Ditch, one of the most unwholesome scars on the face of London. Its very name conjures up pestilence and filth; yet the king has decreed that it be made into a navigable canal. To date, even our finest architects and planners"—he respectfully does not name Mr. Wren—"have not been able to make progress. I have devised a means for clearing the Fleet of its waste and sewage, which will enable the king's desire to be made manifest." He unfurls his second drawing.

At first, as he begins to describe his system of filters, pumps, and barges, he can see that Sir Hugh and the others take little interest in his designs. But he is more than usually articulate this day. His plan for the Fleet is nothing less than a prophetic vision, and elucidations cascade from his tongue with elegance and conviction. After a while he notices with no small degree of satisfaction that his audience is eagerly listening. Even Sir Richard seems to be caught up in his fervor.

"And how would these filters, as you call them, be made secure in the riverbed?" Sir Hugh asks.

Ravenscroft flips through the drawings on his easel. He moves one of the candlesticks closer so they will be able to see the details more easily. The air in the comptroller's chamber is very warm, he thinks, as he tugs at his too-tight cravat and brushes the long locks of his wig away from his shoulders. He turns back to Sir Hugh and points to the relevant area of the diagram. "The filters would be secured in much the same manner as the footings of a bridge, but with additional support extending from the sides, into the riverbank. See here, at Figure D, the cantilever posts are fortified by iron—" He hears a strange crackling noise behind him, a sound like paper being crumpled into a ball. He turns round to look but there is nothing to be seen, only an odd smell of sulfur in the air. His three-person audience utters a collective gasp. Perplexed, he faces them once more, to find an expression of alarm and amusement on Sir Hugh's face, astonishment on the two others.

"Your wig!" Sir Hugh shouts. "It's on fire!"

Ravenscroft's initial reaction is sheer panic, his next self-preservation. He snatches the flaming, smoking hairpiece from his head and throws it on the floor, then tears off his coat and flails at the wig as one might flog a disobedient dog. By this time, now that it's apparent that he's not in any real danger, Sir Hugh, Sir Richard, and even the subdued Mr. Urquhart are hooting with laughter. They double over, unable to speak, making sounds that are better suited to a barnyard than a Whitehall chamber. Ravenscroft extinguishes the fire and waits silently, face reddening, his wispy, pathetic tufts of gray hair only partially concealing his naked scalp. The three men catch their breath, and for a moment it appears that his humiliation is at an end. Then Sir Hugh looks at him once more and roars. The two others quickly follow his lead.

At long last, Sir Hugh wipes tears from his eyes and rises from his chair. "Good show, Mr. Ravenscroft. I do not believe I have ever laughed so hard without so much as one drop of drink."

"But what do you think of my plan for the Fleet?"

"I believe Mr. Wren has it well in hand already. Surely you do not need to trouble yourself."

Trouble? "But it is no trouble. Indeed, it is what I most desire. It could be the pinnacle of my life's work. My destiny, if you will."

"The Fleet Ditch? Your destiny?" Sir Hugh's face appears to be locked in an odd grimace, as if he is holding back another flood of mirthful tears.

Ravenscroft searches the architect's face for some evidence of his empathy, if not for himself then for his intended plan, but he finds none. Could it be that Sir Hugh has completely missed the point of his discourse? Surely the comptroller is not going to reject a rebuilding scheme so worthy of implementation. Ravenscroft cannot resist one last attempt. "Do you not think the king will be interested in my invention?"

"I cannot say, Mr. Ravenscroft. But perhaps," Sir Hugh says as he turns to the two others, his eyes shining, "you should inquire if he is in need of a new jester. I've heard that Mr. Killigrew no longer suits."

The three men hoot and haw and hold their sides. Ravenscroft pulls on his battered coat, places his stinking wig back upon his head, and rolls up his drawings. "Good day, gentlemen," he says as he departs, but they do not hear him, they are too busy laughing.

It is over, he decides. All of it. The trials and the experiments and the days and months and years of conscientious study. If he can accomplish no more than being made sport of by ignorant asses, he wants nothing more to do with philosophy. He trudges through the palace with his chin on his chest, taking little notice of where he goes or what he passes. After he walks through the main gate and out onto Whitehall Street he stops, overcome with fatigue and bewilderment. Where is he and where is he going? Home, he supposes, but why? What point is there in continuing to tread upon the path of his life? It has only led him here, to his mortification and disgrace.

Not far from the gate he eases himself down to the ground, propping his back against the palace's exterior stone wall, not caring that his best coat and breeches will be stained with mud. His mind is occupied with something much more important than his attire: what to do with the remainder of his life. Perhaps it's time for something new. He could take a wife; but even in the depths of his despair Ravenscroft is cognizant of how little chance he has of a wife taking him. He could spend the rest of his days traveling in foreign countries. Or drinking in taverns. Better yet, he could spend the rest of his days drinking in foreign taverns. Or he could simply throw himself in the Fleet and be done with it.

"Am I addressing Mr. Ravenscroft?"

He looks up to see one of the King's Guards staring down at him. "What do you want?" he asks crossly.

"I am instructed to bring you back to court, sir."

Ravenscroft snorts. "Surely you jest."

"Not at all, sir." The guard is so young that he hasn't got a beard. A flicker of worry passes over his countenance: he hadn't expected any difficulty.

"I won't go." Sir Hugh can find another philosopher to humiliate.

The guard nervously shifts his weight from foot to foot. "But you must."

"Says who?"

"I don't know, sir. I only know of my orders. You must come with me, or—or I'll have to summon my captain."

Damn, he would swear that he saw the boy's chin quivering. "Odd's Fish, you aren't going to start blubbering, are you?" Ravenscroft stands up and makes a halfhearted attempt to brush himself off. He realizes the instant his hand sweeps across his backside that he has sat in something more elemental than mud, probably horse manure. He sniffs his hand—definitely horse manure—then wipes it on the front of his breeches. Well, Sir Hugh would have to take him as he is.

"Get a grip, son," he says to the sniveling guard, then motions for him to lead on. He follows the boy back through the gate, back through the crowds in the palace courtyard, back through the covered gallery, then along the stone gallery, past the questioning eyes of envious courtiers, who watch as Ravenscroft is whisked past the curtains at the end of the hall. The guard leads him through a luxurious bedchamber and into a small room full of clocks. There are scores of them, too many to take in all at once, timepieces mounted on the walls, displayed in glass cabinets, or simply set out on top of tables. They make a fantastic noise, each one ticking, tocking, chiming, or clicking: a room full of mechanical birds and insects.

In the center of this cacophony stands King Charles himself. He is a magnificent figure, so tall that Ravenscroft comes up no higher than the middle of his chest. He is the most extravagantly dressed person the philosopher has ever seen, sporting a glossy black wig that reaches to his waist, a jacket of lush scarlet brocade embroidered with gold, cascades of lace at his throat and wrists. His scarlet velvet shoes are adorned with gold bows; gold garters studded with jewels encircle the white silk stockings that sheath his well-defined legs. Strangely, though, the king does not appear foppish at all, but assuredly regal.

Ravenscroft falls to one knee. As he crouches down, he catches a whiff of his own fug: scorched wool, burnt hair, horse shit. How can his luck be so poor, that he should appear in this filthy undone state before the king? Panicking, he drops everything he carries under his arm; the easel clatters on the floor and the drawings roll away from him as if possessed by a spirit. The king approaches, holding out his hand. Ravenscroft has never kissed the hand of a monarch before and is momentarily flummoxed: should he place his lips on the back of the hand or on the fingers? The royal fingers sport two capacious gold rings, one set with sapphires and one set with rubies. The back of the hand is lightly covered by a growth of black hairs. Before he can decide the hand is withdrawn. The king clears his throat and steps back a few paces. From the royal sleeve a scented handkerchief is extracted and briefly held to the royal, obviously affronted, nose.

"Mr. Ravenscroft," the king begins, in a voice sonorous and rich. "Perhaps you will be so good as to show me what you have just shown Sir Hugh." He points across the room. "From over there, if you will."

Chapter Twenty-seven

HE HAS NEVER been squeamish, but Edward Strathern does not like to be stared at by the cadavers he dissects. It makes the process much too personal and intimate, as if the body could suddenly become animate again. He cannot explain why something he knows to be impossible should trouble him, but this queasy fear seems to be securely lodged in the human psyche. Doesn't everyone prefer the eyes of a corpse closed? Once the spirit is gone, one imagines that only something evil could make it return.

He places his fingertip on one of Sir Henry's open eyelids, but it won't budge. Even when a person dies with their eyes closed, rigor mortis can tense the muscles of the eye socket and force the eyelids open again. Unfortunately neither the watchman nor the guards who handled Sir Henry's body thought to close his lids and put coins on them to keep them shut. If Edward exerts too much pressure now he'll tear the skin, and he has been instructed to make Sir Henry more presentable for his surviving relations, not less. It won't be easy: at present he is not looking well.

"Rigor of the facial muscles is well established," he says loudly for the benefit of Mr. Billings, the ancient amanuensis the college has pro-

vided for him. He sits perched at a small escritoire set up on the operatory floor, laboriously penning a wavering script with a palsied hand.
The anatomy theater at the College of Physicians is modeled after the
one at the University of Leyden but, being new, has incorporated some
welcome innovations: a skylight directly above the operating floor and
a dissection table on wheels so that cadavers can be easily rolled in and
out. Otherwise, Strathern could almost forget whether he is in London
or Leyden, the interiors are so similar, with spectator galleries on each
side and low-hanging chandeliers that provide additional light. This
will be his first postmortem performed in relative peace and silence,
without a group of students crowding him and peering over his shoulder. His only other companion this day is his assistant, a newly licensed
young doctor named Gordon Hamish, who stands on the opposite side
of the dissection table upon which lies Sir Henry's brutalized but still
clothed body. Like Edward, he does not wear a wig—it gets too much
in the way—and Hamish's thatch of red-gold hair appears like a halo
when seen against the candlelight. His pale, light-lashed eyes are the
only feature visible on his face, as his cravat covers his nose and mouth.
Hamish is new to dissections and not yet accustomed to the smell of
cadavers. Strathern does not find this corpse particularly noisome, as
Sir Henry has not been dead long and the cold night air has slowed
the process of putrefaction. Despite the young doctor's sensitivity,
Strathern considers himself fortunate in his choice of aide: Hamish's
quick mind and eagerness to learn compensate for his lack of experience. Not to mention that none of the other physicians at the College
wanted the position.

"There is a deep cut through the trachea which has produced some
blood but which does not appear to have severed any arteries," Edward
says, continuing his external examination. Sir Henry's cravat saved him
from worse injury. His waistcoat, however, did nothing to protect him.
The silk vest is ripped in a half dozen places and soaked with blood.
"There are a number of wounds to the chest and abdomen." He unbut-
tons what's left of the waistcoat and opens it, revealing the torn and
bloodied shirt beneath. Dr. Hamish hands him a pair of scissors, and
he splits the shirt up the middle. Five deep gashes, one in the lower left

breast that Strathern suspects pierced the heart, and a diagonal laceration to the abdomen of at least seven inches crisscross the torso in a ghastly pattern of dried, rust-colored blood, purple hematomata, gray integument.

Hamish mumbles through his cravat.

Strathern frowns. "I can't understand a word you're saying."

Hamish tugs his scarf down. "It looks like someone went mad," he says, breathing carefully through his mouth. "It isn't necessary to cut someone up like this just to kill him, is it?"

"No."

"Should I write that down?" the secretary asks.

"No." Edward lowers his voice. "Any one of these injuries might have killed him—if not right away, then soon enough."

"But with only one, he might have lived long enough to tell someone who did it."

"That's true."

Strathern lifts Sir Henry's arm off the table. It doesn't go far. "Mr. Billings, if you will please record: state of rigor mortis is extreme, indicating the time of death is likely to be between twelve and fifteen hours ago." He sets the arm down again. "According to people who saw him last, Sir Henry was still alive at eleven last night, which would put his death at some time between eleven and one of the clock."

"Rigor mortis won't wear off for another twelve hours or more. How're we going to get all his clothes off while he's so stiff?"

"We'll have to cut them off." Edward takes up the scissors again and begins cutting along a jacket sleeve while Hamish removes one of Sir Henry's gloves. "Good God," Hamish says. He holds up a bloodied hand. "Look at this."

The outside three fingers of the right hand have been cut off at the base, just above the metacarpal bones. Edward removes the other glove. The left hand is intact.

"The watchman who discovered the body this morning said that no purse or coin was found on him," Edward says. "Maybe the person—or people—who killed him stole his rings too."

"By cutting off his fingers?"

"It may have been easier than taking the rings off."

Edward strips off the layers of jacket, coat, and vest, uncovering the left half of Sir Henry's torso. Hamish cuts off the garments on the other side. On Sir Henry's right breast, just below the clavicle, the killer—Strathern can only assume it is the killer—has used the point of his knife to carve symbols deep into the flesh: a kind of curved Y, an X inside a square, and a cross.

"Mother of Christ," Hamish swears softly. "What is that?"

The work of a madman, Edward thinks, but he doesn't say it aloud. He shakes his head. "I don't know."

The news crier stands on the corner of King's Street waving a sheaf of crudely printed paper. "Murder in St. James's!" he shouts. "Murder in St. James's Park!"

Moll Harris pushes her way into the crowd and swaps a halfpenny for a handbill. The news crier's gaze lingers briefly on the plum-colored crescent under her eye before quickly moving on to the others eager to press money into his palm. She walks quickly as she reads:

"Heinous Murder Comitt'd in St. James's Park: Under cover of Night this 12th of November an unknown Assailant viciously Attack'd Sir Henry Reynolds and left him for Dead; by which means he did Die; of Wounds so Grievous that his Body was near Decapitat'd; and his Arms and Legs nearly cut Asunder. His Majesty Charles the 2nd calls out his Guard to hunt down the Villain."

Moll crushes the paper in her hand and lets it fall to the ground. Only the murder of a gentleman would cause such a fuss. Londoners meet with unnatural deaths all the time, but for the most part the law can't be bothered to raise a hue and cry for any of them. Especially if they are poor, and especially if they are women. She thinks of a girl she knew named Beth, who once dwelled, as Moll did, in the dark courts and alleys around Maiden Lane. Beth disappeared a few months ago. Like Moll, she'd eked out a living picking pockets and practicing the art of "buttock and twang": picking up a mark in a tavern and luring him into a back alley, where her lover or pimp—in Moll's case, the foul-tempered Seamus Murphy—knocked him down and took whatever was worth stealing. Beth disappeared, and nobody even bothered to look for her. Her shiftless, maggoty-headed husband said she'd run off, but Moll didn't believe him for a second; she'd lay a bet that Beth was pushing up flowers in an unmarked mound in one of the fields around London.

That's what will happen to Moll too if she doesn't escape now. At last she's got money enough, and God knows she's got reason enough: the bruises that everyone can see are nothing compared to the ones hidden under her clothes. Of course, if Seamus discovers that she's gone off with the spoils from last night, her life won't be worth a farthing. But by her estimations he won't recover from his drunken binge for at least another few hours, by which time she'll be gone from this godforsaken city.

She makes her way through the maze of market stalls, heading toward Russell Street on the east end. In sight are no less than six of the King's Horse Guards. Do they imagine that the "villain" will march up to them and give himself up? The thought provokes a bitter laugh. They'll never find the man who done it, never.

A muscular hand grabs her upper arm and twists it painfully. "Just where did you think you were going?" Seamus snarls.

The odor of beer on his breath is so strong that Moll can taste it. "Let me go." She thought he was still out cold when she tiptoed from the room.

"Do you know what the law will do to a woman that deserts her husband and robs him blind? It'll be Newgate for you, without nothing to look forward to but the gallows."

"You're not my husband."

"I am if I say I am."

"Let me go!" This time Moll says it loud enough to turn a few heads.

"First you'll give me that purse."

He grabs her hand, pulling one of her fingers back, hard. She yelps with pain. "Give me the purse," he threatens.

"Stop it." Her finger feels like it's about to break. "I'll give it to you, but you've got to give your word not to hurt me."

The coarse barking sound that issues from his mouth is what Seamus would call a laugh. "You'll get what's coming to you, you will," he says. His free hand grapples at her waist, reaching into the placket between her outer skirt and petticoats to take hold of the richly endowed purse they'd lucked into last night while prowling St. James's Park. Sir Henry Reynolds's purse, Moll knows now. Seamus puts it safely into his own breeches and lets her go, regarding her with an expression she knows too well, one of domination and disgust.

He'll kill her this time, Moll is sure of it. Maybe not today, maybe not tomorrow, but soon. There won't be any handbills about her death, no King's Guards looking for her killer, no justice. Seamus will tell people she's run off, and they'll believe him, because if they don't he'll beat them black and blue. And soon they'll stop asking.

There's only one way out of her predicament. "Help!" Moll screams. "Guards! Over here! This is the man who killed that gent!"

Two of the Horse Guards turn swiftly, urging their mounts toward Moll and Seamus, and call out to the other guards in the square.

"You bitch," Seamus spits.

"There isn't a word nasty enough for what you are," she sneers back. "Over here!" she yells again. At last, she'll be free of him. "This here's the man you want—the man who killed Sir Henry Reynolds!"

Chapter Twenty-eight

To the Rue de Varenne, Paris

Tho' I can think of few, if any, reasons for you to return to your native soil, should you ever step foot on these Shores again I must recommend that you take in the unique spectacle that is an English hanging.

The hordes at Tyburn are near-frenzied with Bloodlust. Not only men but women resort to Blows and Hair-tearing for the best views of the Gallows and to better witness the death of a known Outlaw. The only seats worth having (where your own Neck will not be broken in a scuffle, or your pocket picked by Thieves so impudent they steal even under the gibbet) are those in the spectator stands built by the enterprising Villagers of Tyburn: very dear but well worth it.

From here I have a clear vista of the triangular Scaffold—commonly called the Triple Tree, or the Three-legged Mare, or the Deadly Nevergreen—and the Tyburn road leading back toward London, lined with the sorts that always come out for Occasions such as this: apprentices, laborers, lay-abouts, and riffraff.

Only one neck is destined for the Noose today. In the past week Seamus Murphy's infamy has spread faster than a Pestilence, and so his Execution has drawn a sizable crowd. Not the tens of thousands *one might see on a public hanging day, when as many as twenty-four luckless Souls are strung up, but impressive nonetheless. Murphy's crime quickly escalated from Murder to Barbarianism of the most heinous kind, fueled by the sorts of lurid Fantasies that sell broadsheets. Rumors say that he not only dismembered Sir Henry's body and scattered it all about St. James's Park, but that he feasted on the pieces as well. It's all bitter lies and Falsehoods, of course, grisly tales to titillate the rabble.*

The crowd parts and the Procession comes into view. The condemned Man arrives at Tyburn according to tradition, sitting upon his own black-shrouded Coffin in the back of an open Ox-cart. In the cart with him are the prison Chaplain, the Hangman, and a few Guards. On horse-back ahead of the cart rides the City Marshal, accompanied by the Under-sheriff and a group of Guards and Constables armed with Staves, to protect the cortege on its slow two-mile journey from Newgate. Those Criminals that the people favor are pelted along the way with Roses and ribbons, and cheered by wanton Women leaning from balconies, but those that are despised get another Treatment altogether: no doubt Seamus Murphy has been bombarded with stinking Refuse and dead Cats. The retinue stops first at St. Sepulchre, where the Clergyman rings a bell and gives the condemned a Posie and a cup of wine. Then the cart lingers at tavern after tavern, where the Prisoner, the Constables, and the Guards—except for those who ride on the Wagon, who are not allowed to drink—knock back countless glasses of liquid Courage.

The Constables push the throng away from the Gallows and the cart is driven right underneath. The Chaplain—well-fed and earnestly pious, by the look of him—stands and calls for quiet. Remarkably, the people listen, but then this is the Play-act they have been waiting for.

"Good people of London! Behold the sinner Seamus Murphy, murderer of Sir Henry Reynolds! Now sentenced to be hanged by the neck until he dies. Stand, sinner!"

Murphy struggles to his feet, hindered by his bound Wrists and a snout full of hard liquor. He is a Brute indeed, with a neck as thick as his Head and a heavy Brow shading malevolent eyes. Even now, only minutes away from his own Demise, he appears eager for a brawl. A few rotten vegetables arc out of the crowd and splatter against the wagon. Murphy bellows with rage.

"Good people, desist!" the Chaplain shouts. "You will have your justice!" He holds up his Bible like a beacon and as the crowd calms down he turns to Murphy. "You that are condemned to die, repent with lamentable tears, and ask mercy of the Lord for the salvation of your soul."

The Chaplain moves aside so the Executioner can come forward with his Rope, but the Hangman is as drunk as his Victim, and he mistakenly slips the Noose over the head of the Chaplain. The crowd erupts in jeers, cheers, and shouts. The Chaplain turns in red-faced fury to berate the Hangman, who with a sloppy grin puts the rope around the Neck where it rightly belongs.

There's a moment of hushed expectation as everyone waits for Murphy to begin his last dying Speech. If he knows what's good for him he won't disappoint, and will give them the Show they long for: insouciant Bravado in the face of death and a sorrowful and complete Confession. Otherwise no one will do him the kindness of pulling his Legs and putting him out of his Misery, but will let him choke and swing for what will seem—to him, at any rate— an Eternity.

At first he refuses to Speak: he breathes heavily, like a Runner in a race, and licks his Lips, and uses all other sorts of means to Delay. The Chaplain thumps Murphy's head with the Bible and calls him a scurvy Dog. This encouragement is what finally makes him speak.

"I lived an evil life," he says, glaring at the Chaplain, who nods sagely for him to continue. No doubt they have rehearsed this Speech, for the Chaplain makes a mint selling the printed chapbooks of the Confessions and Last Dying Words of Newgate's condemned. "I never did nothing that was any good. I took what I wanted and spent it on drink. I cheated and robbed, and once I beat a man so

hard he died." Murphy glowers at the crowd. "But I ain't supposed to be here today. I did not kill that gent!"

The crowd bellows in reply and surges forward angrily. This is not what they have come for.

"Good people of London!" the Chaplain shouts, this time to no avail. He motions to the Hangman to get on with his job; the people will wait no longer. He is clearly disappointed by Murphy's lack of eloquence. The Hangman throws the rope over the Gallows, hoisting Murphy into the air, and secures the Rope around the beam. Murphy's body flails and jerks about like a fish on a hook, his legs kicking at the empty air. At the sudden Shock of seeing him rise from the Wagon the crowd pulls back, almost as if they were one giant Body all attached, and Silence ripples through them like a breaking wave.

"It's only a kick, man!" some wiseacre yells.

"A wry neck with wet breeches!" This comment provokes a dark Laughter, and the Crowd is better contented. For the next twenty minutes or so they will watch him Die—a slow, asphyxiating Death—and the people will be Satisfied. They are too Ignorant to know that Murphy is not God's avenging angel, he would never have been entrusted with the Task I hold dear. A task that continues to consume my mind, my soul, my life.

Letum non omnia finit.

Chapter Twenty-nine

Fourth week of Michaelmas term

"BOTH OF YOU, but especially you, Hoddy, should know better," Andrew Kent said angrily. "What the hell did you think you would do in here, anyway?" They stood in the main room of Derek Goodman's set. When Hoddy and Claire had seen who had come in the door, they'd emerged from the bedroom to greet him, even though they'd both known they'd get a dressing down.

"We're looking for the diary Claire discovered. It's all my fault, Andy. I'm the one who suggested coming here."

"Why aren't you looking for it in the Wren Library?"

"We did," Claire said. "It not there."

"And what are you doing here?" Hoddy asked Andrew.

Andrew took a folded sheet of paper from his inside jacket pocket. Claire saw that it was the same one that Portia had given him the day before: a photocopy of the diary page with Derek Goodman's handwriting at the bottom. "I'm looking for the diary too."

"Why didn't you go to the library?" Hoddy asked.

"I'm familiar with Derek's habits. I rather suspect it's here somewhere. Don't you?"

Claire and Hoddy nodded. "We were just about to look through the boxes of materials near his desk," Claire said.

"We could use some help," Hoddy added.

Andrew reluctantly nodded his agreement. They cleared off the dining room table, then brought in boxes from the office. They placed them on the floor near their feet and began taking things from them and spreading them out on the table.

An odd collection it was, with books, papers, dissertations, and journals all jumbled together. A copy of the *Historical Journal,* 1998, vol. 3. *The Tyburn Hanged.* Minutes of a Royal Society meeting from 1672. *Old and New London.* A drawing for a water pump from around the same time with a letter to the Royal Society from the inventor requesting a patent. A dissertation on the Opium Wars of the early nineteenth century written in the 1930s. *The Cabal,* a book about the five ministers who advised Charles II in the late 1660s to early 1670s, after the ouster of Lord Clarendon. A few reports from the College of Physicians. A dusty copy of the London *Pharmacopoeia.* Robert Hooke's *Micrographia.* Claire tried to arrange them in some sort of order, wondering what could possibly connect all these incongruent materials together. Andrew and Hoddy, busy at the same task, didn't seem to have any clearer idea than she did.

A knock sounded on the door and they all looked up, startled and wary. What would the police say if they found them here, going through Derek Goodman's stuff? What would the master say? Strange, but Claire could have sworn she'd seen a guilty look in Andrew's eyes, the same sneaking guilt she felt herself. Was it because it was a little too easy to forget why they were here and simply enjoy the deeply satisfying act of rummaging around in old books and papers? Or was it because there was something immensely pleasurable about the quiet presence of each other's company? Whatever it was, she was not to know, as the person outside knocked more insistently, and Andrew got up to answer the door.

"Dr. Kent." The young man was obviously surprised to see him. He was also obviously a student, dressed in typical garb of sneakers, jeans, and a rumpled corduroy jacket of a dark and indeterminate hue. A bulky neon orange canvas backpack hung from one shoulder.

"Robbie, come in," Andrew said, opening the door wider and stepping aside. "You know Dr. Humphries-Todd. This is Dr. Donovan, a new lecturer who's filling in for Dr. Scott. Dr. Donovan, Robbie Macintosh, one of Dr. Goodman's MPhil students." A graduate student, Claire deciphered, working on his master's degree under Derek Goodman's tutelage.

Robbie entered and looked around uneasily. He looked like he suffered from the usual graduate-student afflictions of too much coffee, not enough sunshine, not enough sleep. "Where's Dr. Goodman?" he asked.

"Dr. Goodman?" Andrew repeated. He exchanged a worried glance with the two others. "Haven't you heard?"

"Heard what?"

"Oh, dear," Hoddy said.

"What's happened?" Robbie asked anxiously.

"I'm sorry to be the one to tell you this, Robbie," Andrew said. "But Dr. Goodman, he . . . had an accident." Andrew shot a meaningful look at the two others: this was the story they were going to stick to for now. "He's dead."

"Dead?" Robbie's head swiveled from Andrew to Hoddy to Claire and back again. "You're joking."

"No, I'm sorry, but I'm not. Dr. Goodman was walking on the Backs, fell, and hit his head. It happened just yesterday morning. Weren't you here?"

"My dad was in the hospital, and I had to go home for a few days. I just got back." He raked his hand through his hair and looked around the room as though lost. "Christ."

"Would you like to sit down?" Andrew asked.

Robbie looked at the untidy room, then at Andrew as though he were crazy. "Where?"

"Take my chair."

Robbie let his pack fall to the floor and slumped into the empty chair across the table from Claire. He swept his hand through his hair again. Claire didn't think he seemed particularly sad; more like he was about to panic and was doing his utmost to keep his feelings under control. But perhaps she wasn't being fair. Wouldn't anyone feel overwhelmed with school starting, a sick dad, a dead supervisor? More than enough stress for one person, certainly.

Andrew leaned against the table next to him. "I'm terribly sorry, Robbie. I know it must be very upsetting to lose your supervisor. You'll be assigned to someone else right away, of course."

Robbie didn't answer, but Claire had the strong impression that he was upset about something more than Derek Goodman's death.

"Tell me something," Andrew asked, "did you always meet him for supervisions here?"

Robbie nodded. "Sure."

"Do you have any idea what he was working on?"

Robbie shrugged. "How would I know?"

"I just thought he might have mentioned why he had so many books in here."

"He was always working on more than one thing at a time." Robbie sighed and seemed to calm down a bit, even offered up a tremulous smile. "The weird thing is, he knew where everything was."

"How so?"

"He had total recall, you know."

"So he told me," Andrew replied dryly. "Many times."

"It was true, though. He used to make a game of it. He'd turn around, close his eyes, ask me to go to a bookshelf or to one of the stacks, pick something at random, and then tell him where I'd found it—say, third bookcase, fourth shelf from the top, and he would tell me what it was. For instance, 'The Letters of Disraeli, published 1939, very poorly edited,' or, 'So-and-so's dissertation from 1953, wrong from top to bottom, he should've been shot.' That sort of thing."

"Very impressive."

"Bloody annoying."

"Do you know anything about a diary from 1672?" Hoddy asked.

Claire saw a gleam of panic in Robbie's eyes. What was he so anxious about? The graduate student scanned the books and documents that covered the tabletop. "What's going on? Are you looking for something?"

"We're looking for this diary," Andrew said. "Did he ever mention it to you? A diary written in code?"

Robbie shrugged. "Once or twice, maybe."

"What did he tell you?"

"Not much. That it was written by a woman doctor who treated the king's mistress for, uh"—he glanced sidelong at Claire—"a malady."

"The mistress of Charles II?"

"Yes."

"Which mistress?"

"He had more than one?"

"Considerably."

Robbie shrugged again. "I don't know."

"Why was Dr. Goodman interested in it?" Claire asked.

"I think he was writing an article on codes and speed writing." He stood up and picked up his pack. "Look, I've really got to go. I'm supposed to meet my girlfriend."

"Hold on a minute." Andrew took a folded piece of paper from his coat pocket—the photocopy of the diary page. He handed it to Robbie. "Do you know what this is about?"

Robbie quickly perused the page, his eyes lingering on his supervisor's scrawled note at the bottom: *I told you so—now PAY UP!* "Isn't this Dr. Goodman's handwriting?"

"Yes."

Robbie shook his head. "Sorry, I haven't a clue." He shifted his backpack nervously. "I've really got to—"

"Is there anything else you can think of?" Andrew pressed him.

Robbie sighed, realizing he wasn't going to get away so easily. "He was kind of secretive about his research. But one night we had a few beers and he told me that the diary was the key to solving a murder."

"Which murder?"

"Let's see . . ." He looked down at the floor, trying to recall. "Osburn? Or Osborne, maybe?"

"Roger Osborne?"

"Yes, that's the one."

Andrew appeared stunned. "Derek Goodman said he was going to solve the murder of Roger Osborne?" he asked with greater insistence.

"I'm pretty sure that's what he said. I didn't have any idea what he was talking about. I don't know much about the Restoration. My thesis is on minorities in eighteenth-century England. Honestly, I just thought he was batty, or drunk."

"Bastard," Andrew said under his breath.

"Excuse me?"

"Never mind. Where's the diary?"

"It's in the Wren Library."

"You sure it's not here?"

"No way. Pilford would never let him take it out." Robbie backed toward the door. "Now, really, if you don't mind, I've got to get going."

After Robbie's exit, Andrew locked the door and resumed his place at the table.

"What was that all about?" Claire asked.

"I spent five years researching the reign of Charles the Second and I was never able to discover the truth."

"About what?" Hoddy asked.

"The murder of Roger Osborne." He could see that Claire and Hoddy required further elucidation. "Osborne was a City merchant who took Cromwell's side against Charles the First, then found it highly convenient to become a Royalist when Charles the Second was restored to the throne. A man not untypical of his time. Osborne loaned money to Charles II and was absolved of his Parliamentarian past. He was present at Charles's reunion with his sister Henriette-Anne at Dover and then at her death in Paris not long after. Some sources state that the princess entrusted him with a secret, and that he worked for the Crown. Others say he was a spy."

"For France?" Claire asked.

"No, for the anti-Royalist faction in England. Some suspected that he never changed his politics, just pretended to. In late 1672, his body was found"—Andrew stood up and looked over the books and papers spread on the table—"in the Fleet Ditch," he concluded with growing enthusiasm. "Look at this: *Springs, Streams & Spas of London,* published 1910; *Old and New London,* an old chestnut from 1881, but with an entire chapter on the Fleet. And here—" He reached down into the box near his feet and brought up another book. "*The Fleet,* published in 1938."

"There are two seventeenth-century maps of London in the bedroom with red stickers on them—," Hoddy began.

"Three near the Fleet," Claire added.

"He was on to something," Andrew said. "How a physician's diary could shed any light on Dover, Henriette-Anne, and Roger Osborne is beyond me, but I'm dying to find out."

"What if Derek Goodman died because he found out?" Claire inquired.

Andrew guffawed. "You think someone killed him because he solved a three-hundred-year-old murder?"

"When you put it like that, it doesn't sound very likely."

"I think not. Academics may be cutthroat, but that's taking it a bit far." Andrew pulled on his jacket.

"Where are you going?" Claire asked.

"To the Pepys Library to see if I can get this letter transcribed right away. Why don't you come with me? You're the one who found the diary, after all."

Claire smiled. "Sure." She turned to Hoddy. "Do you want to come with us?"

"Count me out this time." He held up a book that looked to be about three hundred years old. "'*Advice Given to the Republic of Venice. How they ought to Govern themselves at home and abroad, to have perpetual Dominion,*'" he read from the title. "I've been looking for this for two years. It's a real page-turner. Thank you for the offer, but I think I'll go back to my set and read."

Claire donned her coat. "You're going to have to explain a few things," she told Andrew.

"Like what?"

"Dover and Henriette-Anne, for starters. As you may recall, I've spent the past few years studying Venice."

Chapter Thirty

27 November 1672

LUCY RUSHES INTO the kitchen, her cheeks bright with cold and anticipation. "A letter's come for you, ma'am," she says. Mrs. Wills turns from the stove, and Hester looks up from sorting a basket of rose hips. As Hannah takes the letter, she notices that the maidservant's hands are nearly frozen. The frosty outside air that shrouds her is faintly redolent of tart apples and dried leaves, a fresh breath of winter in the smoky kitchen.

"How long have you been outdoors?"

"Only a few minutes, ma'am—that's all it seemed, anyway." Lucy looks at Hannah and the letter with impatience. "Aren't you going to open it? It's from that gentleman who's been bringing you home in his carriage."

Hannah breaks the seal and turns away to read in privacy.

My dear Mrs. Devlin:

The King has made good on his promise and proposes a dance on Wednesday next. I would be honored to be your escort for the evening. Of course you will want to bring your ladies. Mr. Maitland and Mr. Clarke will be at their service.

I anxiously await your reply.

> *Your most humble and obedient servant,*
> *Ralph Montagu*

Hannah looks up to find all three pairs of eyes fixed on her. "Mr. Montagu tells me that the king is to have a dance," she says calmly. She folds the letter and slips it into her pocket, trying to hide the smile stealing over her lips.

"Is that all he writes?" asks Lucy, perplexed. Even Hester looks intensely concerned with Hannah's answer.

She decides she won't make them suffer long. "In fact," Hannah says, "Mr. Montagu asks if I would like to go. Do you think I should?"

"Of course!" Lucy blurts out. Hester nods her head. Mrs. Wills looks doubtful, but that's to be expected.

"He also asks if the two of you would care to attend."

Lucy gasps and looks at Hester. "Us? At court?"

"Yes, you."

Lucy rushes to Hannah's side, overcome with excitement. "Ma'am, please, you will say yes, won't you? Hester, say something! You do want to go, don't you?"

"Well, Hester?"

Hester looks back at Hannah, round-eyed, a heightened color in her cheeks. "Yes, ma'am, very much, ma'am."

"Then I shall reply that we will be delighted to attend."

Lucy can barely contain her joy. She throws her arms around Hannah, then goes to Hester and takes her by the hands. "We're going to a court dance!" she squeals. "We might even meet the king!"

Hester looks overwhelmed at the thought. "But ma'am," she says solemnly, "we've nothing proper to wear."

Lucy sits down next to Hester. "Oh, no," she cries, suddenly deflated. "I hadn't thought of that."

"It's all right," Hannah reassures them. "Of course you'll need something new. And I can't go to a dance in one of these old work dresses, can I?" She smoothes her ruched skirt over her cotton damask petticoat. "I've been told that gray wool worsted is not the height of fashion this season," she adds in a light, mocking tone. "Why don't you both go over to Mrs. Delacroix's and ask if she can take us for a fitting later."

The girls race from the kitchen in search of cloaks and mittens, and in less than a minute Hannah and Mrs. Wills hear the front door slam.

"I don't think it's wise to take them to court," says Mrs. Wills, slicing an onion with unusual vigor. "It's a wicked place. Meet the king, indeed. Don't you dare let those girls near him."

Hannah smiles. "They'll be perfectly safe, I promise you. It's only for one night. And it's the first time in weeks I've seen Hester look happy."

"It's been even longer since I've seen a smile on your face," Mrs. Wills remarks with a sidelong glance.

"Yes, I know. I'm sorry. I haven't been very good company lately."

"I wasn't complaining, just saying that you work yourself too hard. Taking care of your patients, your mother, the girls, putting food on this table and coal in the grate—it's too much to be both man and mistress of a house."

"But I'm not, really. I have you. I couldn't do it without you."

Without answering, Mrs. Wills continues her assault on the onions.

"Am I doing such a bad job?" Hannah presses.

Mrs. Wills puts the knife down and turns to her. "Don't you think I hear you upstairs in the middle of the night, pacing about and scribbling in your books until all hours? You come down in the morning looking like death."

"I've had trouble sleeping."

"Is that all?"

Hannah sits down at the kitchen table. She sighs and massages her temples. "I have been suffering terrible pains in my head. I suppose I should have told you, but I thought it would go away."

"For how long?"

"For months now. Since Father died."

Mrs. Wills studies her carefully. "Your father had headaches."

Hannah looks up, surprised. She and her father had always been so open with each other. "He never told me."

"He never told anyone. But your mother knew, at least she did back when she was well. She could sense it, I think. She'd make a special de-coction for him. Nettles and willow bark, as I recall."

"Did it help?"

"I don't know. Your father was a stubborn old mule. He'd never admit he felt poorly in the first place. You're just like him."

"Is that so terrible?"

"Hannah . . ." Mrs. Wills regards her with concern. "I've watched you grow up, seen everything you've been through. Life would be easier for you if you married again. Surely enough time has passed. Nathaniel loved you, he wouldn't want you to be alone forever. You're still a young woman."

"Am I?" If only she felt so herself. "I don't know what Nathaniel would have wanted. But I can't discuss this right now, I—I must make ready to go out." She leaves the kitchen with the goodwife's gaze weighing heavily upon her.

French ambassador Colbert de Croissy has an odd habit of examining his fingertips while in conversation, as if he's more intrigued by his perfectly manicured nails than the person with whom he's speaking. A delaying tactic, Montagu reasons, along with a good bit of snobbery. In de Croissy's company one is never allowed to forget that The Most Christian King Louis XIV is the richest and most powerful monarch in Europe, and Charles Stuart little more than a poor country cousin reigning over a backwater court. It's an attitude Montagu would find less galling if it weren't so close to the truth.

"My king has expressed some doubt about the veracity of your claim," de Croissy sniffs. "You must admit, it's hard to believe you don't know the whereabouts of your own courier."

Despite the ambassador's disdain, Montagu knows that de Croissy spends all of his time spying on Charles's court and doing his utmost to bend England's will to French interests. The futility of his work makes it slightly more difficult to dislike him. The two men sit in the ambas-sador's private chambers on high-backed chairs made from ornately carved Spanish wood. Montagu finds them uncomfortable, even in-quisitorial, at least in comparison to the sensual opulence generally exhibited within the French embassy. De Croissy's London mansion is a smaller-scale Louvre, with palatial rooms and galleries that dwarf a man. The ambassador employs a virtual army of domestic servants, footmen, cooks, chambermaids, and coachmen, but the rooms always feel empty—of inhabitants, at any rate. Moving de Croissy's collection of paintings, tapestries, carpets, and furniture from France to England required two ships.

"Did you really think we would fall for such a simpleminded story— missing courier, lost gold?" the ambassador continues. "It sounds more like a brash attempt at extortion." He stares down his long nose in a manner Montagu regards as particularly French. As the brother of Jean-Baptiste Colbert, Louis XIV's financial minister, Colbert de Croissy is about as wealthy and powerful as it's possible to be without being king. He is accustomed to nothing less than the best, from the soles of his shoes—made of the finest leather imported from Italy by his personal cobbler, also imported from Italy—to the Venetian lace at his throat. Everything he wears, drinks, eats, and breathes (a perfumer and a to-bacconist are on his permanent staff) has its expensive origins in some other, finer place. He is the kind of man who complains about the cost of things most people cannot possibly afford, such as how he must host sixty-five people at his table every day, or the high price of gilding a carriage. It's a trait Montagu finds particularly irritating, although if he could himself afford such things he would find it less so. He was eager to take on this chore of extracting funds from the tight-fisted French; when money changes hands, some of it is sure to fall into his own. He only needs to convince de Croissy of His Majesty's need for lucre, and that he is the man meant for the task of transporting it from France.

"On His Majesty's behalf I regret King Louis' misapprehension." Montagu is no longer an ambassador, but the language of diplomacy returns easily to him. "You should know that the relation between our countries is such that we would not invent something so divisive. Roger Osborne is missing, and so is the gold he was carrying. We know not if he absconded with it or if he met with foul play. I can only assure you, as my Lord Arlington assured His Majesty, that everything is being done to discover what is behind this. In the meantime, however—"

"Your king needs money."

"As always."

Colbert leans back, lazily picking up his glass of wine as if he's not certain he's going to drink it; as if it's not a fifteen-year-old burgundy with a heavenly aroma that melts like honey on the tongue. "Why doesn't he reconvene Parliament and ask them for it?"

"Because he is afraid of what they will demand in return—the retraction of the Declaration of Indulgence."

The ambassador swirls the wine in his glass, peering at it as if he can see the future within its rubicund depths. "This godless country seems to enjoy nothing better than persecuting people of the True Faith."

"His Majesty has done what he can to ensure freedom of worship."

"It isn't enough. My king requires more proof of His Majesty's good faith."

"What more can he do? He's passed the Declaration, he's declared war on Holland—"

De Croissy silences him with a skeptical look. "You know very well that he has not fulfilled all of his promises." Even here, away from court, the ambassador dares not speak openly of the agreement, but he won't accept any disingenuousness.

"His Majesty says the time is not right," Montagu says. "English Catholics are too weak in number."

"That will always be true unless he himself takes steps to change it."

"And he will." Montagu seizes the opportunity to steer the conversation in the necessary direction. "He just needs more encouragement. The best way to influence His Majesty," he suggests, "is to influence those closest to him."

"So I've been told for six long years, to the detriment of my purse and my good nature!" The ambassador shifts unhappily in his chair. At last, de Croissy's impassive veneer reveals a few fractures. That they're caused by the king's women doesn't surprise Montagu in the least.

"I've spent thousands—tens of thousands—bribing the king's mistresses and I've little to show for it," the ambassador says testily. "I'm sick of this petticoat diplomacy. Only two weeks ago I gave a jeweled bracelet to the Countess of Castlemaine, and in return she's done nothing but laugh in my face."

"The countess no longer has the king's . . . ear."

"How is one to get anything accomplished here," de Croissy continues, "when your king is incapable of constancy? In France, King Louis has one *maitresse en titre,* and she rules all. It is simple; if one wishes the king to take action on a matter of state, one appeals to either his brother or his mistress—a clear and sensible system of government. After Mademoiselle de Keroualle's recent indisposition, His Majesty is certain to be casting about for someone new. Knowing Charles Stuart, it could be anybody: another actress or a seamstress or some wench who brings him a dish of chocolate. Why should we be expected to deal with women of such low birth?"

"That's exactly why it's so important to continue to support Mademoiselle de Keroualle as head mistress," Montagu says. "She is a lady of quality and His Majesty continues to show her great consideration. Everyone is convinced that he is more in love with her than ever before."

"But she should remember who her friends are! She does not do as King Louis wishes. The mademoiselle will sorely regret ignoring her own king's instruction when Charles loses his regard for her. She will be friendless then."

"I agree, the mademoiselle is not as malleable as we originally thought she would be. She has a great friend in Madame Severin, who sharpened her teeth at the French court and bares them here. As long as she is at the mademoiselle's side, the girl will not be easily managed. But I happen to know of something the mademoiselle desires—something only the French king can give to her."

"And what is that?"

"A tabouret, to enable her to sit in the presence of the French queen."

The ambassador snorts derisively. "For that she'd have to be a countess, not a commoner."

"Exactly."

De Croissy shakes his head. "God save us. I can imagine what the king will say. He has passionate feelings about retaining the purity of the aristocracy."

"Surely the True Faith is worth more than a title or two. And consider this: once she is ennobled, she will have even more influence than before. His Majesty will have more reason to listen when she whispers into his ear the words your king wants him to hear. The mademoiselle still sees herself as Princess Henriette-Anne's maid, and she believes she carries on the princess's good work for the betterment of England and France." Montagu isn't certain this is true; Mademoiselle de Keroualle is disinclined to do anything that doesn't directly benefit her. But it sounds convincing, and Montagu knows that the French ambassador will not approve the transfer of the gold unless he can tell his king that their cause is going forward.

De Croissy sighs. It's almost an admission that Montagu's gained the advantage; all that's left to discuss is how much and when. "So you're to be the new courier?"

Montagu nods. "I have the confidence of Lord Arlington and the king."

"What about Clifford?"

"Sir Thomas? He will be brought around."

The ambassador sets down his glass and looks sourly at Montagu. "Exactly how much is required for His Majesty—and for the others?" he adds with a scowl.

Montagu sips his wine and allows himself a moment of sheer indulgent pleasure. Wine-induced warmth spreads through his limbs, calm clarity descends upon his mind. How much? How much, indeed? As he studies de Croissy's face, the figure rises up, and up, and up.

Chapter Thirty-one

28 November 1672

THE TWO PHILOSOPHERS watch from a lofty vantage point on the Fleet Bridge as workers dig a trench in the muddy riverbank. "So the third of these filters is to be constructed here?" Robert Hooke asks. It sounds more like a criticism than a question.

Ravenscroft nods, biting back his own sharp retort: *As I have already explained more than once.* He has been in the company of the city surveyor all morning, leading him on a tour of the Fleet Ditch building sites, and Mr. Hooke's abrupt manner has vexed him from the first. Some people do not know how to observe the rules of decorum adhered to by men of a certain standing. Hooke makes inquiry after inquiry, most of which appear to have no other purpose than finding fault and disparaging Ravenscroft's project.

Ravenscroft's encounter with the king still lives in his mind as a sort of fantastic dream in which His Majesty stands as tall as a colossus. The king studied Ravenscroft's designs and told him that no other scheme for London had ever pleased him so mightily; on his return in 1660, Charles Stuart said, he could smell the stench of the city two miles off. The philosopher knew then that his life had not been for naught. Everything he had studied, every trial he had made, every previous invention, all had been in preparation for this. The Fleet Ditch project requires money, men, and materials on a scale he has never before imagined, but the king's endorsement and signature are all that is needed to procure everything necessary. Already the lumberyards are cutting and delivering timber and the crews are engaged. There is only one hitch: Mr. Wren and Mr. Hooke must evaluate the project and report their findings to the king.

"The first is just below the Holborn bridge, the next after Fleet Lane. By the time the river reaches the last filter, it will be cleansed of all but the smallest debris: purified all the way from here to Blackfriars."

A bitter gust of wind whips at their coats, transforming their cravats into lace-trimmed sails. Ravenscroft's nemesis makes no reply but continues to look down at the men on the riverbank, his blue, watery eyes inscrutable, his ungenerous lips pressed together so tightly that a knife blade couldn't pry them apart. Hooke is an unprepossessing man, stooped-back and short of stature, with skin the color of congealed porridge except for a patch across his nose and cheeks, where a lacy web of capillaries imparts a perpetual ruddiness that's exacerbated by the cold air. In spite of his humble appearance, however, the man has no deficiency of pride. The way he clasps his hands behind his back and turns his face up to the sky, eyes squinting and head angling this way and that, one would think he stood before an audience who waited rapturously for his erudite revelations; or that he believes that by studying the ominous, low-lying clouds he will be able to determine exactly what will materialize: rain, sleet, or snow. "This is an absurd time of year to begin a building project," he announces.

"The king desires that it be completed with all haste." Ravenscroft cannot help but add, "He expressed some disappointment that the canal project has not yet succeeded—"

"The small difficulties we encountered will be easily overcome when we commence next spring, in a season of agreeable weather, as is sensible."

"Have you suspended all of your building projects, Mr. Hooke?"

"No, of course not."

"Then I see no reason to suspend this one."

Hooke's pale eyes spark with anger. He turns away and paces along the bridge, every few steps peering down into the river. He marches back to Ravenscroft and looks at him levelly. "It won't work," he announces. "I don't believe I've ever set eyes on a more cockamamie scheme, and I am prepared to tell the king exactly that."

He should have realized that Hooke's conceit would never allow anyone to succeed where he had failed. "If you had perused the drawings, sir," Ravenscroft snaps, unable to resist the sarcasm creeping into his address, "you would better understand the mechanics of the plan. It is simple, elegant, and effective, as His Majesty understood at once."

"It goes without saying that the king is the greatest of all men; but there is one thing that he is not, Mr. Ravenscroft, and that is an architect. I have looked at your diagrams, and I tell you that your plan will not work. The structures have not the strength necessary to withstand a flood. Once the winter rains start in earnest, I fear it will be overpowered."

"The Fleet has not flooded in thirty years."

"All the more reason to be concerned. Regardless of the king's support, I remain the city surveyor, and the failure of this endeavor will reflect badly upon me."

Ravenscroft is about to say that he is quite willing to accept responsibility for the failure of his own work, if it comes to that (which it won't), when one of the workmen dashes up to them, pulling his wool cap from his head and making a quick, scraping bow.

"Sorry to intrude, sirs, but we've got a problem," he says, pointing to the riverbank. The men have stopped digging and have gathered around what looks at this distance like a mound of muddy clothes. "A problem for the constable."

"What is it?" Ravenscroft asks.

"A man's body."

"If you're going to retch, do it over there, away from the corpse," Strathern tells Hamish. His assistant reels away from the dissection table and takes two rapid strides to bend over a bucket on the operatory floor.

"Sorry," Hamish says, keeping his head low and resting his hands on his knees until his heaving subsides. Finally he straightens and wipes his face and watering eyes with his cravat. He doesn't look eager to return to the table. "How does one ever get accustomed to the odor?"

"Practice," Edward replies. "Although this one's a challenge, even for me." By his estimate, the body is two weeks old. It's waterlogged, bloated from the internal gasses released after death, and covered with the foul-smelling slime of the Fleet River. Only the clothes make it appear human. The stench is almost indescribable: rotting meat combined with the worst house of office imaginable. "The question is, what do we do first: clean him up, or remove his clothes?"

"I say we take him out back and hose him down." Hamish edges a bit closer, keeping his wrinkled cravat held to his nose.

"Let us see what we can do here first." Strathern takes up a sponge from the water pail at his feet, squeezes out the excess, and begins wiping the mud from the corpse's eyes and cheeks. But before he's cleaned the entire face, he stops and, without being fully conscious of doing so, utters an oath under his breath.

"What's wrong?" Hamish asks.

Strange how, even two weeks gone, swollen and sodden, human faces are still recognizable. Especially this face. The port-wine stain across Osborne's brow is as vivid in death as it was in life. "I know this man," Strathern says.

She left as soon as she was able, Hannah says upon entering the anatomy theatre anteroom, apologizing for her tardiness by explaining that it was not always easy to be excused from the mademoiselle's company.

"I think she's come to believe that having a physician in constant attendance adds to her mystique, rather like keeping an exotic pet," she tells Edward with a wry smile. She bristles with energy, apparently invigorated by the winter weather. "You wrote you had found something intriguing, but you look so serious. Am I too late? Or—" A more disturbing thought occurs to her. "Are women not allowed inside the theatre?"

"I don't know of any such rule, although I don't believe there have been any women here before. In any case, you're quite welcome. Only myself and Dr. Hamish are here today, and at present he is washing up. You are not too late, but I must tell you that I did not reveal everything in my letter. Perhaps you would like to put on a coat before going inside? You may leave your cloak here."

"Thank you." She unties the cord at her throat with a graceful swiftness. He is struck by the agility of her hands, by the way she buttons up the light cotton coat he provides to cover her dress. He has seen those facile, delicate hands carve up a man's leg; a contradiction that occupies his mind so completely he almost forgets to offer her his scented handkerchief as they walk into the theatre. She shakes her head—she's an experienced physician, after all—then the stink of the corpse reaches her, as abruptly as if she'd been doused by a wave of water. Her step falters, and she reaches for his proffered linen square.

"Will you be all right?" he asks. She nods, and they approach the dissection table. He has placed a cloth across the dead man's privy parts, something he would not have done for a male colleague. He isn't sure if he made this gesture out of concern for Mrs. Devlin's modesty or for his own, but feels deeply grateful for his precaution. Her gaze is drawn instantly to the cadaver's chest, punctuated with stab wounds and the three strange markings inscribed in his skin: a trident shape, a backward S, a small circle. She turns her questioning eyes to Strathern.

"His name is Roger Osborne," he answers. "Obviously he was murdered. His body was found in the Fleet Ditch this morning."

"I don't understand. You wrote that you had come across some point of anatomy that might be of interest."

"Please forgive me. I was afraid you would not come if I told you the truth. And I am not ready to put my suspicions in writing."

"What suspicions?"

"A week ago I performed the postmortem on Sir Henry Reynolds. His body suffered wounds very similar to these and had markings like these upon his chest." Strathern plucks a sheet of paper from the unmanned escritoire and gives it to Hannah. She squints at the three symbols copied from Sir Henry's body: a kind of trident shape, an X inside a square, and a cross. "As you see, they're not precisely the same, but they're in the same location on the body." He gingerly lifts one of Osborne's hands. It's as full and round as a glove filled with water—a glove with only three fingers. "Two of Osborne's fingers have been cut off. Sir Henry was missing three."

"Are you saying that the same person killed Sir Henry and this man?"

"Yes."

"But Sir Henry's killer was hanged at Tyburn only two days ago."

"A man was hanged, but I don't believe he murdered Sir Henry. I think the killer is still among us."

"But why are you telling me this? What has it to do with me?"

"Mrs. Devlin, Sir Henry and Roger Osborne were acquainted with each other. As they were with your father. I know this to be true, as I saw them all together in Paris, only two summers ago."

A wry flicker of incomprehension, almost like a smile, curls the corners of her mouth. "You think that the same man killed my father?"

"I believe it's possible, yes."

It takes a moment for his words to fully take hold. When they do, she begins breathing rapidly, obviously distressed. She presses the handkerchief to her face. "May we?" she asks, looking toward the door.

"Of course," Edward replies, inwardly cursing himself for his insensitivity. "Please, let us leave here." He helps Mrs. Devlin to a seat in the anteroom and sits down beside her. "I know this is difficult to discuss, but I need to discover, before I tell anyone of my suspicions, if your father was harmed in a similar manner."

"I cannot say. His body was prepared for burial by the sexton of our church. I could not bring myself to do it."

"I'm sorry, of course you couldn't. But the sexton never mentioned anything unusual?"

"No, but then I never asked. The cause of his death was obvious— he'd been stabbed."

"In the chest?"

"Yes."

"Is it true he was killed in the area around Fleet Lane?"

"Yes. He had gone that evening to visit a patient, a charity case.

Apparently he was on his way home when he was attacked. He was found early the next morning by the watchman, who, with the constable, brought him home. They told us that my father had been robbed, but even after many inquiries we could find no one who witnessed the crime. More than that we were unable to discover."

"Did your father ever tell you why he left court?"

"Not precisely, no. I believe he had a falling out with Lord Arlington."

"Whose good graces are the only thing that stands between you and jail?"

She looks at him sharply. "How do you know that?"

"Sir Granville is possibly the worst physician of all time, but he is keenly attuned to the goings-on of the court. He hears things, and he usually"—Strathern allows himself a bemused smile—"repeats what he hears. Frankly, it isn't so difficult to deduce. You're a woman openly practicing physick."

"An abomination, some say."

"I am not one of them." He leans closer. "Mrs. Devlin, I don't believe your father's murder was a random event. There is something more here than meets the eye. Something that may involve Lord Arlington."

"How so?"

"He was also acquainted with each of these men."

"How can you be certain of that?"

"He was also in Paris." He takes a breath. "Mrs. Devlin, perhaps you and I should come forward—" Edward knows instantly that he has said something wrong, for he can feel Hannah recoil.

"You want me to say that Lord Arlington had a hand in my father's murder? I would be in jail before I had spoken two words."

"I'm not asking you to implicate him in anything. Indeed, I do not know in what way he is involved, but I would ask you to come forward with me to reveal what we know."

"What we know? I know nothing of this, nor do I especially want to, and it seems to me that you know very little indeed. This," she says as she nods in the direction of the theatre, "could be a bizarre coincidence or the work of a madman. You have no proof that my father was in any way connected. Besides, just who would we come forward to?"

Even before he says it, he suspects his answer is going to be incorrect, feeble, futile, but it's the only answer he's got. "The king?"

"I don't believe that would do your cause much good."

"You have so little confidence in him?"

Her silence is all the answer he needs. "Very well, then," he says, frustrated. "But surely you want to find out who killed your father. By gathering what information we can, you have only to gain—"

"I have much to lose," she says. "Do you imagine that I enjoy being one of Arlington's minions, attending to a spoiled girl instead of caring for people who truly need me? I can only hope that when I am no longer required at court I will be allowed to resume my old life. The College of Physicians turned a blind eye toward me as long as I treated patients they cared nothing about. But now that I have been brought so much to their attention—"

Strathern winces. His own uncle is partly to blame.

"—I fear I will never be allowed to practice again."

"But surely you have other things in your life—a husband, children?"

"I have neither. Only my mother is left." She looks at him cautiously. "But even if I had a family of my own, I would still want to practice physick, just as you yourself would wish to continue, with family or without. Do you understand?"

If another woman had told him this, he would have thought her brash and immodest. From Mrs. Devlin it seems wholly natural. "Yes, I think I do."

"If I tell you something I have never told anyone before, will you keep my confidence?"

"Of course."

She casts her eyes to the floor. Mrs. Devlin seems to him the sort of person who is seldom at a loss for words, but it appears that she does not know how to begin. "I must go back a while to fully explain," she says at last. "I met my husband Nathaniel when he came to London to study medicine with my father. I was seventeen and he was twenty-two. We studied and practiced physick together, and became very close. I can't say it was a grand romance, but we were very good friends. We had similar goals, and I believed he would be a good husband to me; and so he was.

"We had been married only a year when he was stricken with small-pox. Despite the best efforts of myself and my father, we could not save him. Soon after he died I found I was with child and, in due time, I gave birth to a girl. I named her Sarah. She was a sweet, plump, happy child, and I doted on her; maybe all the more so since her father was gone. Then she fell ill with pleurisy and a fever. There isn't even a name for what she had, it was no more than a contagious fever that afflicted many people that spring. She was not yet ten months old.

"After Sarah died I was overcome by a great melancholy. Even though I knew that many others had suffered similar, or even greater, losses than my own—it was not that long since the Plague, after all—knowing this made no difference. The melancholy took over my life, and the pain of it was so great it was unbearable. I did not know how to rid myself of it, so one evening I walked to the river.

"I thought I would throw myself in. I could not think of any other way to end my agony. I decided to wait until nightfall, so that no one might see and stop me. I lay down upon the riverbank, waiting for night, and was overcome with grief. Once I'd started sobbing I could not stop. I cried for what seemed like hours. When I finally stopped it was dark, and the sky had cleared and was full of stars. By then I had cried for so long, I had forgotten what I was crying about. I believe I even forgot who I was—if you had asked me my name I could not have told you.

"As I looked up at the star-studded sky I felt it was the most beau-tiful thing I had ever seen. I almost began weeping again—not from sorrow but because of the immensity and beauty and presence of God. And I prayed as I have never prayed before or since, that I might know the right thing to do."

Hannah stops and looks at her hands, carefully folded in her lap, then into his face. Behind the calm sepia of her eyes he senses turmoil.

"I don't know exactly how to describe what happened next except to say that my prayers were answered. I heard a heavenly voice, a voice

I believed was that of an angel. She said that life was too precious to cast away; that even the foulest and meanest expression of life was precious, full of grandeur and inestimable beauty, although we are often too blind to recognize it. I asked this angel, 'Why do we suffer so?' and she told me, 'All souls must suffer in order to learn compassion.'

"When she said this I understood that compassion was the most profound and powerful thing in all the heavens, greater than any love I might feel for another person, even my parents or my husband, even greater than the love I felt for my own child. I asked her what I must do and she said that I must ease the suffering of others. She offered me many words of kindness, and love; and put me at ease, and promised to stay with me as long as I needed her. I lay on the riverbank for a long time, as if in a trance, listening to her. Finally, just before dawn, I thanked her and got up and went home."

She steals a quick glance at him, checking, he thinks, for signs of incredulity. He purposefully keeps his expression neutral, and nods for her to continue.

"You may think that this experience made me feel as if I'd been touched by grace, but it did not. For many days afterward it frightened me to think of it. I believed that I had suffered a kind of lunacy. But a few weeks went by, and a few more, and gradually I found that the recollection of that night gave me comfort. I tried to follow the angel's advice. I devoted myself to my patients, and in this I found some degree of happiness.

"Then my father was murdered. For all your conjecture, Dr. Strathern, I believe it was for no other reason than the few coins he had in his pocket. I have struggled since then to keep my faith in goodness and decency, even at times when there is very little to support that faith. It's only by practicing physick that I find any measure of peace and purpose. If I lose that, I will lose everything, perhaps even my life."

Hannah abruptly finishes her story, the need and urgency suddenly gone. Her tale has left Edward deeply troubled, in his soul and in his mind, in a way he did not expect, could not have expected. He knows that she wants him to say something, is almost daring him to as she removes the cotton coat, dons her cloak, and turns toward the door.

But he can think of nothing that would not be an admission of his feelings.

He is thoroughly and overwhelmingly lost, overcome by a passion so profound that he is afraid to speak, even though he fears she will interpret this the wrong way: as disbelief, perhaps, or disinterest. Nothing could be further from the truth. He is intensely aware of her as he has never been aware of anyone else, aware of her as a unique living creature: aware of her heart drumming, aware of the sibilant blood coursing through her body, aware of the heat of her fingertips and the sweet musk of her skin, the moistness of her mouth and her other secret places. He feels a violent longing to be enveloped in the aliveness of her, the humming thrumming breathing aliveness of her. He calms his fervent feelings by reminding himself that he is a man of the world, he is no newcomer to love. He has known other women, some of them intimately. He has known other women, he repeats sternly. Yes, he has known other women; but now he cannot remember wanting them.

Chapter Thirty-two

5 December 1672

MONTAGU EXPERTLY LEADS Hannah through the steps of the coranto. It's been ages since she's danced, and she's pleased to discover it comes back to her easily. In her new gown, a rich claret-colored velvet with a daring décolletage, movement seems effortless. Under the influence of the music and the sumptuous ambiance of the Great Hall, she feels more carefree than she has in years.

The king's promised fete does not disappoint. Whitehall's Great Hall is as festive as a gift wrapped in ribbon, draped with gold fabric and garlanded with holly. Crystal chandeliers and rows of sconces are illuminated by hundreds of beeswax candles, their honeyed aroma sweetly thickening the air.

"You are extraordinarily handsome tonight, Mrs. Devlin," Montagu says. "I don't believe I've ever seen you so radiant."

Montagu is looking especially fine himself in a new navy silk jacket worked with silver thread, velvet breeches in the same dark blue, and a silver brocade waistcoat. More than any other man she has met at court, he is able to wear such dazzling attire without any loss of masculinity. Tonight he seems especially intent on reminding her of their inherent differences. He cradles her hand in his, warm and dry, and when he holds her waist for the turn his grip lingers, confident and strong but never overbearing. Montagu is a man who knows how to touch a woman.

Hannah discreetly ignores his compliment but returns his smile. "I had forgotten how much I love dancing."

"It's a great shame that you should be allowed to forget. I would never allow it."

"I'm sure I shall not forget being in such elegant company as this."

The courtiers are decked out in their best finery, the men rivaling the women for lavish excess. Hannah has never seen so many jewels before, nor did she know it was possible to display them in so many ways. Not only on fingers, ears, and throats, but stitched onto gowns and gloves, adorning shoes and feathered fans. The courtiers are so unlike the average London denizen that they might as well be another species. They shimmer and glitter and smell of fragrant balsams, and seem to have been generated from a finer, more beautiful world than the one in which she usually lives. In this world, age and unsightliness have been banished.

On the black and white marble checkerboard floor, twenty couples step and turn, glide and swirl. Important members of the court line each side, like ornate chess pieces waiting to be put into play. Queen Catherine sits at the center, surrounded by her ladies, impassively watching. She is a diminutive woman, olive-skinned and thick-browed, her coiffure a nimbus of springy black curls. Though she is short on humor and long on piety, her thrice-daily entreaties to the Virgin have not yet resulted in the blessing of a child. The king seems little troubled by her unfruitfulness, perhaps because even though the queen has not given him an heir, she has, as part of her dowry, given him two million crowns, Bombay, and Tangier.

Montagu notices the source of Hannah's interest and leans closer to whisper into her ear. "The queen looks bored, as if she'd rather be playing cards."

Hannah suppresses a smile; she was thinking much the same thing. "She shows the forbearance of a saint for watching her husband dance with his mistress."

"She has had long practice."

Only four couples away, the king partners Louise. She's still pale from her illness and convalescence, but Hannah has never seen her looking lovelier. Her dress of shimmering gold cloth is topped by a diaphanous fabric covering her arms and shoulders. It sparkles as she moves, as if dozens of tiny mirrors are capturing the light and reflecting it back. "What is it that the mademoiselle wears?"

"The sleeves and bodice of her dress are covered in diamonds," Montagu tells her. "Did you not hear the talk earlier? It is a great scandal. The king's mistress is wearing more diamonds than the queen."

Although Montagu mentions it lightly, Hannah is reminded of the constant undercurrent of tension in the court, the rivalries and factions that never cease. As she turns, she scans the courtiers' painted faces. Beneath the gaiety and the lacquered beauty she can sense the whispers, the rumors, the secrets, the menace. The court is like a pond stocked with sharks without enough food for them to feed upon. Hannah wonders sometimes what they say about her.

But she refuses to let herself be bothered by it tonight; the music, the dance, and her partner's courtesy are too pleasant a diversion. Mr. Montagu is more than usually solicitous this evening. Since the moment he arrived at her house with Mr. Maitland and Mr. Clarke, the girls' escorts, he has been at his most charming, offering his hand or arm as often as possible, and infusing his perfect punctilio with a certain suggestiveness, one that she admits is not entirely unwelcome.

"Every man will envy me my company tonight," he said once she, Lucy, and Hester gathered in the parlor. Although his words included all three of them, he kept his eyes on Hannah, regarding her with such obvious admiration that she felt herself blush. She'd thought herself past the rituals of courtship and romance, yet she is enjoying every second of his attention.

Her eyes sweep up to the balcony, where Lucy and Hester stand in the crush of footmen and ladies' maids watching the dance. She can just make them out by their new gowns. In her blue silk moiré, the fair Lucy is fresh, rosy-cheeked, and lovely as always. Hester is the real surprise, the proverbial swan. Her green velvet dress matches her eyes, and accentuates the pale luster of her skin. What appeared as lankiness in her flannel skirts and apron is transformed into willowy arms, a long neck, sylphlike grace. Hannah would guess they didn't sleep a wink last night in anticipation, but they conceal their excitement well.

She and Montagu clasp hands for the last steps of the dance. "I see your doctor is with us tonight," he remarks.

"My doctor?"

"Strathern, isn't it?"

She looks to the other end of the dance floor, where Dr. Strathern dances with an elegant blonde in a pale gray silk. "So it is. Who is his partner?"

"Arabella Cavendish, to whom he is to be wed. A propitious match, one that caused a great deal of envy in some quarters. Her father owns lumberyards near Deptford."

Hannah steals another glance at the couple, but only a brief one, for she does not want to catch Strathern's eye. She feels uneasy about their encounter at the anatomy theatre last week. What possessed her to tell him that story? He said nothing at the end, nothing at all. He probably thought she was soft in the head, as she in her worst moments feared. The headaches, the melancholy, the sleeplessness—perhaps they were all symptoms of losing her mind.

"Where have you gone, Mrs. Devlin?" Montagu asks, softening his reproof with a subtle smile revealed more in his eyes than on his lips. "One minute I'm dancing with a beautiful woman who looks at me with bright eyes; the next, with a shade who only follows the steps."

"Forgive me."

The dance ends and Montagu pulls her close, wrapping his arm around her as they leave the dance floor. They've barely caught their breath when Lord Arlington appears at Montagu's side, looking the dandy in a gold-trimmed black brocade coat and breeches. "Mrs. Devlin, I see you have at last found some attractions at court."

No doubt his innuendo is meant to embarrass her, but she will not give him the satisfaction. "If only you'd told me of these attractions sooner, Lord Arlington, perhaps I would have come on my own accord."

He responds with a vague harrumphing noise and motions Montagu aside to speak privately. Hannah watches as Montagu's expression takes on the same gravity as Arlington's. Montagu nods solemnly, then turns back to Hannah. "If you'll excuse me, I must attend to a matter that requires my urgent attention. I promise to return as quickly as possible." Montagu bows to her, then disappears into the crowd.

"My apologies, Mrs. Devlin, for depriving you of your gallant." Arlington turns to the dance floor to watch the king, who continues to dance with Louise de Keroualle. "Are you not concerned that the mademoiselle will become overtired? Perhaps you should suggest that she sit the next dance out."

Hannah studies Louise. The mademoiselle has never looked happier. This is her triumph, after all, and her repeated turns on the floor with the king—not to mention her extravagant diamond-studded dress—is a slap in the face to every courtier who believed she would not command the king's heart for long. Nothing short of sudden death is going to make her sit down. "I think she is well enough to do as she pleases."

Arlington nods slowly, accepting her judgment. Perhaps it's his apparent acknowledgement of her superior wisdom that gives her the confidence to begin. "Lord Arlington, now that I have your ear, I should like to ask you—well, now that the mademoiselle's health is improved, I should like to be excused from the court."

"To do what?" The minister is clearly taken aback.

"To resume my former practice, of course." It's an answer that seems to Hannah as obvious as her request.

Arlington snorts with disbelief. "Your practice of physick?"

"Yes."

"That is impossible." He speaks so emphatically that his words feel like a fist against her breastbone. "Now that the College of Physicians is made aware of you, they will never allow you to practice so openly."

"But it was you who brought me to their attention—"

"It could not be avoided."

"A familiar sentiment from ministers who claim that their crooked ends justify any means."

"Do not crack wise with me, Mrs. Devlin." His eyes flash with anger, but only briefly; in fact he seems reluctant to engage in a dispute. It crosses her mind that Arlington might feel something akin to guilt for what he's done to her. Then again, he may possess no finer feelings at all. "What is it you really want?" he asks. "More money?"

"You have already paid me generously. I simply want to return to my former life."

Arlington sighs and looks away.

"I will be arrested, is that it?" Hannah presses him for an answer. "And you'll do nothing to stop it."

"There are too many . . ." Arlington stops, as if remembering he is the secretary of state, she is nobody, and he does not have to explain himself to her. The steeliness she's accustomed to reasserts itself. "I will not stick my neck out for you."

So that's where it stands: once she leaves the court, she'll be on her own, against the College. How long would it be before they brought her up on charges, made an example of her? Two months, one perhaps? Perhaps not even that.

Arlington sighs again and, as if acting against his better judgment, leans closer to speak confidentially. "I may be able to work a solution," he says. "You can't ever be called a court physician, of course, but you could stay on in an unofficial capacity treating courtiers as needed for . . ." His voice grows fainter. "Indispositions of a private nature—"

"Stay on to treat cases of the clap?"

"You would be kept quite busy, I'm sure. And when you are not so occupied, the court ladies are always happy to have new lotions for their face, or potions to help curl their hair, or whiten their teeth . . ."

She tries, with great difficulty, to keep the indignation from her voice. "Is that what you imagine I do, make cosmetics?"

He shrugs. "You are a woman, after all."

A woman, after all. *Something inferior to man* is his implication—

what all men imply when they speak of the "weaker" sex, the "gentler" sex, a woman's "modesty": but it is not really modesty women are rewarded for, it is subservience. It makes no difference that she has spent years learning the art of medicine and could best any man her own age in a test of knowledge and experience; as a woman she is relegated to cosmetic maker. Men may find her useful, but they will never grant her respect, and there is little she can do about it. She cannot even throttle Arlington's throat as a man might, even though it's something that she does, at this moment, sincerely wish to do. But of course that's a fruitless undertaking. Her physical strength is no match for a man's, and Arlington himself is only a symptom of the greater evil that opposes her. She has no choice but to restrain her fury, but all that remains is the numb sensation of despair. "Thank you, Lord Arlington." Her voice rings hollow. "This has been most instructive." She curtsies and turns away, pushing past the courtiers who crowd the Great Hall, angrily brushing at the sudden tears that wet her cheeks.

In the gallery, she accepts a tumbler of wine from one of the servers and looks for a quiet place to collect herself. She should check on Lucy and Hester, but she is in no mood to make idle discourse with Mr. Maitland and Mr. Clarke. She finds a spot in an empty corner, not too brightly lit, where she can dab at her wet eyes and sip some wine to steady her nerves. Why, she wonders, does she have such a deep need to prove herself? Why is she not content with the things most women are contented with? Is something fundamentally wrong with her? As she leans back against the wall—the only seats provided at a function like this are near the dance floor, and reserved for the nobility—her head begins to throb. She knows the signs too well: the initial ache, the burning discomfort, the inevitable pain.

She sets the tumbler on a long, narrow table and retrieves a vial of laudanum from her purse. She will be in agony if she allows the headache to continue, and the anodyne effects of opium work best before the pain is at its worst. Only a few drops, she reasons. She turns her back to the room, unscrews the stopper from the bottle, and extracts the tiny glass wand. The bitter liquid on her tongue is an instant comfort, and she allows herself to savor its acrid taste.

"Mrs. Devlin." The voice behind Hannah startles her, and she hastily attaches the top to the vial and stows it away. She turns to face Madame Severin's nearly perfect yet eerily flawed visage. Dressed in her customary layers of black, tonight she has dispensed with the hood and has laced her upswept white-blond hair with pearls. Her feline eyes study Hannah with their usual cool detachment. Hannah wonders how much she has just witnessed.

But it's only a cursory notion, for what strikes Hannah even more forcefully as she faces Madame Severin is the sense that the widow harbors a secret, and the invisible presence of it seems as evident to Hannah as something she might actually see or touch. She thinks back to their every meeting, almost daily now for weeks, and realizes that this particular feeling always accompanies the madame. In the beginning she'd thought that Madame Severin's air of mystery had its origins in her exalted, almost mocking, attitude of mourning, or the dramatic events surrounding her disfigured face. But these were not secrets; indeed, the widow made certain that everyone knew of her past, which seemed to be a source of pride for her, not shame. It was something else. Something dark, guilty. Something Madame Severin would never willingly admit to. This sudden, certain knowledge unsteadies Hannah, but she quickly regains her composure and curtsies in greeting. Madame Severin dispenses with the niceties altogether.

"Recently a young lady came to you for help." It's a statement, not a question, and Madame Severin requires no sign of confirmation to continue. "There is no need to mention any names. You must forget you ever spoke with her—indeed, that you ever met her at all."

Hannah bristles at being addressed in such an imperious manner, but she won't pretend she doesn't know to whom the madame is referring. Ever since Jane Constable first approached her, Hannah has expected the girl to seek her out again, but she never has. Hannah even made up a list of simples and compounds believed to bring on the terms. Not that she felt comfortable recommending any of them. Some were useless, others were poisons. *Poisons.* A thought nags at her, something she should but can't quite remember, but at the moment she is most concerned about Jane. Why is Madame Severin taking such an interest in her welfare?

"Is this what the young lady wishes?" Hannah asks.

"Indeed it is. It appears that she was mistaken in her beliefs."

"She is well, then? With no . . . worries?"

"I suggest that you put all thoughts of this lady from your mind. You are to relate to no one anything you have heard of her. If I hear even the merest hint of a rumor, I will know that you are the source. My vengeance will be swift and impossible to trace."

Is Madame Severin truly dangerous or simply mad? Hannah decides to err on the side of caution. "You have my promise that what was told to me in confidence will remain so." She curtsies again, signaling an end to their conversation, and makes her best effort at a smile. Her dismissive gesture is not lost on Madame Severin, who gives her one last lacerating look before she turns and glides away.

Good Lord, what a night. Hannah takes another sip of the wine, but it tastes bitter. Perhaps the aftertaste of the laudanum in her mouth has soured it. Or perhaps it's indicative of the way the entire evening is progressing. The ache in her head makes her more aware of the din of hundreds of voices, the smothering, sweet, overheated air. She walks back to the Great Hall, looking for Montagu. If she does not improve, she can always ask him to take her home.

The dancing continues, although the king and Louise have apparently retired for the evening. Montagu too is still absent; she meanders through groups of courtiers on both sides of the dance floor without seeing him. She decides to go check on Lucy and Hester, but as she turns toward the staircase she finds Edward Strathern blocking her path.

"Good evening, Mrs. Devlin."

He is stylishly attired in a velvet coat the smoky hue of a black pearl, paired with a gray silk waistcoat that matches the storm-cloud color of his eyes. He is taller than she remembered, a full head higher than herself, and stands with a dignified bearing. His cheek is smooth, and every groomed hair is in place. His hands are clean and perfectly manicured. She hardly noticed before how handsome he is: those deep gray eyes stare out of an even-featured, strong-jawed face, in which intelligence and good breeding claim equal measure. He's perfect, almost too perfect, she thinks; but it's no wonder that the elegant lady in gray would want to marry him.

"I have desired to speak to you all evening, but it seems you are constantly in Mr. Montagu's company." His manner is strangely accusatory.

"He is my escort for the evening," Hannah replies. "What do you have to say that requires such privacy?"

Instead of answering, Strathern looks past her into the crowd. She turns to see Montagu making his way toward them.

"May I have the next dance?" Edward asks.

She hesitates. She would rather wait for Montagu to partner her.

"The music is starting," he says insistently. "Please, may I have the next dance?"

Hannah is about to turn down his request when Montagu stops to talk to a pretty young lady. Hannah watches the woman flirt with him, tapping him lightly on the cheek with her fan. It's a wanton gesture, but Montagu smiles in return, then takes her hand and kisses it. Hannah knows she should not let this disturb her, it's a common sight in a flirtatious court, but all at once everything feels uncomfortable and strange. The music and the constant clamor slow and echo, the sound breaking over her in waves.

"Are you all right?" Strathern asks.

"Of course," she replies. "Shall we join the dance?"

After the requisite bow and curtsy, Strathern awkwardly takes her hand as they promenade along the dance floor with the other couples. It's odd, but after his insisting that she dance with him, Hannah has the distinct feeling that he does not want to touch her. They return to their original place on the floor and face each other.

"You are in Mr. Montagu's company a great deal, I have heard," Strathern remarks.

So she's the subject of court gossip after all. But it hardly matters when there's nothing substantial to gossip about. Not yet, at least. "Why should this be your concern?"

"Mr. Montagu is not all that he seems. Or perhaps I should say he is more than he seems." He takes her hand again as they step closer together.

"How do you know of Mr. Montagu?"

"He was ambassador while I was studying in Paris. He cut quite a swath through that city. He is known for ruining every woman he is associated with—not only their reputations but their lives."

"Surely you cannot be speaking of the same man. Mr. Montagu has always treated me with respect and admiration."

"I do believe he admires you, but he will never have any serious intentions toward you. Everyone knows that his only true interest is money."

"Odd for you of all people to lay that charge at his feet. You've made a profitable match, why shouldn't he?"

The doctor looks deeply uncomfortable at the mention of his impending nuptials. "Money was not my first consideration. I tell you it will be his only concern when it comes to marriage. Otherwise, he is known to prey on women without friends or protectors, women he can dally with without consequence."

"Do you mean to imply that is the sort of woman I am?"

"That is not at all what I meant. I simply meant to warn you."

"You take an eager interest in this role." Too eager, for a man who's just told her that he is marrying for love. "I do not think it suits you, under the circumstances." The circumstances of his engagement, she means; and by his guilty glance she knows he has understood her. "Please let us drop the subject."

He slips his hand onto her waist for a turn. She feels his hesitation. Perhaps his uncertainty is nothing more than his unfamiliarity with the dance. Although Dr. Strathern appears to know the steps, he does not dance with Montagu's confident grace.

"Have you thought any more about our conversation of last week?" he asks.

"A little." More than a little, but she does not want to let on how much.

"I told Lord Arlington about the wounds on Osborne's body, but

I have not told him of my suspicions regarding Sir Henry or your father."

"Perhaps it's best to keep those suspicions to yourself."

"Do you not want to find your father's killer?"

"I think the past should be left in the past." Except that there's something she should tell him, something important. If she could only remember. She feels overwhelmed by the dancing, the heat, the noise. Faint and dizzy. Dr. Strathern's face appears very far away, then very near.

"Are you all right?" he asks. His voice sounds unnaturally slow. "Mrs. Devlin!"

She attempts to speak, but he is too far away for her words to reach him. The room spins, a sickening blur of light and color, and she hears him faintly calling her name. She cannot answer, for she feels herself falling, falling endlessly, falling soundlessly, falling into darkness.

Chapter Thirty-three

Fourth week of Michaelmas term

I T   W A S   A   walk of only fifteen minutes or so, and a very pleasant one, to Magdalene College and the Pepys Library. They could have gone online to find information about tachygraphy, but why bother when you could go straight to the source? Andrew had queried, and Claire had agreed. It was simply another benefit of living in a library-rich town; Cambridge could boast of more than one hundred.

They decided to take the most scenic route and stroll north along the Backs and through St. John's College. But as soon as they walked out of Trinity, they caught sight of the yellow crime scene tape cordoning off a section of grass near the stream where Derek Goodman's body was found. Claire quickly looked away and saw Andrew do the same. The fiction that they were making their way though the cold, blustery afternoon solely to learn about an obscure form of writing was shattered, and the unpleasant reality reasserted itself. It had been a rather flimsy fiction in the first place, Claire supposed.

All summer she'd been envisioning exactly this, walking with Andrew Kent along the picturesque bank of the River Cam or in the cloisters of medieval courtyards and talking about—well, it hadn't really mattered what they'd have been talking about. She'd imagined watching the changing expressions in his earnest and intelligent eyes, hearing the soothing, low pitch of his voice and the gratifying sound of his laughter.

Her summer daydreams now seemed like a naive fantasy. Her mind wandered back to Venice. On the night they'd deciphered Alessandra Rossetti's letters, she and Andrew had walked together through the Piazza San Marco to a friend's palazzo on the Grand Canal. How comfortable they had been with each other, how close, even. Now, even though Andrew was unfailingly polite, Claire knew that their burgeoning intimacy had come to a full stop. He was cautious around her, never standing too close or looking too long into her eyes. The very air between them seemed weighted with the things they couldn't say.

"The story of Roger Osborne's murder begins with Princess Henriette-Anne, Charles the Second's little sister, his junior by fourteen years," Andrew said. "The English Civil War began while she was still an infant; in fact, when Queen Henrietta-Maria took her children to France to live in exile, Henriette-Anne was considered too young to travel. Two years later she was smuggled out of England by a lady-in-waiting and lived with her mother in Paris while Charles the First waged a losing war against Cromwell and the Parliamentary forces.

"Henriette-Anne lived the rest of her life within the milieu of the French court. At first, while England was ruled by Cromwell, she was considered a poor relation—she and her siblings were first cousins of Louis the Fourteenth. Once Charles the Second regained his throne in 1660, Henriette-Anne came into her own as a proper English princess. In 1661, when she was sixteen, she married Louis' brother, Philippe, Duc d'Orleans, also her cousin. The alliance was political, of course, as noble marriages were, but it was notable for its lack of love or affection, and even cruelty, on the duc's part. By all accounts Henriette-Anne was a sweet, refined, gentle soul. She was a dutiful sister, who revered her brother Charles and her cousin King Louis and she tried to make the best of an unpleasant situation, but I suspect that she was never happy.

"In the latter part of the 1660s, Charles began to seek a closer alliance with France. Although England and Holland, as two Protestant countries, had more in common than England and France did, the

Dutch had been making incursions into English shipping routes that the English had been unable to stop on their own; with France's help they could declare war. But this goal of a closer alliance with France had to be pursued in secret, as it would mean breaking a treaty that England had recently signed with Holland and Sweden, and it meant going against the wishes of a vociferously anti-French, anti-Catholic Parliament. Charles had to tread very carefully, as he needed Parliament to raise funds for his continually cash-strapped treasury.

"Who better to be the liaison between Charles and Louis than Henriette-Anne? She was delighted to be needed by the two men she loved, and she took to the task of uniting England and France with an almost missionary zeal. It took more than a year of negotiations, but in June of 1670, Charles and Henriette-Anne met at Dover, along with hundreds of English and French courtiers. The king and the duchess had not seen each other in ten years, since Henriette-Anne was six-teen and had traveled to England prior to her marriage. It was a joyous reunion for both. Charles doted on his little sister, whom he adored as much as she adored him. This happy occasion was celebrated with feasts, dances, comedies, and ballets. But the true purpose of the re-union was a new treaty between England and France, negotiated by Charles's ministers Lord Arlington and Sir Thomas Clifford and the French ambassador to England, Colbert de Croissy. The treaty was in essence a pact to wage war on the Dutch: Charles wanted to reassert England's maritime supremacy, and Louis laid claim to territories in the Spanish Netherlands.

"The treaty was signed at Dover, and Charles and his little sister bade a tearful farewell. Only a few weeks later, Henriette-Anne was back at Saint-Cloud in Paris when she suffered excruciating stomach pains and suddenly died. There were rumors of poison, which later proved to be unfounded. Apparently she died from the perforation of a peptic ulcer. Her last hours were reportedly quite gruesome."

"But what does all this have to do with the death of Roger Osborne?"

"Osborne had been part of the English contingent at Dover. When Henriette-Anne returned to Paris, he was one of a handful of English courtiers who accompanied her. No one knows precisely why. Right before she died, Henriette-Anne entrusted Osborne with a gold ring and a secret."

"What secret?"

"No one knows. But it's long been speculated that a connection exists between that night at Saint-Cloud and his murder in London two years later."

Exactly how a diary written by an English doctor could provide insight into a centuries-old mystery was not at all clear, but Claire knew from past experience that a careful reading of documents such as these could reveal secrets long obscured. It had certainly been true in Venice, where she and Andrew had found that Alessandra Rossetti's letters to her cousin contained secret, coded messages. Claire felt a tingle of excitement at the possibility of a new discovery. That the diary was written by a female doctor—that's if Robbie Macintosh's memory was accurate—was an additional source of interest. Female physicians had been uncommon in the late seventeenth century, but not unheard of. Claire had read of female practitioners of all sorts: midwives, tooth-pullers, bone-setters, apothecaries, surgeons. But a female physician who'd ministered to the king's mistress? That was promising, indeed. But how could they be certain that Robbie Macintosh was telling the truth? He'd seemed awfully nervous about something.

"Didn't you think that Robbie Macintosh was acting strangely?" Claire asked Andrew as they passed through St. John's Chapel Court and headed toward Magdalene Street.

"Robbie? Why, no, not at all."

"I thought he seemed anxious. Upset, even."

"Of course he was upset. He'd just found out that his supervisor died."

"It seemed as if he was reacting to something more than that. As if—"

Andrew skewered Claire with a skeptical look. "Are you going to suspect everyone you meet from now on of being a murderer?"

"Of course not. But you can't deny that he was acting strange."

"How would you know?"

"Because I saw him. I observed him."

"But you've never met him before."

"So?"

"So you have nothing with which to compare his behavior."

"What difference does that make?"

"It makes a great deal of difference, I should think. How can you know if someone is acting oddly if you don't know how they act normally?"

"It isn't necessary to have a baseline of normal behavior to judge aberrant behavior against. Odd is simply odd—anyone can see it. Or, at least, most people can see it, if they're paying attention."

"What exactly do you mean by that?"

"You don't always pick up on the subtleties, do you?"

"Are you trying to insult me, or are you just doing it inadvertently?"

"I wasn't trying to insult you. I'm just saying that you don't always seem to—"

"Notice the nuances of human behavior?" He made a harrumphing sound as he walked under the archway marked with the inscription BIBLIOTECA PEYPSIANA 1724, commemorating the date the library was installed. "Yes, I'm sure that's a wonderfully attractive quality," he said grumpily as he stomped up the stairs ahead of her.

"Of course I've heard about Dr. Goodman. I'm terribly sorry." Nora Giles, the Pepys librarian, had risen from her desk and walked across the gleaming wood floor to greet them, the tap of her high heels echoing in the otherwise silent room. She was in her late twenties, of partial African descent, with a posh accent that placed her in England's upper crust. She was stunningly attractive, with flawless coffee-and-cream skin and shining black hair that she wore in short, bouncy curls. Her shapely figure strained against her businesslike silk blouse and tight pencil skirt. She was rather glamorous for a librarian. No, Claire corrected herself, Nora Giles was rather glamorous, period. She looked as if she'd be more at home singing jazz standards in a nightclub than babysitting a bunch of old books.

"Had you seen Dr. Goodman recently, by any chance?" Andrew asked. He seemed unaffected by the librarian's potent appeal. Perhaps this quirk of not noticing everything was a positive quality, in the long run.

She took her time answering such a simple inquiry, and a seemingly innocuous one. "Yes," Nora finally said, "in fact I did see him just a few days ago." As she spoke, she twisted the engagement ring that graced her well-manicured hand. Perhaps it wasn't nervous tension, however, but simple discomfort. The ring was rather large, after all, with a center diamond approximately the size of a Mini Cooper. Poor thing, Claire sympathized. Beastly ring probably got in the way when she was trying to shelve books and so forth. "Dr. Goodman was researching seventeenth-century speed-writing and stopped by to ask a few questions," Nora added. The cherry red gloss on her full lips glistened seductively in the warm light from a brass chandelier.

Andrew's eyebrows hiked up. "Really?" Claire had heard that tone before, one that managed to insinuate disbelief without coming right out and calling someone a liar. But why was he using it with Nora Giles? Why was he suddenly so suspicious?

"Yes," Nora answered. "He was writing a paper for one of the journals." She seemed more confident now, as if she was on more familiar territory.

"Coincidentally," Andrew said, "we're also here to pick your brain about the sort of code Pepys used in his diary. But this is Dr. Donovan's first time here. Perhaps we could . . . ?"

"Of course," Nora replied smoothly, then offered to take them on a quick tour. They followed her to the room where the collection was kept in tall glass-fronted oak bookcases, specially designed by the diarist to accommodate his three-thousand-volume library. The books were arranged, rather unusually, from the smallest to the largest.

An alumnus of Magdalene College, Samuel Pepys had bequeathed his library to his alma mater at his death. "His six-volume diary was part of the collection," Nora explained, "but no one knew of its existence. Although he wrote in his diary nearly every day for nine years, he kept it a secret even from his wife and his closest friends. So here they languished until John Evelyn's diaries were successfully published in 1818. The then master of Magdalene decided that Pepys's diaries should be transcribed, so he hired John Smith, a poor, struggling undergraduate, to do it. It took Smith three years, working almost every day. When he finally completed the project in 1822, the three thousand diary pages added up to over nine thousand pages of handwritten text—and, of course, one of the most complete and personal accounts of the Restoration era.

"The sad and ironic footnote to this story is that John Smith never knew that the key to the 'code' was here in the library all the time. It's not really a code per se, but a form of shorthand made popular by a man named Thomas Shelton. The book that Pepys used as a guide is right here."

She crossed to one of the bookcases and opened the glass front, taking out a copy of Thomas Shelton's *Tachygraphy, The most exact & compendious method of short and swift writing that hath ever yet been published by any.* Pepys's binder had bound it in brown calf and stamped Pepys's coat of arms on the front.

"Any chance we could borrow this?" Andrew asked.

Nora laughed. "You should know better, Dr. Kent. Sorry, but no."

Andrew took the photocopied diary page from his coat pocket and opened it for her. "Can you decipher this?"

Nora studied it for a moment. "Not right away, no. It looks like tachygraphy, but it's not exactly like Pepys or Shelton," she said.

"Then what is it?" Claire asked.

"A personal cipher, based on Shelton's system. His method was often used as a prototype, but people tended to develop their own code— their own way of speedwriting unique to themselves. In addition, as I'm sure you know, Dr. Kent, in the seventeenth century there was no such thing as a dictionary or standardized spelling. People wrote words phonetically, and they often wrote the same word in a variety of ways."

"So it's like translating another language," Claire said.

"It can be daunting, but it's not quite that bad. It is English, after all. If you really want to try to decipher this, I'd suggest reading Shelton's book. Although I can't loan you our copy, the text is easy enough to acquire. Not only is *Tachygraphy* available online but so are a few other seventeenth-century books on speedwriting. Early English Books Online it's called. You'll have access through the university."

Chapter Thirty-four

9 December 1672

HANNAH SLIPS INTO a pew at the back of the church as the choir begins the Introit. St. Clement Danes is old, cramped, and dark, with the clammy air of a root cellar and a whiff of putrescence no amount of burning herbs can eradicate. Beneath the buckling stone floors the parish dead are buried one on top of the other. The broken flagstones are most noticeable near the altar, the most sought-after spot for the departed. Although the church filled up long ago, a few extra shillings to the sexton will ensure that old bones are dug up to make room for the new. Hannah's own people—father, husband, daughter—rest in the churchyard near the south wall.

Although the service has just begun and it is not yet time to pray, Hannah quietly sinks to her knees. Her patellae fit into worn hollows made by hundreds of other knees on hundreds of other Sundays. Only a few others have sought out St. Clement's dim sanctuary this morning; they look too lost in their own supplications to make note of hers. She bows her head and lowers her eyes. The voices of the choir rise, their somber Latin harmonies resonating off the moldy stone. *Thou shall purge me with hyssop and I shall be clean.* The guttering candles nod, her closed prayer book hums in her hands.

She soundlessly recites the words of the fifty-first psalm along with the choir without any expectation of an answer. The event that she related to Dr. Strathern was singular; she is no Joan of Arc. Hannah has never even considered herself particularly devout. It's been a long time since she's entreated God for anything. In recent months she has avoided church, using her patients or the care of her mother as an excuse.

Thou shall wash me and I shall be clean as snow. Was it possible to be redeemed? To be a better person, to be wiser, kinder, more compassionate? To be the sort of doctor who could have saved her husband, her child, perhaps even her father? It is no wonder she has avoided coming here, and the weekly reminder of her failure. Failure to be the sort of physician she set out to be, not the one she is becoming, who waits on the king's mistress and brushes up on recipes that make a woman's skin white and soft.

When she collapsed at the dance the other night, Dr. Strathern caught her and carried her from the floor. That much she was able to deduce, although everything after that was confused, unclear. She remembers opening her eyes while she lay on the floor of the Great Hall, seeing Montagu, Lucy, and Hester hovering over her. She remembers vaguely some terse words exchanged between Strathern and Montagu, remembers brief snatches of the ride home interspersed with moments of blackness, as if she was drifting in and out of consciousness. She recalls that the atmosphere in the carriage was tense, but whether it was from Lucy's and Hester's worry about her or from their disappointment at leaving the dance early she could not say; perhaps it was both. She spent the next day in bed with a pounding head and a tremulous stomach, turning away the girls and even Mrs. Wills when she knocked on her door. Montagu sent a note inquiring after her health, which she was unable to answer. The next day, when she was feeling human again, a second letter arrived, telling her that he must go abroad immediately and would be away for some time. He didn't mention how long.

Last night she read over Montagu's last letter, as if it might divulge some secret about him, about who he was or how he felt about her. About his intentions, she supposed, but she could not solve that puzzle with this missive, which was tender without being overtly romantic. *My dearest Mrs. Devlin*, it began, *It is painful for me to relate the following, for it puts such distance between us . . .* That he wrote to her in the first place must mean something; but what, exactly? That he expected her to notice his absence and to long for his return? Or that he felt such longing himself? From their first meeting they had a natural affinity; on the night of the dance their rapport took on new depth. She thought about the way he looked at her, the way he held her while they were dancing, the many compliments and courtesies he paid her. Until the night of the dance, she would have said that she favored no one more than Montagu, and she would have guessed that he favored no one more than she. And then she ruined it all by her embarrassing display. Though she doesn't want to admit it, Dr. Strathern's comments worry her. She knows better than to listen to court gossip—it's meant to slander. She doesn't really believe what he said about Montagu, but she can't help wondering if just a bit of it might be true.

Her night was troubled by vivid, disturbing dreams. Memories from the night of the dance intertwined with fantasies and visions, things that never were and never could be. Montagu holding her hand and smiling seductively; that was real. As was her memory of Mademoiselle de Keroualle making a perfect curtsy to the king, all the while gazing up at him adoringly; or Lucy and Hester, their faces aglow, watching the dance from the balcony. But along with the authentic recollections were unsettling visions: the courtiers' powdered, rouged faces turned grotesque as they spoke and ate and laughed. The queen busily knitted a black and white checkered counterpane that flowed from her lap and metamorphosed into the dance floor. Arlington and Madame Severin loomed overhead, as big as giants, moving the courtiers about like chess pieces. The king winked at her. "It'll be our secret," he said, but when she demanded to know what the secret was, he refused to tell her. Lucy and Hester stood in a garden, arguing vehemently. Madame Severin offered Hannah a glass of wine. She accepted it, but when she looked into the glass, she felt ill. Jane Constable danced with the Duke of York. After a few turns on the floor, the duke was no longer a man but a squalling baby struggling in the girl's arms. Dr. Strathern held a severed foot in his hand. He kept trying to tell her something, but she could not hear him over the sound of the courtiers' laughter.

Edward. She permits herself to say his name. Softly, so that no one else can hear, except God. She went to sleep thinking of one man and awoke thinking of another. All night, her dreams kept returning to Edward Strathern. At first, she envisioned him as he was the night of the dance. Then she recalled every moment she had spent with him—in the tack room, the anatomy theatre, the Great Hall—in dreams that offered an unending kaleidoscopic vision of his face, witnessed in every mood and every light. When she woke, she was on fire with the thought of him, almost as if he had been lying with her. And she realized what she had been avoiding most of all, the feeling that had started the first time she'd looked into his eyes and seen that he was the one person from whom she could not hide, from whom she did not want to hide.

But he is to be wed to another, to a woman who is most likely a better match for him. She remembers the two of them dancing together: both tall and elegant, a seemingly perfect couple. From Strathern's own admission, it's a match based on affection. She does not want to covet another woman's man; she does not want to think of him at all.

Make me a clean spirit, O God: and renew a right spirit within me. She nestles her prayer book in the folds of her skirt, clasps her hands together, bows her head, and prays fervently to rid herself of her preference.

Walking home, she stays close to the buildings, her cloak wrapped tight. The storm that passed during the night is long spent, but the day remains blustery. Wind blows rainwater off the rooftops, whips in moaning, keening fury through the narrow alleys.

She turns into Portsmouth Street to find a private coach parked outside her door. Two roans paw the ground, steamy breath rising from their flared nostrils. The coachman jumps down from his seat to gentle them. When she gets closer, she sees the man who has come to call.

Dr. Strathern stands back from the front door, gazing up at the windows as if expecting someone to appear. She stops, feeling the blood rushing to her face; whether it's from panic, shame, or elation she isn't entirely sure. She has just asked God to help her forget him, and now he is here. Is it a test? Did she mouth the words without meaning them? In her heart, what exactly did she pray for?

Her first impulse is to turn and walk away, but by the time she is close enough to recognize him he has seen her too. There is nothing for her to do but to continue forward, as if his appearance at her house on a Sunday morning is not unusual. She worries that her thoughts, her dreams, her desires are achingly obvious in her face, and she gives a brief thanks that people cannot read minds; for she would blush furiously if he could read hers. But Dr. Strathern gives no indication that his visit is anything other than congenial in nature, and so she decides to welcome him in the same spirit.

The doctor is attired somewhat carelessly for the Lord's Day in a wrinkled wool coat. No wig, just his own shoulder-length hair tied back with a simple ribbon, a few strands breaking free in the gusty winds. The natural hue of his hair is slightly lighter than the wig she has seen him wear, its true color the warm brown of roasted hazelnuts with some early streaks of gray at the temples. She likes the gray, likes the unshaved stubble darkening his cheeks and chin and upper lip. She thinks back to how he looked the night of the dance, the velvet coat and the snowy cravat, his clean hands, his smooth face, how flawless he appeared. Even so, she decides she prefers him like this, mussed and a bit rough. It feels intimate, almost too intimate, both of them still creased with sleep.

"Is no one home?" Hannah asks. To her surprise, her voice sounds perfectly modulated and calm.

"Apparently not."

"That's odd," Hannah says, reaching into her purse for her house key. This is an even greater mystery than the purpose of Strathern's visit. "My mother is never left alone."

She unlocks the front door and lets them inside. In two quick movements she removes the patents from her shoes, then calls out to Mrs. Wills. Receiving no answer, she walks to the door leading down to the kitchen and calls again. The house is silent.

"We take turns going to church," Hannah says as she returns to where Strathern waits in the parlor. "I left a note—they knew I would be back soon."

"Lucy?" a thin, querulous voice calls from above. "Lucy, is that you?"

"My mother," Hannah explains, crossing to the stairs.

"She's ill?"

Hannah hesitates, then decides to tell him the truth. "She is ill in her mind." She starts up the stairs, then stops and looks back at him. "Why don't you come with me? I may need your help."

They find Charlotte still in her nightdress, sitting on the edge of her bed, attempting to pull a comb through her long gray hair. Hannah kneels in front of her to gently untangle it. Though Charlotte is only a few years older than Mrs. Wills, she aged rapidly after becoming ill six years ago. She's an old woman, with liver-spotted hands, knobby knees, delicate bones. Only in her bright blue eyes can one get a glimpse of the girl she once was. "Mother, where have the others gone?"

"Lucy's supposed to dress my hair." She looks at Hannah, confused. "Who are you?"

"I'm your daughter, Hannah."

"I don't remember a daughter. I have a son." She turns to Strathern, smiling as if she knows him. "Two sons." She beams with pride.

Hannah glances at Strathern: *Now you see.* He nods sympathetically. She looks around the room, but there's no sign of dishes or a tray. "Have you had your breakfast?"

"Butterflies and flowers," Charlotte replies, waving her hand as if shooing something away. "Butterflies and flowers."

"It looks like they've gone out without even bringing up her breakfast," Hannah says to Strathern. "This isn't like Mrs. Wills at all." She presses her mother's hands between her own, then bends down to check her bare feet. "You're freezing. Mother, please, get under the blankets." She looks at Strathern and points to a metal box next to the hearth. "Do you mind?"

He stacks more coal in the smoldering grate while she coaxes her mother back into bed. "Stay here. I'm going to make up your morning medicine." She motions for Strathern to follow her and leads him upstairs.

She's relieved that he doesn't recoil at her attic bedroom, hardly that of a proper young woman, but instead calmly takes it all in—the bundles of drying herbs, tables and shelves crowded with bottles and jars, the alembics, the stacks of books. She's relieved that his eyes pass over the unmade bed as if it weren't there. Hannah goes straight to her workbench, picking up a small marble mortar and pinching off bits of various herbs, which she crumbles between her fingers before dropping them in. "How did you discover where I live?"

"I asked an apothecary. The lady doctor of Portsmouth Street is quite well known, it seems. I'm beginning to see why. Do you make all your own medicines?"

"Some, not all."

He stands near the shelves, looking over the books: *The English Physitian* by Nicholas Culpepper; *Theatrum botanicum* by John Parkinson; Robert Burton's *The Anatomy of Melancholy; Rare Secrets in Physick and Chirurgery* by Elizabeth, Countess of Kent; *A Proved Practice for Young Chirurgians* by William Clowes; Peter Lowe's *Discourse on the Art of Chirurgery;* Harvey's *Du Motu Cordis.* "I see you're not entirely opposed to book learning."

"Not at all. I find it very helpful, in fact, especially if the authors emphasize observation over theory. The books on surgery are quite good." As soon as she says this she regrets it; it reminds her of how they met. Reminds him too, she notices as their eyes meet. But that's a dangerous thing to do. She quickly looks away.

"Do you know how to use this?" she asks, handing him a mortar and pestle.

"I think I can manage." He sets it on the table and grinds the herbs into powder. "What are you making?"

"An electuary. I'll put the ground herbs into honey—she won't take it any other way. Dandelion to strengthen her bones, rosemary flowers and juniper for mental clarity, fennel to stimulate her appetite." She brushes her hair away from her face with a gesture both impatient and fatigued. "Sometimes she simply refuses to eat."

"Does this help her condition?"

"Honestly? I don't know. I think it's better than no medicine at all. At least I hope it is. I keep trying new combinations, but none so far has made a huge difference in her state of mind. Somehow it seems better than doing nothing."

He gives the mortar and pestle back to her, his job completed. "I've been thinking about that story you told me."

"Oh." She turns away, self-conscious. "I'd rather hoped you'd forget."

"I cannot." His voice is serious enough to make her look back at him. "You said you were told to ease suffering."

"Yes."

His gray eyes are gentle, worried. "What about your own suffering?"

"I don't know what you mean."

"Are you ill?"

It's bad enough that he's seen her as she was at the dance, seen her mother's invalid state. "No."

"Then why do you carry this?" From his pocket he takes the vial she had on the night of the dance. He holds it in his open palm. "It's laudanum, if I am not mistaken."

She has no choice but to explain. "I suffer from headaches. Megrims, they're sometimes called."

He puts the vial on the table in front of her. "Does it help?"

"Yes. Like nothing else."

"When I was in Paris, I knew a few students who used opium to medicate themselves. One was consumptive, the others had various complaints. Some used laudanum, some took opium in the Oriental manner, by smoking it, something that is becoming more the fashion there. I think they believed it was harmless enough at first, but after a while, these men—men of good understanding and good character, mind you—cared for little else other than the drug. Little by little, every other pleasure was stripped away and replaced by opium. They became sad wrecks indeed, with no future, no hope. I could not bear to see this happen to you."

"Do you truly believe that is a great danger?"

"I suspect it can happen to anyone, no matter how careful one is. Exactly what happened the night of the dance?"

"The laudanum was more potent than usual. Usually such a small amount does not affect me so powerfully."

"Perhaps you took more than you realized."

She thinks back; she is fairly certain she put the dropper in her mouth only once. Then Madame Severin interrupted her. This recollection prompts another thought. "There's something I need to tell you," Hannah says.

"What?"

"I can't remember. Don't look at me that way, I'm not being devious. It's on the tip of my tongue—"

Downstairs, the front door opens and shuts, then a single pair of pattens clatters on the entry hall floor. Mrs. Wills has arrived. Hannah steps past Strathern and hurries down the stairs. Why did the goodwife leave her mother all alone?

"She's gone," Mrs. Wills says even before Hannah reaches her. "She's left and taken all her things. I suppose we'll have to check on the silver, too." Mrs. Wills gives way with a short, choking sob, covering her mouth in a futile attempt to contain it. "She's run off and we have no idea where to find her."

Hannah doesn't need any more explanation to understand that Hester's run away. She has always worried that the girl would succumb to some passing evil. The runaway maid is an all-too-common story in London: everyone has heard tell of a girl who steals away in the middle of the night wearing two of her mistress's best dresses underneath her own, a few spoons clanking in her pockets. Off to a life that may hold some excitement for a while but will never offer anything more than what she's left behind, and usually a good deal less. She's never heard from again, unless brought up before the courts . . . or the gallows.

"Hester's gone?"

"Not Hester," Mrs. Wills replies. "Lucy!"

Chapter Thirty-five

HESTER ARRIVES ONLY moments later, distracted and disheveled. "I've asked everywhere—no one's seen her since yesterday." She turns her red-rimmed eyes to Hannah. "I'm sorry, ma'am."

"It's not your fault, Hester. You'll not be held accountable for what she's done. Did neither of you hear anything last night?"

Hester shakes her head.

"I heard some noise, but I thought it was the storm," Mrs. Wills replies, wiping her eyes. "Why would she leave us in such a way?"

"For the usual reason, I suspect," Hannah says. "She's fifteen and in love, or believes she is. Hester, you must tell me honestly—did anything happen between Lucy and Mr. Maitland on the night of the dance?" She should have kept a closer eye on them; she knew only too well that Mr. Maitland was more forward than he should be.

"What do you mean, ma'am?"

"I think you know very well what I mean. Was there any flirtation or intimacy between them?"

"No, ma'am. I don't think they took at all well to each other. They hardly spoke. She was nicer to Mr. Clarke."

"Was there any intimacy between Lucy and Mr. Clarke?"

"No."

"Were you together all night?"

"Yes."

Hannah sighs, stymied. So much for her suspicions.

Dr. Strathern descends the last flight of stairs and looks on, concerned. "Is there anything I can do to help?"

"I'm afraid not. It appears our maid Lucy has run off." Another red-letter day for her little household. What must he think of me now? she wonders, then brushes it aside; his approbation—or lack of it—is the least of her worries. She places a consoling hand on Hester's shoulder. "You might as well hang up your coat. There's no point in looking for her now. I suspect we won't see her again until she wants us to."

Hester takes a paper-wrapped package from her pocket. "The apothecary bid me bring this to you. He said you asked for it a few days ago."

The Blackhorse Alley apothecary's mark is stamped upon the paper. "Wait," Hannah says. "I saw you and Lucy with a young man in Blackhorse Alley some weeks ago. Near Carter's Lane."

"A young man?" Hester's eyes cloud over, a sure sign that she's hiding something.

"Yes, a young man. Tall, fair. Could be an apprentice of some sort. It seemed as if you both knew him rather well."

Hester's lower lip swells and her chin begins to quiver. "You mean Thomas?"

"Is that his name?" Hannah senses that she's getting closer to the truth.

Hester nods and bursts into tears. "Do you think she ran off with Thomas?"

"You tell me. Did she fancy him?"

Hester nods again, still sobbing. She manages to squeak out a "Yes," and then adds, "we both did."

"I see." Now everything was beginning to make more sense. They'd both been in love with the same boy, no doubt the source of Hester and Lucy's recent friction. Hester is crying about something more than Lucy's disappearance; her heart's just been broken.

"Hester," Hannah says gently, "what is Thomas's full name? Where does he live?"

"Thomas Spratt," Hester manages to say between sobs. "He works for some funny old man who lives over on Bishopsgate."

"What is his name?"

"I don't remember—it's odd, like a bird or a crow or something."

"Theophilus Ravenscroft?" Edward asks.

Hester nods.

"Do you know him?" Hannah asks Edward.

"Mr. Ravenscroft is an acquaintance of many years," he replies. "I've met the young man. Thomas Spratt is his assistant."

Hannah immediately makes up her mind. "Mrs. Wills, Hester, please stay here in case Lucy should return. I'll pay a visit to this Mr. Ravenscroft right away."

"I'll take you in my coach," Edward offers.

"I haven't seen the boy in two days," Mr. Ravenscroft says. "No, make that three. If you should find him, please ask him what has become of my best microscope."

"The microscope is missing?" Edward asks.

"Indeed it is."

The same thought occurs to Hannah and Edward simultaneously: Thomas might have sold the instrument to pay for his and Lucy's elopement.

The philosopher and his two visitors stand in the shadowy clutter of his laboratory. There are no chairs, just two long tables upon which the accoutrements of the philosopher's art vie for space—three microscopes of various sizes, an alembic, boxes of glass slides, an air pump, blocks of wood and carving tools, along with their offspring of small whittled parts. At first, she felt some surprise upon entering a house and finding a laboratory instead, but as someone who has two alembics in her bedroom, she of all people should be the last to take issue: in fact, she feels quite at home. As for the man himself, Hannah guesses that Mr. Ravenscroft is nearing sixty. He is not much taller than herself, partly on account of what appears to be a crook in his spine, and he has the beaked nose and hard, glittering eyes of the bird from which his name is derived. He affects an impatient, preoccupied air, as if they have interrupted him in the midst of some very important task. The only reason they found him at home and not at the Fleet Ditch, he informed them, was that it was the Lord's Day, and the crews cannot be induced to work.

On the drive over, Edward told her something of his friend's unusual character. Less to acquaint her with him, she gathered, than to distract her from worrying about Lucy, but she welcomed the diversion. "His manner is sometimes abrupt and lacking in . . . grace, if you will," he said. "But I have met few people more devoted to natural philosophy. He is very clever, with a fertile mind, and he is actually quite pleasant once you get past the initial impression of . . . well, you'll see for yourself, I'm sure."

Indeed, when Mr. Ravenscroft opened the door he impressed her as pugnacious in manner; his hands were balled tight, as if ready to engage in fisticuffs, rather comical in a person so obviously unsuited to physical confrontation. But the instant he saw Edward his expression changed, and he greeted them warmly and welcomed them inside. She was quite relieved that he didn't ask any awkward questions, such as who she was or what her relation was to Dr. Strathern. These inquiries didn't seem to cross his mind.

"Do you know where we might find him?" Edward asks, looking closely at the empty place where Ravenscroft's missing microscope once stood. He brushes a finger over the tabletop, then studies it curiously, turning his hand under the candlelight.

"Thomas? No, but his father can often be found at Garraway's near the Old 'Change."

"Have you not inquired after the boy yourself?"

"I've been much too busy—at the king's behest, no less. Though I am quite cross that Thomas has not been here to help with the improvements to my design. He is much better at carving these small bits of wood. My eyes are not what they once were." He picks up a silver candlestick and leads them into the adjoining room, which houses an unusual collection of natural phenomena. Hannah studies the shelves filled with the skeletons of small mammals, snake skins, a sheep's head with only one eye. But these are not the focus of Mr. Ravenscroft's attention. On a table in the center of the room is a wood miniature of a complicated contraption. Actually three contraptions, a series of what appear to be latticed gates operated by wheels and cogs. "I have made a model of my invention for the Fleet Ditch. My system," he turns to Hannah, for Dr. Strathern seems to be familiar with this device, "removes waste as it courses downstream, so that only clean water shall flow from Ludgate to Blackfriars."

Hannah takes a closer look. The workmanship is remarkable, the invention quite ingenious. She turns one of the tiny wheels and the lattice gate rises up, then down again. "How is the refuse disposed of?"

"See here," Mr. Ravenscroft says excitedly, "the filters trap the refuse while allowing the water to flow through. Then the refuse is loaded onto barges"—he points to the little wood platforms adjacent to the gates—"and taken downstream to the Thames and then to the open ocean. I believe that in this manner the Fleet may be cleansed of all its pollution—that's if the laws barring the dumping of waste into the river are enforced."

"What a noble scheme," Hannah says. "What a difference you will make in the lives of people who live near this foul place. The number of children who die from pestilential miasmas each year alone is reason enough for your invention, Mr. Ravenscroft."

"You understand," he says with some surprise.

"Very much so."

"Mrs. Devlin is not only educated, she is a physician and a believer in modern philosophy," Edward tells him. Is that pride she hears in his voice, or simply the pleasure of introducing two friends to each other?

"I am always glad to have people of science in my house," Mr. Ravenscroft replies. "If you should ever have need of a laboratory for any trials or experiments you wish to make, Mrs. Devlin, I hope you will call upon me. I have many fine instruments and should be happy to put myself at your disposal."

"That is a most generous offer, Mr. Ravenscroft." Indeed, she is deeply grateful. He speaks to her as an equal, without patronizing;

without, it seems, any belief in the supposed limitations of her sex. It's as if he doesn't even notice, or much care, that she is a woman. Her thoughts and ideas are all that matter to him. If only every man would treat her so. She begins to see the appeal of this odd little man. In Mr. Ravenscroft she senses a kindred spirit of sorts, in that they both revere knowledge more than respectability.

"Think nothing of it," he says, blushing a little, as if he could read her thoughts. "We must encourage the younger people to follow in our footsteps, mustn't we, Dr. Strathern?"

Strathern catches Hannah's eye and smiles. "Yes, we must." But he is not lighthearted for long. "I fear we must be on our way. Where did you say we could find Thomas's father?"

They do not find Mr. Spratt at the coffeehouse but at a tavern on Suffolk Lane, where the coffeehouse owner has directed them. When Hannah and Edward step inside, more than a few faces look up from their pipes and pints. They're all men, of course; no woman of quality ever sets foot in here. A proper young lady such as Arabella Cavendish wouldn't have stepped out of the carriage, Hannah reflects. As they progress through the smoky, low-ceilinged room, silence falling in their wake, Hannah sneaks a quick glance at Edward. She saw his expression of shock when she insisted on going into the tavern, but it passed quickly enough. If he's embarrassed by her behavior, he conceals it well. His dignity is such that he might be accompanying her to church.

The only other woman in the tavern is the proprietor's wife, easily thirty years his junior, who lolls with her elbows on the counter next to where her grizzled husband sits sucking on a pipe, keeping an eye on the patrons. As they approach, she grins lasciviously at Edward and leans forward on the wood counter, revealing more of her well-endowed chest.

"We got us a gentleman here, Mr. Tupper," she says to her husband. "I told you we'd improve our custom once we put that notice in the *Gazette*." She turns to Edward, smiling wantonly, but her husband takes no more notice of her shamelessness than he would a bee buzzing around a flower. "The first pint is on us, sir, just be so good as to tell your friends. And we'll throw in a glass for your lady, too," she adds with a wink.

Edward coughs nervously. He looks away from Mrs. Tupper's insinuating glances and addresses her husband. "We're not here to sample your ale, which is very fine, I'm sure, but in hopes of finding a Mr. Spratt."

With obvious reluctance, Mr. Tupper takes the pipe from his mouth. "Spratt? What d'you want 'im for?"

"We would like to speak to him about his son."

Tupper looks them over carefully. Apparently he finds them harmless enough, for he points to the back of the tavern. "The other room. Tall fellow, head like a boiled egg. He'll be the one losing at cards."

A round table with six men fills the tavern's back room. Judging by the tense silence and the pile of coins in the center, the game is being played for serious stakes. Edward whispers to the tavern boy at the door, who runs to speak to a bald man of middle years. He stands and walks over to them with a wary curiosity in his eyes.

"What can I do for you?" he asks, dabbing at his perspiring forehead with a cotton kerchief.

Edward introduces himself and Hannah. "We're friends of Mr. Ravenscroft, Thomas's employer."

"Yes?"

"It seems that Thomas left three days ago and hasn't been back since. Have you seen him?"

"Why, no. Has something happened?"

"We have no reason to believe that any harm has come to him," Hannah says quickly, dispelling Mr. Spratt's noticeable concern. "But we fear he may have eloped with my maid, Lucy Harsnett. Has he ever spoken of her?"

"Spoken to me about a girl? No, never. But Thomas is almost a man now, he's got his own life. I'm just his old dad. He doesn't confide a thing." He wipes his wet forehead again, smiling ruefully.

"If you should see him," Edward says, "will you ask him to go back to Mr. Ravenscroft's? He is quite anxious for his return."

"Yes, of course. Now if you'll excuse me," he nods at his empty seat, "I've had a run of bad luck and I'm trying to make up for it."

The carriage is passing the charred ruin of St. Paul's before either of them speaks.

"Mr. Spratt did not seem terribly concerned about his son," Edward comments.

"But as he said, Thomas is nearly a man. Perhaps fathers naturally worry less about their sons than mothers do about daughters." Or mistresses about their maids.

"Still, I find it odd. Mr. Ravenscroft told me that both Thomas and his father were reliable sorts, not the type one would expect to find gambling in a tavern." He looks down at his hands, then into her eyes. "I fear we are no closer to finding Lucy."

"And the day is growing dark. I pray she is somewhere safe." She musters a brief, sad smile. "Dr. Strathern, in all this confusion, I never did learn the reason for your visit this morning."

"I hope you will agree there is time for one more stop."

"To do what?"

"To speak with the sexton who buried your father."

Chapter Thirty-six

HANNAH LEADS STRATHERN along a dirt path, only wide enough for one, that winds through the burial plots crowding St. Clement's churchyard. She points to a small outbuilding ahead. Like the church, its stone walls are blackened with soot.

"Mr. Ogle lives there," she says. "One can usually find him here of a Sunday—that's when the parish pays him extra to tend to the graves."

The weathered wood door to Ogle's cottage is closed. Edward raps hard enough with his gloved fist to make it rattle. They stand expectantly for a minute, then Hannah adds her much softer knock to his. "Mr. Ogle?" she calls tentatively.

"Who's askin'?"

They both start at the sound of the voice behind them. The tread of Tom Ogle's boots was muffled by the muddy ground. He carries a rusty shovel, dirt still clinging to the blade. "Oh, it's you, Mrs. Devlin," he says. The sight of Hannah puts him slightly more at ease, but he stares at Strathern with a native suspiciousness. On his scarecrow's frame hangs an ill-fitting suit of work clothes, grimy and threadbare. His skin is so often caked with dirt and coal dust that it's permanently stained a dull, dark brown. Hannah knows that the sexton is not a bad sort, but his presence in the churchyard is enough to make young children cling to their mothers.

Hannah introduces Edward. "We'd like to speak to you, if you have a moment."

Ogle squints up at the sky. "You'd best come in, then. It's startin' to rain."

His cottage is cozier and cleaner than one would imagine, with a neat straw bed in the corner, woven mats on the floor, hooks for his clothes on one wall, and hooks for his grave-digging tools on another. The rapidly fading daylight struggles in through two square windows cut into the thick stone. Ogle hangs up his shovel, lights a long wick by holding it over the burning coals in the tiny fireplace, then puts the flame to a candle set on a table just big enough for one. Next to the table is the only chair in the room, which he offers to Hannah. She thanks him and sits down.

"Mr. Ogle," she begins, "last year you prepared my father's body for burial. Do you remember?"

Ogle shifts his glance from Hannah to Edward and back again. "I remember. I was wonderin' when someone was goin' to ask me."

"Ask you about what?" Edward says.

"About what I seen."

A shiver of foreboding runs down Hannah's back. It took some time for Dr. Strathern to convince her to come here. She agrees with him that the murderer should be brought to justice, but it does not make facing the truth any easier. Who would want to discover that their father was willfully, brutally murdered? She prefers to believe that her father's killer was poor, starving, afraid, and had not meant to kill him. She prefers to believe that he is someone she can forgive in time.

"Did you find anything unusual about my father's body?" She wants Ogle to say no, there was nothing, so that she can press a few coins in his palm for the care of her family's gravesites and leave with an easy mind.

Ogle fixes her with his dogged stare. "Are you sure you want to know?"

Hannah hesitates. She isn't sure at all.

"We can stop right now if you want," Edward says.

Once Ogle tells his story, there's no going back. Will she be tormented by thoughts of her father in his final moments? Perhaps knowing the terrible truth is the price of justice. "I want to know," she says softly.

Ogle steps over to the grate. He stirs the burning coals thoughtfully, as if the action might spur his memory. "When the constable first brought him to me I could see he'd been stabbed. And not just once. He'd been cut up real bad—almost like it was done by some demon. I never seen nothin' like it."

"Can you describe what you saw?" Edward asks.

"His stomach was sliced right open, all the way across. His chest was all cut up. Deep wounds, about this wide." He holds up his thumb and forefinger about an inch and a half apart. "And there were marks cut into his flesh."

"Do you remember what they looked like?" Edward asks.

"Of course I remember. I tried to forget it, but I couldn't. I never wanted to say, knowin' your father was a good man, Mrs. Devlin. But they was like something' made by the Devil hisself."

"Could you draw them for us?" Edward surveys the room and realizes at once that it doesn't hold any writing accoutrements. "I suppose I could fetch some paper and ink—no, wait." He crouches down by the fireplace. With a pair of tongs he withdraws an ashen lump of coal, then brushes off the smooth hearthstone in front of the grate. "Draw them here."

Ogle takes Strathern's improvised writing instrument and kneels down next to him. The rain gently patters on the roof while Ogle slowly draws, the charcoal scraping softly on the stone. When he is finished, Edward stands back so Hannah can see.

The shapes the sexton has drawn are similar to the markings Strathern found on the other bodies, but not precisely the same: a circle with a dot inside, a slender crescent moon, a vertical line adjoining a small half circle at the top.

"I'm sorry, Hannah," Edward says.

Ogle looks up at her, the whites of his eyes bright against his brown skin. "There's something more," he says. "His finger—the little finger on his right hand—it was cut off."

In the carriage they sit facing each other, each of them nearly lost in the shadows.

"I neglected to tell the coachman to put in new candles," Edward says apologetically. "I didn't think we would be out so late."

Night has fallen. Under a steady barrage of rain, the streets are slick and empty. "It is of no consequence," Hannah replies. She doesn't mind the dark. There is a certain comfort in being in Dr. Strathern's carriage, in listening to the rain and to the slow clatter of the horses' hooves along the cobblestones of Wych Street. She feels safe in a way she hasn't felt in some time. It's reassuring to gaze upon Edward's countenance. At regular intervals, the sight of his face emerges from the darkness as the orange glow of a street lantern illuminates the coach, then disappears into shadow again. It occurs to her that they've spent nearly the entire day together. She hasn't spent an entire day in a man's company since Nathaniel was alive. What's most odd about it is that it doesn't seem odd at all.

Edward called her Hannah earlier, saying her name easily, naturally, as if they were already intimate. Something has happened between them, though she cannot say exactly when or where or how. When did it happen? While they were dancing, or before, at the anatomy theatre when she unburdened herself to him, or even before that, as they stood by poor Mr. Henley's bedside? Perhaps it happened at the very start, when they first looked into each other's eyes during the surgery. How could something so momentous result from such small events: a glance, a few conversations, the discovery of a shared passion? She did not imagine that it was so easy to fall in love, but she is forced to admit that it is.

Her whole world has suddenly shifted in a way she didn't anticipate or even desire. It hardly seems fair. Only a few days ago she would have said that Mr. Montagu impressed her as the most attractive of men: worldly, charming, witty, gallant. But she suspects that she would never have told Montagu about the darkest time in her life or allowed him to see her mother in her fragile state. She can't explain even to herself why she trusts Dr. Strathern, a man she hardly knows, except to say that what she first mistook for vanity she now recognizes as a quick understanding coupled with intellectual curiosity. His face has become as dear to her as any she has ever known. She tries to discern what exactly has charmed her so: the cleft in his chin, the strong jaw, the slightly asymmetric but graceful nose, the eyes that betray so many of his emotions? It's the sum of all of these and more. It's in the remarkable feeling of familiarity, as if they met before. Each conversation between them seems as if it has its beginnings in the past and its end sometime far in the future.

Presently, Strathern's gray eyes cloud with concern. "I'm sorry, Mrs. Devlin. About what we discovered about your father, I mean."

So now it's back to Mrs. Devlin; but that's as it should be. Dr. Strathern is much too respectable to disregard the rules of propriety. Nor does she want him to. She has had an entire day to think about the possible consequences of an attachment between them, and heartbreak is the only outcome she can envision for herself. Even though he indicated that his engagement is based on affection, she is certain that money plays no small part, and its appeal shouldn't be underestimated. Furthermore, he is an aristocrat and she is not. Men such as the Honorable Dr. Strathern marry not only for themselves but also for their families. Would he ignore all of that to be with her? Even if he were not engaged to another, would he actually marry her? She may trust his judgment, she may even trust him with her life, but she will not risk putting him to that test.

"Thank you for your kindness."

"I can only imagine how you must feel."

"Indeed, I'm not entirely sure myself. I have so many different emotions I feel they are at war inside me." And that's without including her complicated feelings about him. "I was more content when I thought my father's death was indiscriminate, perhaps even unintentional. And now . . ." She shakes her head in despair. "It's clear we must proceed, but how?"

"I have thought about this. I believe we could benefit by following the principles of modern philosophy. First, we must carefully examine the physical evidence, then proceed to an hypothesis." He leans forward eagerly. "For instance, we know that the manner of your father's, Sir Henry's, and Roger Osborne's murders were nearly identical, by which we can deduce that these killings were probably carried out by the same man."

It's a brilliant idea and a unique approach. Crimes are usually solved by the testimony of witnesses or by confession; to her knowledge, no one has ever considered another method. "Which would narrow the list of potential killers down to someone who knew all three men, someone who had been involved with each of them in some way. But there is a matter that perplexes me. My father was killed more than a year ago, and Sir Henry and Mr. Osborne only recently."

"I wish I knew what to make of that. I can only hope that we'll learn something more that will help us understand why."

"You told me that you saw my father with both those men in Paris. What were the circumstances?"

"They were all at the Palace of Saint-Cloud the night that Princess Henriette-Anne died."

"My father was there because the king asked him to accompany the princess back to Paris after their reunion at Dover. But why were you there?"

"For a completely frivolous reason—a party, or so I'd been told. Sir Granville, who was at that time visiting Paris, insisted that I was too serious in my studies and would benefit from the diversions of the French court. I was by no means convinced of this—which is to say that he practically had to drag me there. We didn't know the princess was ill until we arrived. Apparently, the sickness came upon her quite suddenly. And tragically, as it turned out."

Hannah thinks back to what her father told her of that sad incident. "There were rumors of poison."

"There always are when a member of the nobility dies in such a manner. But your father's postmortem put an end to that."

Hannah nods. "He spoke to me of it. He was certain that she died of an ulceration of the stomach." She pauses thoughtfully. "About the markings—there is one that I recognize. This is what I meant to tell you earlier. I remembered it the night of the dance. The *x* inside the square is a symbol used by apothecaries. It means *month*."

His brows knit together. "Month?"

"As they might write on a recipe—as in, 'use once a month.'"

"And the others, could they also be apothecaries' marks?"

"I didn't recognize them as such."

He stares out the window, ruminating. "Did your father keep records of his patients or his cases?"

"Yes, quite a lot."

"Have you ever looked through them? Perhaps you would discover a reason why someone would want to kill him."

"No, but until today I did not know that his death was due to anything other than a robbery."

Strathern looks chagrined. "Of course."

The coach stops outside her house. Neither makes a move to leave the carriage. Perhaps he knows, as she does, that doing so will mean good-bye. All that must be left unsaid fills the space between them, awkward and painful. But she must know one thing. "Dr. Strathern, why is it so important to you to solve these murders?"

He seems surprised by her question. "A killer is on the loose. Is that not reason enough?"

"No other reason?" The words seem to come from deep inside her.

He takes a long time to answer. "If there were another reason, a more personal reason, would you allow me to speak to you of it?"

She has heard enough; any more would be tempting fate. "I think that would be unwise." She puts her hand on the latch, but he covers her hand with his own before she can open the door. She looks at him steadily. "I must go," she says softly, pulling her hand away. "I must find out if they've heard anything from Lucy." Strathern's disappointment is evident in his eyes. He opens the door for her, steps out, and helps her down from the coach. His hand holds hers for a moment longer than it should. She pulls away and starts toward the house.

"Mrs. Devlin," he says suddenly. Hannah turns around. "Will you allow me to call on you again?"

His entreaty is almost impossible to resist, but she has had an entire day to come to her senses. "I do not think we should see each other, Dr. Strathern. But I promise to read through my father's papers. If I find anything of interest, I will write to you."

She turns and walks to the door, leaving him standing in the dark, in the rain.

Chapter Thirty-seven

Fifth week of Michaelmas term

DURING HER FREE hours Claire read Shelton's *Tachygraphy* on-line and attempted to decipher her copy of the first fifty pages of the diary. She worked at the dining table in the main room of her set, a few printed pages with the symbols from Shelton's book spread out before her. At first, the symbols used in the book and in the diary seemed to have little relation to each other, and for a while she worried that Hannah Devlin had devised her own code irrespective of Shelton's. But gradually, reluctantly, it seemed, the diary divulged its secret language. First Claire searched for the most common words—*a, I, and, the,* then *he, she, they*—copying them down in the same location in which they appeared on the page, with great gaps between them for the still-undeciphered words. After a while she began to see the similarities between the diary's code and Shelton's, and the sentences formed between the pale blue lines of her notebook.

What she found was nothing less than amazing. The book she'd discovered in the Wren Library was as Robbie Macintosh had said: the journal of a female physician in Charles II's court. Hannah Devlin's private observations ranged far beyond medical notes to include her daily activities, her encounters with other people, her private hopes and fears. While not as exhaustive as Pepys, it made for fascinating reading. By the time Andrew Kent stopped by to check on her progress, Claire was transcribing her notes at a slow but steady pace. "It's amazing," she told him. "It's an incredible find."

"A find that's been lost, unfortunately," he replied. "Hoddy and I have gone through most of Derek Goodman's set without discovering it."

"Other than not being where he said it would be, the diary is just as Robbie Macintosh said. Hannah Devlin was a doctor. She treated Louise de Keroualle."

"For what?" He glanced at Claire's notebook and saw the transcribed date at the top of the page. "Of course: 1672. The king gave her the clap, as it was then called."

"You know about this?"

"It wasn't a secret, even then."

"They tried to keep it a secret, though." Claire flipped through her transcription to the beginning. "One of the king's ministers, Lord Arlington, practically kidnaps her and takes her to court. Her father had been a court physician and a friend of Arlington's, but something happened—I don't know what, she doesn't say. She only mentions that her father is dead and that she doesn't trust Arlington at all."

"Smart girl. Who was her father? Dr. Devlin?"

"Her maiden name's Briscoe."

"Dr. Briscoe," Andrew mused. "Never heard of him. Is there any mention of Osborne?"

"Not one."

"Henriette-Anne? Saint-Cloud?"

"Nothing." Andrew looked disappointed, so Claire tried to cheer him up. "But I'm only up to the eighteenth of November. There's still a lot left to decipher."

Andrew asked to read her transcription. She slid her notebook over to him and waited patiently. Near the end, he turned a bit pale and gulped. The amputation, no doubt.

After he finished reading, he stared out the windows at the gray sky beyond. "Robbie Macintosh said that Derek Goodman told him that this diary was the key to Osborne's murder," he said, thinking aloud. "I assumed that meant that the author was privy to all of the details, and had written down precisely who murdered Osborne and why. But what if it isn't that straightforward at all? What if it's something inadvertent? Incidental, even?"

"You mean that Hannah Devlin herself didn't know anything about Osborne's murder?"

"Right."

"Oh," she said, dismayed. That would make solving this puzzle considerably more difficult.

Andrew's expression suddenly brightened. "Have you transcribed the photocopy yet?"

"No. I was so caught up with the diary that I forgot about it." She found it in the inside pocket of her notebook and set to work. It wasn't long before she had reproduced the page in fairly legible English.

> *. . . she said her name was Jane Constable and she was with child by one of the men at court. Though I told her that I was not the sort of physician who could assist her, I could not help but be moved by her distress. I promised, against my better instincts, to consider providing her with the necessary herbs. Am I wrong to fear that she has been sent to entrap me, to embroil me in a scheme that would be my undoing?*

They looked at each other, perplexed. "Still nothing about Osborne," Claire said. "Maybe you're right, maybe the solution to the murder isn't here in the diary. Maybe this is just . . . a guide."

"A guide to what?"

"I'm not sure yet. But think of all the books and papers we found in Goodman's study. The other day, they seemed to have little in common—at least, I couldn't imagine exactly what it was." Claire excitedly flipped through her transcription. "But look—there are direct correlations between what's in this diary and the materials Derek Goodman had in his rooms."

"So you think this is just a starting point, a nexus for the research."

"It could be."

Andrew sighed and studied the floor for a moment. "You want to go back to his set, don't you?"

Claire nodded eagerly and grabbed her coat.

"So what happened to her?" Claire asked as they hurried along a court-yard path. Even though fellows were allowed to walk on the lawn, she had noticed that they seldom did.

"To who?"

"Louise de Keroualle."

"You mean because of the, uh—"

"Yes."

"She survived. For a very long time, in fact. She died in 1734 at the ripe old age of eighty-five, outliving Charles by almost fifty years."

"That's it? She was fine?"

"I don't know if I would say she was fine. She was the king's mistress for another thirteen years, but she never had another child, and there's no evidence that she ever conceived again. That episode of illness left her barren. I'd say she paid dearly for being the king's mistress—but he also paid dearly for his mistake."

"The necklaces?"

"That was only the beginning. Although Charles's first mistress, Barbara Villiers, was the most blatantly avaricious of them all, Louise de Keroualle did very well for herself, acquiring jewels, gold, revenues from estates and taxes, houses, land—although she never showed much interest in living anywhere other than at court. She thrived on being at the center of power and being the center of attention."

Andrew unlocked the door to Derek's set and they went inside. It was much as they'd left it, with books and papers spread out on the dining room table. If the police had been here again, they hadn't been much interested in anything there. Although Claire was keen to get back to work, her thoughts were still occupied with Hannah's story. What a strange and rarified world the court must have been.

"Did she love him?" she asked.

"The king? That's a question that has long fascinated historians, though no one has ever been able to answer it satisfactorily. Certainly she loved being the king's mistress, even though she obviously suffered for it. Louise de Keroualle adored comfort and luxury above everything else. But passionate feelings for Charles? If she ever had any, they were never recorded."

"Did he love her?"

"His true feelings for the mademoiselle, too, are an enigma. Some people believe that his alliance with Louise was political, that she was little more than a French pawn in a game between Charles and Louis. But most think he was blinded by love and quite the fool. Ralph Montagu—the man mentioned in the diary—once famously said that Charles was a fool, and his brother the Duke of York 'a governable fool.' It wasn't an uncommon sentiment at the time. Pepys, Evelyn, the playwrights, the wits—all expressed their disappointment in Charles's character once the first heady days of the Restoration had passed, and they frequently complained about a king who seemed serious about nothing other than the pursuit of pleasure."

"Do you think he was a fool?"

"When it concerned women, he certainly was." Their eyes met, but Andrew quickly looked away, turning his attention to the stacks of books and papers on the table. "Now then. You said there's something here from the College of Physicians?"

They sorted through the materials on the tabletop until Claire found the document she'd remembered. "It's the postmortem report on Roger Osborne," she said. "Performed by Edward Strathern, MD, FRS. What's FRS stand for?"

"Fellow of the Royal Society."

Together they read through the report. Osborne died from multiple stab wounds and had been dead for at least two weeks when his body was discovered. Found in the Fleet Ditch by a Mr. T. Ravenscroft, FRS.

"Another fellow," Andrew commented.

"Is that important?"

"I don't know. But it makes me wonder where Derek found this document—in the archives of the College of Physicians or the Royal

Society? Or somewhere else altogether? It doesn't have an archival stamp on it. I'm also wondering—"

"There's more," Claire interrupted. A couple of the puzzle pieces were beginning to make sense. "More than one."

"More than one what?"

"More than one murder. The London maps. Perhaps Hoddy pointed them out to you. Derek Goodman wasn't trying to solve one murder but a whole series of murders."

The same idea occurred to both of them at the same time, and they rushed to the bedroom to study the maps and the six red dots scattered around London.

"Six murders?" Andrew said skeptically.

"He doesn't seem sure about the fifth. There's a question mark next to it."

"My question is, what do they all have in common?"

"Three of them are near the Fleet," Claire pointed out.

"You think that's significant?"

"There's a lot of material out there on the Fleet River."

"More than we have time to read," Andrew concurred. He paused thoughtfully. "I think I know just the person who can help us."

"Absolutely not," Fiona Flannigan said. "I wouldn't lift a finger for that bastard even if you offered me the chance to tap-dance on his grave."

"But Dr. Flu . . . Fa . . . Fla . . . *Fiona*," Andrew sputtered, flustered by her vehemence. "Dr. Goodman is dead."

"Don't expect any tears from me," she said, rather unnecessarily. From the moment Andrew had first mentioned him, Fiona Flannigan had made no effort to hide her virulent hatred of the deceased.

"What I mean, Dr. Flannigan," Andrew went on, attempting to retrench, "is that you wouldn't be helping the late Dr. Goodman so much as you would be helping us. We simply want to know if you know anything about a few murders. In London. In the 1670s. Near the Fleet."

She folded her arms over her chest and raised her pointy chin, regarding them suspiciously through narrowed eyes. Fiona Flannigan was a petite woman, but formidable. Her incredibly well-defined biceps and triceps bulged from the short sleeves of her black cycling shirt, which was made of some kind of high-tech fabric that reminded Claire of a diver's wet suit. Her short red hair stuck out from her head in a puckish arrangement of moussed spikes, a style that seemed rather revealing of her personality, which Claire would have readily described as thorny.

The walls of Fiona's Clare College office were plastered with copies of old diagrams, drawings, and plans of various pumps, pipelines, gutters, sewers, canals, and a number of mechanisms Claire couldn't even begin to name, all clearly connected with the book she was writing. An important work, Andrew had told her on the walk over. Derek had been wrong to make fun of it. Clearly Fiona hadn't forgiven him, and possibly never would. Just by saying his name they'd aligned themselves with the enemy, not a smart move. If they didn't rectify it soon, it was unlikely Fiona was going to tell them anything helpful. She looked as though she was ready to kick them out of her office. Andrew might not have noticed the fury in her eyes, but Claire certainly did.

"Dr. Flannigan," she said sweetly, "this drawing is very intriguing." She pointed at a nearby diagram of what looked like a canal. "Part of your research?"

Andrew shot her a look, but she ignored him and continued to smile encouragingly at Fiona. She knew as well as anyone that historians liked nothing better than to discuss their work. How many people ever bothered to ask? And, truth be told, she was sincerely interested.

"That," Dr. Flannigan replied, "is the first large-scale system of municipal waste disposal ever invented. It was conceived and designed by Theophilus Ravenscroft, one of the unsung geniuses of his time." She spoke with pride and some lingering hesitation, as if she feared ridicule. No doubt she'd had plenty of that from Derek Goodman.

"How did it work exactly?"

"See here—" She moved closer to Claire and pointed at the relevant parts of the diagram. "These movable gates filter the waste from the river. It's then put on barges and taken downstream."

"Ingenious."

"Yes, it was." Fiona Flannigan looked at them with a gleam of triumph in her eyes. "All the more so for being the first. Until this, no one in London—not even Wren or Hooke—had thought of a method to rid the city of the sewage that accumulated every day." She spoke more pointedly to Claire. "Do you have any idea of the sort of filth that people lived amongst then?"

"A bit," Claire ventured.

"It was worse than you can possibly imagine. People were surrounded by rubbish and their own effluvia. And dying from it, of course, although they didn't know it. It's difficult to conceive of what it was really like, mainly because most of us have only been exposed to a sanitized, Hollywood version of the past. But back in the seventeenth century, town-house basements were used as cesspits, and night soil men carried the unpleasant cargo right through the house. People thought nothing of throwing the contents of a chamber pot out the front window and into the street."

"Did Mr. Ravenscroft's device work?"

Fiona stepped back, the sharp features of her face tightening with distrust. "That's not really the point, is it?"

"Didn't Ravenscroft end up in the Tower?" Andrew mused. "Didn't something go terribly wrong—"

"Ravenscroft was a genius," Fiona insisted. "And I could prove it too if Derek Goodman hadn't absconded with my research materials."

"What do you mean, absconded?"

"What I mean is that too many times when I tried to locate the books or documents I needed, they seemed to have mysteriously disappeared. And Derek Goodman always seemed to have been the person looking at them just before me."

"I see," Andrew said. "I might be able to help with that. Fiona, if I can find the materials you want, would you share with us what you know about any murders committed near the Fleet Ditch? It may have something to do with Derek Goodman's death."

She thought it over, then smiled. "I'll do you one better," she said. "I'll tell you the name of the student he was sleeping with."

Chapter Thirty-eight

HER NAME WAS Ashley Templeton and she was a third-year at Trinity. Fiona had seen her with Derek Goodman in the London Underground only two weeks ago, on the Piccadilly line. They hadn't seen her. How could they? They'd been in constant lip-lock all the way from Knightsbridge to Leicester Square.

As Claire and Andrew crossed West Road after leaving Fiona's office, Andrew was still shaking his head. "A student," he muttered angrily. "The man clearly had no moral compass whatsoever. If he were still alive I'd be tempted to kill him myself." He stopped and looked tiredly at Claire. He seemed to have aged a few years since the morning. "I'm going to have to talk to her. But what am I going to say? Pardon me, but did you have a sexual relationship with Derek Goodman?"

"You can't just blurt it out like that."

"I know, but I can't think of anything else."

"The point is to encourage her to talk, not frighten her into being defensive. Why not ask her if she knows anything about what happened that night? Even the smallest detail could help us discover who killed him."

"Help *them*, you mean." He looked at her sternly. "The police."

"Them, of course," Claire nodded.

They watched a punt filled with Japanese tourists float slowly along the river past Queens' College. Andrew sighed. "Do you mind coming with me? I don't imagine I'll be very good at this."

She was surprised that he'd taken her comment so much to heart. "But I don't even know her."

He shrugged. "I hardly know her myself."

They found Ashley Templeton's set at the top of C staircase in Whewell's Court. As soon as the girl opened the door, Claire realized that she'd already made a whole group of assumptions that weren't going to apply at all. She'd constructed a mental image of an innocent, duped schoolgirl, another of Derek Goodman's victims. Or, if *victim* was too strong a word, someone who had been taken in by his mesmerizing charm; something to which Claire could sadly relate.

But Ashley didn't look like anyone's fool. To begin with, she was exceptionally pretty, with the kind of polished beauty only money can buy, from the roots of her expensively highlighted mane of golden hair to her perfectly manicured toes. Her bare feet, one christened with an ink-blue, star-shaped tattoo, were just visible from under the fashionably faded bell-bottom jeans that rode low on her slim hips. A T-shirt emblazoned with the name of a rock band Claire had never heard of—what else could IronKlad be?—was short enough to show off her diamond-studded navel. Although Ashley had the requisite piercings, tattoos, and wardrobe of her peers, Claire got the impression that the clothes were the pricey, boutique version of Neo-hippy. It wasn't that hard to figure out. Through the open door, she could see an array of shopping bags—Harrods, Harvey Nichols, Selfridges—on the chairs and on the floor, tissue paper and price tags still sticking out of the open tops. Not a typical Cambridge student; not a typical twenty-year-old. More than anyone else Claire had met in Cambridge, Ashley Templeton reeked of money and privilege. Not to mention cigarettes and perfume. The odor of both drifted out into the hall.

"Dr. Kent." Ashley's eyes quickly passed over Claire, ascertaining in an instant that she was no one important. "I've already spoken to the police." She looked at them dismissively and began to shut the door in their faces.

"Do they know?" Claire piped up.

She froze. "Know what?" Despite her blasé demeanor, there was a flash of fear in Ashley's eyes.

"That you had a sexual relationship with Dr. Goodman."

Andrew turned to Claire, his mouth agape with wonder and horror. Ashley looked furtively into the hall, as if she was afraid that someone had overheard.

"You'd best come in," she said. She opened the door for them and turned to the guy slouched on her slip-covered couch. "Clive, it's time for you to go."

Clive reluctantly got to his large, Doc Marten–clad feet. He, too, was dressed in jeans—working class rather than designer, Claire noted—and grubby T-shirt, over which he wore a black leather jacket, the kind with an excess of belts and buckles favored by motorcyclists. His dark hair was shorn almost to the scalp. Part of a colorful and obviously large tattoo crept up his thick neck above his jacket collar. He was an inch or two taller than Andrew and built like a truck. Not the sort you'd want to encounter in a dark alley.

He lumbered past them. "Awright, luv, see you later," he said. He glanced warily at Andrew as he walked out the door.

"Is he a student?" Andrew asked.

"No," Ashley replied. "What of it? Just because I'm a student, I'm only allowed to hang out with poncey students?" She loped over to the dining table, her long pants dragging noisily on the floor, and picked up a pack of Marlboro Lights and a bright pink disposable lighter. The ashtray next to them was so full of butts that ashes had spilled on the table all around it, but Ashley didn't seem to notice or care. She tossed her long, thick hair away from her face and tilted up her chin, putting the cigarette between her lips and lighting it amidst a jangle of silver bracelets.

"So what is it you want to know?" she asked, expertly blowing out a long stream of smoke. With her air of brittle sophistication, Claire would never have guessed Ashley was only twenty.

"We're not here to question you, Ashley, but it's come to our attention that you were involved with Dr. Goodman," Andrew said. "We were hoping that you might know something about the night he died. Dr. Donovan and I are investigating on behalf of the college. It doesn't involve the police." He gave Claire a sidelong glance, and she subtly nodded her approval.

Ashley sniffed and ran her tongue over her teeth, which were brilliantly white and as straight as piano keys. "I saw him at a party. Not a college party—it was over on Pemberton Terrace. Some artist's studio." She took another drag off her cigarette. Claire noticed that the pink, candy-colored nail of her right index finger was short and ragged, as though it had been chewed off. Her one tiny blight of imperfection. "Derek showed up with someone else. He didn't know I was going to be there, obviously. We had an argument." She shrugged. "It wasn't a big deal."

"Did you see him again later?"

"No," she said crossly. "I never wanted to see him again, ever. I'm not one of those idiots who moons about over guys who are two-timing me." Ashley was beginning to look tense, like she was no longer interested in playing along.

"Who did he come to the party with?" Andrew asked.

"That bitch Nora Giles."

Nora Giles, the Pepys librarian? The conspicuously engaged Pepys librarian? Claire tried to suppress her astonishment. She looked at Andrew and saw that he didn't seem surprised at all.

Ashley stubbed out her cigarette in the ashtray, sending a small avalanche of ashes and butts onto the table. She was obviously angry, and her mouth had a mean twist to it, but her eyes were starting to look a little misty. She sniffed again.

"Do you have a cold?" Claire asked her.

"Allergies," Ashley replied.

"Who else was at this party? Any other students?"

"A few graduate students—a girl named Sharon, a guy called Robbie, and another one that Derek called Mousy."

"So you told the police that you had an argument with Dr. Goodman, but you didn't tell them why?" Andrew pressed.

"I don't see why they needed to know. I simply confirmed what other people saw. If they want to know more, they'll have to arrest me. My father's a barrister, I know my rights. I don't have to tell them anything. Or you, for that matter. Keep in mind that if you mention any word of this to the police I'll sue you for violating my student confidentiality rights. You personally, Dr. Kent, along with the school," she added with a triumphant toss of her hair.

"That went well," Andrew said as they walked down the last few stairs and stepped out into the bracing air. It was too obvious a falsehood to bother with sarcasm. Instead, he sounded rather wistful, as if he'd been referring to something pleasant from long ago.

Claire responded with an indistinct harrumph of despairing agreement. They'd been beaten by a twenty-year-old. A sophisticated, intelligent twenty-year-old, but still. Hardly the thing to make them feel proud of their investigative skills. Perhaps they were both better off sticking to books. The blustery wind kicked up, tossing Claire's long hair into her face. She arranged her paisley scarf around her throat and chest and buttoned up her wool coat. Andrew thrust his hands into his jacket pockets. They turned west into the wind, automatically heading back to Great Court.

"Didn't Detective Hastings tell you that Derek Goodman tested positive for cocaine?" Claire asked.

"Yes," Andrew replied glumly. "Is that what you think was going on in there?"

"Could have been."

"I suppose I'll have to tell Portia."

"Yes, you will." Claire could see how upset he was by the prospect— almost as if it was physically painful for him to discover law-breaking behavior at his own school. "This is really tough for you, isn't it?" she asked gently.

"Yes, it is. I guess I'm a bit of a square."

"I'm afraid so. By the way, no one uses the word 'square' anymore."

Andrew smiled faintly. "Damned by my own out-of-date vocabulary. I suppose I am rather old-fashioned sometimes."

"It's one of the things I like about you," Claire blurted before she could stop herself. There she went again, saying what she thought at the moment that she thought it.

"That I'm old-fashioned?"

"Why don't we call it 'traditional' instead?" She paused, wondering if she should risk saying anything more. Andrew looked pretty gloomy; perhaps he needed some cheering up. "I like that you expect people to be honest and trustworthy and honorable."

"You don't think I'm boring?"

"No."

"Thanks." He smiled again, this time with more enthusiasm.

"How did you know about Nora Giles?" Claire asked.

"Rumors, for a start, although I try not to give too much credence to them. But late last term I came over here for an early run and I saw her leaving New Court. It was five-thirty in the morning. It wasn't difficult to deduce where she'd been. I didn't know if they were still seeing each other, however."

Jesus, Claire thought, how many women had Derek Goodman been stringing along?

They walked through the Trinity Gate and into Great Court. "I promised Fiona I'd look for those books in Derek's set. I've been thinking . . . if his work had anything to do with his death, then we need to figure out exactly what he knew. I'll work on finding the materials in his rooms if you'll—"

"Transcribe the diary?"

Andrew smiled. "Meet me at eight for dinner at hall, and we'll compare notes."

Chapter Thirty-nine

16 December 1672

FANNY DOYLE PADS quietly up the thickly carpeted stairs to Sir Granville's bedchamber, breakfast tray clutched in both hands. She's been under-chambermaid for less than a month, but she's already familiar with the bellowing that will ensue if she spills so much as a drop of chocolate. The master's particular about his morning repast: a dish of chocolate and a sugared roll, every single day. The cook-mistress told her this is what they eat in France, but Fanny's not certain she should believe her. Never sardines or meat or a bit of strong cheese? Bread and chocolate seems meager fare, especially for someone as rich as Sir Granville.

Fanny carefully balances the tray on one arm and taps on the door. Her knock doesn't prompt any response. Even though it's well past ten, she's not surprised that the master's still asleep. He keeps whore's hours more often than not. She'll have to wake him, a prospect she doesn't enjoy. Sir Granville doesn't seem to mind if she sees him in his nightgown looking a fright, but it's hardly a sight she appreciates. Fanny slowly opens the door and steps inside. It's always quiet in Sir Granville's bedchamber, a muffled, numbing sort of quiet that exists nowhere else in the house. It's because of all the frills and furbelows, she decides, the swank bed draperies and the damask-covered walls, the thick red velvet curtains. They're drawn shut, but a weak daylight filters through, enveloping the room in a ruby-colored gloom. She sets the tray on a table near the hearth, pushing aside a wine decanter and two gold-stemmed glasses, and crosses to the window, her feet sinking into overlapping layers of plush Turkey rugs.

Fanny pulls back the curtains and looks over to the bed. The silk sheets are all a-tangle; in fact the old goat has fallen out of bed and is sleeping on the floor. She can see his bare feet sticking out from the end of the tester. It isn't the first time she's found him in this condition.

"Sir?" Fanny calls tentatively as she walks closer.

Then she puts her hands to her face and begins screaming.

It's a gruesome sight. So gruesome that none of Sir Granville's servants have gone anywhere near the body. As his closest relation and heir, Edward Strathern is the first informed, and when he arrives he finds the scene unmolested. Despite his shock and revulsion at the way his uncle met his ultimate end, it occurs to him that studying the victim in the milieu in which he was murdered may yield some information about the crime.

Sir Granville's steward stands a good distance away, looking on the tableau with horror. "You can see for yourself, sir, why I thought it best not to summon the night watchman or the constable."

"Yes, Mr. Callow."

"Best to keep it in the family, sir."

Edward mumbles something indistinct that could be interpreted as his assent. The manner of Sir Granville's death would no doubt appear to many as shocking, sordid, even salacious. His uncle is stark naked and sprawled on the floor, with a bedsheet—twisted so it's as strong and deadly as a rope—coiled tightly around his neck. His eyes bulge from his face, looking as if they could be popped out as easily as one might squeeze a pip from a lemon. His tongue, thick and livid, hangs from the side of his mouth. But that's not the worst of it. Although if he had to make a choice between the bloody stab wounds, the long gash in Sir Granville's lower abdomen, so deep he can glimpse slick gray intestines, or the symbols inscribed on his uncle's chest, Edward would be hard-pressed to decide which was the most horrible. There's something deeply discomfiting—atavistic, even—about flesh being cut in such a manner.

He crouches down, trying to stay clear of the dark stain that spreads out in a wide circle around the body. He gingerly touches the warm, wet carpet. When he turns his hand over, his fingertips are bloody. With his handkerchief, he wipes his fingers clean, then rubs away some of the dried blood from Sir Granville's chest. Like the others, he is marked with three symbols: the first is two interlocking triangles, the second is another triangle, inverted. The third is nothing more than a short vertical line. He tips the body back slightly, to free the arm that's trapped underneath.

"Holy Mary Mother of God," Mr. Callow exclaims in a single exhaled breath.

It's as Edward feared: the only digit remaining on Sir Granville's right hand is his thumb.

Only a week ago he told his uncle about the similarities between the murders of Dr. Briscoe, Sir Henry, and Mr. Osborne, and he revealed his conclusions, such as they were. Sir Granville became quite distressed at the news, so much so that Edward suspected he knew something he wasn't telling. He insisted that Sir Granville be especially cautious when he was abroad at night, but he never imagined that his uncle would be vulnerable in his own home. Apparently neither did he.

Sir Granville's bedroom is on the third floor. It's unlikely anyone entered through the window, but Edward checks it anyway. It's closed and locked, and the windowsill is free of dust. Either it's been opened recently or the room is kept spotless. He peers outside. Only thirteen years ago, at the end of Cromwell's reign, this area between Pall Mall and Piccadilly was untamed park and swampland. Now it's one of the most popular areas for the new mansions of the gentry. There's decent street lighting here, and the parishes are wealthier, so they can afford to hire able men for the watch. It's not an area known for its crime—but then again, Sir Henry was murdered not far away, in St. James's Park.

Edward turns back to the room, his gaze settling on the wine decanter and glasses on the hearthside table. "Mr. Callow, could you do me a kindness and have everyone assemble downstairs?"

Sir Granville's staff numbers nearly twenty, not including the stable boys. They gather in the kitchen, the cook-mistress and the kitchen maids and chambermaids sitting at the long table, the footmen, page-boys, porter, and steward leaning against the walls and counters. The cook-mistress sits with a protective arm around a young chambermaid with a tear-stained face—the one who discovered his uncle, Edward surmises.

He stands at the foot of the table to address the group. "Did Sir Granville have a visitor last night?"

The servants shift uncomfortably and exchange cautious looks, but no one answers.

"My uncle is dead," he says. "There's no point to keeping secrets."

The porter, a tall, thin lad of twenty or so by the name of James Turner, speaks up. "Yes, he had a visitor, though that's not what we usually call them." He glances at the others but sees that his attempt at levity falls flat.

Edward misses the inference. "Can you tell me the gentleman's name?"

" 'Tweren't a gentleman. 'Twas a lady."

"It weren't no lady," the cook-mistress says.

"Well—it was a woman, sir," Turner says.

A woman? He can't believe that a woman is capable of the violence inflicted on his uncle. Perhaps she was an accomplice and it was she who let the fiend into the house. He only briefly entertains the thought that the killer is one of the staff. Most of Sir Granville's people have been with him for years. Although his uncle could be haughty and demanding, he was fair, and his servants were loyal to him. And Edward couldn't think of any among them who would have had any contact with Osborne, Sir Henry, or Dr. Briscoe. No, it had to be someone from outside. But a woman?

"I shouldn't of let her in," Turner adds mournfully.

"You were only doing your job, Jamie," the steward consoles him, then addresses Strathern. "You aren't going to hold him responsible for what happened, are you?"

"Of course not. Please, do not make yourselves uneasy. I'm simply trying to find out who came to see my uncle last night. Did Sir Granville often have female visitors?" The servants nod emphatically, surprising him. He hadn't known that his uncle was such a connoisseur of women. He speaks to Turner. "Had this particular woman been here before?"

"I don't think so, sir. Usually they show up just once is all."

"And where do they come from?"

Mr. Callow speaks in Turner's stead. "I believe Sir Granville had an arrangement with one of the bawds in town. She sent him those ladies that she thought would meet with his approval."

"I see," Edward replies. Then turning to the porter, he asks, "Can you describe her for me?"

"Not really, sir. Her face was covered by one of them masks."

"A vizard?"

Turner nods.

"Perhaps there was something else about her that was notable."

"Not that I can think of, sir."

Edward tries to conceal his mounting frustration with Turner's limited powers of observation. "What was she wearing?"

"She was dressed in black, sir."

"Was she young or old?"

"I really couldn't tell, sir. Young, I suppose."

"Tall, short, fat, thin?"

"Tall and sort of medium-size, I'd say. Her hair was red," he adds, happy to remember something.

"Was it a wig?"

"I don't rightly know, sir. It looked real enough to me."

"And how did she arrive here? On foot?"

"Hackney coach, sir."

He pauses and studies the faces staring back at him. Beneath the

bland, inexpressive mask of servitude, they're afraid, and not just because someone has committed a heinous crime in their midst. The sudden death of the master of the house means the sudden loss of their
positions and pay. As Sir Granville's heir, it will be up to Edward to
decide how the house is managed, how many servants will be necessary,
who stays and who goes.

"Thank you, James," he says, certain that the porter has no more
information to impart. "You're all free to go about your duties. Please
carry on as you would any other day, if you can. You'll all be paid through
the end of the month, at which time I shall determine the needs of this
household. In the meantime, there are more pressing things to attend
to. Mr. Callow, if you would come with me?"

Surrounded by stacks of leather-bound journals and yellowing papers,
Hannah sits on the floor of her bedroom reading through her father's
medical notes and observations.

> *Mr. Sadler, aged 60, who labored of a grievous cough, difficulty of*
> *breathing, and loathing of meat, was cured thus . . . The Lady Green*
> *was oppressed with scorbutic symptoms, binding of the belly, mel-*
> *ancholy, watchfulness . . . the child of Agnes Barnes, aged six, was*
> *afflicted with the falling sickness, and by consent was thus freed . . .*

Much of it is instructive, but none of it is pertinent. So far, she has
found nothing that mentions Sir Henry or Mr. Osborne, nothing from
her father's time in France attending Henriette-Anne.

She hears Hester's footsteps on the landing and calls out to her
before she reaches the open door. "You may come in."

Hester lingers uncertainly on the threshold. "You have a visitor,
ma'am," she says with eyes lowered. She's been inconsolable ever since
Lucy left. For all their squabbling, she and Lucy were as close as sisters;
Lucy's running off with the boy Hester fancied must feel like a double
betrayal. Hannah has tried to cheer the girl with special treats of sugared plums, oranges, and chocolate, and she has allowed her to ignore
her chores and even her studies when she wished. Mrs. Wills frets that

this kind of indulgence only makes it worse, but Hannah cannot bear to see her so sad. Unhappily none of it has worked.

"Who is it?"

"Dr. Strathern, ma'am."

Just the mention of his name makes her feel breathless. Only a week has passed since they last saw each other and she asked him not to call on her. Why is he ignoring her request? A small voice inside says that he may have broken off his engagement, but she knows better than to listen to it. Hope only leads to disenchantment.

As she descends the stairs, Edward turns from his study of the chimneypiece, a tapestry her parents bought years ago in France. He is attired much as he was the week before, sans wig, in an everyday coat and breeches and plain silk cravat.

"Mrs. Devlin," he begins as she crosses the parlor, "I would not intrude on your privacy except for a matter of the utmost importance." His expression is grim, his eyes dulled by dark half circles underneath. She knows at once that his purpose here is not romantic, but she is too concerned by his obvious suffering to feel disappointed.

"What is it, Dr. Strathern? What has happened?"

"My uncle was murdered," he says, his voice low but tinged with an unmistakable edge of anger.

"When?"

"Just last night. He was in his own home—actually, his own bedroom."

"I'm so sorry." Hannah shakes her head, baffled. "No words are adequate for occasions such as this. Please sit down. You look quite distressed."

"Thank you." He absently settles into the nearest chair, looking around as if he is just beginning to take notice of his surroundings. "I don't think I realized just how distraught I felt until seeing you. All morning I have been contending with the most horrible . . ." He trails off, not wanting to burden her with the details, but she can see by the stark, pale line of his jaw that they remain fresh in his mind. "It is one thing to clean a stranger's body in the theatre, quite another to prepare one's own relative. Especially after a murder such as this." He sighs and shakes his head. "First your father, then Sir Henry, then Mr. Osborne, and now Sir Granville."

"He was killed in the same manner?"

"I'm afraid so. Although I believe he was strangled first, so that no one would hear his screams."

Hannah shudders. She had no great affection for Sir Granville, but she would never wish such savage cruelty upon anyone. She wants to say again that she's sorry, but it seems unnecessary. Dr. Strathern knows that she of all people understands how he feels. Perhaps that's why he's come here.

She goes down to the kitchen and asks Mrs. Wills to prepare some food and wine. When Hannah returns, Edward is on his feet again, pacing the room.

"Dr. Strathern, please; you are overtired and should rest."

"I am unable to rest. I feel as if I must do something, only I don't know what to do."

"You've already alerted the constable?"

"To what purpose? Even the King's Guards are no help in this matter. Look at what happened after Sir Henry's death—an innocent man was hanged."

"We can't be certain of that."

"You may not be certain, but I am. The only way to find the truth is to search for it ourselves. I came here for a reason: to ask you if you'd found anything among your father's papers."

"I've looked, but so far have come up with nothing."

Edward sits down again, easing back into the chair with a bewildered sigh. "I felt so certain there'd be something—some reference to that night at Saint-Cloud."

"I've found no mention of it. In fact, I have not found any notes on the princess at all, or from that entire period in which he attended her."

"Does that seem unusual to you?"

"Under the circumstances, yes."

He looks down at his hands, interlacing his fingers and tapping his thumbs together thoughtfully. When he looks up, there's a renewed optimism in his eyes. "Did your father correspond with anyone regularly?"

"With many people." She grasps the direction of his thoughts. "But I can think of no one who might be familiar with those events."

Hester enters carrying a tray with bread, cheese, sliced meat, and a decanter of claret. She sets it on the table between them and makes a short, solemn curtsy before hurrying back to the kitchen.

Edward's eyes follow her from the room. "Have you heard from Lucy?"

Hannah shakes her head sadly. "Not a word."

"Have you made any other effort to find her?"

"We have inquired of everyone hereabout, to no avail. Other than that, I know not what to do. Lucy is a free person. She did not steal from us; she took only what was hers. I have no legal or moral grounds for preventing her from doing as she wishes. But it has been hard. My mother asks for her every day. And I worry so; Lucy is very young, and so much more innocent than she imagines she is." She smiles ruefully. "But you do not want to hear about the problems of my little household."

"Indeed, I do not mind at all." His clear gray eyes lock onto hers and she is reminded of the day they met, the first time they truly looked at each other. It provokes a flutter in her chest and a sudden shyness that she would not have thought herself capable of feeling, but with Dr. Strathern she has felt many things that she thought were long behind her. She looks away and busies herself with pouring the wine. "Please, you must eat," she says, pushing the plate with bread and meat closer to him. Judging by the way he eagerly takes up their simple meal, he is famished. "You have not eaten all day," she observes.

"No, it was a bad business. I'll be lucky if any of the servants want to stay on after this. It is so odd. My whole life has—" He stops, seeming to think better of following that train of thought. Instead, he shakes his head as though he knows not what to make of anything anymore. "I had no notion of having a large house and a staff to worry over, not quite so soon."

"Where do you make your home now?"

"My brother's house near Leicester Square. I was planning to stay there until . . ."

"Until your marriage," Hannah finishes for him.

He looks down and slowly rubs his hand across his mouth. "I find it difficult to speak of it to you," he admits. "I feel . . . confused."

Hannah stands up. "Dr. Strathern, perhaps you should go home. You must be very tired after what has happened. It's not surprising that you are feeling so unsettled. Tomorrow you will feel better, I am certain."

As is proper, Edward stands, too, but he makes no move toward the door. "I don't want to go home," he says, his tone as vexed as it was when he first arrived. "I want to find out who murdered my uncle. Your father must have seen something, must have known something—if he had not, I believe he would still be alive." He pauses, calming his impassioned thoughts with a few measured breaths. "Has it not occurred to you," he continues, brow knitting with worry, "that you may also be in danger?"

"Yes. And so may you."

"We must do whatever we can. Perhaps if I helped you read through your father's papers . . ."

"Wait—earlier you asked if my father had any correspondents. I've just thought of someone we should call upon."

Chapter Forty

BY THE TIME they reach Dr. Sydenham's house on Pall Mall it's well after six of the clock and the last vestiges of daylight are long gone. Hannah emerges from the carriage into a cold, clear night and breathes in the fresh tang of flourishing greenery and rich, loamy earth still fragrant from yesterday's rain. This part of London is sparsely inhabited; the aristocratic mansions that have sprouted up in recent years are surrounded by private gardens, public parks, open fields. In comparison to the neighboring estates, Dr. Sydenham's residence is modest in size and lacking ostentation. In the latter respect it resembles its owner, a Puritan among Royalists. Hannah raps the brass knocker in the shape of a caduceus, and soon a woman in a ruffled white cap opens the door.

"Hannah Briscoe!" she exclaims, her eyes wide with delight. "Can that be you?"

"Indeed it is." They embrace warmly. Dr. Sydenham's housemaid has changed little in the years since Hannah last saw her. Grown a bit more plump, perhaps, but her coppery hair is as bright as ever, her broad face welcoming.

"It's been much too long since you paid us a visit." Maureen steps back from the doorway and impatiently waves them both inside.

Hannah introduces Edward and inquires after Dr. Sydenham as they remove their hats and gloves in the wood-paneled hall.

"He's at home," Maureen replies, "though he's been feeling rather poorly all day. But I'm sure he'll be pleased to see you. One moment, I'll tell him you're here."

"Should I be nervous?" Edward asks as Maureen hurries away down the hall. "I've heard the good doctor can be quite imposing."

"It's true you might find yourself arguing the merits of morbid anatomy," Hannah says, "but he has always been kind to me."

"I can't imagine why anyone would be otherwise." His eyes look large in the dim light.

Hannah is suddenly conscious of how close they stand in the narrow hall, aware of Edward's warmth and the faint, spicy-sweet scent of his skin. On the ride over they carefully avoided any further discourse on subjects of a personal nature, an unspoken agreement to put private matters aside while embarked on their pursuit of the truth. But those feelings are right under the skin, ready to surface again at the least opportunity. Edward moves closer, close enough that if she tilts her face up to his, their lips would nearly meet. Bridging that distance is only a matter of inches, and the desire to do so suffuses the air between them. "Hannah," he whispers hoarsely, and for a second she allows herself to imagine it, everything falling away, their cares, their obstacles, this house they stand in, everything disregarded for the sensation of his lips on hers.

Maureen appears at the end of the hall. She must notice how quickly they step away from each other, but she discreetly ignores it. "He'll see you in his study," she says brightly. Hannah follows, hoping no one will notice the flush spreading over her face. Their unconsummated kiss resonates in her body like a missed heartbeat as the housemaid ushers them into a comfortable room with a wood fire burning in the hearth. Dr. Sydenham sits facing the flames, his slippered feet propped on a footstool, a light blanket draped across his legs.

"Forgive me for not rising to greet you," he says amiably. Hannah is pleased to notice that Edward is favorably impressed by the physician's direct yet agreeable manner and his understated attire, a dark woolen suit with a square linen collar. At forty-eight, Dr. Sydenham is still striking, with a magnificent head of graying hair that flows in waves to his shoulders and a strong-featured face absent of the usual marks and furrows of age, except for a deep crease of concentration between his brows. His expression is one that those who are not well acquainted with him might deem arrogant, but Hannah knows he is capable of great compassion. He is also, from her father's own accounts, prone to pigheaded resolve—a charge that Dr. Sydenham often leveled back at his friend.

"My rheumatism has got the better of me today, I fear," he says. He has been troubled with the gout for nearly two decades, and in recent years he has suffered a host of other ills. But he continues to write medical treatises, teach, and practice physick, with a practice so extensive that it includes both the indigent poor of St. Bartholomew's Hospital and persons of quality such as John Locke and Lord Shaftesbury. "Please come in and make yourselves easy." He gestures to the two chairs that help complete a cozy half circle in front of the fire.

"Hannah Briscoe," he says affectionately, his brown eyes merry behind spectacle glasses glimmering with the fire's reflected light. "It seems only yesterday that you were a girl putting my medical students to shame. She used to visit here with her father," he tells Strathern, "and went 'round to his patients with him. She knew more about medicine at sixteen than most young men coming out of Oxford or Cambridge at twenty-two."

Dr. Sydenham's casual reference to the past feels foreign to her; so much has happened since then that the time he speaks of seems very long ago. "You are too generous," Hannah says, although she remembers being astonished by how ignorant the university graduates were.

The sparkle fades from his eyes. "I regret I could not attend your father's funeral last year."

"Your letter of condolence was quite enough," Hannah says sincerely.

"I cannot agree, but I was in the country and unable to travel at the time. A great shame, as there is nothing more salubrious for gout than exercise and fresh air. But my other ailments prevented me."

"Exercise and fresh air is your recommended remedy for gout?" Edward asks.

Dr. Sydenham nods. "Horseback for those who are able, otherwise a daily coach ride will do. Along with the steady consumption of small beer and retiring early of an evening, no later than nine of the clock." He smiles at Edward. "Surprised, are you? Do not credit every wild tale told about me. Most are the extravagant foolishness of prejudiced people. After I recommended a cooling regimen for the treatment of smallpox, the story went 'round that I take those who are so afflicted out of their beds and put them in a bath of ice water. It's balderdash, of course. This is the kind of thing one must put up with if one dares to be different. Some simply don't like the fact that I don't prescribe a great deal of medicine. Often there's nothing better than to leave a sick body alone to allow it to be healed by that prince of physicians, time. But that's not how doctors and apothecaries get rich." He chuckles softly to himself and shakes his head, as if at his own folly. "But I go on too long. I suspect you are not here to listen to my theories of physick."

"Dr. Sydenham," Hannah begins, "Dr. Strathern and I have discovered something very distressing. My father was murdered not by a thief but by someone with a darker purpose, one we do not yet know. But we are quite certain"—she glances at Edward, who nods solemnly—"that my father's death is in some way connected to that of Sir Henry Reynolds and, more recently, Dr. Strathern's uncle, Sir Granville—"

"Sir Granville Haines?" Dr. Sydenham says with surprise.

"Yes."

"I had not heard of this." He looks quizzically at Edward.

"It's only just happened," Edward explains.

"This is distressing indeed." The furrow between his brows deepens as he assimilates their news.

"We believe that these murders have something to do with my father's time in Paris attending Princess Henriette-Anne," Hannah says. "Did he ever speak to you of it?"

The doctor stares thoughtfully into the fire. Finally he looks back at Hannah with resolve. "Did your father ever tell you why he left court?"

"Not exactly, no. Only that he had some sort of argument with Lord Arlington."

"It wasn't precisely an argument. Your father simply refused to do something Arlington asked him to do."

"What was that?"

"Lie." Dr. Sydenham leans forward as if to get up from the chair, but as soon as his feet touch the floor he grimaces with pain. "Dr. Strathern, if you would be so kind?"

"What can I do for you, sir?"

"On the top shelf of that cabinet," he says as he points across the room, "there's a cherrywood box. Can you bring it to me?"

Edward retrieves the box and puts it in Dr. Sydenham's outstretched hands. Inside is a stack of aging papers: legal documents, a few deeds, old letters. From the bottom of the box he extracts a folded page with a broken wax seal. He looks at it intently, as if he is uncertain about what to do with it.

"Sir," Hannah says, "if that letter should shed any light on why my father was killed, I believe I have a right to see it."

"I hesitate not because I would deny you that right but because it occurs to me that at least two people who knew the contents of this document have been murdered. I would not be honoring my friendship with your late father if I put you in harm's way."

"I am determined"—she glances at Edward—"*we* are determined to find out the truth, regardless of the consequences."

Dr. Sydenham looks at Strathern, eyebrows raised. "What she says is true, sir," Edward assures him.

Dr. Sydenham hands the paper to Hannah. "You are your father's daughter."

She unfolds it and begins to read. Almost at once she looks up from the page, her eyes wide. "This is my father's report on Princess Henriette-Anne's postmortem," she says, amazed.

"He gave it to me for safekeeping soon after his disagreement with Lord Arlington," Dr. Sydenham explains.

Hannah pores over the page written in her father's familiar hand. "'Corrosion of the stomach lining, morbidity of the liver, evidence of renal injury . . . ,'" she reads aloud. She looks quizzically at the other physicians. "He does not come right out and say so, but his findings are strongly indicative of poison."

Dr. Sydenham nods solemnly. "Keep reading."

She quickly peruses the rest of the report. "My God," she whispers.

"What is it?" Edward asks. Hannah silently hands him the report. It takes only a moment for him to discover what has shocked her. "'The uterus is enlarged,'" he reads. "'Upon further examination, the princess is found to be with child. Judging from the size of the fetus, about three months gone.'"

"Poisoned and pregnant," says Hannah, perplexed. "My father lied to me. He told me himself that the princess died from natural causes, and he never said a word about her being with child."

"I'm sure he was only trying to protect you," Dr. Sydenham says. "He must have suspected that knowing this was dangerous."

"What did you mean when you said Lord Arlington asked him to lie?"

"He asked your father to destroy this report and write a new one, a report that made no reference to those morbidities that indicated poisoning or to the princess's condition. Your father refused to do it."

"Why would Arlington try to conceal the murder of the king's sister?" Hannah asks. "He could be sent to the Tower."

"Not only sent to the Tower, but executed," the physician adds. "Whoever poisoned the princess murdered not only her but her child— the child of the Duc d'Orleans and a potential heir to the French throne. A treasonable crime in both England and France."

"Perhaps Arlington has concealed this because it is he who is behind it," Edward remarks.

"Why are you so suspicious of Arlington?" Hannah asks.

"He is known to be ruthless in achieving his aims."

"But murder? It seems extreme, even for someone as ambitious as Arlington. Do you believe that the minister is behind this, Dr. Sydenham?" Hannah asks. "Is that what my father believed?"

"I have often wondered about Arlington's role in this matter. Your father did not share his thoughts on the subject with me, so I cannot tell you his conclusions. For myself, I think the minister is unscrupulous and considers nothing other than his own interests, no matter how loudly he brays about his service to king and country, but I have never thought him a murderer. Indeed, I cannot see how the death of the princess benefits him in any way."

"You raise an important point, sir," Edward says. "Who, if anyone, stood to gain from the princess's death? I recall that at the time, rumors condemned her husband's lover, the Chevalier de Lorraine. It went around that he had her poisoned in retribution for being banished from the French court. But those rumors ended once it was put about that she died from natural causes."

"I'm sorry to say, Dr. Strathern, that your uncle helped to spread that particular fiction. Lord Arlington prevailed upon Sir Granville to write a new, false postmortem report that became the official one."

Edward nods slowly. "In exchange for a better position at court, no doubt."

"It appears that these murders are meant to conceal the murder of the princess," Dr. Sydenham sums up.

"Someone is killing everyone who knows the truth," Hannah agrees. The three regard each other soberly as the reality sinks in: they are all potential victims.

Edward reaches into his pocket. "There is something else we cannot make sense of, sir. We would appreciate hearing your opinion on this." He gives a piece of foolscap to the physician, who carefully studies the symbols written thereupon.

"My father and the others were not only murdered but mutilated, all in a similar fashion," Hannah says. "Their fingers were cut off in the same sequence in which they were killed. My father, being the first, had one finger missing, and Sir Granville, being the last—"

"Was missing four," Edward adds. "The symbols you see there were inscribed on the bodies."

"The *x* in the square is an apothecaries' mark," Hannah says.

"Yes, I recognize it. *Menses,*" Dr. Sydenham says, using the Latin word for *month.*

"Are the others familiar to you?" she asks.

"These two"—he points them out to Hannah—"look like the astrological signs Capricorn and Leo." He hands the paper to her.

It's the first time she's seen all the markings together. There are twelve in all, as each body was inscribed with three different symbols. So far, if Dr. Sydenham is correct, they have deciphered only three of the twelve: the astrological sign for Leo, the sign for Capricorn, and the *x* enclosed by a square, the apothecaries' symbol for *month*. No, *menses*. It's Latin. Some of the other symbols, she sees now, are not symbols at all. They're letters.

"Dr. Strathern, the mark on Sir Henry's body wasn't a cross. It's a *T*. And the one on my father's body was a *P*. It's a word, or the beginning of one. P-O-T-I." The answer seems obvious now. "*Potio*. It's Latin for poison."

Edward nods, agreeing with her deduction, then cocks his head, perplexed. "But if the killer is trying to obscure the truth, why would he reveal the method of the princess's murder?"

"Someone who could commit these heinous acts cannot be of sound mind," Hannah points out. "And, I'm beginning to believe, is not a man."

"Not a man?" Edward scoffs.

"Madame Severin," Hannah says. "When I first began treating Louise de Keroualle, she was strangely fearful of the mademoiselle being poisoned."

"She had good reason to be fearful. She'd already seen one mistress die."

"But she tasted my medicines herself, as if she were familiar with poisons." Hannah pauses as she recalls a darker memory. "I thought it was the laudanum that made me faint at the dance, but I have not experienced anything like that before or since. I remember that the wine tasted strangely bitter—"

"You think she poisoned your wine?" Edward asks.

"I don't know for certain, but she had ample opportunity." Hannah shakes her head. "I knew from the moment I met her that she was not to be trusted, that there was something menacing about her. And you yourself said that a woman was seen at Sir Granville's last night."

"An accomplice, perhaps, but not the killer. If you had seen the violence done to my uncle's body, you would not believe that it was carried out by a woman."

"You're going against your own precepts of philosophy," Hannah reminds him. "A woman called on Sir Granville, and then he was found dead. I think we should at least entertain the notion that a woman could be the murderer. I would not put anything past Madame Severin."

"But how can we possibly prove it?" Edward asks.

"I can think of only one course. The only person who may have the answers we seek is Lord Arlington."

"But you yourself said it would be dangerous to confront him."

"But if we do not, we may never know the truth."

"I agree with Hannah," Dr. Sydenham says. "You must speak to him. And it occurs to me that there is yet another reason for proceeding. There are five letters in *potio*, five fingers on one hand. I think this killer means to strike once more."

"But to accuse Lord Arlington of conspiring to conceal the murder of the king's sister? We might never see the light of day again," Edward says.

"I think there may be a way to approach him," Dr. Sydenham says, eyeing Dr. Briscoe's report. "Keep in mind, however, that you'll still be putting yourselves at great risk."

Chapter Forty-one

"SIR GRANVILLE'S BEEN murdered?" Arlington's stony gaze shifts from Edward to Hannah and back again.

"Last night," Edward grimly informs him. "In his bed."

They convene in the secretary of state's baronial chambers. It's the epitome of luxurious officialdom, with gleaming mahogany walls and French carpets as thick as sheep's wool yet silken to the touch. Except for the light cast by the two candles the clerk brought in, the room is draped in shadow. The smoldering remnants of a fire glow red in the huge hearth.

Hannah watches the minister closely for his reaction. Even artful dissemblers such as Arlington cannot disguise their every emotion. Beneath his impassive veneer she detects suspicion, doubt, even fear. She's certain that he knew nothing of Sir Granville's demise before now, but she suspects that the news does not come as a complete shock to him.

"My father, Mr. Osborne, Sir Henry, and now Sir Granville," Hannah says. "What do you imagine all these men had in common, Lord Arlington?"

"I'm sure I do not know," he replies indifferently. He straightens the velvet collar of his embroidered dressing gown; with the palm of his hand he rights his wig, haphazardly donned as he entered the room. "I'm saddened to hear about your uncle, Dr. Strathern, but neither of you has any business bothering me at this hour of the night. It's only out of my respect for the deceased that I have been prevailed upon to leave the sanctity of my privy quarters and meet with you. And now it's time to say good night." He takes a step toward the door to his private rooms only to find Edward blocking his progress. To procure entrée to the minister, Dr. Strathern has already threatened Arlington's clerk with bodily harm, and he has no qualms about using a similar sort of intimidation on the secretary of state, foolhardy though it may be.

"All of those men were present at the Palace of Saint-Cloud the night that Princess Henriette-Anne died," Edward says. "As you were yourself."

"And how would you know that?" The minister's lips press together as if he's just tasted something sour.

"I was there, too."

Arlington looks back and forth between them once more, as if trying to discern precisely what they know or, perhaps, what is wise to tell them. "One word"—his head jerks toward the door to the clerk's office—"and you'll both be taken from here and thrown in the Tower."

"We're aware of that, sir," Edward says. "Why not allow us a few minutes of your time first?"

Arlington's head tilts skeptically. "What good will it do me?"

"It might very well save your life."

The minister remains wary, as if he doesn't really care to know what they have to tell him but decides he must listen. Whether his choice is based upon self-interest or political expedience Hannah can't determine. "All right, then," he says crossly. With his thumbnail he scratches a notch into one of the candles a half inch below the flame. "You have until the candle burns down to there."

Hannah glances at Edward, who nods for her to take the lead. "The Princess Henriette-Anne was poisoned," she begins, "and someone is killing those who know the secret of how she died."

"You think that the king's sister was murdered?" Arlington's voice is inflected with just the right amount of haughty disbelief. If Hannah didn't know that the minister knew otherwise, she might be shamed by his disdain. But she knows the truth, and she will not let him deny it.

"We've seen my father's report on the princess's postmortem."

"That's not possible—I destroyed it myself."

"He made a copy before presenting it to you. Dr. Strathern and I have both seen it. There's no mistaking his hand, or what it implies."

"Where is this report?"

"In a safe place."

"And what did you imagine you would do with it?"

"All we ask, Lord Arlington, is that you tell us what happened so that we may discover the true identity of this fiend and bring him to justice," Edward says.

"And if I choose not to tell you anything?"

"If you do not help us, we'll take my father's report to the king," Hannah adds. It was Dr. Sydenham's idea to use the report as leverage.

Arlington crosses his arms over his chest and huffs with annoyance. "You think you've got me over a barrel, don't you?"

From the sarcasm in his voice and the condescending smirk on his face, Hannah knows that their threat hasn't had the effect they'd hoped for. Edward notices it too and appears equally uneasy. Perhaps Arlington doesn't fully understand the peril he's facing. "You concealed the murder of the king's sister," Hannah says. "Surely that's treason."

"It would be, if you were correct in your assumption that I concealed it from him."

"The king knows?"

Arlington doesn't answer. He doesn't have to—his rejoinder is evident in his eyes.

"Why would the king not speak out against his own sister's murder?" Hannah asks.

"It is not yours to question why the king acts as he does. I suggest you abandon your inquiry. No good will come of it."

"But this killer may strike again," Edward cautions. "Even you could be in danger, Lord Arlington—as is anyone who knows the truth of the manner in which the princess died." Arlington still looks skeptical, but Edward's exhortations appear to have struck a chord. He presses further. "Do you have any notion of who may be responsible for these terrible crimes?"

Arlington sighs heavily. "No," he replies, his voice threaded with worry and fatigue. Hannah suspects that for the first time tonight the minister is responding with candor. "So far our own investigations have come to naught."

"Your own investigations?" Hannah says. "You too have been seeking the killer?"

"Do you imagine the king cares not when his loyal subjects are mercilessly slaughtered? Of course we have been trying to uncover the identity of this knave." He looks at them sharply. "Don't tell me—you already have someone particular in mind."

"Yes, we do," Hannah says carefully. "We believe that Madame Severin—"

"Madame Severin!" Arlington scoffs. "You can't possibly imagine—"

"Lord Arlington, please bear with me. Madame Severin was close to the princess, perhaps closer than anyone else. I am certain she has knowledge of poisons, and therefore had not only the opportunity but the means. She had a sad history in France, of which you are probably aware. Perhaps she desired to quit the princess's household for England but the princess would not give her leave." Hannah thinks back to the dance and Madame Severin's strange behavior. "I fully believe she is capable of carrying out these attacks."

"Do you?" he asks dryly.

Hannah looks to Edward for confirmation and nods. "Last night, a woman called at Sir Granville's—a woman dressed in black."

"And this is what you base your conjectures on?"

"In part, yes." How can she explain that she intuitively knows that Madame Severin is guilty of something?

He arches a brow. "It's an imaginative tale."

"There is more than my imagination at work here."

"I happen to know for a fact that she did not murder Sir Granville."

"How can you be so sure?"

Arlington glances down and shakes his head, sighing. When he looks back at them, there's a spark of anger in his eyes. "Because she was here," he says without breaking his gaze. "With me. All night." He waits for them to comprehend the full meaning of his words.

A guarded glance at Edward tells Hannah that he is as astonished as she. Twice now the minister has surprised them.

"Stay here," Arlington commands. He crosses the room and disappears through the door to his privy chambers.

"What's going to happen now?" Edward asks.

"I have no idea," Hannah replies. "But I suspect he will never forgive us for forcing his hand like this."

"Might he be lying about Madame Severin?"

"I don't think so. Indeed, the first night I came to Whitehall I suspected something between them, but they conceal their alliance well with their bickering."

They don't have to wait long for confirmation. Arlington returns with Madame Severin on his arm. From across the room Hannah can barely distinguish her form, cloaked as it is in black, a shadow among shadows, one that's alive with the whispering rustle of silk skirts. Steadily the indistinct pale oval of her face grows closer, larger, sharper. Both the minister and his mistress look discomfited, as if they have just had a row; and in Madame Severin's expression Hannah detects a petulant anger. But then it's no surprise that the mistress of the bedchamber is not pleased to see her.

"Madame Severin is not to blame for your father's death, Mrs. Devlin, or that of your uncle, Dr. Strathern. Quite the contrary—we are worried that whoever killed them may set his sights on her too." He turns to his mistress. "Madame?"

"I still say that telling them this is unnecessary," she says vehemently.

"And I say it is," he replies calmly but with no less conviction. His subsequent glance says it all—he is the king's counselor, not she.

"Do you know the truth of what happened that night?" Edward asks.

Madame Severin pensively looks away; clearly the recollection is painful for her. Candlelight softly flickers on the precise and elegant planes of her face. The candle has burned well past the mark that Arlington made upon it.

"First," Madame Severin begins, "you must know that Henriette-Anne was very unhappy in her marriage. The duc never loved her, as he could never love any woman. He flaunted his male favorites in front of her, in front of the entire court. Not only he but they treated her scandalously. The duc was jealous of the princess's intimacy with his brother King Louis and sought to keep her his servant and slave. He had relations with her only to produce heirs; what should have been an act of love was instead an act of violence he used to control her. Before she was to go to Dover to be reunited with her brother, your king, the duc forced himself on her with the sole purpose of making her with child so that she would not be allowed to travel.

"She had only just realized her condition when King Louis granted her leave to visit the brother she had not seen in ten years. I was her sole confidante, and I helped her to conceal it. She felt unwell during the entire trip. King Charles asked Dr. Briscoe to attend to her, but the princess was careful to hide her pregnancy even from him. When we returned home, she vowed never to have another of the duc's children. She asked me to procure for her those remedies that would bring on the terms."

Madame Severin falls silent. She dabs at her eyes with a hand-kerchief; within its gossamer silk folds a tiny glint of silver sparkles as the candlelight catches a jeweled band on her finger. In spite of her efforts, two shining, crystalline tears slowly roll down her cheeks. Hannah finds herself captivated by them, and moved by a sympathy for Madame Severin that she would never have imagined she could feel.

"You gave this medicine to her?" Hannah asks.

"No. I did as she asked, but I hid it from her. I was afraid of what might happen to us if the duc or the king found out. We argued fiercely, and I thought that I had convinced her to carry the child despite her feelings for her husband. But she discovered where I hid the medicine and unwittingly took a deadly dose. Only a few hours later she was in unbearable agony, and the doctors could do nothing to save her." She looks at Edward. "As you well know."

So the Princess Henriette-Anne had taken her own life. Self-murder is a mortal sin, and the souls of those who commit it are believed to burn in Hell for eternity. The stigma of it would forever darken her name.

"Now you know why the king should like the truth of his sister's death kept secret," Arlington says. "He will not allow her memory to be tarnished by scandal. You have been told this in the strictest confidence. If you reveal what you have learnt to another living soul you will end up in the Tower, make no mistake."

"But Madame Severin's account begs a question, Lord Arlington," Edward says. "If my uncle and the others were not killed to conceal the murder of the princess, then why, in fact, were they killed?"

"I have no idea. But even if I knew, Dr. Strathern, I would not be obliged to tell you."

"But we are determined to bring this man to justice," Edward says.

"You would do well to remember that there's only one justice in this country, and that's the king's justice."

"You could at least tell us who else is privy to this secret," Hannah says. "Perhaps they will have the knowledge we seek."

Arlington glances at Madame Severin as if seeking her opinion, or perhaps approval. Her tears have dried, and her face is once again set in an attitude of self-regarding hauteur. The minister appears to mull over Hannah's request and come to a decision. "There's only one other I am certain of," he tells them. "Ralph Montagu."

"Montagu!" Edward nearly spits out the name. "Of course, he was in Paris at that time. And where might we find him?"

"I thought that perhaps Mrs. Devlin would know," Arlington replies in an insinuating tone, one eyebrow raised.

"How dare you." Edward lunges at the minister.

Hannah grabs his arm. "Edward, please." She addresses Arlington. "I have not seen Mr. Montagu since the night of the king's dance. Do you not know where he is?"

"I have not seen or heard from him since his return from Paris last week. I assume he's holed up with some doxy in the rooms he keeps near Newgate Market. Or perhaps he's been dispatched like the others." He eyes them suspiciously.

"You can't imagine that we have anything to do with it," Edward says.

"I have not made up my mind about anything, Dr. Strathern. But I do expect that both of you will stop meddling in this matter. The king has asked the Duke of York to oversee an inquiry into the murders." Arlington sighs and scowls. "Which I'm sure he will do, in those rare moments when he is not occupied with his new mistress, Jane Constable."

"Jane Constable?" Hannah repeats, unable to conceal her surprise. She looks at Madame Severin, whose composed expression changes not a whit. "Since when—"

"You have not heard?" Arlington inquires calmly, almost breezily. "She is to bear his child." He looks at Hannah as if daring her to refute him. Madame Severin wears an enigmatic, almost imperceptible, smile.

"The duke's child? But—"

"Yes, felicitations are in order," Arlington interrupts again. "Unhappily you will not be able to deliver them yourself. As of tonight, Mrs. Devlin, your presence is no longer required at court."

Chapter Forty-two

EDWARD'S COACH RATTLES along London's dark, rutted streets. The tapers have been replaced, and they shed a warm, pungent light on the carriage's lacquered walls and satiny brocade seats. Hannah settles back with a sigh. Their meeting with Arlington has left her exhausted.

Edward looks at her with concern. "You seem far away."

She shakes her head. "No. I am only thinking on this strange affair of Jane Constable."

"Who is she?"

"A maid to the late Duchess of York. A while ago she asked for my help, the kind of help only a physician or an apothecary could give her. She was with child, and desperate. She said the father would not marry her."

"That's not surprising, surely. I don't imagine that the Duke of York intends to take a commoner as his second wife."

"But I do not believe that the Duke of York is the father of her child. I am quite certain she would not have sought me out if he were. I remember clearly a remark she made about how only the king's mistresses are allowed to have bastards, who are then made dukes. Something that is equally true for the Duke of York's mistresses."

"You think that this maid has somehow tricked the duke into believing the child his own?"

"With Severin's and Arlington's assistance, I am sure. At the dance, Madame Severin told me to forget Jane Constable entirely—she implied that the girl had been mistaken, and wasn't with child after all. I didn't believe her; I thought instead that Severin was going to procure a remedy for Jane. Although I was concerned for her, I must admit that I felt some relief to be left out of it." She pauses, her brow wrinkling. "Strange, that what I thought the madame had done for Jane she had actually done for Henriette-Anne. And with such terrible consequences." She shakes her head sadly. "If Arlington and Severin have convinced the Duke of York that Jane Constable bears his child, when the child is born he will acknowledge it and it will be made a duke, or a duchess. Jane and the child will be forever in their debt. It is nothing more than a political ploy, meant to extend their power." She remembers her unsettling dream of Arlington and Severin looming over the courtiers on the dance floor. "They move everyone about as if they were pawns. Even us, though you would think we were not so important."

Something tugs at her memory, a tiny, glimmering thing, something she knows is meaningful. Something to do with Madame Severin. Hannah recollects their earlier encounter: Severin dabbed at her eyes, Hannah saw a glint of light, and then the tears. All at once she understands what she saw. The audaciousness of it makes her gasp.

"She was lying," Hannah declares.

"Who?"

"Madame Severin. The story she told about Henriette-Anne was entirely false."

"Not entirely, surely. I think we can be certain that the princess was poisoned."

Hannah leans forward with passionate conviction. "But she's lying about all the rest. It did not happen as she said."

"What makes you so certain?"

"Her tears. She wiped her eyes and *then* there were tears on her cheeks. There was something, a small flagon, I think, concealed in her handkerchief. She put water in her eyes. She faked her tears."

"Are you sure?"

"Yes, completely," she says, amazed. "They're trying to lead us astray. I do not think we can credit her story at all. Which means it's still possible that Madame Severin is exactly as I thought: not to be trusted and very dangerous. What's more, they intend for us to believe that Ralph Montagu is involved—perhaps even that he is the murderer."

Edward's expression darkens. "Or they know it to be Ralph Montagu."

"You are quick to believe in that gentleman's culpability."

"Gentleman," he scoffs. "He does not deserve to be so called."

"Why are you so eager to believe the worst of him?"

"Because he is nothing but a rogue with pleasant manners."

"That does not make him a murderer," she points out.

"As ambassador, Montagu was intimately involved with the French court. A more scheming band of cutthroats is not to be found anywhere on the face of this earth. The French make the goings-on at Whitehall look like child's play."

"So he is to be condemned by association? You have said nothing so far that has convinced me of his guilt."

"I have not had the opportunity," he protests. "There are any number of reasons why someone like Montagu would be involved in this affair. He is perennially short of money and seems willing to stoop to the basest means in order to get it. Because of his position, he was well acquainted with the princess. Some said very intimately acquainted. Perhaps it was he who the Chevalier de Lorraine paid to place the poison in her cup."

"And since then he has murdered everyone who knows or suspects him of this dreadful crime?"

"Precisely."

"There is a flaw in your logic. My father was killed over a year ago. Ralph Montagu did not return from France until a few months ago."

"Perhaps he did not return to stay; but that does not mean he was not in London when your father was murdered. As ambassador, I expect he often traveled between here and Paris. Indeed, I am certain that with little effort we could make a connection between Mr. Montagu and every one of the four men who were killed."

Hannah's face flushes with anger. "You are ready to attribute to Mr. Montagu every evil for reasons I believe have little to do with your philosophical principles. He is a charming man, with many attractions to his person, and I am willing to believe that there may be some indiscretion in his past attachments. But a murderer? If you knew him as well as I do you would know this to be impossible."

Edward's eyes smolder with resentment. "Exactly how well do you know him?"

She rings the coachman's bell with a sharp pull on a braided rope, and the carriage comes to a halt. "I shall walk from here," she says brusquely, gathering her skirts and pushing the door open.

"You don't even know where we are!"

"It doesn't matter. I know how to find my way home." Hannah steps down to the street, slamming the door behind her, furious and confused. She can't recall ever being so angry that she's walked out on someone before. She stops to get her bearings—Portsmouth Street is only a few blocks to the south—and realizes that the coach remains in the street behind her. She hears the door open and shut again, hears Edward's footsteps quickly approaching. She ducks into a narrow alley lined with brick buildings. It's so dark that she can barely see two steps ahead.

"Hannah!" Edward calls. "Wait, please."

She turns to face him. He's a shadowy silhouette outlined in the faint orange glow from the coach lanterns.

"I'm sorry," he says. "The last thing I want to do is to offend you."

"You had no right to say that."

"I know. Please forgive me." He moves so close that she can feel his chest rising and falling, each warm breath grazing her forehead before it dissipates into the star-filled sky. "And allow me to take you home. This is no place for you to be walking alone."

He's right—these murky, deserted alleys near Lincoln's Inn Fields are unsafe, especially on a moonless night, but neither of them makes a move to return to the carriage. They look into each other's eyes, and neither seems able to break away. It feels like the first time they've truly been alone. Perhaps it's the engulfing darkness of this place, its forlorn silence, but as Hannah gazes at Edward she feels as if they are the only two people in the world. Everyone else is a figment, a shade, a fleeting ghost. The world itself is, perhaps, imaginary. Only they are real and warm and alive. She fights an overwhelming longing to touch his face; the obstacles that divide them are too great. Edward is engaged, he is an aristocrat, he cannot marry her—all of this should persuade her to put her feelings aside. And yet she finds herself wishing, *Just this once. If only I could have him just this once.*

"Hannah," Edward says. In his voice she hears both a plea and a confession. "I cannot deny my feelings for you."

"Though you should."

"I do not know anymore what I should or should not do—I only know what I want." His eyes search hers. "You have bewitched me."

"That was not my intent," she says softly. "But whatever I have done to you, you have done to me, too."

Her admission makes him bolder. He grips her shoulders and pulls her closer. It seems to take an eternity for his lips to touch hers. When they do, Hannah feels surprised by their frank, simple warmth, the scratchy reality of his stubbled chin and cheek brushing against her own softer skin. Surprised by how a kiss can mean so many different and conflicting things: longing, desire, hope, regret, the sad awareness that their first kiss may be their last. She is surprised by her own desire, a sudden, ravenous presence in every part of her body: in her hands that reach to touch him, in her breasts that strain against the confines of her dress, in her mouth that returns Edward's kisses in a delicious delirium. Surprised by his passion that equals her own.

Edward breaks away, then embraces her to speak softly into her ear. "Please, let me take you home."

They take the coach to the north end of Portsmouth Street and, like figures in a dream, slip through the street's indigo shadows to her front door. Inside, Hannah lights a candle and holds it aloft as they creep quietly up the stairs, past the closed doors of Hester and Mrs. Wills and her mother. Stepping lightly, they enter her attic bedroom. She carefully shuts the door and sets the candle down on her desk.

They face each other solemnly. "Are you sure?" Edward asks softly.

She understands what his question implies: he has obligations, there is nothing more for them than this one night, no consequences, no ties.

"Yes." It's a bargain she's already made.

"But I regret that I cannot—"

"Shhh." She places a fingertip against his lips. She can accept tonight for what it is, but she does not want to hear him say the words.

First the gloves, then coat and cloak, his cravat, her neck scarf. Slowly, silently, they remove their clothing: shoes are slipped off, his waistcoat unbuttoned and tossed aside. Carefully, quietly, Edward unfastens the clasps on Hannah's bodice, five hooks in a straight line from her breastbone to her navel. He helps her shimmy out of her dress, which settles in folds around her ankles, like a shed skin. There's nothing left to remove except for their blousy cotton undershirts and Hannah's pale stockings, gartered at the thigh. The room is so quiet that when the candle suddenly gutters and sizzles, it startles them.

Edward reaches out and delicately traces the dark areoles of her breasts, visible through the sheer gauze of her undergarment. "May I?" he asks. Hannah nods and he takes hold of her undershirt and pulls it up. She raises her arms, and as the blouse is whisked away over her head it feels like freedom and release. She stands naked before him, shivering a little in the attic's chill air. Edward's gaze roams freely and appreciatively over her small but shapely breasts; the tight curve of her abdomen; her generous, firm hips; and well-turned legs.

"I knew you would be beautiful," he says, "but I did not know you would be this beautiful." He tilts his head down to kiss her, gently at first, then more passionately, and wraps her in the warm safety of his arms. They break away just long enough for Edward to remove his shirt—it falls haphazardly over the chair and then to the floor—and move to the bed, still kissing. Beneath the flickering shadows that play among the rafters, they lay together silently, carefully learning each other's bodies, two musicians inspecting new and wondrous instruments. Edward has a muscular build and strong, elegant, capable hands: a surgeon's hands. Hands that explore Hannah's body with a sureness and sensitivity beyond what she expected.

Sensation leads to sensation. Edward's warm lips on her lips, then on her throat. His lips move slowly down her chest, stopping briefly to take one caramel nipple into his mouth, then travel lower still, teasing, tantalizing. His hands caress her thighs, then gently press her legs open. Edward bows his head, brushing his lips against her most secret and sensitive part, and Hannah shivers with pleasure. He slips both hands under her buttocks and hugs her body to his mouth for a deep kiss that she feels as wave after wave of pleasure, pleasure so intense that she must bite her own fist to silence herself. It is too much, *it is too much,* she shudders violently from the pleasure of it, *it is too much.* Edward tightens his hold on Hannah as she struggles underneath him, *it is too much.* Just when she thinks she must tell him to stop, that it is too intense, that she cannot withstand any more, the little death overtakes her and she is spinning, lost, free, unable to stifle her own cries. It seems an eternity before she is stilled and calm; but even then, the merest touch could set her off again, spinning away, out of control.

Edward looks with solemn delight upon her heaving chest, her flushed face. He kisses her mouth, then carefully lowers himself onto her. Flesh to flesh, arms and legs entwined, he fits his body to hers. She arches to meet him.

"I will be gentle," he whispers.

"Do not spare me," she replies.

Chapter Forty-three

Fifth week of Michaelmas term

AS THE CANDLES on the High Table burned lower, Andrew listened attentively while Claire related the newly transcribed events of Hannah's diary: the death of Hannah's patient, Mr. Henley, and her second meeting with Edward Strathern; her encounter with Jane Constable; Montagu's attentions; the dance and its aftermath. She told him about the growing intimacy between Hannah and Edward, and their search for Lucy. Then on to Sir Granville's shocking murder, and Hannah and Edward's subsequent visits to Dr. Sydenham and Lord Arlington.

"What happened after they left Arlington's?" Andrew asked.

"Edward took her home in his carriage," Claire replied. She could feel her cheeks burn and was thankful that the lighting in hall was dim.

"That's all?"

"I didn't have time to transcribe all my notes," she replied. She felt a bit cowardly for evading his question, but she thought it better to save Hannah's most private revelations for another time.

Andrew and Claire's dinner together was a sort of first date, albeit an unusual one, as they sat at a long table surrounded by more than thirty of their peers. Claire scanned the faces and discovered a few that she recognized: Carolyn Sutcliffe, thankfully sitting some distance away, who was pretending not to watch them; also Radha Patel, Toby Campbell, and Elizabeth Bennet, who sat next to an elderly man she seemed to be doting on. An unusual first date in that Claire was not, by any stretch of the imagination, wearing something seductive but was attired in her dark blue Trinity gown, with the appropriate clothing underneath: a black skirt worn with black tights and a white, long-sleeved shirt buttoned up to the throat. An unusual first date in that she suspected Andrew had distinct reasons for meeting in this particular public place: to show that he harbored no suspicion toward Claire, and to help put to rest some of the rumors that Derek's death had engendered. And perhaps to put to rest any other rumors: everyone could see that they were just two colleagues who happened to sit next to each other in hall.

Claire swallowed the last sip of wine in her glass, and a waiter instantly appeared to fill it up again. The unexpected luxury of Formal Hall still felt foreign to her. At the hall's eight o'clock dinner, everyone was required to wear gowns, and everyone, including the students, was served at table, unlike breakfast, lunch, or the seven o'clock dinner, which were buffet-style. The meal began with grace, recited in Latin by the master (or the vice-master, if the master was absent), and ended with tea, coffee, sherry, or port and a pudding, as they called dessert. In between was a multicourse affair of a much higher standard than Claire had ever associated with college kitchens. Tonight's cauliflower soup, stuffed chicken breast, pine nut and goat cheese tart, roast potatoes, and *haricot verts* were a long way from the fare she remembered from her undergraduate years, even a long way from what she was accustomed to eating at home. That they were dining in a candlelit medieval hall with everyone in academic dress added even more luster to the experience.

"There are two things we're trying to deduce from this diary, correct?" Andrew said, bringing Claire back from her wandering thoughts.

"Two?"

"As I see it, yes. One, what is the significance of the copied diary page Derek had on him when he died? Two, who killed Roger Osborne, and why?"

"Not just Roger Osborne," Claire added, "but Sir Granville, Sir Henry Reynolds, and Hannah's father, too. The suspects seem to have been narrowed down to two: Madame Severin and Ralph Montagu."

"I'd put my money on Montagu. He was also at Henriette-Anne's bedside the night she died."

"Are you sure? Hannah doesn't mention it."

"Perhaps she didn't know."

"But Edward tells her exactly who was present in Henriette-Anne's bedchambers. He doesn't mention Montagu at all."

"Maybe it's a simple oversight. There were a lot of people there that night."

"But Edward suspects Montagu of being the murderer. Don't you think he'd remember if Montagu were there?"

"Maybe he left him out on purpose."

"Why?"

"I don't know. How much do we know about Edward Strathern, except that by his own admission he was at the princess's that night, too? I'm certain that Ralph Montagu was there. In fact, he was the one who came back to London to inform the king of Henriette-Anne's death, and told him her last words."

"Are you sure?"

"Of course I'm sure. I spent more than five years researching that period. Montagu told the king that Henriette-Anne's last words were of Charles—that her 'only regret was in leaving her beloved brother.' I'm certain I've read it somewhere."

"Montagu came all the way from Paris to tell the king that Henriette-Anne had died?"

"Yes."

"Then it must be as Edward said: Montagu often traveled between England and France. He could very well be the man who killed Hannah's father and all the others."

"Yes, he very well could be," Andrew replied, lowering his voice. "I suspect this is exactly what Derek was considering—that Ralph Montagu was a serial killer. A gripping story, all right. Big enough for a book, and not a bad conclusion, I might add. The more I think on it, the more likely it seems."

"What do you know about Ralph Montagu?"

"In a time when honesty, chastity, piety, and caring for the welfare of your fellow men was all but extinct, Montagu—"

"Was a shining example of goodness?" Claire offered.

"Just the opposite, I'm afraid. He was a shining example of just how low a man could go. He was never honorable, charitable, and most certainly not chaste. He never made a move without first determining how he would benefit from it. Even during the early Restoration period, a time when men like Montagu flourished, it would be difficult to find a more scheming and despicable man than he."

"But Hannah didn't think so."

"She doesn't have the benefit of hindsight, as we do. When Ralph Montagu discovered that he couldn't earn enough in bribes from his position as the master of the great wardrobe, he married the heiress Elizabeth Wriothesley. From all accounts, their marriage was troubled from the start. He freely spent her money and made her miserable until the day she died in 1690. Then, still not rich enough for his taste, Montagu decided to court the daughter of the Duke of Newcastle, who was also the widow of the Duke of Albemarle and fabulously wealthy. There was only one problem: the Duchess of Albemarle was completely insane. She insisted that she would not marry again except to a person of royal blood. So Montagu got himself up in exotic garb and presented himself at her house as the emperor of China."

"He showed initiative, at least," Claire said with a smile. "You can hardly blame a guy for trying."

"He not only tried, he succeeded. The duchess married him, and he went through her fortune like sand through an hourglass. He built a grand house in Bloomsbury that was designed by Robert Hooke. About sixty years later, the government bought it to house the country's collections of antiquities, and later still it became the site of the British Museum. While he was married to the duchess, Montagu had affairs too numerous to count. At one point, while in Paris, he was sleeping with the Countess of Castlemaine, King Charles's former mistress, and her daughter—the king's daughter—simultaneously. He blackmailed people, was involved in devious and underhanded political plots, succeeded in framing the Earl of Danby, the then secretary of the treasury, for something Montagu himself had done, and generally sowed discord wherever he went. If he were alive today he would be called a sociopath."

"Unless he was a fellow, and then he would be called 'difficult.'"

Andrew harrumphed.

"Something I don't understand in all this," Claire said, "is why, in a city so crime-ridden, Hannah makes almost no mention of any sort of police. Even the King's Guards don't appear to enforce the law."

"There was no police force, as such, at that time. The English people didn't want one—they associated policing with France and with tyranny. There were night watchmen, but they were usually old and not at all interested in putting themselves in harm's way, and there were constables, usually three or four to a parish, but none of them truly fought crime, although they might testify in court if they'd seen a crime being committed. The King's Guards were only trotted out at the king's behest, usually for crimes of treason."

"I think I can understand why Derek Goodman took the diary," Claire continued, "if he thought that this revelation about Ralph Montagu could be the basis for a book, but it doesn't answer the question of what the note was about. Jane Constable hardly comes into Hannah's story at all. She's just a subplot, a bit player."

"I don't understand it, either."

"Oh, no—I just thought of something. Derek Goodman has mapped out the location and the order of the murders: the first was Dr. Briscoe, the second Roger Osborne, the third Sir Henry Reynolds, the fourth Sir Granville Haines." Claire set down her wineglass and stared at Andrew. "What if the fifth and sixth are Hannah and Edward?"

"Oh, dear," Andrew said as the thought sank in. "How long will it take you to transcribe the rest of your notes?"

Claire stood up and put her napkin on the table. "I'll start right now. Be at my set first thing in the morning."

Chapter Forty-four

18 December 1672

THE JOURNEY TO the College of Physicians on Warwick Lane is slow, held up by the pouring rain and an accident on Fleet Street. Hannah rides alone in the hackney coach, staring out the windows at the inclement weather but taking little notice of what she sees. She has thought endlessly on what happened two nights ago. Even now, after receiving such terrible news, she cannot stop thinking on it. What she tried to forestall has come to pass: she has fallen in love with a man who cannot marry her because of money, rank, and duty to family. Or *will* not marry her, Hannah reminds herself, because of all those considerations and more. Perhaps Edward has no wish to change his life. Now that she has given herself to him, perhaps he erroneously believes that she will become his mistress. Edward does not seem the type of man to seek that sort of arrangement, but he has given no indication that he has broken off his engagement, or is even considering doing so. He has written to her three times in the past two days, letters she has read but not answered, letters full of passionate feelings but empty of promises. Her mind tells her that Edward will need time to think before making such a dramatic change in his life. She does not want him to make a hasty decision that he might later regret. Yet in her heart she expected him to fall to one knee to proclaim his love and eternal fidelity and ask for her hand as soon as their love was consummated. If she could laugh at herself today—if she could laugh at anything right now—she would be amused by her emotions. In some respects, she is forced to admit, she is very much like all other women.

The coach comes to a halt on Warwick Lane outside the front door of the College. The door opens and Hannah steps down, bowing her head against the storm. Rain falls so fiercely that the lane's muddy surface appears to quiver under its assault. She quickly walks past the college's white stone façade, turning into an alley that runs along the back of the building and leads to the anatomy theatre entrance. Overhead, a carpenter's shop sign depicting a row of coffins swings madly in the wind, each movement of its rusting hinges accompanied by a lunatic screech.

She enters the theatre's anteroom, a small, high-ceilinged chamber filled with a sedimentary light and the soft echo of rain drumming above. It's reminiscent of being underwater. But then, ever since receiving Dr. Strathern's urgent letter, she's felt weightless, floating, blank. As though she can only register impressions: her shoes gliding over the marble floor, the animal scent of her rain-heavy cloak as she hangs it on the wall, the alien feel of her leather gloves brushing the rain from her cheeks. She removes her gloves and rubs her hands against her wool-clad arms; the theatre's sepulchral chill is palpable even in here.

A hazy sphere of incandescence illuminates the center of the theatre, courtesy of two chandeliers and a few stout-columned standing candelabra. All else—the perimeter of the operatory floor, the spectator galleries, the paneled walls—falls away into a black eternity. From the doorway she glimpses the dissection table and a few strands of long, sinuous hair hanging down as carelessly as a dress tossed over a chair. She finds herself unable to go any farther.

Dr. Strathern approaches her silently, a dark omen in mourning clothes. He looks at her with a practiced delicacy, such as a warden might eye a resident of Bedlam prone to sudden violence. Behind him stands another doctor, scrawny, ginger-haired, young. She can sense his melancholy mood even before she can distinguish the features of his face; it's in the resigned slant of his shoulders, his disheartened air. Perhaps he is too sensitive for this work.

"This is not the way I would have wanted us to meet again," Edward says, the emotion in his eyes quite evident but his manner restrained in the presence of another. "But I knew you would want to see her." His gentle touch on her arm propels her forward into the room and up to the table.

Hannah brushes her fingers against the girl's cheek, still petal-soft but as pallid and bloodless as an eggshell. "Oh, Lucy," she murmurs. The girl is dressed in a long white garment that gathers at the neck and wrists and extends beyond her feet so that it can be tied at the bottom, like a sack: the flannel robe of death. Hannah's throat tightens painfully, and she is unable to hold back her tears. She brushes a few away, then dabs at her face with Edward's proffered handkerchief. Both men regard her with slight trepidation, such as men often exhibit in the presence of female emotion, as if they fear she will begin to weep copiously, or scream and rend her clothes. It crosses her mind that such histrionics must be consoling in their own way—certainly more satisfying than restraining grief; but for now she has too many questions to give herself over to her sorrow.

"Where was she found?" Her voice sounds so rough that she hardly recognizes it as her own.

"Dr. Hamish, will you please tell Mrs. Devlin"—at the slight pause in his speech, she knows he nearly called her Hannah—"everything that the watchman told you."

"He discovered her in an alley in Southwark. In the area with all the—" He stops, remembering that he's speaking to a lady.

"With all the bawdy houses," Hannah finishes for him. "There is no need to mince words with me, Dr. Hamish."

He colors slightly but continues on. "She was without any effects, or, I'm sorry to say, any clothes. Whether she was left there in that condition or later robbed we do not know. He reported that he saw no blood near the body, by which we believe"—he glances at his superior—"she died elsewhere. He said he inquired of people in the parish, but no one recognized her."

Meaning that the watchman had put Lucy's body in a cart and wheeled it around to all the neighboring shops and houses. Hannah hoped that he'd had a blanket or at least some straw with which to cover her body. It pained her to think of Lucy being so vulnerable, even in death. Perhaps especially in death.

"She might have been brought to Southwark from anywhere in London," Hannah surmises. "Why did the watchman not take her to a church?"

"Because of this," Edward replies. He rolls a sleeve back from her wrist and nods to Hamish to do the same to the other. He steps back to give Hannah a clearer view. Across each of Lucy's wrists are two deep red gashes.

Self-murder. Something terrible indeed must have happened to provoke Lucy to it. Perhaps she and this young man had run out of money, or he had abandoned her. Either of which would have made her prey to the city's madams and bawds, always on the lookout for girls like her: young, destitute, and alone. Whatever happened, it was dreadful enough for Lucy to die outside of the comforting embrace of the church. Such obvious sinners as self-murderers aren't readily granted a church burial. It will require substantial greasing of palms just to get Lucy admitted into St. Clement Danes's churchyard, and even then the best she can hope for is to be buried facedown on the north side, the least hallowed ground. It's cold comfort to know that it could be worse; suicides are still sometimes found at lonely crossroads outside the city walls with a stake in their hearts.

"The watchman brought her here hoping to earn a few extra shillings," Edward says. "Dr. Hamish was disinclined to subject her to any trials but paid him just so she might not fall into less restrained hands. When I arrived I recognized her from the dance—and the rest you know." He seems relieved to be finished telling this sad tale. "What would you like us to do?" he asks.

"Do you truly believe she is a suicide?" Hannah asks.

"There are no other marks of violence on her body."

Her stomach turns at the thought of it, but she must know if Lucy was ravished or hurt. "None at all?" she asks.

"No, I assure you, nothing of that nature."

Small relief, but it is something. She runs her thumb over the ridged cuts on Lucy's wrists. "How well can you disguise these?"

"I don't know, but we can try." Strathern silences any objections Hamish may have with a stern look.

"I'll send someone for her as soon as I've spoken to the priest at St. Clement's."

There is nothing more to say. She gently brushes the hair away from Lucy's face and chokes back a sob. Each time she witnesses death she is reminded anew how changed a body is once the soul has flown. The contrast between life and death is most apparent in those of tender years, as if when we age and lose the vital spirits of youth the distinction between this world and the next lessens and fades. And though she knows this Lucy of eternal repose is not really Lucy, she leans over and presses her trembling lips against the girl's cold forehead.

"May I see you out?" Edward asks. He walks Hannah to the anteroom and takes her cloak from the peg so that he may drape it over her shoulders. Outside, the rain is still falling. "I'll have my coach take you home."

"I'll make my own way, thank you." By declining his offer, they both know she is saying no to more than that. When Hannah meets Edward's eyes, he shakes his head as if he doesn't believe her.

"I must see you again."

Even now, face-to-face and alone, Edward says nothing about the status of his engagement, only that he wants to see her. Does he truly believe she will be his mistress? It would be no life for her; it would be unacceptable, really. That he finds it acceptable must mean that he does not love her in the way she imagined. The thought creates a pain in her chest that leaves her nearly breathless. Sorrow she'll have to live with, now and forever.

"Dr. Strathern—" With her formal address, Hannah puts more distance between them. "I see now that I have made many mistakes. Please let us not make another."

He leans toward her, his brow knit with confusion. "But we must see each other again—if for no other reason than to discover who is responsible for the murders of your father and my uncle."

She places her hand, softly but firmly, upon his chest, allowing him no closer. "Seeing each other will not necessarily help us find answers. What happened the other night should not have happened."

"Do you regret it?"

Of course I regret it, she wants to say. *I've fallen in love with you.* "Don't you?"

"I cannot say that. I cannot say I regret it."

"Yet you are engaged to be married, Dr. Strathern. I will not see you again. If I discover anything that can help our mutual cause, I will write to you."

The depth of her resolve surprises him. He nods once, slowly, as if he does not completely comprehend, but he is a gentleman and presses no further. She raises her hood and heads for the door.

"Mrs. Devlin," he calls as she departs. "May I attend her funeral?"

Something akin to a smile briefly haunts her lips. "That would be kind of you. I fear there will not be many people there."

Mrs. Wills's wide, bony shoulders hunch forward, quaking with the cadence of her grief. Her openmouthed grimace buckles the sharp planes of her face, squinting her eyes until they're little more than two swollen red crescents. The wail that issues from her lips is the primordial howl of a mother for its young. To see the starched, matriarchal Mrs. Wills collapsing under her own bereavement is almost as painful as the source of the sorrow itself. Next to her, Hester stands mute, frozen in her desolation, tears streaming down her face.

Of all the times Hannah has had to relay the sad news of someone's passing, this is by far the worst. She feels like the Grim Reaper for being the harbinger of so much anguish to the people she loves; and she is crushed by the possibility that they blame her for Lucy's death as much as she blames herself. She lowers her face and presses her fingertips against the bridge of her nose. But the throbbing pain that started behind her eyes this morning has reached deep inside her skull, beyond appeasement from such a simple effort at relief.

"How?" Mrs. Wills manages to say. "Why?"

The how, at least, is straightforward. "It appears she has taken her own life." This is, of course, no comfort to the goodwife or maidservant—their keening grief becomes all the more pronounced. The why is more difficult. "She and this young man must have parted ways or fallen on hard times."

"Then why didn't she come back here?" Hester cries.

Hannah shakes her head. "I wish I knew."

Mrs. Wills reaches out her long arms and pulls Hester into her chest, cradling her as if she were still a child. Hannah wishes she could join them; wishes she could be so consoled. Instead she rises from the kitchen table.

"I'll tell my mother," she says.

But when she reaches her mother's room, Charlotte is happily playing with a black-haired poppet that was once Hannah's own, and singing to herself in a sweet, breathy voice. Would she understand if Hannah explained it to her? What would be the purpose? Hannah cannot bear making her mother unhappy, too. Are there not enough oppressed and sorrowful spirits in the house?

Hannah turns away to the stairs. With each step she feels a stab of pain, reaching deep and burning hot behind her bleary eyes. From habit she walks to the workbench in her room and the vial of laudanum waiting there. The amber glass is cool and smooth in her palm. Simply holding it is a comfort of sorts; but she knows now that she cannot be comforted. There is no consolation to be found in this bitter liquid. She has used opium to dull her pain, and it has dulled her senses as well. If she had been more attentive, more observant, she might have foreseen Lucy's involvement with this young man; she might have prevented her from making such an ill-considered choice.

She grips the vial hard, as if to crush it in her hand, then throws it across the room, where it shatters against the wall, leaving a ragged stain as dark as dried blood.

---

20 December 1672

For as long as he can remember, he's believed that what he wants is exactly this, the continuation of the life he's always known. But as Edward stands up from the Cavendishes' dinner table and holds out his arm to Arabella, he is struck and disconcerted by the dull repetitiveness of his quotidian routine: the requisite formality of the midday meal; the polite, empty conversation; the short promenade to the withdrawing room. As he walks with his fiancée in measured pace behind his future in-laws, he cannot suppress an image of himself as a harnessed dray horse trudging unimaginatively along in well-worn traces. In the withdrawing room they will spend an hour or two in each other's company for no other reason than that this is how people of quality organize their days.

The Cavendishes' withdrawing room is stiflingly familiar, not only because he has visited almost daily since his return from Paris but also because there is nothing within its tastefully and expensively well-appointed walls that hints at originality or invention. It is strangely austere, in spite of its efforts to the contrary: bright daffodil yellow damask-covered walls, gilt-framed Venetian mirrors, a ceiling swarming with pink-cheeked *putti*. Arabella and her mother sit down in their usual place on the French-blue silk settee. Sir William lowers himself into the large wingback by the fire, stretching out his gouty ankles and nestling his head into the crook of the chair. He'll be asleep before the servants arrive with the wine and the fruit. Edward gravitates to the armchair nearest the window, where he can peruse the newest additions to Sir William's library, stacked on a nearby parquetry table.

No one except Edward ever reads them. Today's volume, *Observations on Monsieur de Sorbiere's Voyage into England,* seems pleasant enough. He opens the book and runs a finger over its smooth ivory pages. Even before he attempts to read he knows he is much too distracted to do so.

Opening the book makes him think of Hannah. Not because of something specific in the book itself but because he cannot do anything anymore without thinking of her. When he looks out a window, any window, he thinks of her: maybe she will suddenly, magically appear. When he ties his cravat in the morning and stares into the looking glass, he thinks of her: would she approve? When he rides in his carriage he thinks of her, of how beautiful she looked the last time she rode with him (fatigued and distressed, yes, but with more grace and strength than any other woman he has ever known), and imagines what they would say to each other. When he rises in the morning, when he goes to sleep at night, when he is alone, when he is with others. Yes, even when he is in his fiancée's withdrawing room, which he knows smacks of betrayal, but he is not quite sure whom he is betraying: Arabella, Hannah, himself?

All entreaties to his conscience and reason are useless. His desire for her is a constant sensation, like unquenched thirst. Something as subtle as a reflection on the river or a dried leaf scuttling across a barren field can set his mind afire with thoughts of her. Much more than his mind, if he is truthful. He finally understands what the poets have always known: romantic love, even the most noble, selfless sort, is a type of sickness composed of longing and continual sexual desire. It is not a quiescent or especially pleasant state. Memories of their passionate embraces keep him awake at night and preoccupied during the day. He cannot forget the sensation of Hannah's body entwined and joined with his, her deep reserves of passion. He cannot close his eyes without thinking of her lips, her eyes, her voice, the sound of her, the *feel* of her.

He experiences her absence most intensely at the anatomy theatre. He can no longer be there without thinking that he may suddenly see her as he did the other morning, framed in the doorway, just come out of the rain and stricken with the news of Lucy's death. Or as he did the first time, when she told him the story of her past. But more often he pictures her next to him, working with him; which to some may seem a morbid sort of fantasy, but the thought gives him deep and satisfying comfort, even joy.

Only a few months ago he could not have imagined sharing his work with a woman. Unquestionably he would not have believed that he would help a female surgeon amputate a man's leg. He knew that midwives and female bone-setters existed, of course, as well as skilled noblewomen who ably practiced physick among their families, servants, and country-folk, but he never expected to meet a woman whose education rivaled his own and was, he would readily admit, a finer physician than himself. As an anatomist he has few equals, but she is the better healer by far. He has always believed that a man's vocation is something separate from his marriage and family. The thought of sharing his work, his life's passion, with a woman—a woman who could be his wife—is one of the most extraordinary and revolutionary thoughts he has ever entertained.

But it is not to be. She refuses to see him. She refuses, even, to accept his letters; in the past two days since he last saw her, he has sent four, each one more desperate and imploring than the last, all of which she has returned unread. She has given him no indication that she would change her mind about him if he was free. She is independent and proud. He can't imagine her marrying for anything other than the purest reasons. Wealth and position, two congenial traits he has always relied upon to recommend him, seem to count for little in her eyes. Take away wealth and position, and what does he have left to offer? Only himself. It's a humbling thought. It occurs to him that if she can so easily stay away from him now, after what has happened between them, then she may not love him: a notion that falls just short of causing him physical pain.

"Edward!"

He looks up to see Arabella and her mother staring intently at him. The annoyance he heard in his fiancée's voice is quite evident on her face. She must have called his name at least once already. "That must be a very engrossing book," she says with a hint of the pretty pout she makes when she feels Edward is not being attentive enough.

"Not really," he admits.

The effect of his honesty in place of the expected politesse is immediate and profound; at least, it is as profound as anything is allowed to be in the stultifying ambiance of the Cavendishes' withdrawing room.

Arabella looks at him with widened eyes, as if she's just suffered a mild shock. Her mother becomes suddenly, pointedly attentive, like a hound that's picked up a new scent.

"What is wrong with you?" Arabella asks.

He wants to say that he can't breathe, that he is suffocating, that he did not realize until now that he is being smothered alive.

"Edward, what is wrong?"

Instead of answering, he closes the book and returns it to its place on the table. He considers how odd it is, that the one person who's supposed to know him best doesn't have a clue to what's troubling him. His entire life is in turmoil, yet she hasn't noticed. No, that isn't entirely fair to Arabella, or entirely honest. He has allowed his life to go on in its smooth, calm, unruffled way, even though he of all people knows that everything's changed.

He rises and crosses the room. He thinks of the many ways in which he has already disappointed Arabella and the many others in which he is sure to. He will be doing her a great favor, although she may not think of it as such, at first. "Arabella," he begins, brought to a halt by her innocent, questioning gaze. His fiancée is completely unprepared for what he is about to say. Lady Cavendish, however, senses what is to come. She regards him almost mockingly, angry yet resigned. *Think of all the trouble you're going to cause,* she declares with only the slightest tilt of her head and the minutest jut of her chin.

"Arabella," he begins again. "May I speak to you alone?"

Chapter Forty-five

21 December 1672

SOON AFTER ITS excavation, the open grave began collecting rainwater. For three days now the storm has continued unabated, and the pale wood coffin nestled within the hollowed-out ground is already half-submerged. The storm's initial bluster has given way to a monotonous, melancholy sort of downpour, the type that makes Hannah feel as if it's always been raining, as if it always will be. A dreary daylight the color of a ripe bruise broods over the churchyard. The bell tower and the Gothic spire of St. Clement Danes stand out ominously against the sodden sky.

The priest holds the prayer book so close to his face that she can see almost nothing of his countenance except for two shaggy black eyebrows, which rise and fall as he speaks. He is a Welshman with pockmarked skin and a timid manner whose voice is barely loud enough to carry across the gravesite. Nevertheless he drove a hard bargain before agreeing to bury Lucy face up, with her coffin oriented east to west, so that she might rise up with the other saved souls come Judgment Day and take her place in heaven. Mr. Ogle too had to be paid. He leans on a shovel at the foot of the grave, near a mound of fresh earth that's already turned to mud.

Hannah strains to hear the priest's recital. "Man that is born of a woman hath but a short time to live and is full of misery," he says. "He cometh forth like a flower, and is cut down; he fleeth also as a shadow, and continueth not . . ."

She keeps a protective arm around her mother, who whimpers and sobs. She suspects Charlotte knows not why she is crying, only that the churchyard frightens her. Hester and Mrs. Wills stand nearby, huddled together for warmth. They both appear stunned, as if they have no more tears left to shed. Edward looks on from the opposite side of the grave. They are the only mourners present. Although Hannah made a generous donation to St. Clement Danes, the cuts on Lucy's wrists proved difficult to conceal and rumors of her suicide spread throughout the parish. It isn't the rain that's keeping the other parishioners away.

"We have entrusted our sister Lucy Harsnett to God's mercy, and we now commit her body to the ground," the priest continues, "in sure and certain hope of the resurrection to eternal life . . ." Once the burial rites are concluded, he leads them quickly through the Lord's Prayer and the final amen. Everyone except Edward is shivering with cold. Ogle begins shoveling mud into the grave, where it lands with a splash and a sickening thud, like a weighted body heaved into a river.

Mrs. Wills discreetly leads Charlotte away as Edward makes his way over to Hannah. Before he says a word, his eyes search her face; discovering, she imagines, all the subtle and not so subtle signs there.

"You are unwell," he states simply.

"Not precisely, Doctor, but I have taken your advice. I've stopped using laudanum." Three days now. Countless times she has longed to take refuge in it, but she has resisted. Her headache has been as unrelenting as the rain. She feels as though she's hardly slept, but she has dreamt. Strange, disquieting dreams.

"But you're suffering, I can see."

With a single glance that encompasses Lucy's grave, her goodwife, mother, and maid, she shrugs and says, "Does it matter?"

"Yes, it matters. How long are you going to punish yourself?"

She makes no answer.

He lowers his voice. "You are not to blame for Lucy's death."

"How can you be so certain? You hardly know me. Perhaps I'm a monster."

"Lucy made her own decisions." He lowers his voice. "Why have you not answered my letters? There is something very important I must—" He breaks off in midsentence, his attention captured by something on the other side of the churchyard. Hannah turns just in time to see a figure slipping behind Ogle's cottage and out of sight.

"It's Thomas Spratt," Edward declares and races across the yard after him. Hannah follows, with Hester not far behind. By the time she rounds the corner of the cottage, Edward has the young man collared and one arm twisted behind his back. His felt hat has fallen into the mud, and his blond hair quickly darkens in the rain.

Not only rain but tears also wet his face. He's clearly overwrought, too much so to attempt to break free. Edward pushes him up against the cottage wall. "You have much to answer for, young Mr. Spratt."

Even if Hannah didn't recognize him as the young man she saw the girls talking to weeks ago, she would know who he was just by the dumbstruck look of calf-love on Hester's face. He does not appear to be the sort of boy who would lure Lucy away from home; but if he did not, why is he here, and why was he hiding?

"What happened with Lucy?" she asks him. "Did you abandon her?"

He looks at them wild-eyed. "Abandon her? I don't know what you mean."

"You and Lucy eloped together, did you not?" Edward says.

"Lucy? Elope with me?" He shakes his head, still distraught. "No! She wouldn't have me."

Hannah nods to Edward, who releases his hold on the boy and steps back. "Explain yourself," she says.

"I loved her. I asked her to marry me. She turned me down." He tries to collect himself, wiping at his face with his sleeve.

She and Edward look at each other, perplexed. "What happened?" Hannah presses.

"I told you, she wouldn't have me. She laughed at me. Said she didn't need my sort, that there was a gentleman in love with her, and she was going to be a lady."

"A gentleman?" Hannah asks, even more mystified. "What was his name?"

"She refused to tell me. She disappeared after that, but I kept looking for her. I discovered her a week later on Foster Lane, near Cheapside. I told her that ladies weren't kept by gentlemen in a few rooms over a tavern, but she said she was happy. I'd hang about sometimes and see him come and go. It wasn't long before he was gone for good. The next time I went by, I found out that she'd snuck away in the middle of the night, for want of the money to pay her account. He'd left her with nothing. Next I heard," he sniffles, "she was here."

"Did you ever learn the gentleman's name?" Edward asks.

He grimaces as he tries to recollect. "I heard a coachman address him once. It was strange-sounding, foreign-like . . ." His voice fades. "Montagu, that's it. Mr. Montagu."

Hannah feels the blood drain from her face. Hester gasps, her long, freckled fingers covering her mouth, her eyes round.

"Hester," Hannah says, turning to the maid. "Tell me what you know."

"Mr. Montagu kissed her at the dance," she confesses as if she didn't quite believe it herself. "I saw them. Lucy swore me to secrecy. I didn't think it meant anything. He was a gentleman and Lucy was a maid! I never imagined a gentleman would do such a thing as ask her to run away with him. I thought . . ." She glances at Thomas, then quickly looks away. "I thought differently."

"Not all men who are called gentlemen are truly so," Edward says. He turns to Hannah. "What do you think of Mr. Montagu now?"

She wants to protest that one biased eyewitness should not be allowed to condemn him, that Thomas may have recalled the name incorrectly, that there may be more than one Mr. Montagu; but she does not have to protest aloud to know that these arguments ring hollow. She shakes her head and says, "I fear you have been right all along."

If what Thomas says is true, her own complicity in Lucy's death is even greater than she first thought. She brought Montagu to her home, took the girls to the king's dance, allowed them to be in his company. All the while she believed that he intended to court her; instead he seduced her maid. Was that his design from the start, or merely a recent fancy?

"When did you last see Mr. Montagu?" Hannah asks Thomas.

"Over a fortnight ago."

Montagu must have lied to her when he wrote that he was going abroad the next day. She couldn't imagine what his aims were, but he could not have done Lucy any worse harm. He abandoned her to a fate of which he could not possibly be unaware.

"Hester, go with Mrs. Wills and my mother to the carriage," she says. The girl reluctantly curtsies to Edward and offers a solemn farewell to Thomas before she walks away. "Dr. Strathern, we must be leaving. I cannot keep my mother out in this weather."

"Wait," he says. His hand clasps her arm. "What are you going to do?"

"I do not know."

"Yes, you do. I can see that you do. Do not be so foolish as to imagine that you can confront him. Lord Arlington said that Montagu returned from Paris last week, which means he was here in London when my uncle was killed."

"Yes, I understand that." She pulls her arm away.

"Hannah, please. Do not be so hasty. At the very least, allow me to go with you."

"I have little desire to be in the company of gentlemen just now."

"We are not all so untrustworthy." His eyes implore her. "I have much to say to you."

"What could you possibly have to say that I don't already know? That I behaved like a fool? That I should have known that a man could not possibly be interested in me when he might instead have the love of a fresh-faced young maid? Or, in another case, the devotion of a wealthy young lady? I know I have been an idiot. I know it more than anyone. And Lucy paid the price for it." Hannah's voice breaks as her throat tightens and tears threaten to overtake her. She gathers her resolve. "Do not imagine that I will allow his crime to go unpunished. But I do not need your help."

"Hannah, please. I must speak to you—"

She tilts her head defiantly. "Well?"

"Not here," Edward protests. "This isn't the place—"

"Then you will have to find another place, Dr. Strathern, for I must be leaving." She turns and walks to the hackney coach, where the others are waiting.

When they arrive home, Hannah goes at once to her desk. On a sheet of foolscap she draws the markings on the bodies from memory. On her father's body were a dotted circle, a crescent moon, and the letter P. Roger Osborne had inscribed upon his skin a trident shape, rather like a curved *Y* with a line rising up from the center, another mark that Dr. Sydenham thought to be the astrological sign for Leo, and an O. On Sir Henry, the sign for Capricorn, the apothecary sign *menses,* and a T; on Sir Granville two interlocking triangles, a single triangle balanced on its point, and the letter I. It doesn't make any immediate sense, but the longer Hannah studies it, the more she is convinced that these markings tell some kind of story. But who is telling this story, and why?

Could it be Ralph Montagu? Thomas Spratt's revelations have forced Hannah to reconsider her opinion of him. If he could behave so unconscionably toward Lucy, she must concede that he may be capable of anything. Even so, it is hard for her to square her firsthand knowledge of Montagu—a man of wit, even temper, and gallant charm—with the secondhand reports of him. Was he truly capable of inflicting the terrible injuries she saw on Mr. Osborne's body, wounds that she knew were also inflicted upon the others? No matter how hard she tries to imagine it, she cannot picture Montagu acting so violently. She could almost as easily believe that Edward did it. And though she doesn't really think that these arcane symbols are going to indict Montagu or acquit him, they are all she has left to go on.

She draws the letters and signs in different combinations, clustering them in various groups. She annotates the known marks by type: astrological sign, Latin letter, apothecary symbol; all of which, it occurs to her, are used in the practice of physick. Although belief in astrological influence has waned in recent years and has few adherents among younger physicians, there were those, including the late, popular herbalist Nicholas Culpeper, who placed great stock in it. And the other symbols? Perhaps alchemy or chemistry.

She stands up and walks over to her sizable collection of books, the combined result of her father's bibliophilism and her own. Her eyes scan their worn leather bindings. The answers must be here somewhere.

Chapter Forty-six

Fifth week of Michaelmas term

NO, THAT COULDN'T be the end. But it was, unfortunately, the end to what Claire had copied from the diary. After taking her morning shower and getting dressed, Claire looked over her notes and felt the same frustration she'd felt the night before, when she'd finally gone to bed after hours of transcribing.

True to his word, Andrew showed up at Claire's set promptly at 9:00 a.m.

"So?" he asked eagerly. "What happened?"

Claire handed him the notebook. "Read it and weep."

"It ends sadly?"

"No, it doesn't end. That's the end of my notes, but not the end of the diary or the story."

She went to the gyp, the small communal kitchen next door, and brought back cups of hot tea. Andrew sat at her dining room table with the notebook open in front of him. He sipped his tea absently, engrossed in reading. At last, he closed the notebook and looked up at her.

"We've got to find that diary," he announced.

"I agree. Take me back to Derek Goodman's set and let me search for it again."

"I don't think that's wise. The police brought in Ashley Templeton and her friend Clive for questioning yesterday after I made that call to Portia. Their story checks out for the night Derek died—the police can't place either one of them at the scene. So they still don't have a suspect, and I'd rather not give C.I.D. any other reasons to suspect you—like, for instance, having your fingerprints all over his set. In any case, Hoddy and I have already looked through everything. I don't think the diary is there, unless it's hidden under the floorboards, which doesn't seem to be Derek's style. I think we should look in the Wren Library again, and not just in R bay, but everywhere. Didn't Mr. Pilford tell you that Derek often put books back in the wrong places? Perhaps he did it on purpose. Instead of taking the book from the library, he puts it in a place where no one else would think to look for it, which is tantamount to squirreling it away for himself."

"Search the entire library? That could take days."

Andrew arched a brow. "Do you have a better idea?"

"No."

"Then meet me at the Wren in an hour. I promised I'd take some books from Derek's set over to Fiona Flannigan. I'll be there at eleven."

Claire decided to spend her free hour in the Lower Library, researching Ralph Montagu. Hannah seemed convinced that he was the murderer, but according to Andrew, no historian had ever even hinted at such dark strands in Montagu's soul. Blackmailer? Yes. Two-timing womanizer? Yes. Completely unscrupulous? Yes. But serial killer? If it was true, Claire realized, a career-making story had just fallen into her hands.

She walked into the library and turned right into the reading room, lost in her thoughts—so lost that she bumped into Rosamond Mercy, who was bent over a water fountain taking a drink. The collision knocked a plastic medicine bottle from her hand.

"Sorry," Rosamond said.

"No, it's my fault," Claire replied, picking up the bottle that had landed near her feet. She read the prescription as she handed it to Rosamond: alprazolam, ten milligrams as needed.

"Sorry," Rosamond said again, taking the bottle and scurrying away.

Claire sat down at a computer terminal and typed in Montagu's name. It didn't take long to discover that if any biographies of the man existed, they weren't in the Trinity Library—or the University Library or the Seeley Historical Library, either. She tried searching under subject, then keyword. The only document relating to Montagu was a twenty-page letter published in 1679 regarding the Earl of Danby affair, which had nearly sent the lord treasurer to the Tower and sent Montagu running back to Paris, out of harm's way.

But from what Andrew had said, Ralph Montagu had been written about in at least a few books, perhaps even his own. She looked up *Charles II and the Rye House Plot*, wrote down the call number, and located two other general histories of the period. Then she typed in "tachygraphy" to see what might come up—why not write a paper on codes and ciphers and then a second on a female physician and a murderous courtier in Restoration London? "Tachygraphy" didn't yield any results, but after unsuccessfully trying a few words and phrases she hit pay dirt with "cryptography": seventeen listings. One book looked particularly helpful: an annotated 1984 edition of John Wilkins's circa 1694 *Mercury, or, The secret and swift messenger: shewing how a man may with privacy and speed communicate his thoughts to a friend at a distance.*

Claire gathered up Andrew's book, along with the other Restoration histories, easily enough, but she couldn't find the book on cryptography. She wondered if it would turn out to be another of Derek Goodman's acquisitions. She took her books up to the front desk and inquired of the young librarian there, who typed the call number into the online catalogue.

"It's listed as being on the shelf," the librarian said.

"I've already looked. It's not there."

"Oh, hold on—I know where it is." She turned around to scan the titles stacked on the book trolley behind her. "The bloke who's had it checked out just brought it back," she said as she handed the book to Claire. "I hadn't gotten 'round to returning it to the shelves."

"Who checked it out?" Claire asked. What if someone else was writing a paper on the same subject?

The librarian made a few quick strokes on the keyboard. "Here's the record," she said. She turned the monitor slightly so that Claire could read it. "Robert Macintosh."

"For God's sake, doesn't the bedder ever come in here?" Andrew asked, looking around at the chaos of Robbie Macintosh's set. Claire stood next to him and was equally amazed at what she saw. Empty pizza boxes and beer cans littered the tabletops. Books and clothes covered the floor. It looked like the aftermath of a party, but Claire suspected that it was a cumulative mess made by Robbie alone. The graduate student himself appeared as though he'd just gotten out of bed. He wore a pair of baggy jeans, a T-shirt with a large stain on the front, and a dazed expression. It was a bit like coming across a hibernating bear in his lair.

"Sorry 'bout the mess," Robbie said. "The bedder refuses to come in here. I was going to complain, then I realized that she had a point—it didn't really seem fair to expect someone else to clean up after me."

Andrew flipped open the top of a pizza box. Inside was a half-eaten slice covered in green mold. "Good Lord, Robbie, if you can't clean up after yourself, you might think of hiring someone."

"That's what my girlfriend says. She refuses to come in here, too. But I haven't because, you know, this is a good way to keep my own space, right?"

"Sure, if you don't mind sharing it with cockroaches. However, we didn't come over here to discuss your extremely unhygienic lifestyle. Dr. Donovan found out that you checked out a few books on tachygraphy. The day we spoke to you in Dr. Goodman's set you said you knew nothing about it. Why didn't you tell us the truth?"

"It was the truth. I didn't know anything about that note you showed me. As for the books, well, I was just curious."

"You developed an interest in speedwriting right at the same time Derek Goodman did? Seems like an awfully big coincidence. Tell me, Robbie, where were you the night he died?"

"You don't think I have something to do with that, do you?"

"I don't know. You said you were with your father in the hospital. Will your father tell the same story?"

"What are you now, the police?"

"No, but I am the college's liaison to C.I.D. If you don't talk to me, you'll have to talk to one of the detectives."

"Shit." Robbie sat down and raked his hand through his hair in the same anxious gesture Claire recalled from their first meeting. What was he hiding? "Look, I had nothing to do with Dr. Goodman's death," Robbie said. "Can't we just leave it at that?"

"No."

One glance at Andrew's stern expression was enough to know he was serious. "Okay, here's the deal. I spent that weekend with a girl who's not my girlfriend. I told my girlfriend that I was with my dad. If she finds out that I wasn't, she's going to break up with me."

"Perhaps you should have thought of that possibility before you kipped off for the weekend with another girl."

"Thanks for the advice," he said, then sighed and muttered another obscenity. "Before I tell you anything, you need to know that I didn't do it."

"Didn't do what?"

"What I'm going to tell you."

"Maybe you should just tell us first—"

"All right. Just keep it in mind, okay?" Robbie took a deep breath. "I needed money and Dr. Goodman said he would pay me if I helped him."

"Helped him what?"

"Write his paper."

"His paper on codes and ciphers?" Claire asked.

"Yes. Except that as it turned out, he didn't really expect me to help him so much as do all the research and write it myself. Then he would publish it under his own name."

"He paid you to write his paper for him?" Andrew asked, incredulous.

"Look, I didn't do it, okay? I didn't even get started except for checking the books out. When I went over to his set that day, I was going to tell him that I wouldn't do it. I didn't want to risk getting kicked out of school."

"But if you were the one who was going to do the research and the writing, how did Dr. Goodman know what was in the diary?" Claire asked. "How did he know about the murder of Roger Osborne?"

"He'd read it already. He was brilliant, you know."

"That means he must have known something about tachygraphy when I showed him my notes," Claire said to Andrew. "He flat-out lied to me—said he'd never seen anything like it before."

"He'd had a close relationship with Nora Giles," Andrew reminded her. "I think we can assume he knew something about it."

"Do you know what he did with the diary once he'd read it?" Claire asked.

"He gave it to me," Robbie replied.

"He gave it to you?" Andrew asked.

"Where is it?" Claire asked.

"It's right here," Robbie said, walking over to a pile of books on the floor. It was buried at the bottom. "I'm glad to be rid of it," he said, handing it to Andrew. "I tried to put it back in the Wren, but I couldn't get into R bay without Pilford's help—and it didn't seem a good idea to let anyone know I'd had it." He paused while Claire and Andrew looked over the diary. "Dr. Kent, is this going to go on my record? I didn't actually do anything wrong. I thought about doing something wrong, but then I realized it was wrong and I didn't do it."

"This will be just between us for now," Andrew said. "But if I hear so much as a hint that you're not on the path of the straight and narrow . . ."

"Yes, sir."

"Do you know of any other students that Dr. Goodman may have paid to write for him?"

"I don't know any names," Robbie said, "but I got the distinct feeling that I wasn't the first person he'd ever asked."

Andrew shook his head in amazement. "It seems that Derek Goodman broke every moral and ethical code held by this college. Or any decent human being, for that matter." He turned his attention back to Robbie. "Are you still having financial problems?"

"My dad's sick, he can't work. It's been kind of tough."

"I'll call the junior bursar's office and set up a meeting for you, all right? I'm sure we can find a way to help you out."

"Thank you, Dr. Kent."

Andrew gave the diary to Claire. She looked at it with wonder. The end of the story was right in her hands.

"How long will it take you to transcribe it?" he asked.

"A few hours."

"Would you like some help?"

Claire smiled.

Chapter Forty-seven

21 December 1672

IN THE CHAMBER outside Arlington's office, Hannah gives the clerk a sealed letter addressed to the minister.

"Could you take it in to him at once, please?" The clerk looks doubtful, so she prods his memory. "You may recall that I was here a week ago. With a gentleman." She sees the recognition in his eyes as he recalls his encounter with Dr. Strathern. He nods and hurries away, message in hand.

Only moments later he returns and ushers her into Arlington's chambers. The minister waits for her behind a massive desk, arms crossed over his chest, wearing a look of extreme displeasure. His affable expression has become decidedly more peevish of late. Her open letter lies in front of him: *I know who killed Princess Henriette-Anne and why.* "You intend to explain this, I assume," he says sourly.

"Yes, my lord."

"Well? Don't waste my time."

"Henriette-Anne had a lover. Her husband found out about it. He also discovered that she was with child and that he was not the father. It couldn't have been difficult to deduce, as according to Madame Severin they were rarely intimate.

"I suspect this betrayal was not easily countenanced by the duc, who was known to be of a jealous and vengeful nature. The duc poisoned her. Perhaps not by his own hand, but I believe it was done on his behalf."

"And what, pray tell, put these ideas into your head?"

Hannah places a neatly written sheet with all the markings and her interpretations on the desk in front of the minister, then watches as he reads. "I believe it means, in essence, 'The cuckolded son of France murdered the pregnant daughter of England.'"

"Where does this come from?" he asks.

"These symbols were found carved into the skin of the bodies of the murder victims."

Arlington reads her interpretation aloud. "'The son of France, a cuckold.'" He looks up at Hannah. "How did you derive 'cuckold' from this?"

"It's the sign for Capricorn, symbolized by a goat. In Latin, the word for 'goat' is *capri,* or sometimes *cornutu,* which means 'horns,' or 'cuckold.'"

"Ahh." Arlington's mood is not improving, but he continues reading. "And the moon and the sign of Leo signify daughter of England?"

"Yes, my lord."

"And the letters?"

"The first four letters of *potio*—Latin for 'poison.' Seeing as all four victims were at Princess Henriette-Anne's on the night she died," Hannah says, "I think we can assume that this story is about her."

He turns the page over. "Is this all?"

"Unhappily, Lord Arlington, I believe this story is meant to continue. The murderer is by no means finished."

He studies her carefully, as if attempting to judge her earnestness. "And what do you imagine happens next?"

"I can't honestly say. But if I were you, I would not go out at night without an armed guard, and I would be very careful about allowing strangers into my rooms."

"I do not need advice from you," Arlington snorts.

"My lord, I do not know what is to come, but I believe there is someone who knows much more than he lets on. If you care for your own and Madame Severin's safety, I suggest that you arrest Ralph Montagu and question him."

"Montagu? You must be mad."

"You told me yourself that he was the one other person who knew how Princess Henriette-Anne died."

"And you think this makes him a murderer?"

"I suspect that he may know more about this affair than anyone else. I do not want to believe that he is a murderer, but there are a number of things that, taken together, signify his guilt. Dr. Strathern said that it was common knowledge in Paris that Montagu and the princess were close, that there were rumors that they were more than just friends. Montagu may have been her lover—or conversely, he may have been her killer. It's even possible that he was both, as he is a man who has revealed himself to be thoroughly unscrupulous. Also, whoever killed my father and the others is an educated man, who has at the very least a passing knowledge of medicine, astrology, alchemy, and Latin."

"Your conviction is inspiring, but these are not terribly convincing arguments. Keep in mind that you're accusing a former ambassador of England and one of the king's servants. Do you really expect me to arrest him on the basis of your suppositions?"

"Such scruples have never stopped you before," Hannah points out.

Arlington's mouth twists at the corners, as if he's suppressing a smile. "You skirt dangerously close to the edge, Mrs. Devlin. All of my dealings are based on what is best for the king. And right now I would say that it is best for the king that we drop this matter."

"Why are you protecting Montagu?"

"I do no such thing. You simply have not convinced me that there is any need to take action against him."

"If you will not send the guard after him, at least tell me where I can find him."

"His lodgings are on the Scotland Yard."

"I've already asked for him there. Where does he stay when not at court?"

"What need have you to see him?"

"It's a personal matter."

"Ahh," Arlington says. "I'm not entirely surprised."

"It is not quite what you think. He seduced my maid, then abandoned her. After which she took her own life."

"I'm sure that's no more than an unfortunate coincidence," Arlington says, unperturbed. "Montagu's personal life is of no interest to me as long as it does not conflict with the king's business."

"I should like to speak to him regardless."

The minister mulls it over. "He is to depart for Paris again tonight. Mind you, I'll have nothing interfere with that. I'll give you leave to see him, but I insist on sending an escort with you."

"I don't need an escort. I'm perfectly capable of protecting myself."

Arlington snorts again, but she senses respect along with the scorn.

"It's not for your safety," he says grudgingly. "It's for his."

Chapter Forty-eight

AT LEAST ARLINGTON didn't send one of his brutes along as her escort. Jeremy Maitland sits across from her in the minister's coach, pensively studying the floor. Other than what she thought was a rather insincere expression of pleasure at seeing her again and a comment on the luxuriousness of Arlington's carriage, he has not said a word since they left Whitehall. He appears anxious, as well he should be. She suspects that Maitland was aware of Montagu's seduction of Lucy from the beginning. He is one of the few people who can shed some light on recent events, and she intends to find out everything he knows about what happened to Lucy. That Maitland, who aspired to be her friend, should have kept it from her feels like a betrayal.

He sits hunched forward, both hands gripping the upholstered seat as if in preparation for a battery of questions.

"It isn't necessary to make yourself so uneasy, Mr. Maitland. I simply want to know what happened between Lucy and Mr. Montagu."

He glances up at her, wary and perhaps even a little fearful. "There is nothing I can tell you. Mr. Montagu is my patron. I cannot divulge details of his personal life."

"You may want to reconsider with whom your loyalty lies."

He looks at her sharply. "What exactly are you planning to do, Mrs. Devlin?"

"When we find Montagu? I don't know precisely. But I believe when I look into his eyes I will know the truth." About more than just Lucy, she hopes.

"It's as simple as that—you'll look into his eyes and know if he's a good man or a bad man?" A few golden whiskers on Maitland's upper lip and chin catch the candlelight; otherwise his face is as downy as a girl's.

He's so young, she thinks. Like Lucy. Which brings her back to her subject of inquiry. "I fear I know the answer to that already. Did you know that Lucy Harsnett was found in an alley in Southwark four days ago, a suicide?"

"No." He appears genuinely troubled by the news. "I'm sorry to hear it."

"Could you not at least tell me what happened at the dance?" she asks, his sincerity softening her tone. "Did you see Mr. Montagu kiss her?"

He shakes his head. "I cannot say."

"You were her escort. Did you not feel any obligation to protect her?"

"No matter what he has done, I cannot betray Mr. Montagu's trust."

"Even though your silence has contributed to the ruin of an innocent girl?"

His olive green eyes take on a grim aspect. "Innocence is but a commodity in this world, Mrs. Devlin."

Ravenscroft supervises his Fleet Ditch project from the relative comfort of the observation platform. Despite its grandiose name, the observation platform is nothing more than a tarp strung up over a few planks of warping wood set down on the riverbank, and it is neither elegant nor even particularly good at staving off the rain. It makes up for its shoddiness with its location at the north end of the construction, just below the Holborn bridge. From here, Ravenscroft has a view of the entire site. In the half mile from Fleet Lane to Holborn, both sides of the twenty-foot-wide river have been cleared of the pigsties that formerly lined its banks. Now it's crawling with men and machines, home to what looks like an occupying army.

What he most often feels as he observes the progression of the work is not accomplishment—that's something reserved for the vague and distant future—but frustration. Building a structure in a river, even a river as small as the Fleet, is a complicated enterprise. First, an oblong island formed with pilings must be created in the center, dividing the river in two. Massive gates, wide enough to block half the river, are attached to each end of the island. They are moved with the aid of huge counterweights, like those used for a drawbridge. Half the river is then dammed by the upstream gate, and all the water is diverted to the other side.

This they have already accomplished, but nothing has gone quite as he imagined it would; his project is behind schedule and over budget, expending the funds the king has allocated at an alarming rate. The wood frame for the first filter (or purification apparatus, as it is now officially called) stands in the exposed riverbed looking, to the knowledgeable eye, as unsteady as a newborn calf. It has been buttressed with supports, but these are only temporary. He's encountered the same problem that Wren and Hooke faced when trying to build at the mouth of the river: the Fleet produces an uncommon amount of silt. These alluvial deposits, combined with decades, perhaps even centuries, of accumulated waste, have turned the river bottom into a stinking, muddy quagmire that cannot possibly support the weight of the structures he has designed. The riverbed must be dredged at least another four feet so that the filter pilings can be secured in bedrock.

Presently, dozens of workmen wade knee-deep in the exposed riverbed, pumping out rainwater and filling countless handcarts with the sludge of the ditch. A steady stream of laborers pushes the handcarts up to the embankment and the waiting oxcarts. Two hundred and eighty-four oxcarts have been filled since they began digging. There are many more to go, more than he can estimate.

"Mr. Ravenscroft!" His foreman ducks his head as he steps beneath the tarp.

"What say you, Mr. Abbott?" The foreman is a tall, thin fellow whose very protuberant Adam's apple is on the same plane as Ravenscroft's eyes. He does not dislike Mr. Abbott, who is generally diligent in exercising his duty, but unfortunately the man is quite lacking in vision, which has led to some tiresome conflicts in the recent past.

"The river has risen more than a foot since yesterday," Abbott says. "If the rain keeps up like this, the water will rise high enough to breach the gate. The men are worried. They fear it won't hold."

Normally, bisecting a riverbed such as the Fleet would not be so difficult, but the recent rains have swollen the river to more than twice its usual size. It rushes furiously through its narrowed channel, pummeling the gate that dams the west side of the river, eroding the embankment on the east side. If the rain continues, they'll have to open the gate and let the water flow into the exposed riverbed. He knows better than anyone that the filter apparatus will be swept away. It would be a monumental setback, one that could prove fatal to the entire enterprise. Perhaps even fatal to himself. He's heard there's an especially frigid dungeon reserved in the Tower for builders who fritter away the king's money so fruitlessly. At the very least, Robert Hooke will make the most of his failure, and he'll never hear the end of it. There is only one thing to do, and that is to keep going.

"I should think that I am a better judge than those fellows down in the ditch, Mr. Abbott. The rain will stop, I am certain. In the meantime, we must keep on. I will not open the gate until the filter apparatus is secure."

"That could be another two weeks."

"So be it."

"With all respect, sir, I have worked on the construction of many a building since the Fire. I have seen some terrible accidents happen when the architects push too hard and too fast to get the job done. It's always the workers who suffer."

"But this is not a building, Mr. Abbott. Am I not right in believing that this is your first river project?"

"Yes, but that does not mean I cannot perceive problems as they occur. That's what I was hired to do."

"You were hired to direct the crews, Mr. Abbott, nothing more." God save him from small-minded men who attempt to impose their own ideas on his work. He crosses his arms over his chest and rocks back on his heels. As far as he is concerned, their conversation is finished.

But the foreman will not back down. "There's a problem on the other side of the river."

"What problem?"

"The storm has washed a great deal of debris into the water. Tree branches and suchlike. It's getting caught in the supports for the footbridge and damming the river on that side as well. I took some men over there earlier"—he points to the temporary footbridge that spans the river at the center of the island—"to try and remove some of it, but it's too dangerous. The water's moving too fast. And the dam is taking a beating. The river's too high, sir. It's time to get the men out of the Ditch."

"Absolutely not! The king himself has taken an interest in this endeavor, and His Majesty means for us to proceed with all speed." It isn't only the king's good graces that he cares for. If he can't make a success of this, how will he show his face at the Royal Society? They'll say he was beaten by the Fleet Ditch, of all things. London's sewer!

"No doubt the king has his reasons," Abbott says, "but even the king can't control the weather. If the rain continues—"

"I know what will happen if the rain continues, Mr. Abbott. You should keep in mind that there is no greatness without risk. Think of the pyramids. Think of the Parthenon. Think of Westminster Abbey. Nothing monumental is ever achieved without sacrifice."

Abbott lowers his voice. "Don't you think you're getting a bit beyond yourself, Mr. Ravenscroft? This isn't a cathedral, this is the bloody Fleet Ditch."

"If you care to keep your job, you will curb your tongue, Mr. Abbott. If the river rises high enough to breach the dam, we'll talk again."

"Staring out at the rain all day won't help matters," Hugh says, clapping his hand on Edward's shoulder. "This isn't the first time an engagement's been called off." He moves away to the warm center of the room and settles into his favorite chair next to his wife, Elizabeth.

"Yes, I know," Edward concedes, turning from the window. He follows Hugh closer to the fire, looking around the withdrawing room with a feeling of relief. It's smaller, darker, and more cluttered than Arabella's; it appears as though people actually live here. It's been months since he's spent an afternoon with his brother and sister-in-law, and he feels as if he's come home after a long journey. He has that strange sense of disorientation in which everything familiar seems changed. It isn't, of course; it's him who's been transformed. He hasn't told Hugh and Elizabeth about the true origin of his melancholy, that it isn't his split with Arabella that's to blame for his present state.

"Just because it isn't the first time doesn't make it any less serious," Elizabeth says. She is a lovely, temperate woman who is more cultivated and more sensible than his brother, who, Edward believes, is lucky to have found her. God has not seen fit to bless them with children yet, a circumstance that has made her all the more sensitive to others' misfortune. "It's the first time for him, that's all that matters."

"But why should he be downhearted?" Hugh protests. "I don't understand. By his own admission, he's the one who called it off. He should be happy."

"Hugh, sometimes you are completely lacking in tact."

"Why should I have to be tactful? He's my own brother."

Elizabeth rolls her eyes. "Insensitive lout, that's what you are." But she is smiling as she delivers her judgment.

"You do both realize that I'm right here in the room with you," Edward says.

"My apologies, Edward," Elizabeth says. "We are only concerned for your happiness. Please sit down and have some wine."

"It's a lovely Madeira," Hugh adds. He lines up three small glasses and fills them to their gold-rimmed tops. "Straight from the sunny slopes of Spain. If this doesn't put a smile on your face, nothing can."

"Hugh, leave him alone."

"That was tactful, wasn't it?" He looks at her innocently. She purses her lips, ready to scold him again.

"Don't bother, Elizabeth," Edward says. "He's right, I have no business moping around like this. Maybe I should leave London for a while, do some traveling. Greece, perhaps, or Turkey."

"That's the ticket," Hugh says.

Edward doubts it. He can already picture himself trudging through the ruins of ancient temples, distracted and despondent. How far would he have to go in order to forget her? Was it even possible to forget a woman just by putting distance between yourself and her? Perhaps it worked in some cases. He didn't believe it would work in this one. How would he ever be able to forget the other day in the churchyard, when Hannah looked at him with such anger, such hatred? It was only then that he realized how much he had presumed of her good opinion of him. What had she said? "I have no desire to be around gentlemen?" It galls him that she has painted him and Montagu with the same broad brush.

The porter announces himself by a knock on the open door. "A letter for you, sir," he says as he carries in the sealed epistle on a silver tray and offers it to Edward.

The handwriting on the outside generates a small flurry of hope. He opens it eagerly. It's from Hannah, but a quick glance is enough to see that it does not contain any personal sentiments. He goes back to the window, where he'll have more light and some privacy and begins to read.

Dear Dr. Strathern:

I have made a careful study of the markings found on the bodies of all four victims. Enclosed please find a second sheet with these markings and my interpretation of their meanings. I believe what I have discovered may signify Mr. Montagu's complicity in these events. We know that he is capable of the most deceitful and despicable behavior. Whether he is the murderer I cannot yet say, but it is clear that whoever killed my father and your uncle was close to the Princess and knew the most intimate details of her life. And who else but Montagu can claim an acquaintance with all the parties involved?

I'm leaving at once for Whitehall to apprise Arlington of my findings and urge him to arrest Montagu. I have no hope of achieving the latter, but I have learnt that the only way to bargain with the minister is to press for more than is desired, and occasionally he will relent and grant some lesser request. All I truly want is to find Montagu and to see for myself if he is guilty. I must attempt to procure some justice for poor Lucy; you know as well as I that there is no justice except that which we make for ourselves.

I have sent a letter and a copy of the enclosed to Dr. Sydenham. If anything should happen to me, please make certain that this information is put into the right hands.

I remain, &tc.
Hannah Devlin

He looks over the enclosed page with the symbols and their meanings. So the duc poisoned his wife because she was carrying another man's child? It seems a plausible explanation, given what he knows about the French court and the duc d'Orleans. But he doubts that the duc would have carried out the murder himself. He is of royal blood, he does nothing for himself. But who, then? And why did Henriette-Anne's murderer make known the reason and method of her death by way of these markings on his victims' bodies?

Up until now Edward has assumed, along with Hannah, that the person who murdered the princess has also been responsible for the death of his uncle and the three others. But what if the motive for the murders of the four men was not to conceal Henriette-Anne's murder but to reveal it? To make known to the world the manner in which she died and take revenge on those who kept it a secret?

He reads over Hannah's disquieting letter once more. "*All I truly want is to find Montagu and to see for myself if he is guilty. I must attempt to procure some justice for poor Lucy . . .* " It seems as though she intends to avenge Lucy's death herself, but she must know that she doesn't stand a chance against Montagu. A more chilling thought occurs to him. Perhaps she is not in her right mind; perhaps grief has unhinged her, and she no longer cares for her own safety.

Edward walks to the door and summons the porter. "Tell the ostler to bring my horse at once."

"But it's still raining, sir. Would you not prefer the carriage instead?"

"Just my horse. I'm in a great hurry."

Hugh appears at his side, concerned. "What is it? What's in that letter?"

"I've no time to explain. I must make for Whitehall right away." He runs upstairs to fetch his coat and gloves. He must hurry. He must find Hannah before she finds Montagu.

Chapter Forty-nine

MAITLAND'S VEHEMENCE SURPRISES her. "You have become a cynic," Hannah says. "Perhaps you have been at the English court too long."

"You think Charles Stuart's court has made me what I am?" he says with a wry but winning smile. "I would never give credit to such a motley bunch of fools. I lost my father before I was old enough to know him, and if my sister and I hadn't been packed off to relatives in Paris we would have starved along with my mother. Not that it was much of an improvement; we were never allowed to forget that we survived only because of my uncle's charity. What he called charity, at any rate. I believe his dogs were treated better than we were. It wasn't until I was taken into Mr. Montagu's service that I was given anything approaching respect."

No wonder Maitland is so loyal to Montagu. What will he do, she wonders, when he discovers the sort of man Montagu truly is? "How long have you been in service to him?"

"Since he was first ambassador, nearly six years now."

She takes a chance. "He was close to certain members of the French court, was he not?"

"Mrs. Devlin, I have already told you, I cannot—"

"What you know of him may turn out to be immensely important." She leans forward, beseeching him. "There is more at stake than just one death."

His wariness returns. "What do you mean exactly?"

"Please understand that I cannot tell you all, but what you know of Montagu and his friendship with Henriette-Anne may help."

"You will not hear any slander of that lady from me."

"I didn't necessarily mean slander."

"She was the best woman ever to grace this earth," he says passionately.

Hannah carefully settles back into the cushioned seat, keeping her eyes on him all the while. She realizes that she has stumbled across something significant, but what it is she cannot yet imagine. "Perhaps you could tell me about her," she ventures.

Now that Maitland is assured that she does not intend to denigrate the princess, his amiable manner returns. "The princess possessed the most refined and sensitive nature," he says. "She knew what it meant to lose one's father at a young age, to be in exile, to be of high birth but low circumstances. We had that in common. She treated everyone with kindness and charity, and as for me—well, she knew I was a gentleman's son. She was as pure as an angel and as devout as a saint. Unhappily she passed from this earth much too soon. Though in God's eyes, perhaps, it makes no difference. *Vivit post funera virtus.*"

Virtue lives beyond the grave, Hannah translates silently. She feels a prickling at the back of her neck, gooseflesh all along her arms.

Maitland speaks Latin.

Of course; he is a gentleman's son with a gentleman's education. She feels as if she's been knocked breathless. Her heart beats in her throat, the metallic taste of fear floods her mouth. She turns her eyes away from him lest her own expression reveal too much. It takes every bit of self-control she possesses to breathe in again slowly, without gasping for air. She stares down at her hands in her lap, willing herself to breathe evenly, her heart to slow down. In spite of her discipline—or perhaps because of it—a fine sheen of perspiration breaks out over her entire body. She has known fear before, but never like this.

She realizes that Maitland is waiting for her to respond, and if she does not speak soon he will know that something is amiss. "You must have been saddened by her death," she says as calmly as she is able. She forces herself to meet his gaze, even manages a look of sympathy, amazing herself with her ability to dissemble. *How did he do it?* she wonders. *How did he murder my father and the others? He does not appear particularly strong.*

"It was a tragedy," he replies, his eyes cast down, "and a crime." She notices the way his long, thick lashes contrast with his pale skin, his downy cheeks. With the right disguise, his face could easily be taken for a woman's. If he wore a dress, perhaps a vizard, under the cover of night—yes, it would be easy. His victims would be caught off guard by a woman. They would allow her to get closer to them than they might a man, allow her near enough to strike; or, in the case of Sir Granville, even allow her into his bedroom. On the first attempt Maitland would go for the heart, incapacitating his victim so that he could not fight back.

But why? She knows now that he did not kill Henriette-Anne—that much is obvious. His feelings on that subject are too strong. But why her father, Sir Henry, Sir Granville? There must be a reason, but at present she cannot conceive of it. Her fear has clouded her thinking. The only things in her mind are to keep Maitland talking, to make him believe that she suspects nothing, and to leave this carriage as soon as she possibly can.

"You speak as though you cared for her," Hannah says.

"Cared for her? That is too pallid an emotion. What I felt had nothing to do with something so commonplace."

"You revered her, then."

"I worshipped her," he says, his voice edged with anger. "But do not imagine that you can understand what I felt for her—what I still feel for her."

For the first time Hannah detects the anguish and rage that fuel his passionate nature. What did he intend that first night? What she thought was a passing romantic interest may have been something else entirely. If she had allowed him inside her house, what would have happened? Would she have been another of his victims? She shudders to think of it. It crosses her mind that he might have inflicted that cut upon his hand himself to gain her sympathy and trust; what could be less threatening than an injured man? She has misinterpreted so much, from the very beginning.

She berates herself for her foolishness. She should never have gone to Arlington without first being sure of the murderer's identity. She should have never gotten into this coach with Maitland. The carriage's window shades are drawn, and she has no idea what part of London they're in. How will she discover where they are and where they are heading without making him suspicious?

She glances at his hand. "It appears your cut has healed quite nicely," she says. "May I take a closer look?"

He offers it to her, seemingly undisturbed by this sudden change of topic.

"I need more light. May I?" She nods at the window.

He shrugs. "Of course."

She unhooks the ring at the bottom of the window shade and lifts it up, fastening it again at the top. They're crossing the Holborn bridge. Just south of the bridge is a huge construction site. Ravenscroft's project, Hannah realizes at once. Half the Fleet has been diverted to run along the east bank, with the muddy riverbed on the west side exposed. There appear to be dozens of workers in the Ditch; blurry figures move about purposefully in the rain. She wonders if the philosopher is among them as she turns the back of Maitland's hand toward the light.

"I'd say it was almost as good as new," she says. "Do you still harbor such a dislike of doctors?" She hopes to divert him from noticing her true interest: up ahead is a crowded street where the coach may be forced to come to a stop.

"Doctors are charlatans who pretend to know much but in fact do very little. I have never seen a physician save a life, have you?"

"Yes, I have, although not nearly so often as I should like to," Hannah replies. "Is that why you're so angry—because no one could save the princess's life?"

"They pretended that she died from a natural illness, even though they knew otherwise."

"My father did not pretend. He was banished from court because of it."

"That's not what he told me." He's defiant and suspicious, as if he has just caught her out in a lie.

Her face flushes with a sudden, overwhelming anger. Maitland has as good as admitted his crime. "When did you speak to him?"

"Near the end of his life, I should say," Maitland replies without remorse. "I asked him why he did not report what he knew to be true: that the princess died by someone else's hand. He denied it outright, said it was her own sickness that killed her."

"He was trying to protect me and my mother," Hannah says. "And for this you killed him?"

"He knew the truth and yet he refused to tell the world. Now she lies unquiet in her grave. They will pay, I tell you." He looks at her fiercely. "They will all pay."

"Who will pay?"

"All of them: Madame Severin, Arlington, the king—"

"You intend to kill the king?"

"I will avenge her even if it means my own death," he says vehemently. "I can never forget the sight of her in agony, ruined, dying— and everyone standing about as though it was some kind of spectacle for their entertainment. Worse, I had to pretend that I felt as little as they, that I felt nothing." The break in his voice betrays the depth of his emotion. "She was pure, you understand. A saint. Yet in the French court she was treated like a servant."

Hannah glances outside. The coachman has turned the horses away from the crowded street ahead, and into a narrow lane barely wide enough for the carriage to pass. She will have to delay her escape a bit longer. "I have heard that the princess cuckolded her husband and was with child by another man," Hannah says. "Do you still consider her a saint?"

"Do not make light of that lady's purity. She was above the concerns of those people. They never understood her."

"You mean the rumors were untrue?"

"I mean that they have no significance."

"So she was with child?"

"Yes." His eyes burn with a dangerous fury. "With my child."

"Yours?" Hannah gasps.

"Do you imagine that it's impossible for someone like me to win a princess's love?"

Hannah thinks about Madame Severin's story of Henriette-Anne's unhappiness with her husband. The appeal of a younger man who worshipped her so passionately would be strong indeed. "I believe I understand her reasons."

"The duc was abominable to her," Maitland continues. "I showed her tenderness."

"Did the duc kill her?"

"Of course."

"With his own hand?"

"No. But it was done for him, all the same. The day she died, I witnessed an argument between her and Madame Severin. She said the princess must do something about the baby, that as soon as it was born the duc would know it was not his and she would be disgraced. Madame Severin said she had procured some medicine for the princess to take, that it would bring on her terms and no one would be the wiser. Henriette-Anne refused to do it. She said the medicine was poison. The duc was spying on her, of course. He had one of his minions put the medicine in her barley-water."

"But why?"

"The duc didn't want her, but he didn't want anyone else to have her, either. And he most certainly could not allow her to have another man's child—a commoner's child, no less. His minions did whatever he told them to do, and they were happy to see her dead. They hated the very fact of her, that she was young, sweet, beautiful. That she was a woman. That she shared the duc's bed. Now she is in her grave and her murderer walks free. She is screaming for justice. I can hear her.

Don't you understand? They keep her murder a secret for a reason."

Hannah lets her hand sink to the seat, then quietly rummages in the folds of her skirt. Her knife is buried deep inside the pocket. "Who are 'they'?"

"All of them," he answers impatiently. "Arlington, Louis, the king."

"Surely you are mistaken. The king of all people would seek justice for his own sister."

"But he did not. King Louis would not have his brother slandered, and Charles Stuart went along with it."

The coach turns into another lane, this one wider than the last. Hannah sees her chance and reaches for the door.

"No, you don't," Maitland says, grabbing her hand and pulling it away from the handle; with his other hand he pushes her back onto the seat. Then he lunges at her, going straight for her throat. He's stronger than she would have thought. His hands grip her neck with such force that she can feel his thumbs against her trachea, feel the dizzying sensation of the lack of blood to her brain. She gasps for breath as she tries to pry his fingers off. She bends one leg and, with as much force as she can muster, knees him in the groin. Maitland gives out a strangled yelp, and his grip on her throat loosens. She pushes him away. For a moment she imagines that she's free of him, but he recovers quickly and hits her roundly in the face. Her head slams against the coach wall. The impact resounds painfully throughout her head, and the sting on her cheek fills her eyes with tears. The coach lurches forward and Maitland falls on her, his hands finding her throat once more.

Hannah digs deep into her pocket and grabs hold of her knife. Without withdrawing it she takes aim at the nearest target. The knife point pierces petticoats and breeches to sink into his thigh. Maitland screams, and she pushes him away with enough force to send him back to the other side of the coach. She takes the knife from her pocket and reaches for the door. This time when he attempts to stop her she stabs the back of his hand, the same one she mended not long ago. As Maitland cries out, Hannah pushes the door open and throws herself forward, as clear of the coach as she can manage. She lands in a street that's more mud than anything else. Her knife goes flying and sinks out of sight. A few pigs run away squealing.

She picks herself up as the coachman reins in the horses. Any moment now Maitland will be coming out after her. She scrabbles in the mud for her knife and finds it just as the door to the coach creaks open. She gathers her skirts and begins to run, hoping to find a way out of this maze of dark alleys and dead-end courts, the very same streets where her father was killed.

The coach must have crossed the Ditch at Fleet Lane or Holborn, Edward explains. Luckily, Arlington's carriage is as ostentatious as the minister; it hasn't been difficult to track it from Whitehall. Mr. Ravenscroft has come out from under the minimal protection of a dripping tarp and stands squinting up at him, one hand shielding his eyes as if he's saluting. Edward is still astride his horse. He hopes to be on his way within minutes.

"Mrs. Devlin, you say?"

"Yes."

Ravenscroft stalks off to speak to a man who looks to be one of the foremen. Edward casts his gaze over the construction site. The embankment is teeming with men, most of them hauling buckets of water or handcarts piled with soil from the riverbed. Oxcarts line up to take the refuse away. The manner in which the Fleet has been diverted seems to him ingenious, though he knows little of such things. A narrow footbridge runs along the top of the gate damming the west side and all the way to the east bank, spanning the river. On the opposite embankment, a huge hoisting machine with a swing crane, used to drop pilings in the river, stands unmanned and motionless. It looks forlorn, he thinks, like a giant tamed animal on a leash.

Other than that, the opposite embankment is empty. The swollen river rises over the crest, encroaching on the land. Not long ago the area was full of pigpens and dying vats. Only the soot-stained shanties on the far side of the cleared area still remain, their sagging backs turned to the river.

Mr. Ravenscroft returns with the foreman, who tells Edward that a carriage matching that description was seen crossing Holborn bridge. Ravenscroft looks up at the sky with wonder. An expression of pure and ecstatic joy crosses his face. "Mr. Abbott!" he exclaims. "It's stopped raining!"

Mr. Abbott responds with a surprised, I'll-be-damned sort of grin.

"Dr. Strathern!" Mr. Ravenscroft gives Edward's leg, still in stir-rups, a fraternal squeeze. "It's stopped raining!" Indeed it has, though Edward isn't quite sure why it's an occasion for such great happiness. Preoccupied, he nods his farewell and guides his horse toward the Holborn bridge.

He's nearing the stone steps when a woman runs out of a narrow alley onto the embankment on the other side of the river. She stops, as if stymied by the rushing water. The denizens of this area are gener-ally of the lower sort, poverty-stricken and unwashed, but this one is covered in mud. She seems to have rolled in it, in fact; her hair is mat-ted and her face is so thoroughly streaked with grime that only a few patches of skin show through. Something silvery glints in one hand. With the other she pushes her hair back from her face. That one gesture tells him everything he needs to know.

"Hannah!" he shouts. She turns to look in his direction, but her eyes pass right over him as if she doesn't see him. How can she not see him? He's a man on a horse. He calls her name again, louder this time, but she continues to stare blankly across the river. Just as he is about to call out once more, a man races out of the same alley. He runs into her, and together they tumble to the ground.

"Hannah!" Edward puts the spur to his horse.

Maitland's assault knocks the wind out of Hannah, and her head smacks hard against the earth. Her delay has proved disastrous. She would have kept running, but she thought she'd heard Edward's voice. She man-ages to keep a grip on her knife as she falls to the ground, but as they struggle Maitland wrests it from her hand. Her attacker stands up and yanks her to her feet. A horse gallops down the rise leading from the Holborn bridge. By the time she recognizes who's riding it, Maitland has the blade up against her throat.

Edward reins in his horse and jumps to the ground.

"Stay back," Maitland warns.

Hannah swallows nervously, feeling the sharpened steel against her skin. Maitland has her wrists clenched behind her back, holding her as close to him as a lover might. His breath is moist and heavy in her ear.

"Let her go," Edward says, venturing a few steps forward.

"Stay back," Maitland repeats angrily.

"You hurt her and you'll go straight to Tyburn." Edward gazes steadily upon them, as if he imagines that by giving them his absolute attention the unthinkable cannot happen. If only it were true. Hannah knows how close she is to dying. One simple cut and she will have only minutes of life left.

"Let them string me up, I don't care," Maitland says. "Wait until the king gets an earful of my last dying words. I'll tell the entire world what I know."

Edward looks at Hannah, his eyes questioning. She nods almost imperceptibly: yes, he's the one, he's the murderer, keep him talking.

"What do you know?" Edward says cautiously.

"The princess was murdered and her killer allowed to go free. Even Charles, her own brother, sought no punishment for her murderer. His love for her was a lie."

"What has this to do with Mrs. Devlin?" Edward takes another step forward. "Let her go."

"Stay back," Maitland shouts. He threatens Edward with the knife, then points it at Hannah's throat again and pulls her with him as he backs up along the river. "I cannot let her live. She'll try to stop me from doing what I must do, as will you."

Maitland's words send a chill through her. She has seen for herself the results of his deadly attacks; she knows better than to imagine that his threats are empty. And now he is starting to panic. His heart is pounding so hard that she can feel it beating against her back, feel his hand wrapped around her wrists dampening with sweat. Her own heart quickens in response. People do desperate things when they're afraid.

Maitland glances back over his shoulder. At first she thinks he's going to drag her into the water, then her feet touch down on solid wood. The footbridge is perhaps four to five feet wide. There's no rail-ing, just a short, raised beam along each side. The river's risen so high it nearly overtakes the bridge. A bunch of downed foliage is caught in the churning water on the upstream side; downstream, the muddy water roils away furiously, sloughing away the embankment as it flows to the Thames. Patches of algae dot the damp surface of the bridge, which vi-brates from the force of the water rushing underneath. The raging river flings droplets in her face. The water is so cold that it stings.

He's going to slit her throat and throw her into the river. Edward moves forward, but Maitland backs away; he won't allow him to get too close. Any second now, Maitland will do it, will press the knife into her throat and cut the artery. How easy it must seem to someone who has killed so many times.

Is this it, Hannah wonders, my last few moments of life? She feels her senses heightened, an intense awareness of every sound, every scent, every sight: the rushing river, the odors of sodden earth and wet wood, coal smoke rising from chimneys and drifting into the rain-freshened air. Edward's face, in which she sees every bit of passionate concern he has for her; his love, even. Yes, his love. *Edward's face.* Will she forget his beloved face once she is dead? Or is this what she was meant to remember? It's all so precious and fleeting. How could she ever have considered ending her own life?

Edward is poised, ready to lunge and to make one final desperate bid for her freedom. Maitland takes another step backward. Hannah feels a tug on her wrists, almost like a warning, just before Maitland's foot slips. He instinctively throws his arms out to break his fall. The tip of the knife nicks her just under the jaw, a sensation that feels more like a burn than a cut. Maitland lands on his back and the knife sails from his hand, skidding in giddy circles across the bridge's slick surface.

Edward jumps onto the footbridge, going for the knife, but Maitland reaches it first. He's on his feet and has the weapon in hand as Edward barrels toward him. Hannah screams as the blade flashes in the air. Maitland buries it to the hilt in Edward's shoulder. Edward cries out and staggers back, then tumbles from the footbridge into the upstream side of the river.

"Edward!" Even before his name leaves her lips, he's disappeared under the tumultuous surface of the water.

Maitland turns toward her. He's nearly close enough to have her in his clutches again when he abruptly stops and lets loose with a terrifying howl. He looks down in horror to see the knife embedded in his calf. An arm's length away, Edward clings to the side of the bridge.

Breathing heavily, Maitland bends to extract the knife. Soon he will have the weapon in hand and threaten Hannah again, or Edward, who still hangs on to the bridge with both hands. Hannah knows what she must do, but still she hesitates; she has never taken a human life before. Edward sees her uncertainty, her vacillation. "You must!" Edward shouts. "Do not delay!"

Maitland straightens, his head rising up, his large green eyes fierce and resolute. He wields the knife high above his head, ready to strike. Hannah barrels forward, her arms outstretched, and shoves him hard in the chest. He yells, not from pain but from anger, as he stumbles back and falls into the river. Hannah watches, amazed at what she's done, as Maitland is quickly swept away downstream.

Like everyone else on the west bank, Ravenscroft has heard the screams and seen the very end of the struggle on the footbridge. He shoves his way through the men who have filled the narrow span to look with alarm on Hannah and Edward, then he urges his men to pull Edward out of the water.

"It's no use," Edward tells him. "My leg's trapped. There's something else caught down there, and I can't break free."

Ravenscroft kneels down. "Is it one leg or both, Dr. Strathern?"

"Just the one."

"Can you push at the obstruction with your other foot?"

"I've tried. It's something large, a tree stump perhaps. It's wedged in the footings next to my leg."

Ravenscroft peers down into the turbulent river, then gets down on his knees to look closely. Already Strathern's having a tough time keeping his head above water. Even though the rain has stopped, it could be hours before it's low enough for a crew to get at the debris. How long can a man survive in this frigid water?

"Hold on," Ravenscroft says to Edward, then instructs two of the men to keep a firm grip on the physician's arms. Even before Ravenscroft has struggled to his feet and completely unbent his crooked body, even before he has looked into the eyes of Mr. Abbott or into those of Mrs. Devlin, he understands the choice he has to make. He can see quite clearly two divergent paths: one leads to his shining success, the implementation of his unprecedented invention, a changed London, a grateful king, respectful peers. On the other lies the destruction of all he has worked for, ruination, disgrace, imprisonment, and possibly even his own death. How long would he survive in one of the Tower's arctic cells?

Abbott has quickly assessed the situation. "We're going to have to open the dam, sir."

After all Ravenscroft has worked toward, it has come down to this: his own glory, perhaps even everlasting fame, for the life of his friend. It would not be an exaggeration to say his only friend: a man who looks beyond his bent body, his gruff manner, his sometimes unappealing self, to see him for what he truly is, or at least for what he can be. Dr. Strathern has often been more kind in his assessment of Ravenscroft's character than he is himself. He envisions a great, heavenly scale on which he weighs his two choices, and they do not seem at all equal; fame being as light as a feather and as easily swept away. A small, childish voice inside him complains, *It isn't fair,* while his more rational self replies that of course it isn't fair: what is? He must make a choice.

"Mr. Ravenscroft," Hannah says. "Please."

If he had not known it before—for what does he know of this kind of love?—he is in no doubt of it now; if the life of his good friend is lost, so too will be the woman who loves him.

"Of course," Ravenscroft says. "Of course." The outcome he will leave up to God. If it means his total ruin, then so be it. He turns to Abbott. "Get the men out of the Ditch, now. Go on, all of you. Spread the word. Abbott, what are you waiting for?"

The foreman glances down at Edward. "You're going to need help, sir," he says to Ravenscroft.

"I need your help to supervise the men and open the dam. Mrs. Devlin and I will do just fine. You have a family to think of, Mr. Abbott. Now be gone with you," Ravenscroft says crossly.

Abbott nods solemnly. "Yes, sir, Mr. Ravenscroft."

"Why is everyone leaving?" Hannah asks as they kneel down and each take hold of Edward's arms.

"They have their job to do and we have ours. When the dam is opened, the water will rush to fill the empty riverbed and the current will be very powerful indeed. Powerful enough perhaps to take Edward with it. Or, in the worst case, the entire footbridge."

"You mean you don't know if this bridge will hold?" Edward asks. He's shivering now, blue with cold.

"It worked on paper," Ravenscroft admits. "Reality's always a little different."

They hear shouts from the riverbank as the oxen are whipped into action and, with a loping gait, turn the cog attached to the counterweight. As the dam slowly opens, the footbridge begins to shake violently and the ebbing water tugs at Edward's body. The sound of the rushing river grows to a roar as it rages downstream and across stream and into the empty riverbed. It takes every bit of strength they possess to keep Edward in their grasp.

With a thunderous noise, the wall of water meets the wood framing of the filter apparatus, breaking it apart as if it were no more than a toy made of sticks. Monstrous cracking sounds, like bolts of lightning, reverberate across the river. Almost at once the water level falls a few feet, then, inch by inch, farther still. There's a hushed sort of silence as the river settles into its new wider and calmer form. By peering over the side of the footbridge, Ravenscroft can see the tree limb caught next to Edward's leg. He anchors his knees next to the raised beam and bends at the waist to grab hold of the tree limb and work it loose. With one last Herculean effort, he frees the limb from the footings and lets it fall from his hands to drift away in the current. Gasping and panting, he sits back. Then, together with Hannah, he helps pulls Edward out of the river and onto the footbridge. Strathern lays on his back, shivering, as Abbott and some others make their way over the Holborn bridge.

"We'll need blankets and dry clothes, if you can round them up," Hannah says, "and a carriage to take him home." Ravenscroft rises and begins shouting orders as Hannah stays on the footbridge, hovering over Edward.

"Don't worry, we'll get you home soon," she says. She's placed her own cloak over him, but his shivering has grown worse. He seems on the verge of losing consciousness, but he rouses himself and tries to rise up on his uninjured arm.

"Hannah," he says, "your eyes . . ."

"Shhh, my love, not now. Rest easy. There will be plenty of time for that kind of talk."

"No, I mean . . . your eyes . . . your headaches." He stops, struggling for breath. "You need spectacles," he says, and closes his eyes.

Chapter Fifty

Fifth week of Michaelmas term

"So it was Maitland all along," Claire said. She and Andrew sat at the Wren-designed table in R bay with Hannah's diary between them.

"Gone 'round the bend with passion and rage," Andrew said, nodding. "It's clear he loved the princess, though it seems a twisted kind of love. But why did he believe that all those men were conspiring against her? Why would King Charles conceal the truth of his own sister's death?"

"Maybe he was afraid that if he accused the Duc d'Orleans of murder, he would alienate King Louis."

"Except that Charles adored Henriette-Anne. One would think that he'd be willing to endure a bit of a cold shoulder from Louis for something as important as punishing his sister's murderer."

"But what if the price of justice was war? England could never have won a war against France."

"I don't think Louis would have declared war on England just to keep the Duc d'Orleans from the executioner," Andrew said, "no matter how much he loved and indulged his brother. But one never knows. We'll certainly never know unless we find the sequel to this diary."

They had come to the Wren to put the diary back where it belonged, but once they'd arrived they'd felt a distinct disinclination to do so, perhaps because it had left them with so many unanswered questions. Had Edward survived? Had he and Hannah fallen in love? Had she been allowed to practice medicine, or had she been forced to give it up?

Also unanswered was the meaning of the photocopied page found on Derek Goodman's body. Over a week had passed, and the police still hadn't made an arrest. More than a few Trinity fellows groused that Derek Goodman's death was really just an accident after all; with their investigation, the police had done nothing but tarnish the reputation of their school.

The only way to learn the answer to most of these riddles was to find another of Hannah's journals, hopefully one that began soon after the first ended. And there was no other way to find it than to search the contents of R bay.

"I'll start on the upper shelves," Andrew offered, "if you'll take the lower."

For the next few hours they spoke little except for brief exclamations of hope that were quickly dashed or vague mutterings about how, honestly, there were really too many books in the world. A belief that was disregarded when either of them came across something truly fascinating. Andrew spent more time than was necessary poring over *A systeme of anatomy: illustrated with many schemes* by Samuel Collins, Doctor in Physick; Claire spent a rapt quarter hour with *An essay on the art of deciphering* by John Davys. Usually a soft "ahem" from the other was enough to remind them of what they were there to do. By the end of the afternoon, they'd scouted every book that looked even remotely like Hannah's diary without finding its sequel, or anything else written by her.

"So much for the Barclay collection," Claire said. "Who is Barclay, anyway?"

"The Earl of Barclay, I believe. If memory serves, his collection was left to the school in the early nineteenth century."

"So how did the Earl of Barclay end up with Hannah's diary?"

"A good question, but not one I'm sure we'll be able to answer. Back in the seventeenth and eighteenth centuries, the collections bequeathed to the Wren usually came from people who had carefully compiled a private library and didn't want the books to be dispersed or destroyed. Later on, even though the library was filled to capacity, the college still took in donations—only now they tended to be the result of someone's cleaning out the attic, and were comprised not only of books but miscellanea. In fact, in the early nineteenth century, the Wren Library was rather like a giant cabinet of curiosities, displaying rare coins, archaeological finds, Egyptian mummies, a collection of globes, and locks of Newton's hair. Tourists would come in to see not only the books, but these other rarities."

"Where is all that stuff now?" Claire asked.

"Most of it has been sent off to the appropriate museums. However, I think at least one surviving lock of Newton's hair is still here."

"Where?"

"Downstairs in the archive."

So the rumors were true: there were storage rooms beneath the school that housed the college's treasures. "The archive?" Claire asked hopefully.

"You don't believe those stories about gold bullion and precious jewels, do you? It's not a pirate's cave; there are more old papers than anything else. I've toiled away in the archive before, and to be honest it's not all that pleasant. It's bloody cold, and there are—" Andrew stopped midsentence.

"There are what?"

"Spiders. Hold on." The faint vertical line between Andrew's brows grew deeper as he searched his memory. "While I was researching the Rye House Plot—which is the name given to a failed conspiracy to assassinate King Charles in 1683—I came across an intriguing story about Thomas Clifford. I never followed it up, though, as it happened long before the Rye House Plot began and wasn't directly connected."

"Who's Thomas Clifford?"

"He was lord treasurer from 1672 to '73. He started out as a lowly squire from Devonshire, but he became Arlington's protégé and so was often in attendance on the king. The king gradually came to rely upon him; in 1672, Clifford was the one who proposed the Stop of the Exchequer to raise money for the Dutch War, for which Charles was grateful. The king subsequently made him Baron of Chudleigh and appointed him treasurer.

"It was a decision that made Arlington furious, but Charles knew better than to hand the keys to the treasury to someone as profligate as Arlington. The result, however, was that mentor and protégé were enemies forever after, and though both were members of the king's council and part of the Cabal, they were constantly at each other's throats. Although neither was in office long enough to triumph. Not long after Hannah's diary ends, both Arlington and Clifford were toppled from power."

"What happened?"

"In the spring of 1673, Parliament repealed the king's Act of Indulgence, which allowed greater freedom of worship in England, and passed something called the Test Act. It was a repudiation of the religious tolerance the king had tried to encourage, and a direct attack on Catholics in England. Every office holder was required to take various oaths of allegiance and public communion in the Church of England. Clifford, Lord Arlington and even James, Duke of York, resigned their government posts rather than renounce their Catholic religion. Not long after giving up his office, Clifford was found dead."

"How did he die?"

"That's what's so intriguing—no one seems to be quite sure. He died in his own bedroom, that much is certain, but the circumstances surrounding his death are rather murky. John Evelyn, a close friend, hinted at suicide. The first earl of Shaftesbury, another member of the Cabal, swore that Clifford had once told him that his horoscope had foretold that he would rise to be 'one of the greatest men in England, but it would not last long, and that he would die a bloody death.' But as we now know, by 1673 Clifford didn't need a horoscope to convince him of that: just like Roger Osborne, Dr. Briscoe, Sir Henry Reynolds, and Sir Granville Haines, Thomas Clifford was at Dover and at Saint-Cloud the night Henriette-Anne died."

"You think he may have been murdered?"

"Very possibly."

"But Maitland was killed in December 1672 at the Fleet."

"All we know for certain is that Maitland was stabbed and then fell into the river. We don't know if he died."

"How are we going to find out if he lived? There doesn't seem to be a second diary. How are we going to discover what really happened?"

Andrew grinned. "The Clifford family papers are downstairs in the archive."

"Jesus, it really is cold," Claire said, hugging her arms to her chest and wishing she'd worn her coat.

Andrew shut the door behind them and turned on a light switch. Six fluorescent tubes suspended from the ceiling flickered to life. "It used to be the wine cellar," he explained. "But it was turned into an archive when the new cellar was built under Whewell Court."

"When was that?"

"About two hundred years ago."

The archive seemed to be the same size as the Wren Library directly overhead, with a low ceiling that was traversed by thick wood beams. The floor was composed of large flagstones, and the walls looked as though they'd been carved out of rock. To help overcome the inherent problems arising from its aged origins, Trinity had installed an air system that reduced dust and regulated temperature and humidity. Even so, it smelled faintly cavelike: Claire detected a whiff of cool limestone with a hint of damp. Rows of sturdy metal shelves held stacks of cardboard boxes, some brown, some white. Antique oak cabinets interspersed with a few simple wood tables lined the walls. The archive was neatly kept, not quite the jumbled warehouse she had imagined it to be, and it had a homey, old-fashioned ambiance, in part because all the boxes were labeled by hand. Claire followed Andrew into the aisle marked C through E, past boxes marked Cardiff, Cedars, Chesterton, and Childers, before arriving at Clifford. The Clifford family papers took up two entire sections of shelving. Twelve boxes, Claire counted, with no dates on any of them. "When were these left to the library again?" she inquired.

"Sometime around the beginning of the nineteenth century, I be-lieve," Andrew replied.

"And Thomas Clifford died in 1673? That's well over two hundred years of papers." On Andrew's face she saw the same hesitation she sud-denly felt: it was a very big haystack they were diving into, without any real assurance that a needle was even in there.

"Are you sure you want to do this?" he asked.

On the one hand she knew it would be sheer tedium; on the other was the possibility of finding answers to one or two of their questions. "Absolutely," she said, even though her fingers were already cold. "The question is, where do we start?"

"At the beginning, of course." Andrew reached up to remove the highest box on the left. "It stands to reason that the oldest papers would be stored here."

It was a reasonable assumption, but unfortunately not one that was shared by the person who had organized the collection. But perhaps "organized" wasn't the correct word for the state in which they found the papers. Even after examining the contents of the first four boxes, they could discover no rhyme or reason to the way the papers were kept. They found a jumble of tax records and ledgers from the family estate at Ugbrooke, bundles of letters to various Cliffords unfortunately not named Thomas, a few small, well-loved books of poetry, the circa 1764 notebooks of a schoolboy named Henry Clifford, age ten, and a large family Bible from the century before. Inside the front cover, Thomas Clifford's date of birth and death were written in a small, precise hand, along with Thomas's numerous children and many descendants, about three generations' worth.

Andrew pointed to the date next to Thomas Clifford's name. "Fourteenth of August, 1673."

"Then how could Maitland possibly be responsible?" Claire asked. "Even if he lived after falling into the Fleet, Hannah knew enough about his crimes to have him condemned to death. He would have been taken to Tyburn long before August."

"It certainly seems so," Andrew agreed.

They continued sorting through boxes while Claire pondered an odd truth: while she and Andrew Kent worked together, they got on spectacularly well. They shared many of the same enthusiasms and interests, toiled in mutual harmony, communicated well, and in general were at their most pleasant. But the moment things became more personal, it all went awry. Claire had the distinct feeling that if she tried to broach a personal subject—say, why she had been kissing Derek Goodman that night—she would encounter a wall of English reticence. How could they get beyond it if they couldn't talk about it?

She stole a glance at Andrew. He was riffling through a packet of what looked like eighteenth-century legal documents, brow knitted in concentration, that stray lock of hair falling unnoticed across his forehead. Intense, intelligent, attractive, and sexy, in an understated, professorial sort of way. In all honesty, it wasn't just his restraint she feared. What if she tried to discuss their relationship—what else could she call it?—and he told her he was still involved with Gabriella Griseri? She'd look like a fool then, and she'd have to avoid him for another six months. No, better not to say anything at all.

By the time they set box number nine on the table and opened it, Claire was realizing just how cold the archive was and that dinner was about to be served upstairs in the hall. She was on the verge of suggesting they take a break when she dug up a sheath of yellowing papers bound by a slender red ribbon. The date caught her eye first—11 October 1672—then the list of names: Countess Castlemaine, Mlle. de Keroualle, Duke of Monmouth, Nell Gwyn, Prince Rupert, Madame Severin. Along the right-hand side, next to each name, was a series of monetary figures: £700, £500, £1,200.

Claire set the bundle on the table in front of Andrew. "Look at this." He quickly scanned the top page and untied the ribbon. Underneath were a dozen or so similar pages; not identical, but with the same roster of names, with varying amounts of money listed next to each.

"There are weekly intervals between each of these documents," Andrew pointed out. "All of them dated 1672."

"Almost as if it were a payroll," Claire added.

"It *is* a payroll," Andrew said decisively. "A secret payroll. Everyone on the list is very close to the king—his mistresses, his son, his cousin. It would have caused quite a stir if anyone realized that the king was giving money to his, well, let's call it extended family—directly from the treasury."

"Maybe it wasn't directly from the treasury," Claire offered. "What if this was funded by another source of revenue entirely? You said that the king made Clifford a baron for the Stop of the Exchequer. What if that wasn't the only reason he was given a title and named lord treasurer?"

"You think that Clifford arranged a secret source of funding for the king?"

"He was always in need of money, wasn't he?"

Andrew looked thoughtful, then his eyes shone with comprehension. "A secret source of funding in *France*. That's why the English contingent went on to Paris after Dover."

With a renewed determination, they searched the remaining boxes: more tax records, a few wills, innumerable ledgers and letters of little interest.

"For goodness' sake, why don't people save the important things?" Claire grumbled. She was freezing and starting to feel a bit peckish. "Does the world really need another Bible?" She lifted a large, surprisingly lightweight King James edition from the bottom of the final box, and halfheartedly flipped open the cover. Perhaps this one, too, would list the Clifford family's births and deaths. She and Andrew both gaped at what they saw.

The pages of the Bible had been artfully hollowed out. Nestled within this hidden cavity was a cache of folded papers.

"After you," Andrew offered politely.

Claire carefully removed the topmost paper and unfolded it. The two-page document had only one word at the top: *Articles*. Following were eleven numbered paragraphs in English, and the same again in French. It was dated May 20, 1670.

"The Treaty of Dover," Andrew said, recognizing it instantly. "But unsigned, and in Clifford's handwriting."

"It looks like an early draft. See how some of the clauses have been amended."

Andrew nodded. "It makes sense that Clifford would draft it. He was known to be closely involved in the negotiations." He removed a second folded paper from the Bible. "Look here, a copy of the final treaty. It's been signed by Clifford and Arlington for England, Colbert de Croissy on behalf of France."

"There's one more," Claire said. She extracted a third paper, one thick sheet of ivory-colored vellum. Like the others, it was written in Thomas Clifford's small, crabbed hand.

"'The Secret Article,'" Claire read from the top of the page. "'The king of England will make a public profession of the Catholic faith, and will receive the sum of two millions of crowns, to aid him in this project, from the Most Christian King, in the course of the next six months.'" While Andrew listened in amazement, Claire continued reading. "'The date of this declaration is left absolutely to his own pleasure. The King of France will also provide an annual pension of two hundred thousand pounds a year and the services of six thousand French troops for the suppression of an uprising that may follow such a declaration.'"

Andrew leaned back against the table, speechless. This secret article was also signed by the treaty's witnesses—Arlington, Clifford, and Colbert de Croissy—and was stamped with the king of England's seal, followed by his large, looping signature: Charles R.

"Here it is," Claire said triumphantly, handing it to him. "The secret source of revenue from France. All Charles had to do was change his religion."

Andrew shook his head, astonished by what they had found. "According to this, Charles was ready and willing to become a Catholic. The implications of this are huge."

"Did he ever become a Catholic?"

"No, of course not. Not until he was on his deathbed, anyway, when he asked for a priest. But I always thought that had more to do with the queen's desire that he confess than his own." Andrew looked with wonder at the three-hundred-and-forty-year-old document in his hand. "Charles may have signed this, but he never followed through on his part of the deal. Two of his mistresses were Catholic, his wife was Catholic, two of his ministers were Catholic, and even James, his brother and successor, was Catholic, but Charles knew it would have been suicide for him to publicly embrace Catholicism. The country would have been plunged into civil war again, with Charles very likely facing the same dreadful fate as his father—or, at the very least, he would have been deposed and run out of the country, as James was in 1688."

Claire slowly read over the secret article again. "My question is, did he sign this knowing that he would never keep his promise, or did he actually want England to become a Catholic state?"

"Unlike many of his contemporaries, I'm inclined to think that Charles was wily, not foolish. The more I think about it, the more this secret article feels like a concession to Henriette-Anne's desire to bring Charles and Louis closer together. I suspect Charles knew better than to ever imagine that he might be a Catholic and the ruler of England at the same time. I think he signed it for the money, and then later realized it was a ticking time bomb."

"And if he made an issue over Henriette-Anne's death—"

"He inadvertently gave Louis the leverage to keep him in line." Andrew folded the document up again. "At least his faithful minister Clifford kept this a secret—even after he left office, little good though it did him."

"What do we do with a discovery that's going to change the way history is written?" Claire asked.

Andrew shook his head. "I'm not sure I know the answer to that. For now, I say we put it back where we found it, and I'll discuss it with Mr. Pilford tomorrow."

After returning the box to the shelf, they silently and thoughtfully walked back to the archive door. "Oh, God, tomorrow," Andrew said, as if suddenly remembering. "I'm supposed to give Derek Goodman's eulogy at his service in the chapel."

"Why you?"

"Everyone else refused to do it. The master wasn't even all that keen on having the service, not after all we've discovered about Derek

Goodman since his death. But Derek's brother is arriving tomorrow especially for this, and we don't want to disappoint him."

"Disappoint him?"

"Well, you know, make him think that we didn't care about Derek."

"You're not going to tell him the truth, are you?"

"Good God, of course not."

"Why not? Maybe he should know what kind of person his brother was."

"Perhaps you're right. But I'm certainly not going to be the one to tell him." Andrew jiggled the lock of the ancient, apparently very stubborn, door.

"What's wrong?" Claire asked.

"Key's stuck." He worked on it some more, jiggling the key and twisting the handle with all his might. "Christ!" he finally exclaimed. "It's stuck. The door won't open." He sighed. "Bloody hell."

"Is there another way out?"

"No." Andrew took his cell phone from his pocket, flipped it open, scowled at it. "No service down here," he said. A mournful tone crept into his voice. "What about yours?"

"I didn't bring my phone."

"Christ," he said again, rather passionately. He looked at Claire and attempted a smile. "Sorry. Didn't mean to lose my temper. But I'm afraid we might be stuck here."

"There's really no other exit?"

"The only way out is through this door."

"Any chance we could break it down?" Claire asked hopefully.

"This door has been here for more than three hundred years," Andrew scoffed. "Frankly, I don't think that our combined strength is going to make so much as a dent in it."

The scope of their dilemma was beginning to sink in: they were locked in a stone basement. Claire was chilled to the bone, a bit tired, and very hungry, now that she thought about it. Unless someone just happened to pop down to the archive—not a likely prospect at this time of night—they would be there until morning.

"This is a fine mess I've got us into," Andrew said, sighing. "Guess what news will spread like wildfire tomorrow: 'Drs. Kent and Donovan were freed from the archive this morning after spending the entire night together. Inquiring minds want to know: did they have it off?'"

"Have it off?" Claire asked, confused.

"In American vernacular, I believe the phrase is 'get it on.'"

"Ah. Don't people here have anything better to do than gossip?"

"Of course they do, but as far as I can tell that's never been an impediment anywhere. I can practically hear the tongues wagging already."

"Why do you care so much about what people say?"

"After witnessing so much bad behavior since you came to Trinity, you may think that no one here cares about honesty, trust, and honor, but most people at this college value those things very highly, as I do. It's impossible to stop people from talking, but you can live your life in a way that doesn't give them anything to talk about."

"You're planning to spend your entire life basing your decisions on whether people will talk about you or not? That's a ridiculous way to live."

"Is it?" Andrew harrumphed. "Would you like to know exactly how many people knew that you'd snogged Derek Goodman less than a day after it happened?"

"Not particularly, no. You're still angry about that, aren't you?"

"Not angry, but it did seem a bit odd. I mean, you were hardly here two weeks, and I find you kissing Derek Goodman, of all people—"

"You *are* angry."

"Not angry, but I did wonder what you could possibly see in him—"

"Admit it, you're angry."

"Okay, maybe I am a little bit angry."

"I'd love to know what makes you think you have the right to be." Claire felt her pulse rising. "Maybe I wouldn't have kissed Derek Goodman if you'd deigned to acknowledge my existence. I'd been here two weeks and you'd hardly spoken two words to me. You could have done something to make me feel welcome, at least offered to show me around. Instead, you acted like you were sorry I was here."

"Oh, dear," Andrew said. He leaned against the wall and crossed his arms over his chest. "I've really mucked things up, haven't I?" He shook his head, sighing, then looked up at Claire dejectedly. "Everything, from the beginning."

"What do you mean?"

"I wanted everything to be just right for you. Maybe I wanted it a bit too much. Before you arrived, I made sure you'd have all the privileges of a fellow even though you're not actually a fellow, technically speaking. I made sure you'd get an F key, and could dine at High Table, and reserved that nice set of rooms for you. I didn't realize just how resentful some people would feel about all that. Some started questioning my reasons for hiring you, even implied that my motives were personal, even though your credentials and your dissertation speak for themselves. By the time you got here, I felt that the best thing I could do for you was to avoid you."

"You might have at least told me why you were avoiding me."

"I didn't really know what to say. 'Everyone thinks I fancy you' might have seemed a bit unprofessional, under the circumstances."

"So why did you hire me?"

"Because I thought you would be a great asset to the college." He paused and looked down at the floor, as though he was unsure whether to continue on. Finally he looked up and gazed steadily at Claire. "Also because I was afraid that if I didn't hire you, I might not see you again."

"Oh." It took her a moment to realize exactly what he was saying. So Andrew Kent did fancy her after all. It was a confession she'd been waiting to hear for weeks now. She felt a faint but very pleasurable flush rising in her cheeks. "Really?" she asked.

"Really."

"What about Gabriella?"

"We broke up a couple of months ago. She has her life, I have mine, and it turns out that they don't work so well together."

"But Carolyn Sutcliffe—"

"Carolyn Sutcliffe is the biggest gossip in all of Cambridge. I make a point of never telling her anything about my personal life. And I would suggest that you do the same, unless you enjoy hearing your deeply personal secrets parroted back to you by total strangers. I have no idea why Gabriella didn't tell her about our breakup—I suppose she has reasons of her own. Suffice it to say that it's prudent to be especially cautious around Carolyn. Unfortunately she happens to be the wife of one of my oldest friends, and it's difficult for me to avoid her, especially at college functions. Simply begging off her company would have had consequences enough, but sitting next to you would have started an avalanche of rumor. That's why I didn't sit with you at the fellowship dinner, as I would have liked to."

"And all this time I thought you were avoiding me because you disliked me."

"Not the case."

"So what do we do now?" Claire asked softly.

Andrew shook his head again, this time in apology. "The rules are pretty clear on this point. I don't think there's anything we can do, except stay away from each other. Not as colleagues, of course, but in any other way. Understand, it's not just myself I'm concerned about, it's you." He suddenly lifted his head and cocked an ear to the door. "Did you hear that?"

"Hear what?"

"Footsteps."

A second later, the door handle turned and the door was slowly pulled open. Mr. Pilford stood in the doorway.

"My, my," he clucked. "What are you two doing down here so late?"

Chapter Fifty-one

SHE WAS RUNNING late for the service. Claire hurried across the Great Court as the chapel bells tolled. Up ahead, a group of four men stood beneath the arch of the Clock Tower. Even at a distance, she could see there was something odd about them: the men did not appear to be speaking. As she got closer, she recognized the master, the dean, and Andrew. They stood absolutely still, as if bound by some invisible force, staring at a man whose back was turned to her. When she was only a few feet away, Andrew noticed her and looked away, and the man, following his gaze, turned around.

Claire gasped; her step faltered; her heart skipped a beat: for the man was none other than Derek Goodman. Looking tanned and trimmer than she remembered, sporting a well-groomed mustache and wearing a well-tailored suit. Unmistakably Derek, yet slightly different, as though he had just come back from a vacation in Capri. How was this possible? She'd been on the Backs the morning when the police had carted his body away. But here he was, standing in the Great Court under a typically gloomy November sky while the chapel bells chimed for his very own funeral.

Her arrival seemed to break the spell that had rendered them speechless. "Dr. Donovan," Andrew said quickly, as if to preempt anything untoward Claire might say, "may I introduce Mr. David Goodman, Dr. Goodman's brother." He paused. "His identical twin brother. From Los Angeles."

"Nice to meet you," David Goodman said.

"Likewise," Claire replied, still not quite believing what she saw. Mr. Goodman must have only just arrived, as the two older members of the college were still tongue-tied. In the master's eyes she saw unmitigated horror; clearly he believed that Beelzebub had sprung fully formed back into their midst. And she'd been in England long enough to interpret the tight expression that the dean wore: it was rather, well, *unseemly* for two brothers to look so much alike, wasn't it? She could almost hear him say it: *It's just not on!*

Despite the distinctly uncomfortable undercurrents, David Goodman appeared very chipper, especially for someone about to attend his brother's memorial service. "What's a nice American girl like you doing in a place like this?" he quipped. "Har!"

"Mr. Goodman," the master finally said, flinching slightly as he looked their guest of honor in the eye, "please allow me to extend our condolences on the tragic death of your brother."

David Goodman let loose with a deep chuckle. "You must be joking." He looked at them incredulously. "You mean you're all actually sorry that he's gone?"

"Of course we are."

"Well, Lord Liverton, I can't say the same. I haven't spoken to my brother in over fourteen years. Not since he stole my car and my fiancée, drove one into a ditch and the other to drink, and then asked to borrow money." He guffawed again, as if he was having the time of his life. "I'm only here to make sure the bastard's truly dead."

The master and the dean gulped simultaneously. "Shall we all go inside?" Andrew said.

The chapel was filled to capacity: senior fellows in the front rows, junior fellows farther back, students ringing the walls. Claire scanned over the faces that were now familiar to her: Carolyn Sutcliffe, Mr.

Pilford, Elizabeth Bennet, Robbie Macintosh, Ashley Templeton, Rosamond Mercy, Nora Giles. Even Fiona Flannigan was there. Perhaps, Claire mused, like David Goodman, she just wanted to make sure that Derek Goodman was dead. Portia Hastings was also in attendance, standing in the back with a dark-haired man about her own age who looked like he might be another representative of C.I.D. Claire soon spotted Hoddy, and they found two empty seats at the rear of the chapel.

"Good Lord," Hoddy said softly as he watched David Goodman make his way down the center aisle to the front row.

"It's his brother," Claire whispered.

"It's like he's come back from the dead."

"Eerie, I know."

They weren't the only ones who thought so. The wave of shocked whispers in David Goodman's wake rose to a crescendo that didn't die down until well after he took his seat. It didn't seem to bother him at all; he smiled blithely as he sat alone in the front pew. Apparently he was Derek Goodman's only surviving family. Or the only one who cared enough to be there.

The master uttered a few platitudes and introduced the dean; the dean led everyone in a prayer and introduced Andrew. He stepped up to the podium with a few index cards clutched in his hands, looking rather grim, Claire thought. He adjusted the microphone, took a deep breath, and cleared his throat.

"What can one say about Derek Goodman?" he finally began, looking out across the chapel as if he was hoping for an answer. "First and foremost, as most of you know, he was an extraordinary scholar. He completed his PhD at twenty-five and, to no one's surprise, soon proved himself a brilliant historian with his books *Reform and Revolution: The Roots of British Democracy* and *Heads Will Roll: Capital Punishment in the Reign of the Tudor and Stuart Kings*. Both were published to wide acclaim and helped establish Dr. Goodman as one of the leading experts on English history." Andrew paused and checked his notes. "He was a frequent contributor to influential journals such as *Past and Present* and the *English Historical Review* . . . "

Andrew fell silent. He checked his notes some more, cleared his throat again, and grimaced a bit, yet he didn't speak. Everyone in the room could feel him faltering. Perhaps, Claire thought, Andrew was wondering just how many of those articles Derek Goodman had actually written himself. Or even if he'd written his books himself. "Dr. Goodman was . . . ," he said, only to pause again. "Derek Goodman . . ." He tried once more, then stopped and simply stood there, blinking at the crowd.

"I don't think I can do this." He rubbed a hand across his forehead. "No, the truth is, I don't want to do this. I've spent years cleaning up after Derek Goodman's messes, and frankly, I'm tired of it. Derek would have a good laugh knowing I was up here singing his praises when all he ever did was try to make my life a misery. My life and everyone else's here." He paused and looked at David Goodman in the front row. "I sincerely hope that I'm not offending you, Mr. Goodman, when I say that, in all honesty, your brother was an absolute ass."

"Not at all!" David Goodman practically beamed with joy.

"I'm afraid that the rest of the eulogy will be rather more in this vein," Andrew warned.

"Do go on," David Goodman urged happily.

"I see Derek Goodman didn't rate the sit-down supper," Hoddy remarked as he and Claire stood in the hall, where the reception was being held. People gathered together in groups, talking, laughing, and lining up for the buffet tables. The remainder of Andrew's eulogy had gone over exceptionally well. There had been a spirit of lightness in the air not usually found at a funeral. It seemed that everyone had had their own Derek Goodman story, and they'd been eager to add it to his legacy. After the service, a few had approached Claire and told her that they, too, had wanted to punch Derek Goodman in the face, and they'd thanked her.

Claire glanced over at Andrew, who was standing near the High Table talking to Portia Hastings.

"Don't worry," Hoddy said once he noticed where Claire's attention had wandered. "She's here with her husband."

Claire looked at Hoddy sharply. "What makes you think I'm worried?"

"I heard that *someone* was working very late with *someone* in the archive last night."

"For God's sake, isn't anything a secret around here?"

He arched a brow. "I tried to warn you."

"Keep it to yourself, all right?"

"I'll try," he said as he snagged a glass of white wine from a passing waiter.

Claire looked around the hall. Mr. Pilford stood talking with the master; by the smile on Mr. Pilford's face, she knew that the master was reassuring him that all the books Derek Goodman had taken from the library would soon be returned. Robbie Macintosh sat in the student's section with one of his two girlfriends. Carolyn Sutcliffe was sneaking an extra portion of pudding onto her plate: diet be damned. Nora Giles and Ashley Templeton were engrossed in what looked to be a chummy and very private conference. Elizabeth Bennet helped an elderly gentleman to a seat at High Table. Claire recognized him as the same man she'd seen at dinner only two nights ago. "Who's that with Dr. Bennet?" she asked Hoddy.

"Her father, Professor Rutherford. Bennet's her married name," Hoddy explained, "though she and her husband divorced about ten years ago, I think. The professor used to teach ancient history here. He's retired now, spends most of his time at the family pile in Bedfordshire."

"The family pile?"

"Giant country house. One of those National Trust behemoths. He's the eleventh—no, twelfth—Duke of Kendal."

Claire craned her neck a bit. She'd never seen a duke before. At least not one who was alive and not a figure in a painting.

"Descended directly from James the Second," Hoddy went on.

"Really? Does Dr. Bennet become a duchess when he dies?"

"No, the title passes on to the male heir. Her son, Brendan. A nice lad, though a bit rebellious—he's going to school at Oxford," he said with a horrified shudder.

It was easy to see that father and daughter were related: the same lofty forehead and pronounced cheekbones. She wondered if they looked anything like James II. If they stood next to a portrait of the king, would the resemblance be noticeable? What did it feel like, being descended from a king? Did they feel different from other people? Have a different outlook on life? Or did it just feel oppressive? After all, James's reign had ended disastrously. In 1688, he was deposed and run out of the country, and spent the rest of his life in exile in France.

And then it hit her.

"Hoddy!" she exclaimed, grabbing his arm. "James the Second was the Duke of York."

"And?" He peered down his nose at her. She'd nearly upset his wineglass.

"Before he was king, he was James, Duke of York. You said the Duke of Kendal was descended from him. Who was the mother? The queen?"

"I don't think so. I think their ancestor came from the wrong side of the blanket, as they say."

"He was the child of one of James's mistresses?"

"Yes."

"Jane Constable."

"What?"

"Jane Constable, Hoddy. The note that was in Derek Goodman's pocket. It wasn't a bet. It was blackmail."

With red-rimmed eyes, Elizabeth Bennet looked around at the others in the Combination Room. "I didn't mean to do it," she said, sniffling and dabbing at her nose with a tissue. "I actually loved him—as a friend, I mean. He could behave abominably at times, usually when he was drinking. But he could also be wonderful. Derek was like a little brother to me. A bratty little brother."

"Can you tell me what happened between you, from the beginning?" Portia Hastings asked. She sat across from Elizabeth Bennet in one of the wingback chairs. Andrew, Claire, and Hoddy looked on silently.

"A few weeks ago, Derek told me he'd discovered proof that my family wasn't descended from James the Second, or so he said. He showed me that diary page. According to the author, Jane Constable was pregnant by someone other than the Duke of York. We argued—I said it wasn't proof—and regardless, the dukedom wouldn't be taken away from us, not this long after the fact. But Derek wouldn't let it go. He was horrid about it, said we were descended from a whore, not a king. He threatened to write a paper on it. For myself I didn't care, but I didn't want my father or my son to be held up to ridicule."

"How did you happen to be on the Backs so late at night?"

"Derek came to my set about one o'clock in the morning. He was drunk and loud and making a big fuss. I told him I would talk to him outside, and he said he'd meet me at the Trinity Bridge.

"He was out of his mind, really—drunk or high or both. He just kept saying that if I didn't give him money he would write this odious paper about how the dukedom should be taken away from my family. He said that Jane Constable was a whore who with the help of Lord Arlington had put one over on the Duke of York. Derek could be the most charming person at times but also the most vicious. One never knew with him; his mood changed more frequently than the weather. We had had some terrible arguments in the past, but he had never done anything like this before. Needless to say, I was very upset. I slapped him, and then we fought. Just a tussle, really, but I pushed him down." She sniffed and brushed at her eyes. "It never occurred to me that he wouldn't get up again."

"He fell into the stream off the Cam?"

"It was dark, I couldn't tell."

"Did you hold his head down after he fell?"

Elizabeth Bennet looked horrified. "No, of course not."

"What did you do?"

"I ran off. I went back to my set."

"So, to the best of your knowledge, Derek Goodman was still alive when you left the scene?"

"Yes, absolutely."

Claire tried to visualize it: Dr. Bennet pushes Derek Goodman, he falls, struggles to get up, crawls forward a few feet . . . then collapses again in the water as the drugs kick in and he loses consciousness.

The drugs. What had the toxicology report said? Marijuana, cocaine, Vicodin—and something else.

"Detective Hastings," Claire piped up, "you told us that Dr. Goodman tested positive for a number of drugs—"

"Yes, he did."

"You said he had prescriptions for some of them. Do you remember which ones?"

"Vicodin, which is a painkiller, and a couple of antidepressants. The other drugs were street drugs—marijuana and cocaine."

"But there was one other, wasn't there?"

"Alprazolam—or Xanax, as it's usually called."

"He didn't have a prescription for that?"

"Not that I recall."

"But that isn't the kind of drug someone uses at a party, is it?"

"I wouldn't think so. It's an antianxiety medication."

Andrew looked at Claire skeptically. "Where are you going with this?"

"There was someone else on the Backs that night," Claire replied. "Someone else who was also at the party." Someone who either loved Derek Goodman or hated him or both, though Claire doubted that he had ever noticed. Someone whose delicate sensibilities had been deeply disturbed by being ignored on the one hand and cruelly teased on the other. "Someone who put Xanax in his drink, followed him home, witnessed his argument with Dr. Bennett, saw him fall down—and then held his head in the water until he died."

"Who?" Hoddy asked.

"Rosamond Mercy."

"She's outside in the hall," Andrew said.

They found Rosamond Mercy sitting by herself at one of the student's tables, forlornly pushing bits of food around her plate. When she saw Andrew and Claire approaching with Portia Hastings in tow, she carefully set her fork down on the table and looked up at them, her eyes appearing unnaturally large behind her wire-rimmed glasses. She was very calm, as if she had been expecting this for some time now.

"Sorry," she said.

———

A few hours later, when the reception was long over and the police had taken Rosamond Mercy and Elizabeth Bennet to the station, Claire walked with Andrew through Nevile's Court on their way to the Wren Library. To her surprise, he opened the door to the basement stairway and waved her through.

"Where are we going?" she asked.

"Back to the archive."

"Oh, no. It's cold, and there are spiders."

"And a new lock and key, so there's nothing to worry about." Andrew unlocked the archive door and ushered Claire inside. "This morning, before the service, I did some detective work of my own. It turns out that the Barclay collection, like a number of the Wren's collections, contains items other than books."

Andrew led Claire along the archive's periphery to one of the antique cabinets. He opened the doors with a flourish. Inside, resting at the front of a stack of paintings, was a portrait of a lovely, dark-haired woman dressed in a Restoration-era gown of gold and red silk. "Behold Lady Barclay."

Claire remembered the letter she'd come across in the folio in R bay when she'd first begun researching women artists. It seemed ages ago now. "The same Lady Barclay who was painted by Mary Beale?"

"The one and the same."

"This is all very interesting, but I don't understand its significance."

Andrew smiled. "Before she became Lady Barclay, she was known as Mrs. Hannah Strathern."

Claire's eyes widened with delight. "It's Hannah?"

"Yes, it's her."

Claire knelt down to look closely at the woman in the painting. She was beautiful, with a mass of dark curls that spilled over her shoulders, large, golden-brown eyes, a wise but gentle expression. Of course Edward had fallen in love with her.

"But she never mentioned that Edward was an earl."

"He wasn't when she met him. The title passed from his father to his older brother, Hugh. Sadly, Hugh died rather young, in 1677, and the title went to Edward."

"So they did marry."

"And had children. The collection was left to the school by their great-great-grandson, the ninth Earl of Barclay. There are probably a number of other things in the collection worth looking at."

"And the books upstairs—they must be from Hannah's own library."

"And her father's and Edward's. You've uncovered a few of the most interesting stories to come out of the Wren in a very long time."

Claire stood and shrugged. "Beginner's luck."

"I would attribute it to something more than that." He paused and took on a more serious tone. "It seems to me that you're going to have to write about this. And I don't think you could do justice to it in a paper. You'll probably have to write a book. Of course, that would mean staying here longer than three terms. Might take a couple of years or more. You'll probably have to become a fellow."

Claire mulled this over, enjoying the sense of perfect contentment that it produced. Stay in Cambridge and become a fellow? She couldn't think of anything better. Especially when it meant she'd have ample opportunity to find answers to all the questions that still remained concerning the fates of Hannah and Edward, Maitland, and Thomas Clifford, et al. Not to mention the splash that the discovery of the secret article to the Treaty of Dover would make.

"There's only one problem," Claire said.

"And that is?"

"Fellows aren't allowed to kiss each other."

"I'm afraid that's true," Andrew said with obvious regret. He bowed his head. "But sometimes, they break the rules," he added, lowering his lips to hers.

Epilogue

21 April 1673

To the Rue de Varenne:

My dear sister:

No doubt you have heard stories of my Capture, even my Death, stories that I hope were so illogical and Absurd that you knew them at once to be False. It's true I have been Taken, and am not Free, but I am not in Newgate or even the Tower where I properly belong; but more of this later.

You should know that Montagu has completely deserted me, his former Man-of-all-trades. He has shown his true Coward's colors—he has tried to put as much Distance between us as he can, and does nothing to ease my Imprisonment, even though he is now a rich Man and has the Means. I hear he has finally achieved his Ambition, and married the first Heiress he could lay his hands on, and has gone back to Paris with his English bride—there to reside in a most Unhappy and acrimonious Matrimony. It may seem Strange to you once you learn where I am Lodged, that we hear the best Gossip here; it is almost like being at Court. But I will not keep you in Suspense much longer. On with my story.

I nearly succeeded in Revenging our beloved Princess, to whom we owe so much: I, for her love and tenderness; you, for your *advantageous marriage, for if she had not introduced you to the Duc d'Alencon you might still be living with our parsimonious uncle in that dingy town house he calls home instead of your palatial villa on the rue de Varenne. Alas, I was tripped up by a pair that I never meant to Harm, though their Interference had made it necessary. But it is not for them that my Hate is harbored. Indeed, it is due to Mrs. Devlin's—or, I should say, Mrs. Strathern's, as she has gently corrected me on her visits—Generosity that I may write to you, for she has provided the ink, paper, quill and candle, along with some hot Victuals that I may not Perish too soon.*

You may have heard that I fought to the Death; Dr. Strathern stabbed my leg, and Mrs. Strathern pushed me into the Fleet. At first they thought I was Lost, doomed to Drown, or so Mrs. Strathern has told me. But after my submersion in the raging river I grabbed onto a bit of flotsam. My makeshift Raft took me safely downstream through the horrible Muck of that channel—indeed, the Wound on my leg was made no better by coming into contact with the foulness of the Fleet Ditch—but otherwise I was unhurt, and was determined to depart via the East shore and make my way to the docks at Deptford, where for a few guineas I could hire a seagoing berth to France.

But the King's Guards were waiting for me. As soon as I crawled up on the muddy bank near Fleet Street, they set upon me. They had already been given their Directive—either by Arlington or by the King himself—and brought me straight here to Bethlehem Hospital, or Bedlam, as it is known, and locked me up with the Lunatics and Madmen.

The whole dreary place reeks with the fetid Odors of urine and dung and the pervasive sour scent of Sickness. Everyone is half-Starved; the thin Gruel they feed us wouldn't keep a kitten alive. People of Quality like to visit of an afternoon and stare at us as though we were Animals in cages instead of human Beings trapped behind the bars of our Cells and within whatever Madness ails us. The men have a good Laugh and the women a pleasant sense of Trepidation, one that puts into their heads all sorts of dark Terrors and dread Imaginings, and this makes them cling to their Escorts in a way that must be most satisfactory. The man in the cell next to mine has what I am told is Catatonia, and does not speak or move himself; though the Guards will charge a few Shillings for arranging his Limbs in bizarre Poses, in which he remains until they move him again. The woman in the cell opposite moans day and night in the most piteous Fashion and bangs her head against the wall. A visiting physician has told me that she has no disease per se, only a deep and abiding melancholy that no Physick can cure. The man two cells away from me has the Falling Sickness, for which they keep him strapped to his bed so that he will not hurt himself; and in another cell is a man who has chewed away at his own Arm, so much so that in some areas between the wrist and elbow the Bone is exposed; but he suffers so much from his Insanity that he cannot be stopped.

And then there is me. They say I am also Mad, for I rant unto the King; not just the English King but also the French King. It is no Accident that I have been shut away here. Charles Stuart fears not my Life so much as he fears my Death and what I would say in my last dying Speech at Tyburn. Though I have much to tell my Visitors, they treat my Exposé as little more than a comic turn they might see in a Theatre. Even after I am set free, if there be such a time, the taint of Madness will be upon me; and whatever I say will be met with Laughter and Scorn. I will always be considered a Madman; even though my story is (God is my witness) the Truth.

For I have had time to think, dear Sister. What I suspect of Princess Henriette-Anne and her sad Fate could tear apart Countries and topple Kings. The fetes, dances and theatrical spectacles enjoyed by King Charles and Princess Henriette-Anne and their courtiers in Dover that golden summer were all a charade, I see that now, a means to conceal the true reason for the long-anticipated reunion of brother and sister: the making of an agreement that promised French gold to Charles Stuart. An agreement that was known only to those closest to both Kings. How do I know this? In part, from the loose lips of our erstwhile friend Montagu, who boasted to me that he was taking over the job of ferrying gold from Paris to London, a task first bestowed on Roger Osborne by the Princess, who sealed her

Request with her gold ring so that Louis would know that Osborne
came to him by her command.

I have that ring now. I stole it from Osborne's corpus vile, that
these conspirators may not think they will go unpunished for their
role in Henriette-Anne's disgrace. For it is these very men who al-
lowed her to Die, then concealed the truth of her death; concealed
it for the sake of this secret agreement. Not even King Charles will
accuse the Duc d'Orleans of murder; clearly his need for French gold
outweighs his obligation to his sister.

I ask you, could I have done anything other than what I have
done? No one but I, not even her own brother the King, sought
justice for her death. I know you of all people will understand
my rage. But my Task is not yet completed, sister; there are those
who are still breathing who have not yet paid the price: Arlington,
Severin, Clifford, the King himself. I throw myself on your Mercy
and beg you to work for my release. I will be free: no matter how,
no matter when. It should not be impossible; lucri bonus est odor
ex re qualibet: the smell of money is good wherever it comes from.
Please do not desert me.

I remain, &c.

"Mr. Maitland." Hannah stands in the corridor outside his barred cell.
"The warden requests that you return the ink and the quill to me."

Maitland looks up from his makeshift desk, a small plank of wood
set over the top of a close-stool. "Without your assistance, I would not
be able to post letters, so what is the use?" He folds his letter, seals it
with wax from the dripping candle, and wraps the wet quill in a spare
sheet of paper. With effort, he rises to his feet. A wide iron cuff rings
his right ankle, and the chain that secures him to the far wall scrapes on
the floor as he limps to the front of his cell. His matted hair has grown
well past his shoulders; his green eyes stare feverishly from his haggard
face. Four months in Bedlam have left Maitland gaunt as a skeleton,
with filthy clothes that are quickly becoming rags. He hands the letter,
ink, and quill through the bars.

"Your leg has healed, and my work here is finished," Hannah says, slipping the letter into her coat pocket. "I will not be returning for some time."

"You are going away?"

"No, not away." She feels herself blush slightly.

Maitland cast an eye over her figure. "You are with child," he says. "I should have noticed earlier." He steps back a bit and narrows his eyes. "It suits you, Mrs. Strathern. As do the spectacles."

"Thank you." Hannah is gracious, but she never forgets what Maitland is capable of; she has seen the brutal results with her own eyes. She bends down to open her medicine case and places the writing accoutrements inside, then straightens and buttons her coat.

"You are not leaving so soon?" Maitland says.

"I'm afraid I must. Our friend Mr. Ravenscroft is back in the king's good graces and is being released from the Tower today. We go to meet him."

Maitland clutches the bars of his cell and brings his face closer, so close that she can smell the lingering aroma of the chicken fricassee he has just devoured. "Was it you who returned him to favor?" he asks sharply. When Hannah doesn't reply, he smiles shrewdly; a smile that sends a cold shiver through her. "Of course it was you. Why can you not use your influence with the king to release me?"

"You have committed murder, Mr. Maitland. You have brought pain and death and suffering to many people. By law, you should have been hanged. Why the king chooses to keep you here I know not, but my clemency does not go so far as to interfere with his justice."

Since January, Hannah has three times been honored with a private sitting with the king. He feels some indebtedness for her successful treatment of Louise de Keroualle and, in return, has protected her against the College of Physicians. He has also allowed her to practice at Bridewell Hospital, where the poor go for physick. She has thought many times on the strange and horrible events of the past months, of the charges that Maitland made as he threatened her life. Almost everyone who knew the king's secret—if Maitland's suspicions are true—is now dead, and they have taken the secret of Henriette-Anne's death to their graves. Is the king outraged over these crimes, or have

Maitland's murderous acts suited the king's own ends? Hannah studied the king's eyes as he spoke to her, and she saw how sharply they glittered behind his devil-may-care façade. The yapping dogs, the foppishness, the insistence on constant merriment and diversion: it was a beautifully crafted performance, she suspected. Although she could never be certain of the truth, she would never again think the king a fool.

"*His* justice," Maitland spits angrily. "The king knows nothing of justice. I am God's instrument, and I will not let his work go unfinished, Mrs. Strathern." Maitland reaches through the bars and seizes her wrist with his bony fingers. He remains surprisingly strong, with a grip tight enough to hurt as he pulls her closer. "I will be free, I tell you, with your help or without."

His eyes lock on Hannah's. In them she sees his rage, his resolve, his madness. Hannah wrenches her arm away and steps back, shaken. She should have known better than to stand so close to his cell without a guard present. "You will never be free, Mr. Maitland. I will post your letter, as your sister deserves to know where you are, but more than that I cannot do." She shakes her head. "No matter where you are, you will never be free of what you have done." She picks up her medicine case. "God have mercy on your soul."

She turns away and walks past the shadowed cells with their sad occupants, many of whom she has treated in the past months. So much pain. Not every sickness can be cured, but she is able to ease the suffering of some. And her own suffering? Her hand instinctively cradles her rounded belly. Her past can never be forgotten but she has discovered, to her solemn delight, that its sorrows can be diminished.

She walks past the warden's office, through the vestibule, and then outside, where Edward waits for her in the warm spring sunlight and the sweet, rain-freshened air.

Author's Note

The Devlin Diary is a work of fiction based on two real events: the signing, in May 1670, of a secret treaty between Charles II and Louis XIV, and the death of Henriette-Anne, Charles's sister and Louis's sister-in-law, a month later.

In May 1670, Charles and Henriette-Anne met at Dover for a long-anticipated reunion. Unbeknownst to the few hundred members of their courts, who were kept busy with feasts and fetes, the king's ministers Lord Arlington and Sir Thomas Clifford and the French ambassador Colbert de Croissy worked behind the scenes to ratify the articles of a treaty between England and France that had been the subject of clandestine negotiation for more than a year. Because of her close relationships with both her brother and Louis XIV, Henriette-Anne had been instrumental in bringing about the rapprochement between the French and English kings. For months prior to their meeting, Charles and Henriette-Anne had exchanged coded letters (all the important participants were assigned three-digit numbers) in which they'd discussed the salient points of the agreement. In short, Charles and Louis agreed to wage war on the Dutch (breaking England's existing treaty with Holland) in exchange for England's receiving a subsidy from France of 3 million *livres tournois*. In addition, Charles agreed to publicly announce his conversion to Catholicism "as soon as the welfare of his kingdom will permit," for which Louis would pay another 2 million *livres,* half to be paid three months after the exchange of ratifications and half three months later.

After ten days of festivities, Henriette-Anne returned to France, to her husband, and to her palace at Saint-Cloud. (Henriette-Anne had a dazzling variety of names: Henriette, Henriette-Anne, the Duchesse d'Orleans, Madame, as she was known in the French court, and Minette, as she was affectionately called by her brother; for clarity's sake, I have chosen to refer to her only as Henriette-Anne or the princess). She was indeed trapped in an unhappy marriage to Philippe, Duc d'Orleans, Louis XIV's brother. The duc was a homosexual who loved dressing up in women's clothes and jewelry; unfortunately, these were his least objectionable traits. He was also childish, cruel, domineering, jealous, and vindictive; he enjoyed parading his lovers in front of his wife and seemed to be happiest when she was miserable.

Henriette-Anne had been ill during her time away, but when she was stricken with excruciating stomach pains on the morning of June 29, she was the first to believe she had been poisoned. She even believed she knew the instigator: her husband's favorite, the Chevalier de Lorraine, whom Louis had banished from the court (the French king was fond of Henriette-Anne, and often dismayed by his brother's treatment of her). Henriette-Anne's agonized sufferings and the speed of her demise—she was dead less than twenty-four hours later—reinforced this belief. A postmortem was performed the next day by a group of English and French doctors, who attributed Henriette-Anne's death to *cholera morbus;* but one onlooker declared that he did not approve of the way the autopsy was carried out, "as if the surgeon's business were to hide the truth rather than reveal it."

The results of the postmortem did little to squelch the rumors of poison, which spread quickly through the French court and then to London. Charles was reportedly so grief-stricken at the news of his sister's death that he collapsed and spent the next few days in bed, an unusual event for such a vigorous man. The news of an English princess dying in suspicious circumstances in France was more than enough to inflame English sentiments, already volatile, against the French. This was hardly in keeping with Charles's aims; he wanted instead to turn the people against Holland. Henriette-Anne's death was a political liability, and it placed the newly minted agreement in jeopardy.

No one knows Charles's true feelings on the subject, but within a few weeks he appeared reassured by Louis's assertions that there had been no foul play. And there was simply too much at stake to make an issue of it (although his dislike of his brother-in-law never waned). Charles, Arlington, and Colbert de Croissy took the lead in quashing the rumors, and the loss of the closest link between Charles and Louis did not affect the pact they had made. But Charles soon realized that if he wanted to make war on Holland he needed the support of all his ministers, not just Arlington and Clifford. The Duke of Buckingham was sent to France on a fool's errand. For the next few months he negotiated a treaty with France that he wrongly believed to be completely of his own doing, while Arlington and Colbert de Croissy laughed behind his back. It was nearly identical to the previous treaty, except that it did not include any references to Roman Catholicism. The new treaty became known as the *traité simulé*. It was signed by all five of Charles's ministers—the infamous Cabal—three of whom were never aware of the earlier agreement. A few months later, in March 1672, Charles declared war on the Dutch, hostilities which cost England much but gained them little. As Charles never did announce his conversion (although, on his deathbed, he requested a Catholic priest, who performed last rites), the secret treaty remained a secret for one hundred and fifty years. In 1830, Dr. John Lingard published his *History of England,* which included the entire text of the secret treaty, generously provided by the sixth Lord Clifford of Chudleigh.

When Thomas Clifford resigned his office in 1673 in the wake of the Test Act, he took the most politically sensitive documents, including the secret treaty, to his estate at Ugbrooke. (Arlington, who also resigned following the Test Act, was apparently uncomfortable having such incriminating papers in his house.) In 1930, a century after Lingard, another historian, Keith Feiling, discovered a wealth of additional papers at Ugbrooke, which included correspondence between Louis XIV and Charles II, a letter from Henriette-Anne to Clifford, copies of the secret treaty in both English and French, and a signed copy of the secret article, which together make a fascinating narrative of seventeenth-century political intrigue. These documents are known collectively as the Clifford Papers, and they are now in the possession of the British Library, not in the Trinity College archive, where I have placed them.

Even though most historians believe that Henriette-Anne died from acute peritonitis, suspicions about her untimely death have never been completely vanquished. (The Duc d'Orleans's second wife, Elizabeth-Charlotte, Princess Palatine, was firm in her belief that her predecessor had been poisoned.) Certainly there's enough mystery surrounding these events to allow generous room for speculation and invention.

The Devlin Diary blends real and imagined situations along with real and fictitious characters. Hannah Devlin, Edward Strathern, Jeremy Maitland, Madame Severin, Theophilus Ravenscroft, and each of the murder victims are fictitious; Louise de Keroualle, Lord Arlington, Sir Thomas Clifford, and Ralph Montagu are real, as is Dr. Thomas Sydenham and, of course, Charles II, although most of the events in *The Devlin Diary* in which they are involved are entirely fictional. It is true, however, that Louise de Keroualle was stricken with gonorrhea passed to her by the king (although this happened in 1674, two years later than in the narrative), from which she suffered terribly. Eventually she was cured, or at any rate was no longer acutely ill from the disease. But Louise never conceived again, even though she remained the king's mistress until he died in 1685. Dr. Sydenham was in reality a forward-thinking physician of the time who helped nudge the theory and practice of medicine toward a more enlightened age. Anyone familiar with seventeenth-century scientist and architect Robert Hooke will understand that Theophilus Ravenscroft, while a fictional character, is not only Hooke's nemesis but also his doppelganger. Ralph Montagu was known to be a "ruthless gallant" who used women to get ahead. It's true that after the death of his first wife, he courted the very wealthy but certifiably insane Duchess of Albemarle by posing as the emperor of China. With her money he rebuilt his Robert Hooke–designed house, which had been gutted by fire in 1686. Montagu House, which stood in what is now Bloomsbury, was bought by the British government in the 1750s and used as the first home of the British Museum.

I am indebted to numerous sources for assistance in replicating the world of Restoration-era London and present-day Cambridge. For general English history and insights into seventeenth-century London, I found the following books to be most helpful: *1700: Scenes from London Life* by Maureen Waller (Four Walls Eight Windows, 2000); *A History of London* by Stephen Inwood (Macmillan, 1998); *The Diary of John Evelyn* edited by John Bowle (Oxford University Press, 1985); *The English: A Social History 1066–1945* by Christopher Hibbert (W. W. Norton, 1987); *History of the Royal Society* by Thomas Sprat (London, 1667); *The Illustrated Pepys* edited by Robert Latham (University of California Press, 1978); *Intelligence and Espionage in the Reign of Charles II, 1660–1685* by Alan Marshall (Cambridge University Press, 1994); *Ladies-in-Waiting: From the Tudors to the Present Day* by Anne Somerset (Knopf, 1984); *The Literary and Cultural Spaces of Restoration London* by Cynthia Wall (Cambridge University Press, 1999); *The London Hanged: Crime and Civil Society in the Eighteenth Century* by Peter Linebaugh (Verso, 2006); *Restoration: Charles II and his Kingdoms* by Tim Harris (Penguin Books, 2005); *Restoration London* by Liza Picard (St. Martin's Press, 1998); *The Shorter Pepys* edited by Robert Latham (University of California Press, 1985); and *The Weaker Vessel: Women in 17th Century England* by Antonia Fraser (Knopf, 1984).

The following biographies brought the people of the time to vivid life: *Aubrey's Brief Lives* edited by Oliver Lawson Dick (David R. Godine, 1999); *The Cabal* by Maurice Lee, Jr. (University of Illinois Press, 1965); *Charles II and Madame* by Cyril Hughes Hartmann (William Heinemann, Ltd., 1934); *The Curious Life of Robert Hooke* by Lisa Jardine (HarperCollins, 2004); *Dr. Thomas Sydenham, 1624–1689* by Kenneth Dewhurst (University of California Press, 1966); *The Forgotten Genius: The Biography of Robert Hooke* by Stephen Inwood (MacAdam/Cage, 2003); *The Lives & Times of the Duchess of Portsmouth* by Jeanine Delpech (Roy Publishers, 1953); *Lord Rochester's Monkey: Being the Life of John Wilmot, Second Earl of Rochester* by Graham Greene (The Viking Press, 1974); *Louise de Keroualle, Duchess of Portsmouth in the Court of Charles II* by H. Forneron (Scribner & Wellford, 1888); *Nell Gwyn: Mistress to a King* by Charles Beauclerk (Atlantic Monthly Press, 2000); *Royal Charles: Charles II and the Restoration* by Antonia

Fraser (Knopf, 1979); and *Samuel Pepys: The Unequalled Self* by Claire Tomalin (Knopf, 2003).

The following books provided the sometimes comic and frequently gruesome details of seventeenth-century medicine: *The Admirable Secrets of Physick & Chyrurgery* by Thomas Palmer, edited by Thomas Rogers Forbes (Yale University Press, 1984); *Blood & Guts: A Short History of Medicine* by Roy Porter (W. W. Norton, 2003); *Culpeper's Complete Herbal & English Physician Enlarged* by Nicholas Culpeper (Meyerbooks, 1990); *The Early History of Surgery* by W. J. Bishop (Barnes & Noble Books, 1995); *English Medicine in the Seventeenth Century* by A. W. Sloan (Durham Academic Press, 1996); *Heal Thyself: Nicholas Culpeper and the Seventeenth-Century Struggle to Bring Medicine to the People* by Benjamin Woolley (HarperCollins, 2004); *John Hall and His Patients: The Medical Practice of Shakespeare's Son-in-Law* by Joan Lane (The Shakespeare Birthplace Trust, 1996); *Opium: A Portrait of the Heavenly Demon* by Barbara Hodgson (Greystone Books, 2004); *Opium: A History* by Martin Booth (St. Martin's Griffin, 1996); *Quacks: Fakers and Charlatans in English Medicine* by Roy Porter (Tempus, 2001); *Women as Healers: A History of Women and Medicine* by Hilary Bourdillon (Cambridge University Press, 1988); and *Women Healers: Portraits of Herbalists, Physicians and Midwives* by Elisabeth Brooke (Healing Arts Press, 1995). *Forensics and Fiction* by D. P. Lyle, MD, provided helpful answers to a few tricky medical and forensics questions.

My memories of present-day Cambridge were greatly enhanced by *A Concise History of the University of Cambridge* by Elisabeth Leedham-Green (Cambridge University Press, 1996); *Trinity College: A History and Guide* by G. M. Trevelyan (Trinity College, 1967); *Central Cambridge, A Guide to the University and Colleges* by Kevin Taylor (Cambridge University Press, 1994); and *The Making of the Wren Library* edited by David McKitterick (Cambridge University Press, 1995).

The Whitehall Palace Plan of 1670 by Simon Thurley (London Topographical Society, 1998) and *Whitehall Palace: An Architectural History of the Royal Apartments, 1240–1690* by Simon Thurley (Yale University Press, 1999) were indispensable guides to a place that no longer exists.

ACKNOWLEDGMENTS

I've received a great deal of help and support during the writing of this book. My sincere thanks go to Keith Moore at the Royal Society for the wonderful tour of the Society library and archives; to Rhiannon Markless and Liz Hore at the National Archives at Kew Gardens for their research assistance; to Dr. Rod Pullen at Trinity College, for finally agreeing to speak to me; to D. P. Lyle, MD, for his fast answers to my forensics questions; to Clay Bowling for his excellent mechanical illustrations of a seventeeth-century building project; to Jonathan Smith of Trinity College Library and Phillipa Grimstone of the Pepys Library for their assistance; to Briana Baillie and Cynthia Phillips for their helpful comments; to DeAnn Hughes, Howard Hughes, Nancy Oliver, and Nick Lyster for their generous hospitality and for making our stay in London so much fun and so memorable; to dream agent Mary Evans, for always being the sweet, calm voice of reason at the other end of the line, and for her unwavering belief; to Maggie Crawford, for being the kind of editor all writers hope for: smart, dedicated, tireless, and full of good ideas; to Louise Burke and everyone at Pocket Books for their understanding during a difficult time; and to Julie Wright and everyone at Simon & Schuster UK for their support. A special thanks to my assistant, Birgit Kaufman, for taking such great care of us. And, always and forever, my love and gratitude to Brian Beverly, for everything.

ABOUT THE AUTHOR

Christi Phillips is the author of *The Rossetti Letter,* which has been translated into six languages. Her research combines a few of her favorite things: old books, libraries, and travel. When she's not rummaging around in an archive or exploring the historic heart of a European city, she lives with her husband in the San Francisco Bay Area, where she is at work on her next novel, set in France. Visit her website at www.christi-phillips.com.

READERS GROUP GUIDE

This reading group guide for The Devlin Diary *includes an introduction, discussion questions, ideas for enhancing your book club, and a Q&A with author Christi Phillips. The suggested questions are intended to help your reading group find new and interesting angles and topics for your discussion. We hope that these ideas will enrich your conversation and increase your enjoyment of the book.*

Introduction

Teaching history at Trinity College, Cambridge, is Claire Donovan's dream come true—until one of her colleagues is found dead on the banks of the River Cam. The only key to the professor's unsolved murder is the seventeenth-century diary kept by his last research subject, Hannah Devlin, physician to the king's mistress. As Claire and historian Andrew Kent follow the clues Devlin left behind, they discover the life of an extraordinary woman and a hidden conspiracy involving King Charles II that might still have deadly consequences today.

Questions for Discussion

1. What is your first impression of Claire Donovan? What did you think of Andrew Kent at the beginning of the novel? How did your feelings about these characters change throughout the story? What were major turning points for you?

2. *The Devlin Diary* has two major settings: the court of Charles II and present-day Trinity College, Cambridge. Each of these places has unique characteristics, yet they share a few similarities. How are these two communities similar and how are they different?

3. Claire Donovan and Hannah Devlin are both strong women in predominantly male cultures. How does each woman approach difficult or delicate situations throughout the book? Compare and contrast Claire's and Hannah's situations and personalities. Which female character did you relate to more? Why?

4. What motivates Hannah Devlin to step beyond the circumscribed role of a respectable woman in seventeenth-century London society? What does Hannah appear to sacrifice by flouting society's conventions?

5. Lord Arlington tells Hannah, "You are a woman, after all," and Hannah thinks, "A woman, after all. *Something inferior to man* is his implication—what all men imply when they speak of the 'weaker' sex, the 'gentler' sex, a woman's 'modesty'" (pages 253–254). Do you believe that either Claire or Hannah is a feminist? Why or why not? What does it mean to be a feminist?

6. Many of the characters in this novel harbor secrets from others, and many characters are not entirely honest with themselves. Which characters in both the historical and contemporary stories seem straightforward and at ease with themselves and their desires?

7. Ralph Montagu and Edward Strathern, two very different male characters, are attracted to Hannah Devlin. Do the same aspects

of Hannah's character attract each man? How did your opinion of each man change during the course of the novel?

8. What is the role of Theophilus Ravenscroft in the novel? Does he have a counterpart in the contemporary story?

9. How is Colbert de Croissy, the French ambassador, different from the English courtiers at King Charles's court? What differences between French and English cultures during the late seventeenth century do you infer from the novel?

10. How does the author use language and imagery to bring the characters to life? Did the novel's characters or style remind you of another novel in any way?

11. Several characters during the course of the novel seem to have ulterior motives or act oddly. "Odd is simply odd—anyone can see it. Or, at least, most people can see it, if they're paying attention" (page 264). Claire points out that Andrew Kent does not seem to have the ability to notice when someone is acting oddly. Do you believe that women have this innate ability more often than men?

12. Whose story is *The Devlin Diary*? If you had to pick one, is it Claire's story or is it Hannah's? Why? Who changes the most from the beginning to the end?

13. How did this book touch your life? Did it inspire you to do or learn something new?

Enhance Your Reading Group

1. To visit or learn more about the community in Cambridge visit: www.trin.cam.ac.uk/.

2. During the reign of Charles II, theaters reopened after having been closed during the protectorship of Oliver Cromwell, Puritanism lost its momentum, and the bawdy "Restoration comedy" became a recognizable genre. In addition, women were allowed to perform onstage for the first time. Some notable plays that your group might enjoy reading include Charles Sedley's *The Mulberry-Garden* (1668), George Villiers's *The Rehearsal* (1671), and John Dryden's *Marriage a-la-Mode* (1672).

3. Author William Somerset Maugham once said, "To eat well in England, you should have breakfast three times a day." Nevertheless, your reading group might enjoy a traditional English Sunday roast. This meal includes roast potatoes accompanying a roasted joint of meat such as beef, lamb, or chicken, and assorted vegetables, generally roasted or boiled and served with gravy.

Author Q&A

Authors often remark that they put a little bit of themselves into their characters. How strongly do you identify with each of your main characters? How are you different?

I do identify with my characters. I learned something about the failures of medicine and the mysteries of the human body early on, when my oldest brother died from oral cancer at the tender age of twenty-two. Hannah is going through a dark, soul-searching period in her life, to which I can relate. Some of her experiences in the novel are taken from my life. Hannah is someone who isn't easily blown off the course she's set for herself, and I would say that is also true for me.

Claire and I share a number of traits; for instance, we're both studious and can spend hours reading and writing. But in a few fundamental ways she's quite different. She's less of a risk taker than I am, and she is often uneasy around other people, which I rarely am.

I never intended for Claire to be completely likable. I always imagined her as a bit obsessive and neurotic (not that there's anything wrong with that). Sometimes she's unaware of her own motivations, and she doesn't always know how to best negotiate the situations she's in. She's somewhat guileless and not always entirely self-controlled. She herself would admit that she's a work-in-progress. To me, these negative attributes are quite common in life, if not fiction. Perfect characters have nothing to learn and no place to go in the dramatic sense. They bore me.

In another way, however, Claire is a kind of alter ego who allows me to do something I love doing—historical research—and to vicariously live out the fantasy of being an academic. Being almost entirely self-taught, I'm fascinated by academia—especially the ivy-covered, hallowed-hall sort that Claire inhabits. After visiting Trinity College and learning about its history degree program, I was convinced that if I had another life to live I would choose to spend it there, getting a doctorate in Early Modern History and spending the rest of my years cloistered in a cozy set. In spite of the many terrible fictional things that happen at Trinity College during the course of *The Devlin Diary*, I found it and the people there absolutely charming. Cambridge is at least as lovely as I have described it. It's the ultimate college town, although residents of Oxford might disagree.

Why did you set the book in the place and time that you did?
The Restoration Era—which begins in 1660 and ends in 1685, essentially the reign of Charles II—can be thought of as the 1960s of the seventeenth century. Both eras ushered in sweeping social changes, a blossoming of creativity in the arts and sciences, and greater freedom for women. There was also lots of sex, drinking, drugs, and really, really bad behavior, which makes for great stories.

Your novel is tremendously engaging and can easily be read in one sitting. Claire and Hannah go through a whirlwind through the course of the book. Did you work on the book for a long time or finish it very quickly?
In the broad scheme of things, it didn't take long: a little over two years. But there were occasions when it felt like much longer. I have a theory that the natural limit of the human attention span is nine months. Anything that takes longer than that really begins to feel like work.

How was writing this novel a different experience from writing your first book, *The Rossetti Letter*? What was harder about writing this novel? What was easier?
It was harder from the very beginning. I'd been researching a completely different idea for about six months when I discovered

that a novel with a remarkably similar concept was being published, and I had to come up with a new idea. Eventually, when this other book came out, it was quite different from anything I would have written, but I think I made the right choice. Very soon after I began researching it, I felt that my new story was much more intriguing than my original idea.

There were some personal issues that also made *The Devlin Diary* more difficult. When I had completed about two-thirds of the novel, my father unexpectedly fell ill and passed away about three weeks later. After he'd been in the hospital for ten days it was clear he wasn't going to pull through, and we took him home to my parents' house. My mother, brother, sister, and I took care of him until he died. It was almost as if by writing about such difficult subjects—pain, death, and grief—I had prepared myself for them in some way. But of course my father's death was devastating. I didn't begin writing again for at least two months. I couldn't.

It was a great lesson to me. Writing a novel isn't just a mental exercise but an emotional journey. Fiction requires conviction, which arises in part from your intellectual belief in your story— but even more than that, I believe, this conviction springs from your emotional investment in your story. Fiction requires a big investment—it simply won't ring true without it. This also helps to explain why writers are so sensitive about their work.

When your personal life is emotionally demanding, it can be difficult to enter the life of your novel. Fortunately, my editor read the uncompleted manuscript and made many helpful suggestions. Following her notes, I was able to rediscover my belief in the story and find my way to the end.

Do you see your book as more of a mystery or a story about two strong women?
I don't put any labels on it. For me, it's a story about Claire, Andrew, Hannah, Edward, Ravenscroft, Montagu, Charles II and Henriette-Anne.

The characters in your novels seem so vibrant—from your protagonists Hannah and Claire to minor characters such as Seamus Murphy and Mr. Pilford. How do you manage to breathe life into such a wide and varied group of characters?

For the historical characters, researching the period is crucial. The more research you do, the more you have to draw upon. Conflict is always key when it comes to character. Whether historical or modern, characters who "breathe" usually want something. They want it very much, and some sort of obstacle keeps them from getting it. From this conflict, all action arises—and characters reveal themselves through their actions.

As you relate in your author's note, much of the book is centered on actual history. What was your research process like?

I started with general English history, so I could understand how the past led up to the Restoration. Then I read books on the seventeenth century and the Restoration, and numerous biographies of the people of the time—Charles II, Pepys, the Cabal (Charles's ministers), Thomas Sydenham, and many others—and books on seventeenth-century medicine. For *The Devlin Diary*, I relied primarily on books aimed at a general reader—popular works, not scholarly articles—many of which are listed in the author's note. I also relied on reprints of seventeenth-century works: Aubrey's *Lives, The Diary of Samuel Pepys*, Culpeper's *Complete Herbal, The London Spy*. I have found that anecdotal history is usually more helpful for creating stories and characters than, say, an academic treatise.

A sense of place is also very important to me. I went on a two-week research trip to London and Cambridge and toured the sites I would be writing about. I also went to the British Library, where I could take a close look at some of the primary sources for the books I'd already read. In the rare manuscript room, I examined the Clifford papers, which includes an early draft of the secret Treaty of Dover and letters exchanged between Charles II and Louis XIV. They're considered so valuable that I was asked to sit at a desk where I could be watched over by two librarians.

I also visited museums for background information. The Old Operating Theatre in London was particularly helpful. It's this wonderful old attic decked out like an apothecary's garret, with alembics, jars of dried frog legs and bird beaks and so on, adjacent to a Victorian operating theater. It's called a theater because it actually is a theater; it's a small amphitheater made of wood, with stair-stepped bleachers overlooking the floor upon which stands only one item: the operating table. The table is not very big, about two-and-a-half feet wide by four feet long, because only the unfortunate patient's torso was situated on the table; his or her limbs were held by the surgeon's assistants. The operating table reminded me, rather nauseatingly, of a butcher block table. Next to the theater is a lovely display of really gruesome antique surgical instruments.

Was it difficult to write the story in two different time periods? Which was easier to write?
The present day is always easier to write, because I don't need to provide so many details—I can assume that the reader has a basic understanding of the world in which Claire and Andrew live. In fact, if I wrote the modern sections with the same level of detail as the historical sections, people would find it redundant.

How did you learn about all the herbs and medicinal substances Hannah uses in the novel?
Two of the first books I read were biographies of scientist and architect Robert Hooke, which included excerpts from his diaries. In them he recorded every ailment he ever suffered from and every medication that he experimented with, and there were a great many of both. Of course none of these "medications" helped him at all, and some of them undoubtedly made him much worse. He was not at all unusual for his time. Many people—intelligent men and women, who were otherwise quite sensible—used a wide variety of substances that we now know have no curative power. What's fascinating is that they didn't figure it out then, even though they would continue to be unwell after ingesting these supposed

remedies. My personal faves were "powdered stag's pizzel" and "the stinking fumes of a burnt horse's hoof."

I often consulted two reprints of seventeenth-century medical books: *John Hall and His Patients* by Joan Lane, and *The Admirable Secrets of Physick & Chirurgery* by Thomas Palmer, which contain numerous "recipes" and treatments.

Did you know how Hannah's story would end when you started writing the novel, or did her fate change as you got deeper into the story?

Even at the very start, when I first begin imagining a novel, I have a sense of how it will end. If I don't have this sense, I know that I don't have a story yet. For Hannah, I didn't know precisely what would happen, but I did know the note I wanted to strike. I had an image or two and an accompanying emotion that I worked toward.

Who is your ideal reader for the book? What do you hope they take away from your novel?

I'm the ideal reader. I write about what interests me, and I hope that other people will be interested too. I hope people come away feeling that they've gone on a journey—one filled with dramatic situations, memorable characters, and historical interest.

What authors do you enjoy reading?

A short list of my favorite historical authors: Iain Pears, David Liss, Philip Kerr, Rose Tremain, Arturo Perez-Reverte, Sarah Dunant.

What books influenced you to become a writer?

The books I read as a child had the most influence. As a child, I couldn't imagine anything better than being a writer. Still can't.

Do you have plans for your next book?

Yes, I'm already working on it. My next novel will be set entirely in the past, in seventeenth-century France.

Also by
CHRISTI PHILLIPS

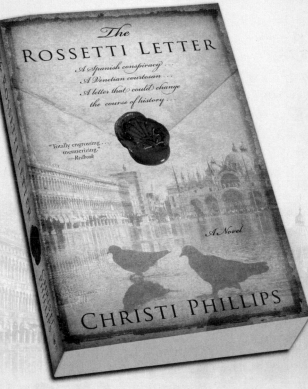

"Reading Christi Phillips's lush,
beautifully written novel is like enjoying
a sumptuous meal in the Venice it describes with
such loving detail. You want to savor every moment."
—Ayelet Waldman, author of *Love and Other Impossible Pursuits*

GALLERY BOOKS
A Division of Simon & Schuster
A CBS COMPANY

www.simonandschuster.com